THE ULVERSCROFT FOUNDATION
(registered UK charity number 264873)

was established in 1972 to provide funds for research, diagnosis and treatmer of eye diseases. Examples of major projects fur d   h Ulverscroft Foundation

- The   Moorfelds Eye Hosr
- T   e   eat Orn   ick ildr
- Funding research into eye diseases and treatment at the Department of Ophthalmology, University of Leicester
- The Ulverscroft Vision Research Group, Institute of Child Health
- Twin operating theatres at the Western Ophthalmic Hospital, London
- The Chair of Ophthalmology at the Royal Australian College of Ophthalmologists

You can help further the work of the Foundation by making a donation or leaving a legacy. Every contribution is gratefully received. If you would like to help support the Foundation or require further information, please contact:

THE ULVERSCROFT FOUNDATION
The Green, Bradgate Road, Anstey
Leicester LE7 7FU, England
Tel: (0116) 236 4325

website: www.ulverscroft-foundation.org.uk

CHRISTMAS WITH THE CORNISH GIRLS

It's 1941, and Christmas is approaching in St Ives. Shy Lily wishes she could hide from the war. But when her friend Eva asks if she will join her in working at a servicemen's convalescent home, Lily can't refuse. Eva came to St Ives to be near Max, the American pilot who risked his own life to save hers. Now, though, he just keeps pushing her away. Meanwhile, Rose suspects that the orphanage next door is mistreating its charges, and Eva is the only one who can help her uncover the truth. Can the Cornish Girls give children and servicemen alike the Christmas they so deserve?

BETTY WALKER

CHRISTMAS WITH THE CORNISH GIRLS

Complete and Unabridged

MAGNA
Leicester

First published in Great Britain in 2021 by
Avon
London

First Ulverscroft Edition
published 2021
by arrangement with
Avon
A division of HarperCollins*Publishers* Ltd
London

This is a work of fiction. All characters, organizations, and events portrayed in this novel are either products of the author's imagination or are used fictitiously.

A catalogue record for this book is available from the British Library.

ISBN 978–0–7505–4921–9

Published by
Ulverscroft Limited
Anstey, Leicestershire

Printed and bound in Great Britain by
TJ Books Ltd., Padstow, Cornwall

This book is printed on acid-free paper

1

Porthcurno, West Cornwall, October 1941

It was almost dusk by the time the all-clear finally sounded. Wearily, Lily followed her gran and Aunt Violet up the stairs and out of the massive cellars that served as an air-raid shelter for Eastern House, Porthcurno. Her younger sister, Alice, straggled behind, her nose still in the book she'd been reading during the long hour they'd spent locked up safe underground while the enemy searched the coast for the secret installation where they worked.

Outside, all the buildings seemed intact. The large white edifice of Eastern House loomed above them, camouflaged against enemy planes, and the quiet village and their own small cottage were just visible across the valley.

Like Lily, Aunty Violet had also turned her gaze towards their home upon leaving the cellars. Her sigh of relief was profound. 'Still there,' she said, and smiled.

'Oh, thank Gawd,' Gran said, clasping her hands to heaven in a fervent prayer. 'It's a miracle, that's what it is. When you remember all the nights we spent in London, hoping to goodness none of them nasty German bombs would hit the Anderson shelter . . . And all the neighbours we lost, poor souls.' She crossed herself, and then wiped away a tear. 'I swear, it don't bear thinking about.'

'Probably best *not* to think about it then,' Alice

pointed out in a matter-of-fact tone, still studying her book.

'Don't cheek your gran,' Aunty Violet told her. 'Apologise.'

Alice lowered her book. 'Sorry, Gran.'

'Cheeky little whippersnapper.' Gran made a face, and ruffled Alice's hair. She was missing her café in the East End, that was obvious. But it was far safer living here than back in London. 'You're an odd girl, aren't you? If only your dad was here . . .'

Alice glanced at Lily, but said nothing.

Their dad, Ernst Fisher, whom everyone back in Dagenham had called Ernest, was half-German. That had caused them a lot of heartache back home when the war started. Other kids had bullied them at school and thrown stones in the street, calling them 'Huns!' Dad had quickly enlisted and gone to fight, maybe to prove their neighbours wrong. When he was reported missing, Lily had cried for a week, until her eyes were red and sore. And then, Mum had been killed in a bomb blast, having left the shelter just for a few minutes . . .

So they were half orphans, as Lily sometimes said to Alice. Poor Mum was dead and buried, God rest her soul. But they still didn't know if Dad was alive or dead. And maybe they never would.

Lily stood yawning in the gathering Cornish dusk while the others streamed past them, back to their homes and billets around the valley. She knew many of the officers and government employees in Porthcurno would have spent the air raid in the confines of the top-secret tunnels behind Eastern House, rather than the cellars, which couldn't accommodate everyone. Those outside the top brass weren't supposed to know about the cliff tunnels, though most people around the village did, of course.

Lily herself wasn't quite sure what lay inside the tunnels, as she had never been allowed in there, but apparently it was a 'listening post'. That meant it housed complicated machines that carried British war communications back and forth around the globe — and that was as much as she wanted to know, given that loose lips sink ships.

'I'm starving,' Alice grumbled, finally pushing her book into her coat pocket. 'I hope there's something in the house for tea.'

Violet laughed and gave her niece a quick hug. 'Let's find out, love. Come on, work's over for the day. Let's head home.' They began to walk across the narrow valley towards the little whitewashed cottage, one of a row going up the hill away from Porthcurno, where they'd been billeted during their stay in Cornwall. 'At least the sirens only go off a few times a month down here. Not every bleedin' night, like in Dagenham, eh, Mum?'

Gran nodded. 'We can't complain, that's for sure.'

It was four months since they'd left their home in the busy East End and taken the train down to sleepy Cornwall. Lily remembered how lovely it had been, waking up that first morning to birdsong and the lowing of cows on her great-aunt's farm, not another soul in sight outside. It had felt like a miracle, escaping the nightly bombardment of the Blitz, even if the price had been trudging the fields until all hours and learning to milk cows!

But then her great-uncle had tried it on with her, and they'd been forced to leave Chellew Farm. Aunty Violet had been furious with Stanley for his nasty groping hands, and so had Gran when she'd come down to join them in Cornwall that summer. But to Lily's relief, nobody had blamed her for what happened. Except for Great-Aunt Margaret, of course.

Left suddenly homeless, they'd been taken in by Hazel Baxter, now a widow expecting her second child, her husband having been killed in service while they were staying with the family. Hazel was a darling, but Lily wasn't so sure about her son Charlie, who was younger than Lily and had an awkward crush on her.

'Hang on a bit!' George Cotterill called out as he closed up after them, and they stood waiting until he'd caught them up.

Mr Cotterill was their boss at Eastern House — well, not Gran's, because she was staying home these days to keep house — after he had kindly offered them jobs as cleaning staff at the base. He more or less ran the place, and since Hazel Baxter had been widowed, he'd been discreetly courting her. They intended to marry, though Hazel, who was showing her pregnancy now, kept putting off the wedding for one reason or another. Perhaps she wasn't keen on wedding another man while carrying her dead husband's baby, or maybe they couldn't agree on a date. All Lily knew was that Hazel's husband hadn't been very nice to her, and she hoped Hazel would be happier with George.

'I thought I'd better check how you ladies are doing in the cottage?' George asked, smiling uncertainly at Aunty Violet. 'Got everything you need?'

The cottage belonged to Eastern House, but they had been allowed to move in there when things got overcrowded at Hazel's place.

Violet nodded vigorously. 'Right as rain, Mr Cotterill. Me and Mum share one room, and the girls share another. Snug as bugs in a rug.'

'I'm glad to hear that.' George hesitated, frowning, then transferred his gaze to Lily. 'I say, are you feeling all right, Lily?' He sounded concerned.

'I'm fine, thank you,' Lily said, looking hurriedly away. She had been feeling a little out of sorts lately, truth be told. Restless and unhappy. But she did not want to discuss that with their boss.

'It's all this diving underground whenever the siren goes off, Mr Cotterill,' her grandmother told him. 'It's not natural. But this bracing Cornish air will soon set her to rights, pretty young thing that she is.' Gran stroked Lily's long fair hair, which she always said reminded her of Betsy, Lily and Alice's mum, though saying so only ever seemed to make her sad. 'Not to mention her dinner, eh?'

'Honestly, I'm not that hungry,' Lily insisted.

'I'll have Lily's dinner,' Alice jumped in quickly. 'I'm so famished, my stomach thinks my throat's been cut.'

They had nearly reached the barbed wire barricade at the bottom of the hill, and the guard had already shuffled out of his little hut to see who was coming.

'Um, just a moment, ladies.'

George cleared his throat loudly, and they all stopped, turning to look round at him. Even in the thickening light, Lily could see he was embarrassed. Their boss looked away, towards the pale glimmer of sea still visible between the cliffs, and thrust his hands into his trouser pockets like a schoolboy.

'You feeling all right, Mr Cotterill?' Alice asked curiously. 'What's wrong?'

5

'Alice!' Lily hissed.

But it seemed something was indeed wrong. 'There is something else I need to talk to you about. All of you.' George made a face. 'You see, I've been asked to cut down on some of our expenses, since the war's been going on rather longer than expected. Budget requirements, you know. Need to run a tight ship. And we haven't got as many men stationed here as we did before, not now the top brass are gearing up to . . . Well, I won't go into details.' He cleared his throat again. 'It's hard, but it's been suggested to me that we don't need as many domestic staff as we have currently. So I need to let somebody go, I'm afraid.'

Gran gave an anguished gasp. 'What?'

'Let somebody go?' Aunty Violet also stared at him in horror, her eyes wide. 'You don't mean . . . you have to sack one of us?'

'But you can't do that,' Alice exclaimed. 'We're good cleaners, Mr Cotterill. The best. We always get the job done. Ask anyone.' She paused. 'Well, don't ask Sergeant Robbie, because he doesn't like me. Not since I left that bucket out and he stood in it. But ask anyone else and you'll see.'

'I know you're all good workers, Alice,' George said gently, trying to smile at the girl. 'And I feel terrible about this. But the sad truth is, I need to lose at least one of you if I'm not to go over budget this quarter.' He grimaced. 'I'll leave you to decide among yourselves who's to be dismissed, shall I?'

'Oh, please, Mr Cotterill.' Gran shook her head, her eyes pleading and full of tears. 'Can you not at least wait until the New Year? Christmas is coming, and my girls need that money to get by. *All* my girls.'

'I'm awfully sorry, ladies. I truly am.' And with that,

6

George hurried back up the hill to Eastern House, his hands still in his pockets.

There was a long silence.

Gran was choking back tears and muttering under her breath. Alice put an arm about her and said something comforting. Aunty Vi just stared after Mr Cotterill as though she wanted to shoot him in the back. Which would definitely get them all dismissed. Not to mention banged up for murder.

Lily bit her lip; she didn't want to lose her job at Eastern House. She enjoyed working there with her sister and aunt. But only a week ago she'd received a letter from Eva Ryder, the Colonel's daughter who'd gone off to become a nurse. Eva was working at a convalescent home on the outskirts of St Ives and had written to tell Lily that they might have a place for her there as an assistant nurse, owing to staffing shortages.

Lily hadn't yet replied to Eva's letter, because she knew Alice was still grieving for their mum and she didn't want to leave her little sister behind.

But now this . . .

'Come on,' Aunty Violet said briskly, herding them through the barbed wire barrier and on towards home. 'No point crying over spilt milk. We . . . We'll manage somehow. Like we always do, eh, Mum?'

But her aunt sounded worried.

★   ★   ★

As they reached home on the other side of the valley, Lily came to an abrupt halt, suddenly recognising with dread the muddy, open-backed truck parked outside their cottage.

'Oh hell,' Alice muttered, also staring at the familiar vehicle, and shook her head. 'I'm not talking to *those two*. I'll go in and put the kettle on.' And she vanished indoors.

'Hello, Sheila,' Margaret said with a forced smile, getting out of the passenger side of the truck.

Lily's great-aunt looked embarrassed, as well she might, having behaved so badly to them over the summer. The last time she'd come to call at the cottage, Gran had been fuming and barely spoken to her sister. It seemed Margaret still hadn't given up.

'What are you doing here?' Gran demanded, instantly on the defensive.

'I wondered if you'd had a chance to reconsider my offer of coming to live on the farm. It's only up the road, if Violet wants to keep working at Eastern House, and you know you'd be welcome with me and Stan.' Margaret looked round at Lily, though the words clearly stuck in her throat. 'The girls too, I suppose.'

Gran stuck her chin in the air. 'Like I told you before, you can take your offer and stick it where the sun — '

'We're happy where we are,' Violet interrupted, hurriedly moving between the two sisters. They had nearly come to blows last time, and Lily's aunt probably didn't want a repeat performance for the neighbours, one of whom was already peering out at them through her net curtains. 'I don't know why you've come back. You're not welcome here.'

'Considering the help we gave you and the girls, Violet, that's very ungrateful of you.' Margaret's voice was icy with dislike. 'As I was trying to explain last time, before you so rudely slammed the door in my face, we need help on the farm. We got three so-called

8

Land Girls to cover the rest of the summer, but they moved on after harvest. Only, we've still got livestock to care for and the work on a farm doesn't stop dead because winter's coming. Truth is, we could do with one or two extra pairs of hands around the place, and . . . ' She paused, clearly reluctant. 'We'd consider a small payment this time, along with bed and board. But no more than's fair, mind you. We're not made of money.'

While Margaret was talking, Lily had crept a little forward to peer inside the truck cab.

Great-Uncle Stanley was sitting at the wheel, looking as grim and unpleasant as ever, his beard and whiskers uncombed, a woollen hat pulled down over his thick grey hair.

Just seeing him again took her straight back to that awful day in the barn when he'd attacked her. Stanley had leered and pawed at her body, ignoring her struggles and her cries for help, until Violet had finally arrived to save her . . .

Lily shrank back out of sight, breathing fast, her tummy so bad with nerves, she feared she might retch. She felt angry and scared at the same time, a confusing mixture. But the thought of others knowing what was going on in her head was somehow worse than these sickening feelings. She clapped a hand to her mouth and struggled to control her fear and horror.

Nobody else seemed to have noticed her reaction, thankfully.

Gran shook her head. 'And I'm telling you, we're not interested. So you can hire someone for a change. Pay them a decent wage this time.'

'But we're *family*.' Margaret was flush with indignation. 'Me and Stan are struggling to make ends meet,

9

especially with this war on. We took Violet and the girls in when they came to Cornwall, no questions asked, even though the girls' father was a filthy Hun. Now it's your turn to help us.' Her voice rose. 'I'm your sister. You can't just turn your back on me. It's not right.'

'Now listen here,' Violet began heatedly, but this time it was Gran who stepped forward.

'What isn't right, Mags,' Gran exploded, her eyes alight with fury, 'is that you let your bleedin' husband touch my innocent young granddaughter. You're lucky my Violet didn't dob you in with the police when it happened. The only reason I don't now is because you're my flesh and blood. But give me one excuse — just one! — and I'll be off to that police station in Penzance before you can spit. So you can crawl back to your farm and take that horrible lecher with you!'

Margaret's eyes bulged as she stared round at them all. Her gaze halted on Lily's face. 'You,' she choked. 'You and your lies ... My Stanley never touched you.' Her accusing finger jabbed towards her. 'And even if he did, it was only because you kept giving him the eye. Dirty little trollop that you are!'

Lily glared and shook her head vehemently, but found she could say nothing, too paralysed with fear and loathing even to speak to the woman.

He was in the truck.

He was right there in the truck, listening to every word ...

Blinking away tears, Lily folded her arms defensively across her chest and tried to stop shivering. It was strange; the weather wasn't even that cold.

Gran gave her sister a shove. 'How dare you speak to Lily like that? Go on, get lost!'

'Get your hands off me!' But Margaret had hurried back to the truck. 'Well, if we do get a visit from the police, Sheila, I'll be sure to tell them all about your German son-in-law. *Missing, presumed dead*, my eye! Did they ever find his body? Of course not. Because he's gone back to his own people.' Her sneer was triumphant. 'With a Christian name like Ernst, it was always obvious whose side he was on, and it was never ours.'

Hearing those words, Lily swayed. She felt hot and cold at once, like she was going to pass out. Her great aunt could badmouth her all she liked, but not her daddy, who had so bravely joined up to fight for his country and was missing, presumed dead.

Gran put her arms about Lily and hugged her tight. 'Now don't you listen to a word she says, ducks,' she whispered in her ear. 'Nasty piece of work, my sister. Whenever she opens her mouth, a load of ugly toads hop out. She and that man deserve each other.'

Margaret had given up at last and climbed back into the truck without another word. It pulled away and moved noisily up the hill, disappearing into the dusk.

'Oh, pet, are you crying?' Violet shook her head, rummaging in her bag for a hanky. 'Here, dry your eyes. She's not worth it, that mean cow. Nobody believes her lies. Not about your dad and not about you either. Besides, I know what her Stanley's like,' she said, adding in a dark undertone, 'And what he tried to do to you that day.'

'I'm all right, Aunty Vi,' Lily insisted, with more

11

bravado than truth, and gave a loud sniff before crumpling the hanky in her fist.

But she thought about her dreary cleaning job at Eastern House, the cramped quarters she shared with Alice, and the awful fear she'd felt on seeing Stanley again.

Maybe Eva was right and a job in nursing would suit her better.

Plus, it would be a chance to get away from this place and its bad memories.

Alice would understand.

'I think it's time I left Porthcurno though,' Lily announced abruptly. 'Let Mr Cotterill sack me, I don't care. I know what I'm going to do instead.'

2

Eva was horribly late, and she knew it. She hurried up the steep lane above St Ives, glad of her nursing cape, so dashingly lined with red, that kept out the chilly breeze sweeping off the Atlantic. She ought not to have worn her uniform to town, but with only three hours between lunch and her next shift, there had been little time to change. It was mid-October, and lights were already on in the country house perched high above St Ives, its solemn Victorian edifice emitting a ghostly glow in the afternoon gloom. The tall windows at the front overlooked the ocean, though all the patients well enough to visit the garden room would have been chivvied out by now and returned to their wards.

Symmonds Hall would look wonderful at Christmas, she thought, imagining those windows festooned with colourful lights and garlands, and the wards redolent with pine tree fragrance for days. And there wasn't long to wait now before the decorations could go up, barely two months. That would not only brighten the old place up, but help staff and patients alike forget there was a war on.

No doubt Sister Gray would be on the warpath, demanding in every ward, 'Where is Nurse Ryder?' and getting no satisfactory answer.

But a lengthy scold would be worth it. For Nurse Ryder had achieved her mission and acquired an item

13

of such precious value from her trip into town that not even a dressing-down from Sister Gray, that infamous Tartar, could spoil her mood.

Eva, passing the entrance sign to Symmonds Hall Convalescent Home For Wounded Servicemen, and hearing the faint sounding of the supper gong, hastened her steps along the drive. Oh dear, she was definitely for the high jump.

But her smile still didn't falter.

Even now, in autumn, the gardens of Symmonds Hall were as beautiful as when Eva had first laid eyes on them at summer's end, vast banks of rhododendrons shading the gravelled drive and a monkey puzzle tree taking centre stage on the neat green lawns. The owner, old Lady Symmonds, had insisted on turning the place into a home for war convalescents, having lost her only grandson, Francis, in a naval engagement early in the war.

'Francis would have wanted this,' her ladyship was reputed to have said, bravely watching her antiques put into storage and hospital beds trundled in to the high-ceilinged rooms instead. 'Besides, I'm seventy-five now, and this will give me some company, won't it?'

A burst of laughter from an upstairs window in the red-brick orphanage next to the convalescent home — actually a modern annex of the hall itself, another endowment by the generous Symmonds family — made Eva raise her head.

Three pale curious faces peered down from the window, and then one of them raised a hand in greeting.

Eva grinned, waving back at the orphans in her usual friendly fashion.

Running lightly up the steps into the home, Eva began to breathe a little easier, unbuttoning her navy cape. But she stopped in the entrance hall, confronted with a glowering, sharp-eyed figure, and instinctively drew herself up to attention, quite as though she were a soldier and Sister Gray her commanding officer.

'Good evening, Sister,' she said deferentially, crossing her fingers for luck under the folds of her cape.

'And where do you think you have been, Nurse Ryder?' Sister Gray asked icily. 'Apart from gallivanting about the countryside, apparently without a care in the world. Have you seen the time?'

'I'm sorry I'm late, Sister . . . ' Eva began, but was waved to silence.

'Is it common practice, would you say, for nurses at Symmonds Hall to set their own hours? Or to wander in and out of these premises as though they owned the place?'

Eva blushed.

Oh yes, Sister Gray was a Tartar, all right.

'No, Sister.'

'I should think not, Nurse Ryder.'

Sister Gray, whose Christian name was Rose, was a formidable creature. That much had been impressed on Eva within hours of her arrival here, some six weeks previously. Not much higher than five foot, at a rough estimate, the petite redhead nonetheless ruled the convalescent home with a steely will and flashing green eyes. At the brutal clack-clack-clack of her low-heeled shoes on the wards, nurses and orderlies quaked, and even the two Dr Lanyons, Edmund and his grandson Lewis, lost their cheery nonchalance. The only person unmoved by her approach was, in fact, her immediate superior, Matron.

Nobody had the power to disturb Matron's stiff-necked poise, though she had been known to unbend a little in old Dr Lanyon's presence. It was even rumoured that she occasionally gave him cocoa in her office during interminable night shifts. Sometimes more than just cocoa was offered, a few brave souls had dared to whisper. Eva could not imagine such a tryst between stern Matron and the grand old doctor who had served the tiny seaside community of St Ives for almost half a century. All the same, she could not help liking old Dr Lanyon herself; the kindly twinkle in his eye reminded Eva of her father, still in Porthcurno, further down the coast.

But as for his grandson . . .

Well, all the nurses were madly in love with Dr Lewis Lanyon. Except for Eva, of course. Her heart was already engaged elsewhere.

'I most sincerely apologise, Sister,' Eva said. 'I'm terribly late, I know. But I missed the bus back up the hill from town and had no choice but to hoof it here on the double. That awful hill . . . At the steepest point, I nearly gave up the ghost. It felt like I was training for an assault on Mount Kilimanjaro.'

'Your cap is askew.'

Chagrined, her hand flew to her cap, which was decidedly off-centre. Her heart sank at the supercilious look on Sister's face.

'I'll tidy myself up, Sister.'

'You most certainly will. And what have I told you about wearing your nurse's uniform into town? Civvies only outside this building.' As Eva began to protest, Sister Gray froze her out with one of her chilling stares. 'Cross-contamination, Nurse Ryder. Didn't they teach you anything about germs during

16

your student nurse training? Or were you not listening that day?'

Eva's father, the Colonel, had sent her to Birmingham for three months over the summer, to complete a rigorous training course in nursing before she could apply for work at Symmonds Hall. It had irked her, not being able to start straightaway. But like Eva's father, Matron had been adamant that, unless she wanted to work there as an assistant nurse — with lower pay and rather too much skivvying about for Eva's tastes — then she would need proper training at a modern hospital. And the Queen Elizabeth hospital in Birmingham had just opened its doors to new trainees, so off she'd gone. They would normally not have accepted her for training when she was not yet twenty-one but owing to the pressing need for trained nurses, along with a strongly worded letter of recommendation from her father, they'd approved her application.

She knew the rules about uniforms. And instantly felt guilty.

'Yes, they did teach us, and I'm very sorry. Should I change my uniform before going on shift, Sister?'

'Of course you must. It must be put into the laundry basket at once. And wash your hands and face thoroughly after that, before starting work.' Sister Gray shook her head. 'I shall have to report this infraction to Matron.'

Eva bit her lip, but said nothing. It had been careless of her not to change out of her uniform before leaving.

'That's the problem with taking on young nurses. I swear, if we weren't so short-staffed . . . ' Sister continued darkly, but stopped on seeing Dr Lewis Lanyon coming up the steps into the home. Her demeanour changed at once, and she dismissed Eva with a brusque wave of her hand. 'Very well, girl. Run along, and get onto the wards as soon as you can.'

'Yes, Sister.'

Relieved to escape that furious glare, Eva scurried through a side passage to the back stairs up to the nurses' quarters, housed in a separate wing of the large Victorian building.

It was true they were short-staffed. That was one reason she had recently penned a letter to young Lily Fisher, suggesting she should apply to Matron for a training post at the home.

Eva had made friends with Lily earlier that year, while staying at Eastern House in Porthcurno, a top-secret listening post near the southernmost tip of Cornwall. A war orphan, Lily was a sweet girl with a heart of gold, who still lived in Porthcurno with her remaining family.

Lily was too young to train as a registered nurse, of course. Being short-handed though, Matron might take her on as an assistant nurse, to be trained on the job. And Lily was bound to get a glowing recommendation from George Cotterill, her employer at Eastern House, for she was trustworthy and a hard worker.

Alone in her room, Eva extracted her precious cargo from a side pocket before throwing her soiled uniform in the laundry basket. She washed her hands and face with carbolic soap and stinging hot water for several minutes, and then changed into a fresh uniform, along with a clean cap and apron, careful to place the little bundle back into her pocket.

She was singing to herself, she realised with a

start, and almost laughed out loud at her own giddy excitement.

What would Max say when he saw what she had brought him?

She had high hopes of seeing the American pilot smile properly at last. And not just the sad twitch of his lips that passed for humour since he'd been wounded, but a real smile, like the ones she remembered from their one glorious evening together in London . . .

3

'Good evening, Dr Lanyon.' Rose had instinctively straightened as the familiar figure of the doctor came through the entrance door, whistling and with his hands in his coat pockets. Lewis took off his hat on seeing her, and smoothed back short, dark hair. She clasped her own hands firmly behind her back, as though afraid what might happen if she permitted them to wander freely. 'I didn't expect you back until tomorrow. Is everything all right?'

Dr Lewis Lanyon served St Ives as General Practitioner, with his semi-retired grandfather helping out too. Among their duties was the oversight of Symmonds Hall and its patients.

There was a deeper link between them too. Her sister, Elsie, had been walking out with Lewis before she'd gone up north to work in a factory, and had often indicated in her letters that they would be married once she returned.

Rose had fallen in love with Lewis back when they were growing up together. But as soon as he came back from his medical training, and Elsie had noticed how awkward Rose was around him, her sister had gone out of her way to attract the young doctor herself. Too shy with men to know how to deal with that situation, Rose had stupidly allowed Elsie to snatch him away from her.

She still felt the same about him, much to her anguish, but these days she'd learned to rein in those softer feelings, aware of her sister's prior claim.

'My grandfather forgot his pipe, that's all,' Lewis said easily. 'He likes to have a puff after dinner, so I said I'd drive back up to collect it. He thinks he probably left his pipe and tobacco tin in the staff room.'

He gave her his usual charming smile; the same smile he gave everyone. It was hard for Rose to remember that at times, and not misinterpret that twinkling look as a sign of special interest.

If only Lewis were not quite so dashing . . .

'By the way,' he added, 'I heard there was a German plane spotted along the coast yesterday. St Ives has already seen a few bombs dropped on it. We can't keep ducking under beds and hoping for the best. How are those plans going for an air-raid shelter?'

'You'll have to ask Matron. I believe she and Lady Symmonds have been discussing a joint shelter with the orphanage. They have a substantial cellar next door, and it's only a short walk from the back door. Though, of course, many of our patients will not be able to evacuate, owing to their condition. I'd therefore stay behind, to ensure everyone follows government guidelines for hospital air raids.'

Lewis grimaced. 'What, hide under the bed like the patients have been doing so far? What good would that do, I ask you, if a bloody great bomb blows the lid off this place?'

Rose agreed wholeheartedly. She had felt like screaming when she'd read the idiotic guidance for hospitals under attack by the enemy. But she had a duty not to question the rules. There was a war on. Somebody had to stay calm and hold things together. However ludicrous and futile it felt at times.

She raised her eyes to his face. 'Nonetheless, it's official advice, and probably the best we can do for patients that can't be moved in time.'

'I suppose you're right. But don't *you* stay behind to help those patients, you hear me? Designate one of the orderlies as an air-raid warden instead. Old Tom would do it, perhaps. He's a good sort.' Lewis turned towards the senior staff room, touching her shoulder gently as he passed. 'We can't afford to lose you, Sister.'

Hurrying into the nurses' washroom after he'd gone, she splashed her face with cool water and took a few moments to compose herself again.

Her mind turned back to Nurse Ryder, a welcome distraction from Lewis. Walking into town in her uniform, for goodness' sake! And the young woman had seemed almost nonchalant about it, not even penitent at being caught in the act.

It had been clear from Eva's first arrival at the home that she already knew one of their long-term patients, Max. Not only knew him, in fact, but was head over heels in love with the young man!

Rose remembered the first day Flight Lieutenant Max Carmichael had arrived at the convalescent home. His looks had been quite striking, for one side of his face was handsome while the other had been badly burnt, a thick red scar running down from his temple to his eye. A difficult spinal injury had confined the young man to a wheelchair, which she could see frustrated him.

'Oh, you're American,' Rose had said in surprise when he greeted her with a distinct transatlantic twang.

'Born and bred, ma'am,' Max had replied with a

grin, and then explained how his grandfather had emigrated from Surrey to become a farmer in Missouri. Frustrated by America's refusal to join the war, Max had crossed the border into Canada. Eventually, he'd joined the RAF and come to Britain to help fight the Germans. 'I'd be flying now, if a bomb hadn't caught me one night in London. But I'm going to walk again, you hear me?'

'That's the spirit, Flight Lieutenant,' she'd told him encouragingly.

Despite his injuries, the young pilot had smiled and laughed at first, as though he didn't have a care in the world. That cheerful demeanour had changed, however, as the weeks wore on and his condition showed little improvement.

Then Eva Ryder had turned up, clearly mad for the boy. But the more the young nurse doted on him, the darker and grimmer Max Carmichael's mood had become. In the end, Rose had decided to move the rotas around, to prevent Nurse Ryder working on his ward. Eva wasn't a bad nurse; she just wasn't much good at following rules and regulations. And sometimes her flirtatious ways with the patients reminded Rose of her sister Elsie, which made her uneasy.

Rose frowned, aware of a nagging headache despite her peaceful morning off, which she'd spent reading a book in her bedroom. Her room overlooked the adjacent red brick of the orphanage buildings and the soft green Cornish countryside beyond. It did her heart good to hear the voices of children at play.

Rose tidied her unruly red hair as best she could and straightened her dress uniform, eyeing herself critically.

She had lost her own parents young, too. She and Elsie had even spent a few years at the orphanage next door while growing up — though not under the Treverricks, who ran it now — so she knew how it felt to be an orphan, with all the hardship and undeserved social stigma that could entail.

Rose made her way to the senior staff room, and settled at the desk to study the list of medications she would be required to administer later that evening, as the most senior nurse on duty.

They'd lost two nurses recently to the war effort, both women signing up to join the British Red Cross. She herself had considered heading overseas to do her bit, but Dr Edmund Lanyon, Lewis's grandfather, had asked her to stay on, insisting that top-notch doctors and nurses were sorely needed in their quiet corner of Cornwall too. That was why he had delayed his own retirement, despite being in his seventies.

Dr Lewis had wanted to join up too, keen to 'have a go' as he frequently put it. But a congenital hip problem that gave him a permanent limp meant he'd failed his medical.

A knock on the door interrupted her thoughts.

'Come in,' she said.

It was Tom, their longest-serving orderly, grey-haired and bent, but excellent at his work. 'All the dinners have gone out now.' His deep Cornish accent echoed about the empty room. 'Thought you'd want to know, Sister.'

'Thank you, Tom.'

'I'll collect the empties in half an hour, shall I?'

'Yes, could you? Then you had better go home. I'm sorry to have kept you so late tonight. I don't suppose Nurse Kettering has turned up yet?'

24

'Not seen hide nor hair of her.'

'Gosh, what a dreadful nuisance.' Rose felt worried for the first time. Unlike Nurse Ryder, it was unusual for Becky Kettering to miss her shift. 'Wherever can she be?'

'I'll keep an eye out on my way home, in case she's a-coming up the hill. Meanwhile, Nurse Hardy's come on duty to take up the slack.' He paused. 'By the way, Matron's on the prowl. Just gone into Carbis Ward.'

'Thank you, Tom,' she said with a nod. 'Though please don't describe Matron as being 'on the prowl'. It's disrespectful.'

Tom shrugged, and withdrew without comment.

After the door had closed behind the orderly, Rose closed her eyes for a count of ten and willed her nerves to stop fluttering.

Damn and blast Matron!

She *would* choose tonight of all nights to spring a surprise early inspection on the wards. First, Nurse Ryder had been wandering about the countryside in her uniform as though the rules didn't apply to her, and now Nurse Kettering had gone AWOL. She hardly dared wonder what other delights lay in store for her tonight.

The telephone on the desk rang loudly in the silence, startling her. Who on earth could be ringing at this late hour?

Rose lifted the receiver, frowning. 'Symmonds Hall Convalescent Home For Wounded Servicemen,' she said clearly. 'Sister Gray here. How may I help you?'

4

As she was leaving her room, Eva bumped into Mary Stannard, one of the other nurses, coming along the narrow corridor. Mary was older than her at twenty-two, a doleful girl with a permanently worried expression.

'I take it the she-dragon found you, then?' Mary eyed Eva's flushed and harried countenance with a knowing look. 'Did she threaten to turn you out on the street? That's what happened to me the one time I was late for my shift.'

'Oh, I'm not scared of old Graysides,' Eva told her airily, though in truth the encounter had left her a little intimidated. 'She can threaten whatever she likes. She can't turn any of us out, she's been short-staffed since Agnes left.'

'Poor Agnes,' Mary said unhappily. 'I wonder when she's due.'

'Not till next year, at least.'

'Sister tore such a strip off her. Anyone would have thought Agnes meant to get into trouble, not that it was an accident.'

'Well, accidents are precisely what happen when you mess about in the linen store with a patient.'

Mary gave her an odd look. 'Now you sound like Sister.' Her gaze dropped to the slight bulge in Eva's pocket that spoiled the line of her crisp uniform dress. 'I say, what have you got there?'

'A present.'

'Who for?' Mary's eyes widened at Eva's smile and

she gasped. 'Not your dashing airman? But you know Sister's forbidden you to go anywhere near him. First turning up late for your shift, now this?' Mary shook her head in flat disbelief. 'She'll have your guts for garters if she catches you, mark my words.'

'Then I'd better not get caught.'

'I wish I was as brave as you; Sister terrifies me.'

'Oh pooh, who cares what Graysides has to say about anything? I went into town specially for this present, and nobody's going to stop me handing it over.' The rattle of the tea trolley doing the round of the wards below them snapped her back into work mode. 'Sorry, have to run. Talk to you later!'

Eva could feel Mary watching in dazed awe as she strode to the top of the nurses' staircase, hoisted herself onto the smooth rail of the banister, and then slid gracefully all the way down to the newel post at the bottom — keeping her legs tucked neatly together, in case anyone below happened to be watching.

Dismounting with a hop, Eva straightened her dress and winked up at her fellow nurse, who remained speechless.

That was when she caught sight of Matron heading purposefully in her direction, and grimaced. No doubt she was about to endure another thundering scold, courtesy of old Graysides.

Matron was a tall, willowy brunette in her fifties whose dark hair was attractively silvered, her severe black belt kept pulled in tight at the waist, as though to emphasise her angular hips. She would not have looked half bad in a ballgown, Eva often thought, a little enviously. In general, Matron wore no make-up, as this was expressly forbidden at the home, and didn't really need any, having an immaculate complexion.

But she did indulge in two exquisitely pencilled eyebrows that arched high over large, rather expressive blue eyes.

In general, Matron was friendly, but she could turn nasty in a second, and had a reputation for coming down hard on nurses who flirted with patients

But it seemed Sister had not yet complained to Matron about Eva.

'Nurse Ryder.' Matron handed her a used bedpan; thankfully, it was covered with a cloth. 'Get this cleaned out at once. And after you've washed your hands, I want you to take vitals on Atlantic Ward.'

'I'm not permitted on Atlantic Ward, Matron.'

Matron's thinly pencilled eyebrows rose. 'I'm aware of that. Nurse Kettering was supposed to have done the rounds an hour ago, but I can't find her anywhere, and one of the orderlies has told me she didn't report for her shift tonight. So the task must fall to you.'

'Yes, Matron.'

Eva bit her lip in an attempt to stifle a triumphant smile. So she was to be allowed on Atlantic Ward, and wouldn't have to sneak in and risk being caught. What a lucky chance! But as she turned towards the ground floor washrooms, unable to hide the spring in her step, Matron called her back.

'Nurse Ryder,' she said. 'I seem to recall there's a patient in Atlantic Ward who is in some way *known* to you. You will take the vitals of all patients and note the results down on each chart, *without* making conversation, other than what is necessary to perform your duties. Is that clear?'

'Yes, Matron.'

'Hmm.' Matron searched her face, but apparently saw nothing there except docile obedience. 'On your way, then. And if you see Nurse Kettering, send her directly to me.'

★ ★ ★

Goodness, Eva thought as she hurried away to empty the horrid bedpan, poor Becky Kettering is for the high jump tonight, and no mistake.

Having washed her hands and tidied her hair again, Eva studied her reflection in the tiny ancient mirror over the sink, which was all the nurses were allowed in the washroom. Her shoulder-length hair was arranged in soft blonde rolls under the starched white cap, and although in her opinion she usually looked washed-out without make-up, the long walk today had brightened her complexion and given her cheeks a becoming flush.

'You'll do,' she told herself.

Eva headed for Atlantic Ward, so-called because it overlooked the ocean on all sides, unlike the other two wards, which had views of St Ives itself, and beyond that, the impressive expanse of Carbis Bay.

This side of the house had once been dominated by the music room, large enough for dancing at parties, but Atlantic Ward now occupied that space, its vast windows draped with white, its ceilings so high that ladders would be required to dust the chandeliers. Not that they used the grand chandeliers, which had been carefully wrapped in tied-up dust sheets for the duration of the war. The ward was lit at intervals with modern lamps instead, beds separated from each other with screens, so that each little alcove glowed with light in the evenings.

The other two wards, Carbis and St Ives, dealt

29

with short-term patients and emergency arrivals, respectively. Patients came and went in those wards, sometimes only staying with them a week or two before being fixed up and sent on elsewhere, or home for recuperation.

Atlantic Ward housed the longer-term residents, those who had been sent here with serious injuries to convalesce over a number of months. Most were able to move about the home themselves, but others were bedridden and needed to be taken out in a wheelchair to enjoy the sea air or join in with therapeutic group activities.

'Good evening, Nurse.' The man in Bed One looked up in interest when she passed, his head so heavily bandaged he could only see out of one eye. 'I say, you're not usually on Atlantic Ward. Where's Becky?'

'That's Nurse Kettering to you,' Eva said, stalking past with her head high. 'And she's been delayed. So I'll be taking your vitals tonight.'

The man grinned. 'Can't wait.'

Fearing Sister might arrive and spoil everything before she could achieve her mission, Eva headed swiftly to the far end of the ward.

The man in Bed Ten was lying propped on pillows, his head turned away from her. He appeared to be staring out through a gap in the curtains, down towards the dark swell of the ocean. Her heart thumped at the sight of that familiar dark head, and she drew the screen further round the bed with a shaking hand.

'Flight Lieutenant,' she whispered, bending over him as she straightened his pillows. 'Penny for your thoughts.'

He turned his head with a slow, delicate movement, frowning up at her in surprise. 'Miss Ryder?

My dancing angel, come to see me at last?'

She smiled at his reference to the night they had first met, earlier that year, when she'd been a chorus girl at The Upside-Down Club in London, and he had come to the club with his pilot friends.

It felt like centuries ago now.

'I'm sorry, I know it's been a while. I've had to duck around Sister to see you.'

His hand clenched into a fist on the top sheet, and Eva realised with a pang that he must be in pain. No doubt his afternoon medication had begun to wear off, but it was not yet time for his nightly dose.

'You really shouldn't, you know. Not now Sister Gray has put her foot down.' His smooth American accent was so very different from the other soldiers convalescing there. His voice was so mellow and hon-eyed, she could listen to him all day. 'You'll be on basic rations for a week if she catches you.'

'It's *Nurse* Ryder now,' Eva reminded him. Everything inside her ached to see him so stricken. 'And I love basic rations. Terribly good for the figure.'

'Eva,' he breathed, his eyes closing. 'Please don't, there's a darling.'

She took his pulse and wrote the number down on the clipboard at the end of his bed. 'I told you before, I'm not afraid of that old dragon.'

'Sister Gray is not old. She can't be more than thirty, at a pinch.'

'You sound as though you prefer Sister's visits to mine.'

'Maybe I do,' he said lightly, his eyes still closed. 'She is quite a looker.'

'That's enough of that nonsense. Do stop trying to

31

make me jealous. It won't work. Besides, I've brought you something.'

'Brought me something?' Max opened his eyes and fixed them warily on her face. 'Not more of Nurse Stannard's rock cake? I nearly broke a tooth last time.'

'This is far more exciting than rock cake. Do you want to sit up?'

He hesitated, then nodded.

She dragged him higher on his pillows, and tucked the sheets about him again, ignoring his averted face. She knew he hated being so helpless. But she wasn't ready to give up on him yet, even if he was.

Max had saved her life, after all. That magical night when they'd first met, he'd pushed her to safety and taken the brunt of a bomb blast himself. She'd landed in hospital herself, but thought he must have died . . . until her father had sheepishly passed her a month-old letter from Max; he had survived and was convalescing here in Cornwall.

Making the decision to brush up on her nursing skills had been easy. Getting Max to see they were meant for each other was proving rather more difficult.

Daringly, after a quick glance round the screen to check nobody else had entered the ward, Eva perched on the side of his bed, which was strictly forbidden.

'Here.' Eva drew a cloth bag from her pocket. Inside was a coiled, long black cord, with a padded leather loop at one end. 'I read about this in one of Dr Lanyon's medical magazines, and found a shop in town that was able to make it to fit your height exactly. You attach this loop to your big toe, and then pull on the cord rhythmically, to stretch out the muscles and tendons in your foot and lower leg.' She smiled at him

32

winningly. 'Shall I give you a demonstration?'

'No, thank you.'

'It can help strengthen your muscles and get them working again.' She placed the cord on his palm. 'Keep it. Maybe you'll have more energy later.'

His hand tightened compulsively about the cord, and then he pushed it back towards her, his expression tortured. 'I don't want it.'

'Max . . . '

'No,' he said thickly, his gaze clashing with hers. 'My spine is broken. The muscles in my legs no longer communicate with my brain.' She tried to interrupt, but he held up a hand. 'It took me a good few months to understand what that means. What it *really* means for me as a man. But I've come to terms with my future, and I'm not going back to hoping that . . . ' He choked on the words and grimaced impatiently, clenching his fist again. 'I should never have sent you that letter from London, telling you I was coming to Cornwall to convalesce. It was wrong of me; I see that now.'

'But I'm glad you wrote to me,' she said, tears in her eyes. 'And I'm not ready to give up on you, Max.'

'That's because you're an angel. But there's no point in you coming to me with all these damn books and gadgets, trying to jolly me out of this bed. Don't you understand?' Max looked away, his chest heaving with emotion. 'My life is over, Miss Ryder. I'll never walk again and that's an end to it.'

'Nurse Ryder!'

The sharp voice brought Eva's head round in surprise. To her horror, she found Sister Gray a few feet away, her arms folded tightly across her chest.

'I was just — '

'You were just sitting on a patient's bed, Nurse Ryder, which is not permitted. And you don't appear to have completed your rounds. You leave me no choice. I'm putting you on a disciplinary charge.'

'But, Sister — '

Sister's green eyes flashed fire at Eva. 'Don't waste my time with excuses, Nurse Ryder. If I had my way you'd be dismissed. But I just received a phone call from Truro hospital. Nurse Kettering spent her day off yesterday with her parents, and somehow managed to fall off a ladder and break her leg.'

Eva stared, horrified. 'Oh no, poor Becky!'

She hoped Becky wasn't in too much pain, poor thing.

'Why Nurse Kettering felt she needed to help her father paint a wall is beyond me. But the fact remains she won't be back at work for several months. So you're going to be taking up the slack, is that understood?' When Eva nodded, still shocked by the news about her friend, Sister looked grimly satisfied. 'Now, there are other patients here in need of care. Go about your duties at once.'

'Yes, Sister.'

Suppressing an urge to argue back, Eva began to take vitals, aware of the other woman's glare between her shoulder blades. Why did Sister Gray have such a problem with her? She'd been on her case since Eva's first day at Symmonds Hall. But there was no point making matters worse by defying her openly, especially now she'd received her first disciplinary charge!

Getting a charge had been worth it though, to spend time with Max again and try to encourage his recovery. Eva refused to give up hope. She only wished he wouldn't either.

5

Hazel Baxter pulled up outside Symmonds Hall, saying cheerfully, 'Here we are, Lily. This is the place.' She peered out through the dirty windscreen. 'Large, isn't it? Bigger than Eastern House, I'd say.'

Lily stared out at the hospital, not sure what to think. But there was a hollow feeling in the pit of her stomach, as though she was already homesick. She kept wishing Alice was there to say something funny, or her Aunty Vi to give her a hug. And she hadn't even seen inside yet . . .

Hazel was right. Symmonds Hall was a large and intimidating building. There was a conservatory at the front, its tall windows overlooking the town of St Ives and the cool grey sweep of the bay below. Inside, she could see men wandering about in pyjamas, some on crutches, and one in a wheelchair. The nurse pushing him wore a neat white cap and uniform consisting of a pale-striped dress topped with a generous white apron.

'Well, what do you think?' Hazel turned to smile at her. 'Your new home, Lily, and a possible career in nursing ahead. You must be so excited.'

Excited?

Lily swallowed, wishing she could tell her friend to turn around and drive her straight back to Porthcurno. But that would be cowardly, wouldn't it? And what would her gran say, after looking so proud waving her off that morning? Other girls her age were doing their bit for the war effort. Now it was her turn.

Yet she still felt queasy.

'I'm a little nervous, to be honest,' she whispered.

'Nervous? Don't talk such rot, Lily!' Charlie, Hazel's sixteen-year-old son, was sitting behind her in the old ambulance that Hazel used for transport. He leant over the seat, peering out enthusiastically at the convalescent home. 'You said you couldn't wait to escape Porthcurno. Well, you've done it. No point getting cold feet now.'

'And St Ives is a lovely place to live,' Hazel pointed out, nodding towards the pretty town that lay below them, bathed in soft afternoon light.

'I know, I'm just being silly. My first time away from home . . .'

'It's bound to feel strange at first without your sister Alice around. Or your Aunty Violet.' Hazel patted her shoulder. 'But I've promised to drive them both down for a visit later this year. Maybe around the time of your aunt's birthday.'

A woman had emerged on the front steps of the home, staring in astonishment at the aged ambulance they'd travelled in. The red cross on the side panel was faded but still visible. Judging by her fiery red hair and short stature, Lily decided this must be the woman Eva had mentioned in her letter.

Sister Gray is the one to look out for, she'd written to Lily. *She's a complete dragon and runs the place like a military barracks.*

The woman did look rather stern.

'I-I'd love that,' she stammered. 'And thank you so much for driving me here, Hazel.' Lily managed a grateful smile, though her tummy was still turning somersaults. 'I'll be fine once I've unpacked, I expect,' she added stoutly. 'I'm eighteen now and this is what I want.'

'That's the ticket.'

They got out in a chill gust of wind that nearly blew Lily's hat off, messing up her carefully arranged hair. Charlie carried her bags towards the house while Lily followed behind with Hazel. The nurse waiting on the steps looked them both up and down, her lips pursed.

Lily had to remind herself that this new life was what she had chosen. A place where she could escape all those difficult memories. She only wished she could be as brave as those nurses on the frontline. Oh dear, now her teeth were chattering. How embarrassing.

'I'm Sister Gray,' the woman said by way of welcome, her tone not particular friendly. 'You must be Lily Fisher.'

'That's right,' she said, nervously holding her hat in place. 'Pleased to meet you, Miss Gray.'

Sister Gray frowned up at her, for although Lily was only eighteen, she was several inches taller than the nurse.

'Here, we refer to each other by our titles. While still under twenty-one, you can only be a nursing assistant. But for convenience's sake, you will be known as Nurse Fisher. Anything else would only confuse the patients. You will address me as Sister or Sister Gray, and Matron strictly only ever as Matron. Is that clear?'

'Yes, Sister Gray.'

'As I explained in my letter, you will receive instruction in nursing while here. But you cannot qualify as a nurse until you are old enough to pass a nationally registered course.' Sister Gray had a frightening intensity about her, Lily decided, thinking it would be best not to cross her. 'Remember, Nurse Fisher, you are now a trainee and on probation. Any funny business and it will be back to Porthcurno with you in a trice.'

Tongue-tied, Lily merely nodded. She'd never met such an intimidating woman before. She had hoped to make friends with Sister Gray eventually, but now doubted that would be possible.

Beside her, Hazel stirred. She shook hands with the nurse, smiling. She didn't seem overawed by Sister Gray's forbidding attitude.

'I'm Mrs Baxter. But please, call me Hazel. I'm a friend of Lily's aunt. And of Lily too, of course.' She nodded to her son. 'That's my boy, Charlie. We've come to help Lily get settled in, if that's all right.'

'Perfectly.' Sister Gray glanced at Hazel's prominent bump under her winter coat. 'If it's not presumptuous of me, Mrs Baxter, when's the baby due?'

'Oh, a few months yet.'

'Well, best of luck with it. Now, if you'll come this way — ' Sister Gray turned to lead them inside, but broke off, her smile fading. 'Yes, Nurse Ryder?'

Eva Ryder stood in the doorway to the home in a tightly belted uniform, a bold smile on her face, her fair hair tucked away under a starched white cap.

She looked pale without the make-up Lily was accustomed to seeing her wear, but was still full of life. Eva had been a good friend to their family and Lily was hugely glad to see her. The daughter of Colonel Ryder, who was in charge of guarding the listening post at Porthcurno, she'd often pulled strings to help them out in times of trouble.

'Eva!' Lily dashed up the steps past Sister Gray and into her friend's arms to give her an unashamed hug.

A friendly face at last! 'How are you? I have so many messages for you. Alice says hello — you remember my sister, of course? — and Aunty Violet,' she gabbled breathlessly. 'And even your dad — Colonel Ryder, I mean — who asked me specially to pass on his regards. Or was it his best wishes? Oh, I don't know. Only that he loves you and misses you, I'm sure.'

'Dearest Daddy,' Eva said, a laughing twinkle in her eye. 'You must tell me how he is. And Alice and Violet, of course. But later, all right?' She said a warm hello to Hazel and Charlie too, shaking their hands, and then linked arms with Lily. 'First, I'll show you up to your room, if Sister Gray will allow it, and get you kitted out.'

From her expression, Sister Gray did seem to disapprove of Eva's intervention. But she didn't refuse. 'Come and see me first thing tomorrow,' she told Lily stiffly, 'and I'll outline your duties. No doubt Nurse Ryder will tell you where to find me.'

★　★　★

After a quick peek into the wards, where every bed seemed to be occupied, they went upstairs to the nurses' quarters. Lily felt daunted by the sheer scale of Symmonds Hall. Despite having worked at Eastern House, which had seemed a large house, she had never actually lived there, and this property was far grander.

'It's dead posh here,' she whispered to Eva as they climbed a second flight of stairs, uneasiness raising her voice, 'ain't it? Who used to live here?'

'Lady Symmonds. Though she still lives here in a private apartment. You may meet her at some point.'

Lily's eyes widened. 'Lord.'

'Oh, she's a lovely old soul. She's turned over the whole place to the war effort. The orphanage next door belongs to her too, though she founded that some years ago.' Eva grinned at her. 'The younger kids tend to hang around the hall at times. Matron isn't too keen on them, so don't let her see you talking to them.'

Several nurses and orderlies passed, giving them a smile and a wink.

'Everyone's very friendly,' Lily said, surprised.

'They're glad you've come to join us, that's all,' Eva told her, opening the door into a bedroom and nodding her inside. Hazel and Charlie followed, looking about, equally curious. 'We've been short-staffed for weeks, especially since Becky broke her leg. Now you're here, things will be easier.'

It was a small, plainly furnished room with whitewashed walls, an iron bedstead and mattress, a chest of drawers, and a single armchair. There was a small sink too, with a fresh bar of soap in the soap dish and a mirror above it, and even a towel rail with a white towel already in place.

'I'm right next door,' Eva continued cheerily, 'so if you ever feel lonely or need a chat, just knock on the wall.' She demonstrated. 'And I'll come running.'

'You mean, all this . . . It's just for me?'

Eva nodded, smiling.

Charlie deposited the bags on the mattress, looking about wide-eyed. 'I thought you'd be sharing a room, Lily.'

'Me too.' Lily was stunned. 'I've never had a bedroom all to myself.'

'Oh Lily, how lucky you are. This is wonderful.'

Hazel wandered about the room, running a hand across the top of the armchair and then gazing out of the window. 'And is that the orphanage?'

Eva and Lily joined her.

'That's right,' Eva said, pointing to a red-brick building just visible to the far left of Lily's vision. 'The children look so sweet when they're playing outside. And we share their cellars when there are air raids. Symmonds Hall has no shelter of its own.'

Hazel looked at her strangely. 'What about the patients?'

'Those men who can walk usually join us in the shelter. But the ones who can't . . . Well, I'm afraid they have to hide under their beds.' Eva pulled a face, nodding. 'I know, it's absurd and appalling. But it's ministry policy and the best we can do in the few minutes we have to clear the building when the siren goes off.'

Lily sat down on the mattress next to her bags. She couldn't quite believe this room was to be hers alone. But she was here, and she had somehow survived her first meeting with Sister Gray. And she was determined not to make a mess of things. It would be too horrible to end up being sent home in disgrace.

Charlie was talking enthusiastically about his job in a factory near Penzance. He would be billeted near work, but allowed to see his mum on weekends. And when she and George Cotterill got married —

Eva interrupted. 'When is the wedding, Hazel? I want to be there if I can wangle the time off. And I expect Lily would love to attend too. We could both go together.'

Hazel gave a faint smile, her hand dropping almost

instinctively to her bump. 'We put it off again. Maybe sometime in the New Year?'

'Second thoughts?'

'Oh gosh, nothing like that.' Hazel blushed. 'It's because of the baby. George wanted to marry me before it was born, but I decided against that. Folk were already gossiping as it was, and if we'd married too soon after Bertie's death, I was afraid that . . .'

'People might say it was George's child, not your husband's?'

'Exactly.'

Charlie looked away, his hands in his pockets. Lily watched him compassionately; he found such conversations about his late father difficult, of course.

Eva nodded sympathetically. 'You know best. And I'm sure you and George will be very happy together.' She glanced at Charlie. 'A proper family.'

Hazel thanked her with a smile, but looked anxiously towards Lily, still perched on the bare mattress. 'We need to head back, I'm afraid. Would you like me to make up that bed for you before we leave?'

'Oh no, I can do it myself.' Lily jumped up and hugged Hazel very tightly. 'Thank you for driving me here. It was very thoughtful of you, especially in your condition. I hope you have a safe journey back.' She turned and hugged Charlie too, ignoring his embarrassed expression. 'Look after your mum, won't you?'

'Of course!'

'And thank you for carrying my bags.' Lily blinked away tears. 'I shall miss you both terribly. And I shall miss Alice and Aunty Violet and Gran. You will tell them I said so, won't you? And about my room, how I've got one all to myself.'

'Of course, I'll tell them everything.' Hazel laughed,

and then bundled Charlie out of the room. 'I think you're going to be very happy here, Lily,' she said over her shoulder as they went.

'Goodbye, Lily,' Charlie called back as his mother shooed him along the corridor. 'Good luck!'

Eva went to the door. 'I'd better see them out. Sister doesn't like visitors wandering about unattended.' She looked at Lily closely. 'Will you be all right on your own for a bit? I have duties. But I'll come back in an hour and show you where the washrooms are, and the uniform stores.'

Lily insisted that she would be fine. 'Go, I'll see you later.'

Once the door had closed and Lily was alone at last in her very own room, she sat for a long time staring at nothing. She decided that she ought to chop her hair to shoulder-length like Eva's, as it would be easier to look after; her Gran would be horrified, no doubt, but she couldn't worry about that now. She remembered how her great-uncle had grabbed at her long hair, dragging her towards him. She could hear the distant sound of children playing, and a bell sounding below, perhaps on one of the wards. Then the sound of male laughter drifting through an open window.

Her vision blurred and Lily cried for a while, for no particular reason. Then she blew her nose and dried her eyes, and started to unpack her bags.

6

Three weeks after the new assistant nurse had arrived, making the home run a little more smoothly, Dr Lewis declared one of the patients fit to be discharged. This was always one of Rose's happiest moments, when a patient she had cared for, often for months on end, was finally free to go home or rejoin his regiment.

Young Johnny Cooper had lost his hearing in a bomb blast, and been badly burnt as well; he would never hear again, sadly, but his scarred back was no longer red and swollen, and he was free of the pernicious skin infection he'd been suffering from on arrival. In the entrance hall, with his parents waiting by the door for him, Johnny had thanked everyone profusely, even shaking Rose's hand twice. But he rather spoiled her pleasure at his gratitude by kissing Eva on the cheek, despite the fact that she had barely treated the young man.

It was plain to Rose who the patients favoured out of the nursing staff.

She had informed Dr Lewis of this fact, but he'd merely laughed and insisted that it did no harm for the men to look forward to Nurse Ryder's ministrations as they did.

'They're wounded soldiers, Rose, stuck inside for months instead of out there with their regiments, fighting the enemy.' Lewis had shrugged. 'Of course they like Eva. She's friendly and fun. It doesn't mean anything untoward.'

She could be friendly and fun too, Rose had thought unhappily, glancing at the doctor sideways, but saying nothing.

Despite his reassurances, she couldn't help feeling a little uneasy. She feared some might try to take their admiration for the pretty young nurse beyond mere flirtation, and that could cause serious trouble, not only for all the female staff but especially for Eva herself. She knew only too well what could happen when a man got the wrong idea . . .

Johnny's departure left a bed free in Carbis Ward.

There were several potential candidates for the empty bed. Most of the patients hoping for a place at the home came from beyond Cornwall, but Matron, who, like Rose, had been born in St Ives, put in a plea for someone more local this time.

'We've taken enough patients from London and the Home Counties. I know Cornwall is a peaceful place for these lads to recuperate, but there must be other convalescent homes closer to those patients.' Matron had turned to Dr Edmund with a winning smile. 'Let's take someone with proper Cornish roots this time.'

Dr Edmund, wiry and silver-haired, looked a little uncertain. 'We may not have a choice. This is the shortlist we've been given. I'm afraid those kinds of decisions are made at Ministry level.'

His grandson frowned. 'I agree with Matron, let's push for a local chap this time. Why do we always have to accept what the Ministry tells us?'

His grandfather looked at him over his spectacles. 'You know why, Lewis. We only look after servicemen here and we are well-funded by the government for our work. This isn't the time to start a revolution.'

'Asking them to send us a Cornish-born lad is hardly revolutionary.'

'Very well.' His grandfather sighed. 'Let me make a few phone calls.'

Rose watched the two doctors with quiet sympathy. Lewis's father, also a doctor, had joined up in a rush of patriotic enthusiasm and died last summer out in North Africa, rather ignominiously from fever. His death had stunned the family, and left Lewis with a dilemma. He might have gone to one of the big London hospitals, where he had done his medical training, if it hadn't been for his grandfather.

Dr Edmund was not in brilliant health. His wife was long dead, and his daughter-in-law, Lewis's mother, had also sadly passed away a few years ago. They had a housekeeper, Mrs Delaney, who kept the home ticking over, their clothes washed and ironed, and both men properly fed. But it wasn't the same as a family member, and Rose could understand why Lewis had chosen not to leave St Ives.

Matron beamed, having got her way, and turned to the next item on that week's agenda. 'Now, what about our plans for Christmas?' she asked. 'The boys always need a lift at this time of year. Last year's concert was a marvellous success, but some of the patients complained that it was too highbrow for them. I say we ring the changes this year.'

'How about a dance?' Eva suggested brightly.

Rose glanced at her disapprovingly; Nurse Kettering's accident had left them with an empty seat at the senior staff meeting and that was the only reason Nurse Ryder was there.

'Not all the men can dance, Nurse Ryder,' Dr Edmund pointed out.

46

'A Christmas party, then? With dancing for those who can, and games for those who can't.'

'Sounds splendid,' Matron said with a smile, making a note on her agenda. 'Thank you for volunteering to organise that. Shall we say, about a week before Christmas? To give the patients a chance to calm down before any family visits.'

Rose decided it was time to put her foot down. 'Nurse Ryder will be too busy to organise a party,' she said firmly. 'Since Nurse Kettering broke her leg, I cannot spare any trained nurses from their duties.'

'What about Lily, then?' Dr Lewis suggested. 'Nurse Fisher seems like a bright young thing.'

'Good idea, Doctor.' Eva nodded enthusiastically. 'Lily helped me organise a dance in Porthcurno earlier this year. She'll know just what to do.'

'Then that's settled,' Matron said.

Looking from Lewis's smiling face to Eva's, Rose experienced an unexpected stabbing of jealousy and bitterness that made her feel quite unwell.

Despite her sister Elsie's claim on Lewis, Rose still sometimes harboured hopes that one day, when the war was over . . .

But the way he kept looking at Nurse Ryder left her feeling flat and dejected. Who was she kidding? If Lewis ever turned from Elsie to another woman, it would not be Rose he found attractive.

Eva was an elegant blonde from the big city, a woman who towered over her and made all the men's heads turn without even trying. Her flirtatious ways reminded Rose so strongly of Elsie, it was hard not to let her long-buried resentment toward her sister bubble up and spill over into what she felt towards

Nurse Ryder.

Even their names sounded eerily similar, so that when she heard one name in her mind, she thought instinctively of the other.

Eva . . . Elsie . . .

Rose looked down at her hands, no longer listening to the meeting. If only she could stop being haunted by her sister, by mistakes she'd made through being too trusting . . . But there was always a taunting voice inside, telling her it was too late, that a solitary life as a nurse was all that lay ahead for her.

Others might find happiness and fulfilment in love. Rose never would.

7

Lily, when told that she was now in charge of Christmas festivities for Symmonds Hall, gulped and stared at Eva, aghast. 'Organise a party? For Christmas? But I can't do that, Eva. I wouldn't know where to start.'

They were upstairs, sorting through bundles of clean sheets in the linen store.

'Goodness, why ever not?' Eva handed her a stack of pillow cases, smiling. 'You helped me with the dance in Porthcurno, didn't you?'

'I washed the dishes and made sandwiches.'

'And you were very good at that. Look, I'll draw up a list of things you need to sort out, how's that? And I expect Mary will give you a hand too.'

Mary Stannard was one of the other nurses at the home, a young woman with naturally curly chestnut hair and a round, homely face. Lily had only spoken to her a few times, and had got the distinct impression that Mary didn't think much of her. Probably because of her East End accent.

She'd had no comments about her Dagenham roots in Porthcurno, perhaps because she hadn't been the only one. But most of the staff at the home were Cornish-born and it seemed they found her way of speaking amusing, for they often smirked when she spoke up. Thankfully, some of the patients were from Essex too, and had welcomed a fellow Londoner onto the ward with warm smiles and winks.

Lily tried to protest, but Eva took up an armful of fresh white sheets and chivvied her down the stairs.

49

'Hurry up, Lily, or Sister will tear a strip off us. We don't have long to change the beds.'

Most of the patients in Carbis and St Ives Wards were outside in the hall grounds, since the autumn day was dry and sunny. Dr Lewis had taken those who could leave their beds outside for fresh air and something he called 'Recreation Hour'. So they were taking advantage of two near-empty wards to refresh the bed linen.

The men in Atlantic Ward were mostly unable to walk, of course, or found it difficult or distressing to leave the home. So their bed linen had to be changed as quickly as possible during wash time or while the patients were still in bed, which could be awkward.

Matron was just emerging from Carbis Ward, instructing one of the orderlies to turn the stripped-down mattresses. She stopped with a smile at the sight of Lily, laden down with linen. 'Ah, Nurse Fisher. Settling in nicely, I hope?'

Lily liked Matron, though her high, pencilled eyebrows were a little terrifying. She had never seen someone draw their own eyebrows before, and without lipstick the effect was decidedly odd. But she had a nice smile.

'Yes, thank you, Matron.'

'Excellent.' She glanced enquiringly at Eva. 'Have you had a chance to tell Nurse Fisher about the Christmas Party yet?'

'Yes, Matron.'

'And you're up to the challenge?' Matron asked Lily directly.

'Erm, I . . . '

'Christmas is a very important time for the patients. It's often when they miss home and family the most.

So we need Symmonds Hall to feel like home for them, and we do that by making everything as festive as possible.' Matron began to list her requirements on her fingers. 'Carol singing round the Christmas tree, coloured lights, silver and gold decorations, sprigs of mistletoe, holly wreaths for the wards . . . I'll be interested to hear whatever you're planning, so make sure you —'

The telephone began to ring shrilly in the senior staff room along the corridor, and Matron broke off at once, her head turning. 'Excuse me.' She headed in that direction, muttering mysteriously, 'At last . . .'

When she'd gone, Lily turned to Eva. 'Carol singing? Where on earth do I get carol singers from? I don't know the first bleedin' thing about organising a party. You've dropped me in it good and proper, and no mistake.'

'You'll be fine. Come on, let's finish this work.'

★ ★ ★

They made up the beds in double-quick time, Lily carefully following Sister's instructions on how to tuck the starched sheet under the mattress correctly and fold the corners under in the approved manner. Her beds never looked as tightly made as Eva's, though, however much she struggled with the stiff cotton.

'Here, like this.' Eva bent to help her, then gave Lily a curious look. 'What's the matter? You've got a face like a month of wet Sundays.'

Lily felt embarrassed. She wasn't happy about being lumbered with the party arrangements. But equally she didn't want to let Eva down. She only had this job thanks to Eva's recommendation to Matron.

'I . . . I suppose I'm feeling homesick, that's all.'

'Don't try to fool me, Lily Fisher.' Eva folded her arms. 'You're scared about making a mess of this Christmas party, aren't you?'

Lily nodded silently.

'Oh, don't worry so much. It'll be a breeze. And, honestly, I'll help where I can.' The sound of children laughing outside the window made them turn. Eva smiled. 'Listen to those little darlings . . . They are so sweet.'

Eva pushed the window wider and leant out, looking down. Joining her, Lily laughed at the sight of a group of children playing in the yard below. One of the older boys was pretending to be a plane, probably a Spitfire, and was racing about with his arms wide, repeating, 'Vroom!' The others were mostly girls, who were clutching each other and giggling.

Then a door banged below, a woman spoke sharply, and the children fell silent. The older boy stopped 'vrooming' and stared, sombre-eyed, at the woman in the doorway. Then they all trooped inside, heads lowered, arms by their sides.

The door shut behind them and, in the quiet of the morning, Lily heard the crack of a bolt being driven firmly home.

'Horrid, horrid woman,' Eva said crossly.

'Who?'

'Mrs Treverrick. She and her husband run the orphanage between them, though 'prison' would be a better word for the place. I couldn't swear to it, but sometimes I've heard what sounds like crying.'

'Oh no!' Lily was horrified.

'I mentioned it to Dr Edmund a few weeks ago, but he told me not to get involved. He says children often cry for no reason or over some minor upset. And that it's none of our business.' Eva sounded bitter. 'But I wouldn't call what we saw just now misbehaving, would you? They were only messing about.'

'Surely Mr and Mrs Treverrick wouldn't tell a child off for playing?'

'I don't know. Maybe not.' Eva hesitated, and then pulled the window shut. 'Look, will you help me keep an eye out? If you see anything that doesn't look right, you'll tell me? And then I can report it to Matron.' Eva touched her arm, a pleading look on her face. 'In return, I'll help with the party arrangements, I promise.'

'Of course I'll tell you if I see something untoward.' Lily bit her lip. 'Only . . . you won't mention my name in any reports, will you? I don't want to risk being dismissed. This is my first job and Aunty Vi would be so disappointed in me.'

'I perfectly understand. We'll keep it between ourselves for now.' Eva gave her a winning smile. 'Besides, it may just be my imagination. Daddy's always complaining about it. Says I've got no business being so interested in what other people get up to. And I suppose he's probably right.'

They finished changing all the beds, then Eva glanced in a mirror to straighten her white cap and smooth her fair hair.

'I say, shall we pop into Atlantic Ward while Matron's busy?' She winked at Lily. 'I haven't spoken to Flight Lieutenant Carmichael in days, not since Sister Gray gave that ward to Mary to oversee. And all because they think I'm soft on Max.'

Lily grinned.

She had finally met the infamous 'Max' after

months of hearing about him from Eva, the American pilot she'd thought dead in the explosion that nearly killed her, but who had in fact only been wounded. If it hadn't been for Max coming to convalesce in St Ives, Eva would never have pursued a job here at Symmonds Hall, and then Lily wouldn't have got her position either.

'But you *are* soft on Max,' she pointed out.

Eva laughed. 'Is that so?' She put a hand on one elegant hip and sashayed out of Carbis Ward like a film star. 'Maybe I am, maybe I'm not. All I know is, he makes my heart beat a little faster whenever I see him.'

Lily gurgled with laughter.

'Better not see him too often, then,' she whispered, catching up with her friend in the corridor. 'Dr Edmund might panic and think you're having a heart attack.'

8

Eva was climbing the stairs to the nurses' quarters at the end of her shift when the distant eerie wail of a siren brought her to a shocked standstill. For a few dreadful seconds, she was back in London, running to the shelter with Max beside her, when the world went black and she was lifted clean off her feet . . .

It was just a memory but so powerful, her heart began to thud, her hand on the banister suddenly clammy.

'Nurse Ryder!'

Still in a daze, Eva looked over her shoulder. Matron was standing below her, holding a torch. The hall was dark, for it was long past lights out and all the men in the wards were asleep, or ought to be.

'Matron,' she whispered.

'Don't you hear the siren?' Matron shook her head impatiently. 'Quick, nurse. Ring the bell. Everyone who can walk is to be helped to the shelter.'

Snapping out of it, Eva ran back down to the hand-bell that sat permanently on the hall table. The bell was heavy, but Eva got it swinging with a little muscle, and kept ringing it as patients came staggering out of their beds and nurses appeared on the stairs, most in dressing gowns and slippers, their hair rolled up in rags. Matron was organising a line out of the back door into the yard that adjoined the orphanage, clapping her hands to hurry the stragglers.

'Ah, good.' Matron had spotted Sister Gray in a belted dressing gown, her jumble of red hair trapped in a net. 'You remember the drill from last time, I'm sure. Get these patients out to the orphanage cellar as quickly as possible. But don't allow anyone to run. That's how accidents happen. And the steps may be tricky for those on crutches.'

'We'll be careful.'

'I expect the children will be going down there too with Mr and Mrs Treverrick. Better make sure they're all accounted for before closing the door.'

'Of course, Matron.'

Eva saw Lily, who had been on the night shift, emerging from Atlantic Ward with a frightened expression. She put the bell down and hurried down the hall. 'Don't worry,' she said, touching Lily's arm. 'You go with the others.'

'But the patients in Atlantic Ward . . . Most of them won't be able to get to the shelter in time.'

'I'll stay with them, make sure they all shelter under their beds.' Eva saw Lily's wide-eyed horror and tried to smile, failing pathetically. 'I know, it doesn't seem right. But it's the best we can do for them. And honestly, the chances of a direct strike are remote. We have red crosses on the roof to identify the building as a hospital.'

'But in the dark . . . '

'Try not to fret. Just go with Matron.'

But it seemed Matron intended to stay behind too. 'Right,' she said briskly, watching as the last of the mobile patients were helped out of the building to safety, 'now let's see about these men in Atlantic Ward.'

'You don't need to do this, Matron,' Eva said quickly. She had seen old Tom, who also lived at the hall, approaching with a muffled light. 'Tom and I can

56

manage Atlantic Ward. There's no point us all being in danger. And when we practised the air-raid drill, we only needed two to help the least able out of bed. Not three.'

'I'm Matron, I should be the one to stay.'

'Please,' Eva begged her. 'I know it's a bit irregular. But I want to do this. And the men will worry if you're not down there. Not to mention Sister Gray.'

The wail of the siren sounded across the Cornish countryside, and now they could hear the heavy, menacing drone of approaching aircraft, like a swarm of bees heading their way. The sound throbbed through the walls of the old building, chilling in its intensity. Eva thought of the families in St Ives, hurrying to their own shelters and wondering if their homes would still be there when they came out. The two doctors lived together in a lovely big townhouse overlooking the bay. No doubt they too would be wondering about the patients up at the hall, and hoping everyone made it through unscathed.

Matron hesitated, then sighed. 'Very well,' she said.

It was dark in Atlantic Ward. All the blackout curtains were in place as usual, but one of the patients had an army torch he was using to guide the others as they laboriously climbed out of bed. But not all of them could get out on their own, of course, including Max Carmichael.

Max was still in bed, though his nearest neighbour, Raymond, was attempting to take his weight so he too could reach shelter of some kind. Which was ridiculous, since Raymond himself only had one leg, the other one having been amputated only a month ago, and was leaning precariously on crutches.

'Remember the drill, gentlemen,' Eva said clearly,

and their heads all turned, a thin beam of torchlight briefly illuminating her face as she ran into the ward. 'Everyone under their beds and use pillows to guard against blast debris.'

She helped Peter in Bed Seven to clamber down under his bed, and handed him a couple of bolster pillows. He looked quite agitated, so she stayed briefly to calm him down, while the noise of the planes grew ever louder.

'Tom, can you help Simon?' she called to the orderly, seeing the patient in Bed Two struggling to get under cover.

'You make sure you get under a bed too,' Tom warned her.

'I will.' Reaching Max, who was still half in and half out of bed, she flashed Derek a quick smile. 'Best get that torch turned off as soon as everyone's out of bed. I know the blackout curtains are up, but let's not take any chances.'

'Whatever you say, Nurse.' Derek gave her a quick grin, and lowered the torch beam.

'I'll take over here, Raymond, thank you. Can you make it to your own bed all right, or do you need help?'

'Oh, I can manage.' Raymond winked at Max, who was perched uncomfortably against his pillows. 'You won't be needing me anymore, old chap. Not now you've got Nurse Ryder to look after you.'

They could hear anti-aircraft guns going off in the distance. But the enemy planes continued, relentless.

'You shouldn't be here, Eva. Get down to the shelter!' Max was trying to get out of bed unaided. 'Damn my legs!'

'I'm not going anywhere. Besides, it's too late. The

Jerries are almost on top of us.'

Tom appeared beside them, breathless, wearing his air-raid warden's helmet. 'Can you support his legs, Miss? I'll take his upper body.'

Working together, she and Tom lowered Max to the pillows already strewn on the floor, then manoeuvred him into position beneath the bed, his only possible protection from a bomb strike in the time available.

'That's it, easy does it,' Tom muttered.

From somewhere below them in the town came an explosion.

Then another, slightly louder.

Eva felt her heart judder, and had to repress a strong desire to cry.

The Jerries were bombing St Ives.

'You should get under a bed too, Miss,' Tom said urgently, abandoning protocol and not calling her 'Nurse Ryder'. He pointed down the ward. 'See? Beds Three and Four are both empty. Private Piper and Corporal Rogers were able to go down to the cellar.'

'Thank you, Tom,' she told him, trying to sound cheerful. 'I'll be fine here. But you should shelter.'

With a shake of his head, Tom scurried away, and Eva crawled swiftly under the bed beside Max, though she could see from his face that he disapproved. From under his own bed, Derek snapped off his torch at last, and Atlantic Ward fell into a profound darkness. The enemy airplanes sounded terrifyingly loud.

She could hear her own heart beating hard, but was comforted by Max's presence. 'Well, this is cosy,' she whispered, not wanting any of the other men to over-hear. 'Just like old times.' She was joking, of course, referring to the bomb in the West End that had nearly killed him when he had saved her life by pushing her

59

to safety. 'Though if my father could see me now, under this bed with you, I doubt he'd be so happy that I chose a nursing career.'

'If your father could see you now, sweetheart, he'd punch me in the face,' Max drawled, his American accent seductive as ever. 'And I wouldn't blame him if he did.'

Eva wriggled, turning to face him in the enclosed space, though in the darkness she could barely see a thing. The blackout curtains were certainly doing their job.

'Don't talk such rot, Flight Lieutenant Carmichael.' She found his hand and gripped it, adding daringly, 'You know how I feel about you.'

'And you know what I've said about that,' Max replied in his dogged way. 'You're a wonderful girl, Eva. But I'm not the man for you.'

'Because you can't walk?'

'Because I'll *never* be able to walk.'

She felt a wave of frustration flood through her, and struggled not to let it overwhelm her. This was hardly the time and place for a scene, after all.

'Listen, I don't care that you can't walk,' she told him, still in a whisper. 'For goodness' sake, when will you believe that? Anyway, I haven't given up hope that you'll recover the use of your legs.'

'Then you haven't been listening to the doctors.'

'Doctors don't know everything.'

He was silent for a short while, then gave a soft groan. 'Oh, Eva . . . You should have kept yourself safe and gone with the others. You're wasting your time with me.'

'Is that so?' Eva gave a brittle laugh, and had just opened her mouth to explain why he was wrong when an explosion rocked Symmonds Hall. 'That one fell right next to us,' she gasped, dropping his hand. Her mind ran through the possibilities and came up with an appalling realisation. 'Oh my God, the orphanage!'

'I don't think so. It wasn't that close.'

'I'm telling you, it had to be next door. Those poor children . . .'

She tried to scramble out from under the bed, desperate to help. But his arm came fiercely about her, dragging her back against his body.

'Stay where you are, honey,' Max insisted. 'This bed may not provide much protection against a direct hit. But it's better than nothing. I'll be damned if I'll let you risk your neck with the Nazis overhead.'

Eva did not continue to argue but lay still, listening in fear and horror as the enemy planes moved beyond the headland, their heavy droning engines eventually fading away.

The only thing that kept her sane for the next interminable half hour was Max cradling her in the darkness, and the memory of his low voice in her ear, calling her 'honey.'

9

Rose stood in the overcrowded, dimly-lit cellar of the orphanage, watching over the patients sitting or lying all about her. Those who were able to stand were doing so, leaning against the walls or each other, since floor space was at a premium down here. The children were mostly sitting cross-legged in shabby-looking pyjamas and nightgowns, though some of the older boys were also on their feet, staring silent and wide-eyed at the wounded men around them.

Across the narrow space, she caught Mrs Treverrick's eye and gave her a tentative smile.

Mrs Treverrick, a thin rake of a woman with greying hair set in curlers under a hairnet, did not smile back.

One of the younger girls had seen her smiling though. She glanced up at Mrs Treverrick, and then at Mr Treverrick, a stout man in glasses with a small moustache that looked eerily like Hitler's, and then looked hurriedly away. The girl was very pale, hands clasped tightly in her lap. Rose thought she looked terrified, poor thing.

Early that morning, Rose had woken to the sound of a child crying somewhere in the adjacent orphanage, and had lain there in the grey light before dawn, wishing she could comfort that child and solve whatever was wrong. It was not the first time she had heard the sound of unhappiness from the building next door, of course; nor would it be the last.

It was a hard life, being an orphan. And even harder

in times of war, as she knew only too well.

At that moment, an explosion sounded nearby, louder than the earlier explosions from the town, and the walls shook violently.

Brick dust fell from the ceiling, coating everyone's hair. Several of the smaller girls let out piercing shrieks or hid their faces in their hands.

'Bloody hell, that was close,' Private Piper exclaimed.

Matron fixed him with a disapproving stare. 'Language, young man. And I'm sure we don't need your commentary. There are children present.'

'Sorry, Matron.' Private Piper turned his head, looking contrite, and winked at the sobbing girl nearest him. 'Now don't you fret, precious. I didn't mean anything by it. We're safe enough down here, you'll see.'

That ought to have calmed her down. But the girl, lifting her head to see who was addressing her, took one terrified glance at Private Piper's hands, burnt red-raw and only recently released from swathes of bandages, and cried even harder.

In the strained silence that followed, a boy of maybe eight or nine years old scrambled to his feet. He was rubbing his eyes, looking distraught. 'I . . . I don't like it down here. I want to go back to me bed.'

'Don't be foolish, boy.' Mr Treverrick took off his glasses and wiped them on his dressing gown. 'None of us can leave until the all-clear has been sounded. Sit down like the others, and be quiet.'

'N-No,' the small boy stammered defiantly, his lip trembling. 'I t-told you, I don't like it down here. It's smelly and cold . . . and I need the toilet.'

Mr Treverrick exchanged a meaningful glance with his wife.

Her lips pursed, Mrs Treverrick grabbed the boy by one skinny arm and shook him like he was an eiderdown. 'You stop that whining, Jimmy, and do exactly what Mr T tells you. Else you'll be going without rations for three days straight. Do you hear me?'

Jimmy said nothing but burst into noisy tears.

'Stop that right now,' she insisted, and to Rose's horror she gave his bottom a smack. Luckily, Jimmy was wearing flannel pyjamas, but he yelped all the same.

'Here, go easy on the lad,' one of the other patients called out, frowning. 'He's just scared, that's all. No need to treat him so harshly.'

'I'll thank you to mind your own business,' Mrs Treverrick told the man, but didn't smack the boy again, dragging him close instead. She bent down to whisper hoarsely in his ear while Jimmy listened, a fist stuffed in his mouth. Whatever she said, it had an impact, because the boy nodded and quickly sat down again without speaking, red-eyed and sniffing.

Mr Treverrick watched all this without any apparent concern. 'Mrs T knows what she's about,' he reassured the man who had commented.

'Of course I know,' his wife agreed. 'Big grown-up lad like that making a fuss over a few bangs in the night? I've never heard of such a thing.' But she ruffled the boy's hair. 'There, there, boy. It'll soon be over and you can go back to bed.'

Rose opened her mouth to speak, but caught Matron's eye and, with difficulty, suppressed her desire to give the woman a piece of her mind. But she brooded internally, watching the Treverricks closely after that. If that's what they were like when being watched by others, what were they like with the children in private?

Eventually, the raid ended and they heard the all-clear from St Ives with gratitude, the sound faint and muffled underground.

The cellar entrance was in the orphanage yard, accessed via a large trapdoor in the ground. One by one, they climbed the narrow wooden stairs to get out, letting the children go first, led by the Treverricks.

Outside, to Rose's huge relief, the buildings all seemed intact. It was still dark, of course, but a pale sliver of moon was just visible at the edge of clouds, its fragile light reflected in rows of unbroken windows, the familiar red brick walls and Cornish slate roofs untouched by destruction.

Wherever that final bomb had fallen, she thought, it hadn't dropped as near to Symmonds Hall as she'd feared.

One of the nurses had found a night light, and was guiding people back inside by its misty glow. Rose glanced over her shoulder, but the last of the children had already vanished back inside the orphanage. Mr Treverrick followed them, shouting, 'Shut up, Buster!' at his furiously barking dog, who must have been left inside during the air raid.

Ahead, Rose spotted Matron and hurried after her. 'Matron, did you see how Mrs Treverrick treats those children? Smacking a frightened child like that . . . It's disgraceful.'

Matron put a weary hand to her forehead and said, 'Let's talk about this in the morning, shall we? Help the patients in Carbis Ward back into bed. Nurse Stannard is dealing with St Ives Ward, and I'll check on those left behind in Atlantic.' Her smile was strained.

'Then maybe we can all get some sleep.'

'But that poor little boy — '

'Our patients must come first, Sister Gray. I'm sure the Treverricks are doing the best they can in trying circumstances.' When Rose still did not move, Matron raised her brows. 'Carbis Ward. That's an order.'

Rose forced herself to obey, though anger at Jimmy's treatment was still sparking through her, her whole body on fire with indignation.

In the darkness, Rose trod around Carbis Ward with a night light, taking each man's vitals in turn, and reassuring more than one patient that none of the buildings around them had been hit.

'Try to sleep now,' she told one patient, an agitated young man who had been admitted with shrapnel wounds to the chest and abdomen that had become infected. 'I'll ask Dr Edmund to come and see you as soon as he arrives tomorrow.' Dr Edmund tended to look after Carbis Ward, as the cases there were usually quite straightforward. 'Unless the bandaging has come undone, it's best to leave it until morning.'

'I've told you before, Sister, I don't want old Edmunds,' the young man insisted. 'I want Dr Lewis. He's bang up-to-date with these new medical techniques.'

'I'll see what I can do,' Rose said soothingly, but she knew it wouldn't do much good. Dr Lewis was much in demand, and there were far more pressing cases for him to look after in the limited time he was able to spare to visit them.

Rose finished her rounds and put out the night light.

Matron was right, she thought, slipping softly out of the dark ward. The men were tired and disoriented after the air raid, and their welfare had to be her first concern. And she too felt fatigued and on edge. Perhaps she had overreacted down there, mistaking an error in judgement by Mrs Treverrick for an act of deliberate cruelty. The woman might have been quite scared herself after all.

Before she could make her way up to bed, there was a hammering sound.

'That's someone at the door,' Tom said in surprise, emerging from Atlantic Ward with his grey hair dishevelled, no doubt from sheltering under one of the beds during the raid.

'Better see who it is then,' Rose told him, with more composure than she felt.

Matron came out of the ward too, looking worried. 'Was someone hurt in the air raid, do you think?'

But when Tom unlocked the door, it was Dr Lewis who came limping in, wrapped in a thick coat, a scarf about his neck. Seeing them in the hall, he took off his hat.

'Thank you, Tom,' Lewis said with a brief nod, and glanced round at them. 'Matron, Sister Gray, how are you? I hope nobody was hurt.'

'Of course not.' Matron clasped her hands, clearly anxious. 'Why have you come? Is your grandfather safe?'

'Perfectly, thank you, and the planes seem to have moved on up the coast. There was bombing in the town, some damage to property. Two people were taken to the cottage hospital before I got there, but I don't believe they were seriously hurt.'

'How awful,' Rose said, hugely relieved to see him safe and well. 'A bomb fell somewhere near us, I'm sure of it.'

'Garrett's Farm was hit, but only a disused cottage. Not the farmhouse itself. I stopped by there for a few minutes. No injuries, thankfully.'

Matron smiled. 'Well, I'm very glad to know you and Dr Edmund are safe. But I must finish my rounds.' She hurried away, taking Tom with her.

Rose stayed.

'Since I was in the area, I thought I'd better check on the hall too.' Lewis came closer, his face sombre. 'You look pale.'

'It's late and I'm tired, that's all.' She had probably spoken too sharply, she realised. 'But thank you. We're all unhurt here, as you can see. You should probably go home.'

'I just wanted to be sure that you were all right, Rose. But you are.' Lewis nodded, and put his hat back on. 'Goodnight, then.'

After he'd gone home, Rose trudged slowly up to bed, her mind whirling with hope and confusion. Had she imagined the look in the doctor's eyes when he said he'd come to see *that you were all right*, as though singling her out from the others?

She was so weary, it was possible she'd misunderstood his meaning. Though he'd also called her Rose instead of Sister Gray, something he rarely did these days.

10

Lily was thankful to receive a letter from her sister a few days after the air raid. Ever since that night, she'd been imagining those enemy planes moving past and dropping bombs on peaceful Porthcurno too. But to her relief they had not done so. Alice did mention a recent air raid a little further away at Penzance. It had taken place during the day a week before, and no bombs had fallen, though the seafront had been strafed with bullets.

Nobody had been killed in the attack on Penzance, Alice wrote in her letter, but several people had been hurt and taken to the hospital there.

The worst thing is, these raids are becoming more frequent, which is making life bloody difficult for everyone. Gran says she's not walking all the way up to the shelter in Eastern House next time the siren goes off in the night, because it's too far to walk. Instead, she's persuaded the man next door to dig out a small bunker for us in the garden, and plans to shelter there instead, under a sheet of old tin. Aunty Violet told her not to be so silly, but you know Gran. She's too stubborn to change her ways, and she says if she survived the bombs back home, she can survive this.

Please let Gran stay safe, Lily prayed, closing her eyes. It was hard not to remember what had happened to her mother, who'd left the shelter during an air raid and never came back. Gran always claimed she'd left something on the stove, but Alice believed she went back to rescue the cat. Either way, there'd been a direct hit on their house while she was gone. Her mum's body had been found in the ruins the next morning . . .

Those horrid Germans, she thought hopelessly. They didn't seem to care who they hurt or killed. And though she'd escaped the frequent bombing raids in Dagenham, it was obvious she would have to face them in St Ives as well. Her heart thumped as she relived the terror of sirens going off in the dark, then the agonising hours spent in the cellar, crowded in with the patients and children, trying to smile when she felt more like crying.

She had never felt so homesick as at that moment, wondering if the whole building was about to crumble around their ears, fearing she might die with all these people, most of whom she barely knew . . .

Lily returned to the letter, suppressing a sob.

I'm well, by the way, and so is Aunty Violet. The big news is, she and Joe Postbridge are walking out together. He's not over his mum's death yet but he knows Aunty Vi wasn't to blame for any of that. And she's got a promotion! George Cotterill came by the other day and offered her a new position on the domestic staff at Eastern House. The housekeeper left recently — that old woman with funny hair, do you remember? — so Violet's got her job. No more slopping out for her! And she's going to be supervising the other domestic staff as well. Mr Frobisher had a tantrum about that, silly old codger, but George overruled him. So we've got more money coming in.

Oh, and Hazel's so big now, Charlie says she looks like a Zeppelin. Though he's only in Porthcurno on weekends now.

Lily grinned, reading between the lines during that last sentence. Alice had developed a soft spot for Charlie over the summer, though wild horses wouldn't have dragged such an embarrassing confession from her, of course. Her sister had always been book-mad rather than boy-mad.

But Alice was growing up. She was sixteen now, going on seventeen, and it was about that age when Lily too had started to notice the opposite sex.

Alice signed off her letter, *With all our love from me, Aunty Vi and Gran.*

It was several minutes before Lily was able to dry her eyes and put the letter away, getting ready for her shift.

She was deeply pleased about Joe Postbridge courting her aunt again; he was a handsome Cornish sailor who'd lost his leg in the war and come home to inherit his uncle's farm near Porthcurno. He and Violet had made friends at first. But then the farm had been bombed and his mother killed, leaving Joe heartbroken. There'd been a ridiculous suspicion about Aunty Violet going around at the time, that she was an enemy spy, and all because of her connection with Lily's German father, who was still missing. Lily was relieved Joe had finally come to realise the rumour had been malicious and untrue.

★ ★ ★

71

When she got downstairs, she was told to look after Neil Bottomley, a heavy-set sergeant in his thirties whose right leg had been amputated below the knee, and who was still too weak to use crutches, owing to other injuries.

It was Recreation Hour, and most of the men were outside, enjoying the bracing sea air and getting a little exercise as they walked about the grounds or played a gentle game of cricket with Dr Lewis on the leaf-strewn lawn.

Lily helped Neil into a wheelchair, and pushed him outside. It was a glorious autumn day, but there was a sharp breeze off the sea at times, making Lily wish she had worn her cape. Neil was in his dressing-gown and slippers, and didn't seem to feel the cold so much.

'Look at that!' Neil pointed out to sea, where the grey mass of a warship could be seen on the horizon. 'Our lads, off to fight for us. God bless them.'

Lily said nothing, gazing at the warship with a heavy heart. She knew he was right, of course. Somebody had to stand up to Hitler. But she feared for the men on that ship. She had seen so many terrible, life-changing injuries since coming to Symmonds Hall . . .

As they walked, she passed Harriet, shy Nurse Hardy, deep in conversation with Private Fletcher, poor man, who could only speak in a whisper most of the time, owing to chemical damage to his lungs. And Eva was also out on the lawn today with a wheelchair, bending to talk to its occupant, Max Carmichael, who seemed to be watching the others playing cricket.

'Oh, Sergeant Bottomley,' Eva called out cheerfully, spotting Neil being pushed towards them, 'just the person we need. You know all about cricket, don't you? Flight Lieutenant Carmichael is an American and doesn't know a thing about our national game. All he's ever played is something called baseball, which sounds quite different to me.' She turned Max's chair slightly to face them. 'But I'm sure you can explain the rules better than I can.'

Max was in dressing gown and slippers too, but Eva had shown foresight by draping a blanket over his knees as well, Lily realised, wishing she had thought of that.

The two men began having a conversation about the differences between cricket and baseball which Lily instantly tuned out, her interest in sport being minimal.

'I heard you had a letter from home today,' Eva said, taking her aside.

'How on earth . . . '

'Walls have ears in this place.' Eva grinned at her expression, then relented. 'Dr Lewis mentioned it, actually. He came in as Tom was sorting through the post.'

'You and Dr Lewis seem very chummy these days,' Lily said, teasing her back.

Eva's eyes widened. 'What does that mean?'

'Oh, nothing. Only that you might want to watch out with that one.' She winked, lowering her voice to avoid the two men overhearing them. 'I'm told Sister Gray has a long-standing interest there. And her claws are sharp.'

Eva shook her head. 'She won't need to use them on me, I'm not after Dr Lewis.' Her gaze flicked to Max, who was still talking to Neil. 'I've got other interests.'

Lily stifled a giggle. 'So I see.'

'Have you thought any more about the Christmas party?'

Knocked off balance by the question, Lily felt herself blush. 'I'd completely forgotten about it,' she admitted. 'Sorry.'

'Don't worry, I should have reminded you. I promised to help, didn't I?'

'But you've got your own duties.' Lily glanced back at Max, adding softly, 'And your own worries. How is he? Any improvement?'

Eva shook her head, a sad look in her eyes. 'Let's talk about Christmas, shall we? That's a more cheerful topic.'

'Of course. I didn't mean to upset you.' Lily thought for a moment. 'You suggested games for those patients who can't dance, or don't want to. Did you have anything in mind?'

'Blind man's buff?'

Lily stared, bemused. 'What's that?'

'One person is blindfolded and spun around while everyone else scatters, and then they have to find someone else to be 'it' without peeking.'

'Like hide-and-seek?'

'That's right.' Eva chewed on her lip. 'Though that won't work for the patients who can't walk. No, we'll have to think of something else.'

'How about pass-the-parcel? I used to love that game at parties when I was little. We could wrap up a small gift in newspaper, and have the patients throw it to one another until the music stops.'

'Splendid idea. And while we're talking about music, have you considered what kind of music we should have? For the dancing, I mean. Obviously, we'll have to sing carols. It wouldn't be Christmas without them.'

'Yes.' Lily brightened. 'I remembered what you and Hazel did in Porthcurno, and asked Tom about musicians in St Ives. He gave me a list of people to ask. Only, I haven't had a chance yet.'

'Give me the list; I'm going into town tomorrow with Mary to see if they have any nice stockings in the shops. I might be able to track down some of these musicians for you.'

'Thank you, I'd forgotten it was your afternoon off tomorrow.'

'Oh, I've been waiting for days to escape this place.' Eva made a face. 'Last time I went hunting for stockings in St Ives, they'd run out completely, and I'll be damned if I'll wear these woollen nurses' stockings to the Christmas party. So thick and prickly, and I've had to darn this pair three times. Not exactly alluring. The other day, Max was telling me about the girls back home wearing 'nylons'. I get the feeling he'd like to see me in a pair.'

Lily was a little shocked by that admission. But she didn't want to appear prudish. 'Nylons do sound marvellous. No ladders, and all that.'

'Nurse Ryder?'

They both turned guiltily to see Sister Gray striding across the lawn with a fierce expression on her face.

'Oh blimey,' Lily muttered.

Eva sprang back to Max and hurriedly wheeled him further down the lawn, ignoring his protest that he was still halfway through his conversation with Neil. 'Yes, Sister?' she asked innocently when Sister Gray reached them. 'Is everything all right? You look a little flushed.'

'This is the Recreation Hour. You are supposed to be allowing your patients fresh air and exercise. You know the rules. In dry weather, even those who cannot walk should be escorted about the perimeter of the grounds.' Sister Gray looked quite incensed, her sharp green gaze taking in Lily as well. 'Not abandoned like a piece of luggage while you two girls enjoy a cosy chat.'

'Sorry, Sister.' Lily gulped, and rushed to Neil's side, her cheeks on fire.

'Please don't blame the nurses. It's my fault, not theirs.' Max had turned his head, addressing Sister Gray in his smooth American accent. 'I asked to be left alone with Neil, just this once, so we could talk cricket.'

'Doctors' orders, Flight Lieutenant Carmichael. No exceptions.'

Max stared back at her, frustrated. 'Look, I don't want to be rude, Sister. But I've been pushed around these damn grounds all summer and I'm getting a bit sick of the same view.' Lily had assumed he was fibbing to get Eva off the hook with Sister, but his voice had suddenly deepened, and there was a raw emotion in his face as he slapped one of his thighs through the thick plaid blanket laid over them for warmth. 'Let's be honest here. No amount of fresh air is going to fix these legs. So what's the point of these damn outings?'

Lily bit her lip, sure he would get a strip torn off him for speaking like that to Sister, who never allowed patients to be impolite to the nursing staff.

But Sister Gray studied him in silence for a moment, then said in a milder tone, 'In that case, I shall ask Dr Lewis to speak to you. He will know what's to be done for the best.' She nodded to Eva. 'Take the patient inside, Nurse Ryder. It seems his Recreation Hour is over.'

Eva wheeled Max about without another word, but Lily could see tears sparkling on the ends of her lashes. Poor thing, she was so eager for her dashing American pilot not to give up hope of walking again . . . But from the way he'd just spoken, it was obvious that he had.

Lily braced herself for Sister's reprimand, knowing it must be coming, but was saved by the sound of an ambulance ringing its bell as it made its way laboriously down the drive.

'Hello, what's that?' Neil asked, looking at the ambulance in surprise. 'Expecting a new arrival?'

'Yes.' Sister Gray frowned. 'This must be our new patient for the bed vacated by Johnny Cooper. Though he was not supposed to be here until four o'clock. I do not believe his bed is freshly made up yet.' She blinked, then headed off to greet them, saying over her shoulder, 'Take the patient down to the formal garden and back, Nurse Fisher. No more standing about in that idle fashion.'

Lily obeyed, though rather more quickly than was safe for her patient, causing an exasperated Neil to exclaim, 'Watch it, Nurse, you nearly tipped me out there!' as the wheelchair teetered at a sharp bend.

But she was so curious to see the new arrival, she simply couldn't contain herself. And her sudden turn of speed was rewarded. For on pushing Neil back towards the house a short time later, she caught a glimpse of the new patient being shown around the conservatory by Matron and Sister Gray.

He looked very young for a soldier, Lily thought, slowing down to study him. In fact, he was probably

77

only a few years older than herself. A fair-haired lad in a trench coat and trilby, he seemed able to walk on his own without difficulty, so that she wondered what his injuries could be that had brought him to Symmonds Hall.

But then, as she came closer to the house, the young man turned to stare back at her through the conservatory windows, and Lily had to stifle a gasp. To her shame, despite having seen many dreadful injuries since coming to the home, it was all she could do not to recoil.

The left side of the young man's face had been badly burnt. It no longer resembled flesh, but was deep-carved in dark red whorls instead, like a painted mask on some grotesque pantomime character.

'Oh, I say,' Neil muttered, also having spotted him. 'That's damn rotten luck for him, don't you think?'

Lily nodded, though she thought it brave of Neil, who had lost half his leg, to consider another more hard-done by than himself.

'Awful rotten,' she agreed, unable to take her eyes off the new arrival.

11

In a blustering wind, Eva and Mary walked down the muddy lane from Symmonds Hall and caught the bus into St Ives when it trundled past a short while later. They could have walked the whole way into town, but Mary, who unfortunately for a nurse suffered from fallen arches, kept complaining that her feet hurt.

Having been brought up near London, far from the sea, Eva loved the view from the bus, staring out over Cornish slate roofs to the wide, windswept bay beyond. She didn't say much, leaving the other nurse to do most of the talking, which didn't seem to bother Mary.

Once away from the restrictive atmosphere of Symmonds Hall, Nurse Stannard was a voluble soul: she chattered on about her family, and her hairstyle, and her newfound crush for one of the younger patients, until the bus finally juddered to a halt on the main street, and everyone bundled out into the chilly November day.

'Where shall we go first?' Mary asked as they rounded a corner above the row of shops at the town centre, cautiously holding her hat in case it blew away. 'I'd like to go to the lending library. But if you want to shop for stockings first, I don't mind.'

'Or we could split up.' Eva could see her friend was eager to take back her books and find some new reading material.

'If you like.' Mary smiled shyly. 'I wouldn't mind, actually. It takes me ages to choose a new book, and I know you're not a big reader. I wouldn't want you to be bored, waiting for me.'

'That's settled, then. Let's meet up at the tea shop over there.' Eva pointed to the tea shop with old leaded windows and a brass kettle hanging over the door. 'Shall we say, an hour and a half from now?'

While Mary hurried off to the lending library, books tucked into her shopping basket, Eva turned the opposite way and wandered along the row of shops. It was all very Cornish, she thought. Up ahead, a stout dairy farmer was delivering large milk churns from the back of a van, whistling as he worked. A weather-beaten old chap leant in the doorway to the pub, pipe in hand, to watch the people coming and going, heedless of the sea winds. And high above their heads, seagulls wheeled in groups, crying noisily before heading out to sea again.

Further down the street, long lines of housewives were queuing outside the butcher's and greengrocer's to do their daily shopping, covered baskets over their arms, their hair-do's protected by headscarves. Some of the women had drawn and worried faces, while others chatted cheerfully enough, wrapped up against the cold in coats and scarves. Several glanced sideways at Eva, unsmiling, for it was a small town in wartime and locals were not always welcoming towards those they didn't recognise. But a soldier, perhaps on leave, touched his cap as he passed her, saying, 'Morning, Miss,' and she replied with a ready smile.

After buying a pair of fine new stockings for the Christmas party, together with a pretty but warm woollen frock that set her back six months' worth of clothing coupons, Eva still had forty minutes or so to kill before she'd agreed to rejoin Mary Stannard.

Checking the list of names of musicians that Lily had passed on to her, she decided to visit the Post Office, where the gentleman in glasses behind the counter viewed her query with undisguised suspicion.

'And why would you want to know the whereabouts of these individuals?' he demanded with a frown. 'I don't believe we've met, Miss. I'm guessing you must be from up country.'

He said 'up country' in a vaguely accusing way.

'I'm from London,' she admitted, though she was sure her accent must have given her origins away as soon as she opened her mouth. 'But I'm living up at Symmonds Hall at the moment.'

'The convalescent home, would that be?'

'That's right. I'm a nurse.'

'I see.' His frown had cleared at those apparently magical words. But he still hesitated. 'I'm not sure I understand though. What's this about, Miss? Why do you need to find these musicians?'

Aware of several women waiting impatiently behind her in the queue, Eva briefly explained about the Christmas party and her mission to find a suitable band or group of musicians to provide entertainment on the night.

'So if you know where I can find any of those people, I'd be very grateful. We'd be willing to pay them, of course.'

* * *

Five minutes later, she was following a rough-drawn map on the back of an old envelope, up a narrow, cobbled lane, down a windy street, and round a corner to where she found a tall, lean timber house

81

with white boards adorning the front. There, she knocked and waited until the door was answered by an elderly lady in a cap and apron, who must have been ninety years old at least.

'Good day,' Eva said politely, and making sure to raise her voice, as the Post Master had warned her the lady was a trifle deaf. 'My name is Miss Ryder, and I'm looking for a Mr Stuart Shrubsole. I hear he's an excellent musician.'

The old lady cackled, nodding. 'Aye, he's a dab hand on the fiddle, is our Stuart.'

'Is he at home?'

'What's that?' She cupped a hand to her ear, frowning.

'I said — '

But Eva was relieved from having to repeat herself, for they were interrupted by a giant of a man shuffling along the passageway with a flat cap on his hand.

'Who is it, Gran?'

'A stranger,' the old lady croaked.

'And what have I told you about not answering the door to strangers? We're at war with Germany. These days, there could be Nazis on the doorstep.'

'She's not a Nazi.'

'I'll be the judge of that, Gran.' A heavily bearded man peered out at Eva, his brows twitching together. She had an impression of sharp blue eyes in a round, red face, with a wild burst of ginger hair that enveloped everything from his crown and ears to his thick jowl. 'Yes, and who are you? Not a Nazi, she says. But you could be one. I've never seen you before and I know everyone in St Ives.'

'I'm Miss Ryder, as I was trying to explain to your grandmother,' Eva said, struggling against the impulse to laugh, for she could see that he was serious. 'I'm a nurse at Symmonds Hall. They don't let us out very often, I'm afraid, which may account for you not having seen me before.'

'And what do you want with me, Miss Ryder?'

'Somebody told me you're a musician, Mr Shrubsole, and a fearfully good one at that.' She held up Lily's list. 'And that you know all the musicians in St Ives.'

'Is that so?'

Undeterred by his stern expression, Eva continued with a brisk smile. 'We're organising a Christmas Party at the convalescent home in December. There'll be singing and dancing, and we were hoping that you and your friends might come and play for us.' She paused. 'For a modest fee, of course.'

At the mention of money, Stuart Shrubsole's face changed. 'In that case, Miss Ryder,' he said, suddenly cheerful, 'you'd best come in and tell me all about it.' He turned to the old lady. 'Gran, put the kettle on.'

★ ★ ★

By the time she met Mary at the tea shop with the brass kettle over the door, only ten minutes later than planned, Eva had already eaten a homemade scone with jam, bravely downed several strong cups of tea, and been regaled with anecdotes of all the places in Cornwall where Mr Shrubsole and his companions had previously played their musical instruments. For both large and modest fees alike.

'Well,' she told Mary with satisfaction, 'that's the musical side of things arranged. I feel sure I can leave Lily to do the rest on her own.'

Mary, who had ordered them both a pot of tea and two disappointingly thin slices of Cornish hevva bread while she was waiting, was less convinced.

'Lily's a sweet girl,' she said, peering into the tea-pot before stirring it again, for apparently there were barely enough leaves in there to make half a cup of tea. 'But she doesn't strike me as having much backbone. She'll never make much of a nurse.'

'She's been very good with the new boy though, don't you think?'

Mary shuddered. 'His face . . .'

'Quite a mess, isn't it? Even old Tom looked taken aback, and he must have seen everything. He fought in the Great War. And the Boer War in South Africa.'

'I think he was in the Crimean too.'

'The poor man would have to be over a hundred years old to have fought in the Crimean,' Eva pointed out, then realised Mary was chuckling disrespectfully. 'Oh, very funny. Now don't be mean, I like Tom.'

'I like him too. But he is ancient.' Mary shrugged, thinking. 'I suppose Lily is quite compassionate, now you mention it. Especially with the lost causes.'

'Lily's a darling,' Eva said firmly. 'Though have you noticed? Sister's much nicer to Lily than she is to the rest of us. Well, than to me. Sister Gray is always so cross with me, I don't know what I've done to deserve her sharp tongue.'

'Oh, come on. You must know she's depressed as hell.'

Eva raised her eyebrows, astonished. 'Over what?'

'You and Dr Lewis, of course.' Mary lifted the heavy teapot and began to pour out tea for them. 'Splash of milk?'

'Yes, please. Sorry, what are you talking about? Me and Dr Lewis?'

'Everyone knows the doctor's absolutely *nuts* about you.'

'Good God, what an out-and-out fib.' Eva stared at her in disbelief. 'How on earth could anyone have come up with that nonsense?'

'Well, for starters, he's always smiling at you like this, with all his teeth.' Mary demonstrated, then resumed her usual dour expression. 'And that only means one thing with a man.'

'Is that all? A funny way of smiling, and he's in love with me?'

'Plus, he's started haunting the wards recently. Coming up in the evenings without there even being an emergency.' Mary gave her a knowing smile. 'Only since you came to Symmonds Hall though. He never did that before. We've all noticed.'

Eva took a little nibble of the hevva cake, which was tasty even though it contained hardly any dried fruit, and sat back, considering what her friend had said. This was the second time someone had suggested that Dr Lewis had a romantic interest in her.

Once, she might have reciprocated that interest.

But these days, her whole world revolved around Flight Lieutenant Max Carmichael; whether he was getting better and would be able to walk again soon, or if he could at least be persuaded to flirt with her again, as he had flirted that fateful night in London. So Dr Lewis could look all he wanted, he was never going to get anywhere with her.

'Rubbish,' she said lightly.

'Maybe so.' Mary leant forward over her cake plate, which now held only crumbs. 'But a word of warning.

85

Dr Lewis belongs to Sister Gray. That's common knowledge among the nurses, even if the doctor doesn't know it himself. So he's stolen property, and you'd better give him back unless you want old Graysides to dream up a reason to send you packing.'

'I don't care what she says or does, I'm not going anywhere,' Eva said hotly, suddenly realising it wouldn't be so funny if she lost her position over a misunderstanding. 'I'm not interested in Dr Lewis. But I do intend to stay here in St Ives with Max, and that's final.'

Mary gave her an old-fashioned look. 'Then you'd better pray Dr Lewis can somehow be persuaded to fall for Sister Gray. Because, at the moment, he's only got eyes for you.'

12

Rose had been preparing to do her evening rounds of the wards as usual, but for some reason she couldn't face it. She stood at the window in the senior staff room, though the blackout curtain was in place and there was no view of the night sky to enjoy, only the distant roar of the sea. She felt restless and on edge, her head throbbing.

What was wrong with her tonight?

A quick knock, and Tom popped his head round the door. 'Sorry to disturb you, Sister. But I thought you'd like to know Matron is on the wards.'

'Already?' Rose's eyes flew to the clock. Matron ought not to have come down to visit the wards for another hour. 'But — '

'She's on the warpath. Something about a tub being left to run over in the nurses' quarters. Made quite a mess, by the sound of it. I think she's looking for you.'

'Oh good grief, why didn't she . . . ' Rose stopped and forced herself not to finish that sentence, aware of his knowing gaze on her face.

An overflowing bathtub up in the nurses' quarters was not her concern while she was on duty. The nurse in question should have been reprimanded and an orderly sent to clean it up. But that didn't mean she should display her irritation in front of Tom.

People needed consistency and calm from those in leadership positions; that had been drummed into her over her years as a nurse.

'Could you take a mop and bucket up there, Tom? See what you can do?'

'On my way now, Sister,' he said, and showed her the mop in his hand. 'Don't you fret, I'll soon get it sorted.'

'Thank you.'

Tom nodded and disappeared again, metal bucket clanking by his side, his footsteps moving slowly away down the corridor. More slowly than usual, she realised.

Matron had mentioned something about his leg troubling him recently, which would account for it. An old war wound. She wondered if he would ever retire. Perhaps he was waiting for this new war to end first. A part of the fixtures and fittings at Symmonds Hall, it would be hard to imagine the place without him. His surname was Reed, she recalled. But nobody ever called him that. He was just plain Tom to every-one, even the doctors.

As Rose left the senior staff room, she saw a shadowy figure slip down the stairs from the nurses' quarters and enter Atlantic Ward. It looked like Nurse Ryder. Except Eva was not on duty tonight. Which meant any visit to the ward was unauthorised.

Rose had just set off in a hurry after her, heart thumping with irritation, when the door to Carbis Ward rattled open and Matron came out and stopped her.

'Sister Gray,' Matron said in a low voice, for the ward lights were about to go out and some men would already be sleeping. 'Where are you going? I need to speak to you on a matter of some urgency.'

Rose nearly blurted what she had seen, then thought

better of it and bit her lip instead, worrying it between her teeth.

Much as she would have liked to earn Nurse Ryder a dressing-down from Matron, it would make her look bad too, allowing off-duty nurses to wander about the wards.

She raised her chin. 'I was about to check on the patients. What is it, Matron?'

'A bath was left running upstairs. One of the off-duty nurses, I naturally assumed. But it was not so.'

'I don't understand. If not a nurse, then who?'

'You may well look surprised. As did I, on hearing a noise in the adjacent linen store, which for some reason had been left unlocked. On closer investigation, I discovered a child was hiding there.'

'A child?' Rose was shocked.

'A small boy. One of the orphans from next door, in fact; very possibly the one we saw making such a nuisance of himself during the air raid the other day.'

'*Him?*' Rose stared at Matron, horrified. 'Where is he now?'

'I have no idea, unfortunately. I tried to lay hands on the intruder but he was too quick for me and fled downstairs. By the time I'd locked up the linen store and followed him down, there was no sign of the little pest anywhere. However, I found the yard door had been left open and was banging in the wind, letting in freezing air . . . ' Matron shook her head, her annoyance evident. 'I expect he's back in the orphanage by now and boasting to his friends, proud of himself for having evaded capture.'

Rose did not know what to say. But the story distressed her, and not in the same way it had clearly upset Matron. She recalled the boy's thin, pinched face and the terror in his eyes as the enemy planes flew over.

'Poor thing,' she said instinctively.

Matron frowned. 'Far from being a poor thing, he's a vandal. It must have been he, after all, who ran the tap until the bathtub overflowed, causing Tom extra cleaning work just when he was ready to retire for the night. I think you might reserve some of your pity for Tom.' Matron searched her face, and then sighed. 'Well, I suppose no *real harm* was done. And boys will be boys. But it cannot be allowed to happen again.'

Rose said nothing, but wondered what had happened to drive the child out of the orphanage.

'In the morning,' Matron continued, a little uneasily, 'I shall have to write a letter to the Treverricks and send it round with Tom. They will know best how to control this boy.'

'Oh no, please don't!'

Rose could have bitten her tongue out, seeing Matron's expression. But the cry had slipped out before she really knew what she was saying.

'Why ever not?'

'Because I am afraid the Treverricks will punish him,' Rose said bluntly.

'I expect they will, yes.' Matron hesitated, frowning. 'But is that a bad thing? The boy must learn about the laws of the land, after all. He trespassed, and did some damage, albeit of a temporary kind. How else is he to learn except through punishment?'

It did not seem right to Rose that young children should be punished for the mistakes they made, even though she knew most people considered such things commonplace. She herself had received the rod as a child, often for quite trivial misdemeanours and once

90

for something she had not even done. Now, years later, she could still remember the pain and anguish it had caused her. There had to be a better way to guide children as they grew, she felt, than to hurt them.

'Maybe the boy was scared, and thought he might be safe here. And maybe he ran the bath so he could clean himself.' Rose was trying to make sense of his actions herself. 'Those children in the cellar the other night did seem rather grubby and unkempt.'

'That's true. But it still wouldn't make it right.'

'Matron, please, perhaps just this once . . .' Rose tailed off, not sure if begging would do any good. And why was she begging, anyway?

The boy meant nothing to her. Though she remembered his sad, scared little face, and his name.

Jimmy.

Matron shrugged. 'Very well. On this occasion I shall let it pass. But if I catch another child causing havoc about the place, I shall take the matter straight to the Treverricks. And the cost of any future damage will be deducted from your wages, Sister Gray.'

Rose felt an immense sense of relief, knowing that she had saved that little boy from whatever punishment the Treverricks would have meted out for trespass. Yet she should find Jimmy and warn him never to trespass again, as a painful fate might await him if he did.

'Of course, Matron.' Rose managed a smile. 'Thank you.'

Matron rustled away in her stiff, immaculate uniform, and Rose hurried about her rounds, now running ten minutes late.

After checking each bed, she snapped out the lights in St Ives Ward and Carbis Ward with barely a word to the occupants, though that didn't matter, since most of the patients had already gone to sleep.

Carefully, she pushed aside the image of the little boy that kept haunting her. Matron was probably right; the Treverricks were best left to their own business. What did she know about raising and disciplining a child, after all? Jimmy had broken into the home, hidden in the linen store, and left a mess behind for Tom to deal with. There was only so much poor behaviour you could excuse before punishment became necessary. Besides, it was foolish to feel a rush of maternal protectiveness for a boy she did not know.

She entered Atlantic Ward last, hoping the figure she'd seen entering earlier would have left by now. She did not feel strong enough tonight for a confrontation.

But as she slipped quietly inside, not wishing to wake anyone, she caught Eva bending over Max Carmichael's bed, seemingly about to kiss him on the lips.

'Nurse Ryder!'

Eva jumped back at that piercing whisper and put a hand to her face, no doubt shocked at having been discovered.

Clad in civvies rather than her uniform, the leggy blonde had styled her hair in soft, rounded curls, and even at that distance Rose had a suspicion that she was wearing lipstick. Which, of course, was forbidden for nurses. But it was easy to see why Lewis might be in danger of falling for her, a thought that left her feeling quite savage.

Crossing the ward, Rose dragged the screens about the bed to protect them from curious eyes, for the lights were still on.

'What on earth do you think you're doing, Nurse

92

Ryder?' Her gaze swept Max Carmichael's pale figure, lying motionless against the pillows. 'This man is under our care. It is not permitted for nursing staff to indulge a personal relationship with patients. What do you have to say for yourself?'

'I'm sorry, Sister, it won't happen again.'

'It certainly won't happen again if you're dismissed.'

Eva Ryder's eyes widened in dismay. 'Please, Sister, it was a mistake. You're right, I shouldn't have done it. It was quite dreadful of me. But please don't tell Matron.' She looked at the man in the bed, her eyes shining with unshed tears. 'I couldn't bear it if I had to leave Symmonds Hall.'

'Sister,' Max said in a low voice, looking at Rose.

'You do not need to say a word, Flight Lieutenant,' Rose said quickly, bending to adjust his pillows and straighten his covers. 'Nurse Ryder knows the rules. You are not to blame.'

'I need to make a request,' he insisted.

'Very well.' Rose straightened, clasping her hands at her waist, expecting to hear some impassioned plea on behalf of Nurse Ryder. The woman certainly seemed to attract admirers wherever she went. 'I'm listening.'

'Eva told me about Nurse Kettering having broken her leg. She says her duty rota will include this ward in future.'

'That's likely, yes,' Rose said grudgingly.

'Well, I don't want that. I'd rather not see Miss . . . I mean, Nurse Ryder, again.' He sounded calm, but his hand had clenched compulsively into a fist on top of the covers when Eva began to protest. 'Is that possible, Sister? Am I allowed to ask that?'

'Ordinarily, no,' Rose told him flatly. 'There's a war

on, Flight Lieutenant. The wounded may not pick and choose who cares for them.' She saw something akin to despair in his eyes, and added more gently, 'However, in this particular case, I agree it would be best if Nurse Ryder were not permitted on Atlantic Ward while you're still in residence here. It's clear that her visits are upsetting you and may even be hampering your recovery.'

Eva looked distraught. 'No, that's not true!'

'Please return to your room, Nurse Ryder,' Rose told her. 'I can see you're upset, so I shan't mention this to Matron. But only so long as I never catch you in here again.'

'But, Max . . .' Eva looked at him, tears running down her cheeks. 'Why would you do this to me? After everything — '

'That will be all, Nurse Ryder,' Rose said sharply, and watched as Eva turned with a sob and fled from the ward.

In the silence that followed her departure, Rose took his temperature, which thankfully was normal.

'You've done the right thing,' she commented, checking his pulse too. It was faster than she would have liked, but that was hardly surprising. The doctors had warned them to monitor Carmichael's vitals closely in case of infection to his spinal wounds. 'It's clear Nurse Ryder's feelings for you are getting out of hand.'

The American pilot said nothing, staring straight ahead with a brooding expression on his scarred face.

'Is there anything you need before lights out, Flight Lieutenant?' Rose asked softly, removing the screens from about his bed.

Max Carmichael shook his head.

13

Lily was disturbed to hear a whisper going around that old Graysides had caught Eva kissing Max and forbidden her to enter Atlantic Ward again. It seemed horribly unfair. Especially given that Eva had bravely hired a number of musicians for the Christmas party, and even squared their fees with Matron. Lily herself would have been far too shy to wander about St Ives, boldly knocking on doors and explaining what was needed, so she was deeply grateful to poor Eva and thought it a shame that she was being punished.

But that still left her the headache of organising party games for non-dancers, and deciding which refreshments were to be served, and whether these should be hot or cold. Cook would not be happy to learn she now had to squeeze festive food out of the already squeezed weekly rations allotted to patients and staff.

Meanwhile, her jumbled and slightly feverish thoughts kept returning to their newest resident at the home. Since the young man had moved into Atlantic Ward, she'd only managed a few glimpses of him from a distance. But she had asked a few questions of Tom, who always seemed to know everything about everybody, and had learnt that his name was Private Daniel Orde, and he'd been on a training expedition in Wiltshire when enemy planes attacked. His squad had taken shelter in the nearest building, but incendiary bombs had been dropped, setting the place alight. Daniel had escaped, but then returned twice, leading trapped soldiers to safety, and become so badly burned his own mother hadn't recognised him afterwards. The army had awarded him a medal for bravery, even though Daniel was still only nineteen and had never seen action.

'Goodness, how brave he must be,' Lily had gasped on hearing this, her heart bursting with admiration.

Tom had winked at her. 'Now, don't you go falling in love with him, Miss,' he'd said, and laughed when she blushed. Tom never called her Nurse Fisher like he ought, but Lily didn't mind. He was a nice old fella and she liked him.

The other patients seemed to like Private Orde too, perhaps because he didn't talk all the time, unlike some of the other young men.

'He's a quiet chap,' she'd heard Raymond say in the conservatory the day after Daniel arrived, 'though that's only to be expected with a face like that. Doesn't like to draw attention to himself, I daresay.'

Some had expressed surprise that Daniel hadn't been taken to a special burns hospital, or perhaps one of the larger hospitals in London that dealt with those badly wounded soldiers who had been brought home from engagements overseas.

Questioned about this, Sister Gray had explained that young Private Orde had already spent time at a specialist hospital and had refused further treatment. He was now awaiting discharge, which couldn't be granted until the swelling and chance of infection had subsided. The swelling caused him considerable pain, it seemed, so he was on medication to help with that.

Lily was intrigued by the suggestion that he had refused more treatment. Why on earth would anyone do such a thing, especially with such terrible disfigurement?

Standing beside the medicine store, Lily asked Sister Gray about him, trying not to seem too curious. 'Why did Private Orde refuse treatment for his burns? That is, I expect there's not much that can be done with burns that bad. But surely something is better than nothing?'

Her eye flicking down the list of medicaments, Sister Gray said impatiently, 'I have no idea what goes on inside a patient's head, Nurse Fisher. But I imagine there must be a good reason for it.' She counted out a number of round white pills into a dispensing bowl, and placed that on a tray alongside the other medicines and dressings. 'Perhaps the unfortunate young private simply had enough of being poked and prodded, and knew it was hopeless anyway.'

'I can't believe it's hopeless. Doctors are so clever these days.'

'Ours not to wonder why.' Sister Gray covered the dispensing trays and dressings equipment with a clean white cloth, and handed her the tray. 'Take this at once to Dr Edmund and Matron in Atlantic Ward, and wait for their instructions. You will be assisting them in Atlantic from now on.'

'Me, Sister?' Lily was horrified, forgetting in her panic to conceal her East End accent, which she feared would hinder her career. 'But I ain't trained for dispensing medicines. I don't have the first clue how to do that.'

'Good God, girl, calm down.' Sister frowned at her. 'Nurse Stannard will be there to dispense. You will merely be cleaning wounds and changing dressings.'

'Sorry, Sister.'

'I've moved Nurse Stannard permanently to Atlantic, with Nurse Bailey and Nurse Ryder overseeing Carbis, while I cover St Ives on my own.' Sister Gray shook her head, clearly exasperated. 'Now, hurry along and be careful not to spill any of those.'

Trying not to walk above a brisk trot, Lily found the older doctor with Matron in Atlantic Ward as she'd been told, and presented them with the tray. She was aware of the new patient lying behind her in Johnny's old bed, but did not so much as glance in his direction, fearing she might gawp idiotically and make a fool of herself.

Dr Edmund had been talking to one of the patients about an abdominal operation he'd undergone to remove shrapnel. The site of the incision was still not healed a month after admission, and the man was worried. But Dr Edmund had such a soothing manner, it wasn't often he couldn't reassure a patient.

'Ah, Nurse Fisher. Today's medications.' He took the tray she was holding out, his look admiring. 'Thank you.'

Dr Edmund was polite and well-mannered, what her Aunty Vi would call a 'proper gent'. The man always had a smile on his face when he toured the wards, and Lily rather liked his plummy accent and distinguished looks. The elderly doctor always made everyone feel they were in safe hands.

'My pleasure, Doctor,' Lily told him, smiling shyly in return. 'Oh, and Sister Gray said I'm to wait for your instructions.'

Matron, who had been taking the patient's vitals, laid down the man's wrist with a disapproving frown. 'That will be all, Nurse Fisher.'

'But — '

'Go and assist Nurse Stannard.' Matron nodded down the ward to Bed Eight, where the screens had been drawn to shield the patient from curious eyes. 'She is giving Sergeant Christian a bed bath, since he is unable to walk to the washroom. I'm sure she'll be glad of your help.'

Lily hurried away.

But Nurse Stannard stared in amazement when Lily poked her head around the bed screen. 'I don't need help, thank you,' Mary replied shortly, while Sergeant Christian looked mortified, poor man, and tried to cover himself with his sheet. 'You can take Private Orde's vitals and make sure he's comfortable. I didn't get a chance yet.'

Lily nodded, but could not seem to move her feet.

'What is it now?' Mary demanded, turning with a dripping sponge in her hand. 'Private Orde. Bed Three. Or have you decided today's a holiday?'

Hot-cheeked, Lily made her way back down the ward to Bed Three. The new patient's chart was fixed to the clipboard on the end of the bed. She made a big deal of picking it up and flipping through the various sheets that listed the patient's personal and medical details.

'Water,' came a croak from the bed.

She'd been so focused on his information that she didn't at first realise it was Private Orde talking. Raising her head, she stared at him.

'S-Sorry?'

Her chest was constricted, and she couldn't seem to speak properly. She only realised what he'd said when his gaze moved to the water jug and glass on the bedside cabinet.

'Right you are.' She replaced the chart with unsteady

hands, then poured a glass of water and handed it to him. 'There.'

The private drank a little, and then lowered the glass. His eyes rested on her face, sharp blue and ironic, one badly bloodshot.

'And who are you?' he croaked again, and she realised his voice must have been affected by the fire that had ravaged his good looks.

'Lily,' she whispered, her own voice barely audible, then cleared her throat and tried again. 'Nurse Fisher. I'm an assistant nurse. Still being trained.'

'Learning on the job, are you?'

'You could call it that.'

She busied herself with tidying his pillows and straightening his sheets, as she had often seen Eva do. It was a good way of avoiding looking at him directly.

'I'm Daniel Orde,' he told her, stretching across to put the glass back. 'Danny to my friends.'

Lily came to the end of her nips and tucks, and straightened, hoping he would imagine any breathlessness or colour in her cheeks was down to her bending and stretching. Nothing to do with her embarrassment and her odd, tongue-tied response simply to standing next to him. She had no idea what was wrong with her. But she dreaded being mocked for it.

'Well, Private Orde,' she said briskly, and took his wrist between her fingers and thumb, glancing down at her wristwatch to calculate his pulse, 'let's see how you're getting on.'

He studied her face while she counted, his gaze thoughtful and unnerving. Lily lost count, of course, and had to start again, impossibly distracted.

Private Orde wasn't even remotely dishy, that was the strangest thing. That is, he must have been quite a looker before the fire. But he wasn't now.

One side of his face was striking in its clean-cut, boyish attractiveness. He would have turned her head in the street with that profile, and no mistake. But the other side of his face was buckled and raw, a mishmash of ridges and bumps and misshapen contours. It was hard to look at one without seeing the other. Whenever she started to stare dreamily at the untouched side of his profile, she was instantly jerked back to the reality of his injuries.

Lily felt a little tear creep out from under one eyelid.

She blinked it back crossly, staring down at the clipboard as she scribbled a pulse rate on the chart that was pure fantasy.

It hurt awfully to see such terrible burns, it really did. Especially on someone so close to her own age. But he must be hurting more, she reminded herself.

'Aren't you going to take my temperature, Nurse Fisher?'

She replaced the chart and dangling pencil on the end of the bed. 'Of course I am, Private,' she said more boldly, trying to imagine how Eva would behave in her position. 'Just hang on a tick, would you?'

'Is that a London accent?' When she ignored his question, he added with a grin, 'You don't say much, do you? And my name's Danny, remember? Not Private.'

Lily found her thermometer and stuck it in his mouth without any response. She counted, meeting his eyes briefly, looking away in a panic, then finding it impossible not to glance at him again.

Private Orde — Danny — watched her throughout with a steady gaze.

Her heart was beating fast. Did he look at all the nurses so intently? None of the other girls had mentioned it, and usually when there was a lecher on the ward one of the nurses would soon report him. But he'd only been here a day. Maybe she'd be the one who would have to say something to Matron . . .

He mumbled something, jerking his head.

'Sorry?'

Then she realised he was saying she'd left the thermometer in too long.

'Bloody hell,' she muttered, and whipped the thin glass tube out of his mouth, almost forgetting to check the mercury reading, she was so flustered.

'Everything all right, Nurse?' He was smiling faintly.

'Absolutely smashin', thanks.'

Lily nearly ran back to the chart to fill in his temperature, which was normal. Her own was probably another matter, she thought, her cheeks flaming hot.

So much for staying calm and collected!

14

Eva tried to stay optimistic, but now that Atlantic Ward was completely off-limits to her, not merely as a nurse but also as a visitor to Max's bedside, the world seemed a little greyer and more depressing. She had come here expressly to be able to see Max Carmichael, to thank him for saving her life and to look after him as he recovered. And now she was not even permitted to speak to him.

The worst of it was, Max himself had asked for her removal.

'Don't be downhearted,' Lily told her over breakfast, though she herself was looking agitated these days. 'Maybe Sister Gray will change her mind, you never know.'

The girl had grown up over the past few weeks since coming here, Eva thought, studying her flushed face and over-bright eyes. She came from the East End and must have seen some grim sights in the Blitz, of course. But perhaps the strain of nursing the more severely wounded soldiers at the home — most of whom would never fully recover or lead a normal life again — was taking its toll.

'Sister Gray is like a battleship. She won't turn around for anyone.' Eva poked her minuscule helping of porridge with a spoon and wished Cook would be just a teensy bit more generous with the sugar. Which reminded her of the task in hand. 'By the way, have you sorted out refreshments for the Christmas party yet? Cook's right there.' She nodded towards the hatch into the kitchen, through which Cook, a large woman clad in voluminous whites, could be seen bustling about. She could occasionally be heard too, raising her voice at Piotr, the skinny Polish boy who helped in the kitchens. 'You could speak to her now.'

Lily looked horrified. 'Now? Over me breakfast?'

'When you've finished.' Eva relented, seeing her expression. 'Well, soon anyway. Cook will need plenty of warning. It took us weeks to decide what we would serve at the dance in Porthcurno and to save up coupons for luxury goods. Like the cake ingredients, do you remember?'

Lily's face brightened. 'It was good fun baking that cake, wasn't it? Though such a shame what happened after.'

The dance at Porthcurno had been interrupted by an enemy attack, their bombers flying low over the cliffs, and a local woman had been killed.

'Of course, I'd forgotten about that.' Eva gave up on the porridge and put down her spoon. 'Strange how quickly one pushes such horrors aside. But the whole war has been made up of moments like that, don't you think? Piled up one on top of the other.' She shook her head. 'I suppose it's no wonder we choose to forget the bad things. If we didn't . . . '

She saw Lily's face and decided not to finish that thought. The girl had slightly known the dead woman, and that kind of thing made a difference. When a death wasn't just a number — another gloomy statistic in the papers — but a face and a name you recognised. Then it became all too real.

That was how she'd felt about Max, when she'd thought he was dead. Now he didn't even want to know her.

Eva groaned, and hid her face in her hands.

'Oh, please don't cry.' Lily got up and gave her a hug. 'Everything will work out, you'll see. Come on, let's go to the meeting. We're late as it is.'

They left the staff canteen, which was essentially part of the old kitchens, and made their way to the senior staff room. Lily was allowed in because it was a training exercise day. Inside, they found Matron handing out new gas masks and Sister Gray demonstrating how to put them on. Dr Lewis was there, with most of the other nurses and orderlies. There was no sign of Dr Edmund.

'These new masks have finally arrived,' Sister was saying, 'as replacements for those that were no longer useable, and also for any patients and staff who don't have access to a working gas mask. If you need one, please take it away, label it with your name, and always keep it to hand. For those who live in the home, that means storing it in your bedroom and bringing it to the ward with you every day. Please follow the Ministry rules strictly and without exception.'

Sister held aloft a booklet of Ministry instructions that had come with the delivery, and then handed it to Matron to study.

'Masks for patients are to be kept under each bed,' she continued, 'and in the event of a gas attack drill or, heaven forbid, the real thing, staff are to put their own masks on first, and then help each patient to don theirs. Starting with the most infirm, of course.'

'I hate the smell of masks,' Mary muttered, quickly pulling the one she had been trying on, off her face.

'They're made of rubber. That's what you can smell.' Eva tried to put one on, but found it knocked her cap askew. 'Oh, bother!'

Dr Lewis, who had been watching them in some amusement, came over to help Eva with the mask. She removed her cap, then he put the mask on her and helped her adjust the straps, which were loose.

'Thank you,' she said huskily, glad that at least one man in the place didn't seem to hate her, and then caught Sister Gray's icy green stare cutting into her from across the room. Oops! Too late, she remembered Mary's warning about Sister's particular fondness for Dr Lewis and decided she ought to back off; it would be a bad idea to make an enemy of the woman for no reason. 'But, erm, I can manage on my own. We were forever doing gas attack drills in London. Perhaps you should help Lily instead.'

But Lily had her hand up and was already asking a question. 'Sister, how are we supposed to know when there's a gas attack?'

Sister Gray did not answer, still glaring at Eva and Dr Lewis.

'If there's no siren, but we suspect gas,' Matron replied instead, giving Sister Gray an odd look, 'then the big bell will be rung in the hallway, and somebody will go about the building, shouting, 'Gas attack! Put on your masks!' Probably Tom or one of the other orderlies. That's the best course of action.'

Dr Lewis lounged on the edge of a chair, frowning. 'Will there be a regular drill for gas attacks? We hold them at the cottage hospital once a week.'

'Regular gas drills are mandatory. We should have been carrying them out at least once a week too, but we simply haven't had enough masks before now to make a drill worthwhile.' Matron gave a helpless shrug. 'Too many patients have arrived without one.'

Sister Gray cleared her throat. 'Well, we have masks for everyone now. Meanwhile, the official guidance says all hospitals and convalescent homes need to designate a warden for gas attacks. Someone to conduct drills once a week, and also oversee the safe deployment of equipment and counting of heads in the event of an attack.' With pursed lips, she looked pointedly towards Eva. 'Thank you for volunteering, Nurse Ryder. You can collect the guidance booklet from Matron.'

'Volunteering? But I — '

'Bravo, Nurse Ryder.' Dr Lewis smiled at her, laughing at her confused expression. 'You did say you'd had plenty of practice in London. I'm sure the nurses will all rest easy in their beds, knowing you are in charge of preserving them from mustard gas attacks.'

Eva managed a smile in return. She suspected that Sister Gray didn't share his confidence, if that martial light in her eyes was anything to go by.

★ ★ ★

During her time off, Rose liked to walk out to the cliffs that looked down over the grey, churning Atlantic Ocean. So she was glad when a week of rain stopped and she was finally able to don her boots and coat, and head out across the green wilds. This time, she was careful to add woollen gloves to the hat and scarf she always wore and was glad of the additional warmth once out in the wind.

The weather was turning colder as each day took them deeper into autumn. Mists drifted across the fields and hedgerows in the early mornings, spiders' webs laden with frost became thin silver chains, and winter eiderdowns were brought out of storage for the nurses' poorly heated rooms.

People were beginning to talk excitedly about Christmas, looking forward to the festivities. Some of the patients kept begging the doctors to confirm their discharge date so they could get home before the holidays, and two of the nursing staff had asked Matron if they might be permitted leave over Christmas; just a few days to visit their families and exchange gifts.

'Are you planning to go home and see your folks too, Sister?' Lily had asked Rose the other day. She was wide-eyed with excitement, for the girl had received a letter from her aunt about their own preparations for Christmas.

'No,' she'd said.

She had spoken sharply. But Lily had not taken the hint. 'Oh, that's a shame. Why ever not? Do they live too far away?'

Rose walked to the cliff edge and peered over, taking care not to get too close to the sheer drop. The sea below boiled and foamed, crashing against the rocks. Further along the coast, St Ives curved about a sheltered bay; she had wandered its narrow, winding streets as a child, never quite feeling as though she belonged.

That was the lot of an orphan, she thought grimly. Home is where the heart is, where the family lives. But when there is no family, no warm heart to return to for love and comfort, how can any place be called home?

'I don't have a family,' Rose had told Lily flatly. 'Enough chit-chat now. Get on with your duties, Nurse Fisher.'

As a young orphan, she'd looked forward to marrying a nice man one day. To making her own family and holding it close until she died, surrounded by children and grandchildren, and perhaps even great-grandchildren.

A silly girl's fantasy, that was all it had been.

For here she was, over thirty now and still unmarried, and with little prospect of ever finding a husband, since the war showed no signs of stopping and she was not getting any younger. Even Lewis, who was the closest she had to a friend in this world, had barely looked at her in days, his smiles seemingly reserved for Nurse Ryder.

She wanted to weep.

But what good would tears do? She blinked them away impatiently and set her face back towards the convalescent home, aware that her next shift would begin in less than an hour. There were more things in life than marriage and children. Her nursing work must be its own reward.

As she neared the home, she saw a child's face pressed against a window pane high up in the orphanage. It was a sad, lonely face, and she thought she recognised it.

Was that Jimmy?

On impulse, buffeted by the wind, Rose raised a gloved hand in greeting.

There was a tiny hesitation.

Then the child raised a small hand in return. Briefly, so briefly. Then the face vanished, and he was gone.

★ ★ ★

Having finally plucked up courage to speak to Cook about the Christmas party, Lily was met with a look of fierce astonishment.

'You need me to do what, lovie? Prepare party food?' Cook, a vast woman with a chest that strained her uniform buttons, shook her head of thick, curly brown hair, which was barely restrained under a net. 'You must be crackers. I'll be lucky to get a few portions of turkey for those senior staff who are working over the Christmas season, and maybe ingredients for plum pudding. Now you want more? You're like Oliver Twist, you are.'

'Maybe if we was to approach the Ministry for help — '

'The Ministry? How do you think I wangled the turkey? The rest will be on mock turkey, same as last year. That's rabbit to me and you, though you won't know the difference under a dribble of gravy with a side helping of sprouts.' Cook laughed at her expression, giving Lily a dismissive wave. 'Off you go now, Cockney. I've enough to do without listening to your nonsense.'

Lily, stopping hesitantly in the doorway, felt quite disheartened. She'd blown it this time, and for sure. At this rate, they'd be lucky to be offering round tea and dry crackers at this party. If only Matron had found someone else to organise this party, she thought unhappily.

But she recalled Eva's cheery resilience to difficult people and situations, and raised her chin, returning to the fray.

'Look 'ere, Cook,' she began firmly, then corrected herself, 'I mean, Mrs Penhallow,' and saw the woman turn, rolling pin in hand. 'I was sent here by Sister Gray.'

It was only a little white lie, she told herself. But it had a useful effect, for Cook was visibly shaken. It seemed everyone was afraid of old Graysides.

'I'm awful sorry. I know it's a nuisance and you're busy, but Sister told me I weren't to come back empty-handed. And you know what Sister's like when she's got the bit between her teeth.' She paused, more confident now, seeing Cook's eyes narrow. 'So I thought maybe we could have a few sandwiches — '

'*Sandwiches*?' Cook barked.

'Only with meat substitute,' she added hurriedly. 'I know some good recipes. I'd be happy to help you make them on the day.'

'I don't need your help to make a sandwich, my girl.'

'And perhaps some fruit?'

'Oh, is that all? In the middle of bloody December?'

'Tinned fruit, of course. With a dollop of custard on top.' Lily backed away as Mrs Penhallow lurched towards her with the rolling pin raised. 'If you can spare it that close to Christmas, of course. I've got some other suggestions. I'll bring you a list. And I can ask Matron to beg the Ministry for some extra help. You might even get some extra rations out of it for Christmas.'

Cook lowered her rolling pin. 'Hmm.'

★ ★ ★

On returning to her bedroom, Lily found a postcard had been shoved under her door. It was from her friend Hazel Baxter, back in Porthcurno.

111

She tore off her nursing cap and threw herself down on her bed, eagerly scanning the few scrawled lines several times over, hungry for news of home.

It made her quite homesick to think about everyone in Porthcurno going about their lives without her, though she was glad that Hazel sounded so healthy and looking forward to the birth of her child in a few months' time.

Dearest Lily

Hope you are settling in at Symmonds Hall. Apols for the postcard but they are all the rage these days. I wish you were here to see how large I've grown, by the way. It's dreary, not being able to work anymore. But I wouldn't be surprised if Baby makes an early appearance.

Your Gran and Aunty Vi miss you. We all had lunch last Sunday. Not much food but great company. Charlie asks, are you coming home for the Christmas hols? Please say yes.

Write soon!

Your friend, Hazel

Lily got out pen and ink, and two sheets of paper from her meagre store, and replied to Hazel's postcard, listing all the tasks she had to do on the wards every day, the weather they'd been having in St Ives, and how she was still scared stiff of Sister Gray. She also told her about the Christmas party she had been asked to organise, and how she'd practically skipped back to the wards that day after tackling Cook about extra party rations.

Who would have thought it? Standing up to a woman as intimidating as Cook and even persuading her to lay on sarnies for the party ... It was not like her to be so brave.

Lily grinned as she described the encounter in her letter, still proud of herself for not running away as soon as Mrs Penhallow opened her mouth. Truth be told, talking to Cook had taken her right back to her Porthcurno days, working alongside Alice, Hazel, and Aunty Violet at Eastern House. Her eyes misted over as she recalled how happy they'd been together, messing about with mops and buckets in their break times ...

Do you remember when scary old Mr Frobisher used to terrorise us like that in the kitchens? Though I suppose Frobisher has to be polite to Aunty Vi now that she's housekeeper there. What I wouldn't give to have seen his face when he heard the news of her promotion!

Towards the close of her letter, she returned to the tricky question of whether she'd be home for Christmas.

I'm not sure I'll be allowed time off this year. It all depends on who else wants to go home for Christmas. But I'll be sure to ask Sister soon — maybe when she's in a better mood with me!

Which might be never, Lily thought, biting the end of her pen.

What she didn't mention to her friend, however, was the obsession she was developing with a new patient at the hall, a certain Private Daniel Orde. Or 'Danny,' as he preferred to be known.

Perhaps because she wasn't ready to admit that to herself.

114

15

Eva waited until she saw Mary pushing Max out into the garden for Recreation Hour, then slipped out of the side door of Carbis Ward and hurried across the lawn towards them.

'Mary? Can you wait a minute?'

Nurse Stannard, surprised by her request, cast a guilty look down at Max in his wheelchair, whose face was like stone. Mary knew perfectly well there was not supposed to be any contact between them, of course. But Eva was counting on their friendship to help her see past that cruel injunction.

'Erm, I suppose so,' Mary said reluctantly. 'What is it?'

'I need to talk to Flight Lieutenant Carmichael. Alone, please.'

Mary's eyes widened. 'Oh, I'm not sure.'

'I'll whizz him round the woodland path and straight back to the house.' Eva glanced about the garden, where various patients were walking or sitting on benches in the chilly sunshine. 'Sister and Matron are having tea in the senior staff room. They won't see if I'm quick. So nobody needs to get into trouble.'

Max was shaking his head. 'Eva, I told you before — ' he began to grind out, but she interrupted him.

'Ten minutes,' she said breathlessly. 'That's all I'm asking. I only came to St Ives because of you, Max. I trained as a nurse for three whole months just to be able to spend time with you. Surely you can spare me ten minutes of your time?'

He looked at her grimly, then shrugged.

That shrug was as good as a yes, she decided, and so she nodded to Mary to go back inside. 'I'll bring him to the conservatory when we're done,' she promised.

'You'd better not be long. I'll catch it if Sister realises what I've done.'

'Thank you, Mary.'

Eva hurried away with Max, wheeling him swiftly along the path beside the lawns and towards the woodland ahead.

After passing under an archway of evergreen hedge, a narrow track wove between clusters of trees with occasional small clearings where benches had been set for the enjoyment of patients. Alongside delicate silver birches, ash, elder and beech trees filled the woods, with shrubs spilling over onto the paths.

Earlier in the autumn, this woodland wilderness had been a favourite spot for patients during their recreation time. But it was colder now and the paths were empty, the damp ground thick with fallen leaves.

Max said nothing, staring straight ahead, his hands clenched on his lap.

Eva kept glancing over her shoulder, ridiculously nervous. What if one of the other patients or a member of staff had spotted Mary relinquishing Max into her care, and told Sister Gray about it? Her career as a nurse might be over. And then she would never see Max again. Not only that, she enjoyed her work at Symmonds Hall, and the thought of being sent somewhere else filled her with dread.

'Here, this will do.'

Fearing discovery and punishment at any moment, Eva stopped beside a bench in a clearing off the main path. She sat down and looked at him, her heart pounding.

Max turned his head, studying the trees nearest to them, most stripped bare by recent winds but some still hanging on to a few old dry leaves. The ridged scar that ran down his temple to the corner of his eye was beginning to fade, she realised.

'Get it over with, then,' he said roughly. 'What do you want to say?'

Eva clasped her hands together tightly. 'Max, what is this about? Why did you tell Sister Gray that you never want to see me again? To have me care for you again?' Her voice broke slightly, and she had to swallow hard to stop from crying. 'I don't understand.'

He said nothing, sitting motionless as the cold wind lifted his dark hair. He might as well have been made of granite, she thought despairingly.

'I mean, I know you've never said that . . . ' She drew in a shaky breath. 'That is, I thought we had an understanding, at least. That we were friends. What have I done wrong?'

'Nothing.'

She stared, wishing she could work out what was going on in his head. 'Nothing? But why push me away, then?'

There was a long silence. Then he growled, 'I told you. I'm not what you need. Look at me. I'll never get out of this chair.'

'Of course you will.'

'That's what I'm talking about.' He turned his head, meeting her gaze at last. 'Your blind optimism. It's very inspirational, Miss Ryder. But it's misplaced. And cruel.'

'Cruel?'

'It gives me — and you — false hope.' He groaned, and hid his face in his hands. 'Don't you see how hopeless this is, Eva?' He sounded broken, just like her. 'I can't be the man you want me to be. I can't live up to your ideal. I want to but . . . These legs don't work. I've faced that truth. But you still refuse to admit it. And I won't keep on pretending with you.' He looked up at her, his face bleak. 'It's finished between us, it's over. I'll always be stuck in this wheelchair. And I'm not going to spend the rest of my miserable existence knowing I tethered you to it as well.'

'Max, for goodness' sake!' Eva stood up, agitated, then sat down again, her mind whirling. 'Tethered me? What on earth are you talking about?'

'This. Here. Now.' Max slammed the side of the chair with one almighty arm, and the whole structure shook and creaked beneath him. 'You pushing me, washing me, looking after me.' He sounded almost out of breath. 'I'm not going to watch you steer me around in this damn chair for the next thirty or forty years!'

Tears were spilling down her cheeks. But she understood at last.

'Oh, Max.' She reached out and put her hand over his. 'You drove me away so I wouldn't marry you.'

He was still staring into the woodlands, not meeting her eyes. 'You can't waste your life on me. Don't you see that?'

'I don't see that, no.'

'Eva, somewhere out there is a man who could make you happy. The kind of man you deserve. Don't stay here in St Ives. Go and find him, and make yourself a life.'

'I have a perfectly good life here, thank you.'

Max looked round at her gloomily. 'I may never be able to father a child,' he said after a long struggle. 'Dr Edmund said it's highly unlikely.'

'Dr Edmund is a lovely man but he's a family doctor, not an expert in conditions like yours. You need to see a specialist.'

'I saw a specialist in London,' he insisted. 'He said there was nothing more he could do for me, and sent me here to convalesce.'

'Then he was a blithering idiot.'

'Eva,' he protested.

'No, I won't listen anymore.' She leant over and kissed him on the lips, and felt him freeze up, a statue beneath her. Pulling back, she looked deep into his eyes. 'I love you, Flight Lieutenant Carmichael. And I intend to stay by your side for the next thirty or forty years, whether or not you're still in this blasted chair. Which, by the way, I don't happen to believe you will be.' Eva raised her eyebrows at him pointedly. 'There, I've just proposed to you and it's not even a leap year. Now, are you going to shut up and kiss me, or not?'

'I'm not going to kiss you,' he muttered, shaking his head. 'Not now, not ever. I appreciate what you've done for me, Eva. But I'm not the right man for you.'

'Well, I . . . I refuse to believe that.' Eva rubbed away her tears, trying not to collapse in a heap at his rejection. 'But I'd better get you back before Mary has a blue fit. We've been gone much longer than ten minutes.' She hadn't won him over but she wasn't about to give up either. 'This conversation isn't finished. You can't keep me at arms' length forever.'

'Watch me,' he said grimly.

16

Rose wandered from ward to ward, still searching for things to do even though her shift had finished some thirty minutes before. She was feeling down and a little lost, she realised, yet couldn't pinpoint why. Perhaps it was the endless nature of this war. The constant worry that Britain and her allies might lose the fight, leaving this green and pleasant land to be invaded and destroyed.

It was hard not to fear such things, living so close to the coast and looking out each day on an ocean that could at any moment bring the enemy to these shores.

But then she would see the grateful smiles of patients as she straightened their pillows, brought them fresh dressings, or checked their vitals. If these brave men, who had suffered so much and were still suffering, could find a way to smile, then surely she could too.

'How are you today, Sister?' Corporal Pinning asked with a cheery wink. The wound in his abdomen was healing well and she felt sure Dr Edmund would soon permit his discharge. 'Looking forward to this Christmas party I hear is being planned?'

Rose smiled, tidying the sprigs of autumn flowers one of the cleaning staff had kindly brought in to brighten up the wards. 'I certainly am, Corporal,' she agreed. 'However, I doubt if you will still be here for that. Not at the rate you're improving.'

'It would be good to get home in time for Christmas.' His smile faltered. 'Though I lost my mum only a few

120

weeks before this happened,' he added, nodding to the bulge of bandaging under his pyjama top, 'and it won't be the same without her. Just me and my old dad. I don't know how we'll get on.'

'That's awfully sad.' Rose glanced across the ward, hearing one of the other men coughing hard, seemingly unable to stop. She would have gone to help him, but halted, seeing the look in Corporal Pinning's eyes. 'What happened?'

'Bloody Jerries bombed the factory she was working in, didn't they? Mum and about half a dozen other women were killed. Didn't stand a chance.'

Rose's heart ached for the man. 'I'm so sorry.'

'What about you, Sister?' he asked, looking at her curiously. 'You got any family to go home to this Christmas?'

'Goodness no, I'll be here over the festive season. Like last year and the year before.' Rose hesitated, then said, 'I only have a sister, anyway. Nobody else. And Elsie's gone away for the war effort. She works in a factory, just like your mother did.'

'Ah, now that's a crying shame, you two being separated.' The corporal was frowning. 'When you've no one but her, I mean.'

'It's not easy,' she admitted.

'Still, you must be proud of your sister. All you ladies . . . Doing such hard jobs, mucking in, working all hours, taking on men's work.' He made a face. 'Some of the fellas don't like it, of course. They say it's not right, a woman doing a man's job. But fair play to you is what I say. That's how we'll beat Hitler, isn't it?'

'I pray you're right,' she said fervently.

Making her way hurriedly across the room to the

patient who was coughing, Rose helped him sit up and take a few sips of water.

'That's it, Private Fletcher, keep up the deep breathing like the doctor showed you. Nice and slow, to a count of five.' She patted and rubbed his back as he leant forward and breathed deep, helping him bring up phlegm to clear his airways. 'You're doing well.'

Private Fletcher had been caught in a chemical explosion at a munitions factory and his lungs had never quite recovered. Dr Lewis had confided in her that he thought they never would, and the poor man would probably die an early death from pulmonary scarring and congestion. Even with the medications he'd been prescribed, and despite a range of physiological treatments intended to open and expand his lung capacity, he still constantly struggled with his breathing. It was tragic.

At the next bed, hidden discreetly behind bed screens, she could hear Nurse Stannard talking to Nurse Ryder as they turned Corporal Hunter over onto his side, presumably so they could change his soiled dressings.

Eddie Hunter, a red-faced man in his late forties from Truro, had been hit with flying shrapnel in his back and buttocks on active service. He needed his dressings changed regularly, as one of his deeper wounds had become infected, forcing his re-admission only a few weeks earlier, after having been discharged for home care.

Rose kept rubbing Private Fletcher's back, making soothing noises, but her ears were pricked, listening to the two women behind the bed screens.

'Now, do lie still, Corporal,' Mary Stannard was

saying, 'or I'll make a right mess of this.' She paused. 'Come on, Eva, stop being so coy.' Her voice dropped, suddenly conspiratorial. 'You were alone with him for bloody ages and when you came back, you were lit up like a bloody Christmas tree. You can't pull the wool over my eyes. Tell me everything!'

Rose stiffened.

Eva, alone with a man? Here at the home?

But which man?

'For God's sake, Mary, keep it down,' Eva warned her, as though aware that Rose was nearby and might be able to overhear them.

Rose was so shocked, her brain wouldn't seem to work. It couldn't be Flight Lieutenant Carmichael, she decided. He had made it abundantly clear he didn't want to speak to Nurse Ryder again.

'I won't keep it down, I did you a big favour there. And you won't even tell me what happened.' Mary tutted. 'Eddie, I told you not to move. Now I've spilt the solution on the sheet.'

'Look, nothing happened, all right?' Eva sounded cautious. As well she might be, Rose thought, her teeth gritted. 'Well, nothing much.'

'Aha!' There was a short silence. Then Mary giggled, as though Eva was smiling. 'You dark horse. So he does like you. I was sure he must. And did he . . . you know?'

'Hush,' Eva hissed again, though it sounded as though she too were laughing. 'Someone might hear us.'

'It's all right,' Mary told her blithely, 'old Graysides should be off shift by now. Tucked up in her room with some dreary improving book, I daresay. And Eddie here won't say anything. Will you, Eddie?'

The corporal muttered something incomprehensible, and Mary replied in kind, settling to her task without further comment.

Her cheeks burning, Rose settled Private Fletcher against his pillows again, made sure he had fresh water and a handkerchief, and then left the ward.

She slipped out into the corridor and stood there a moment, breathing hard. Her hands were trembling and she hid them under her apron, trying to regain some composure before heading upstairs.

Mary was bad enough. A dreary, improving book, indeed!

But she badly wanted to shake some sense into Eva. A nurse spending time alone with a man was strictly forbidden by the rules, and could cost the foolish young woman her career.

Yet at the back of her mind was a growing sense of panic. Who on earth 'liked' Eva enough to risk being caught alone with her? And what was it they'd done together to make Mary giggle like that?

Rose felt like crying.

Faced with her sister's long absence, had Dr Lewis lost his heart to yet another woman who wasn't Rose?

17

It was a cold, wintry afternoon when Lily heard the
large handbell being rung violently in the hallway
outside Atlantic Ward, and stopped what she was
doing, staring about herself in consternation. 'Bloody
hell, what's that clanging? Are we being invaded?'

The patient she had been caring for chuckled at her
expression. 'Nothing so exciting,' Private Piper reassured her, pushing back the bed covers and swinging
his legs out of bed. 'It's the new gas drill, nurse. Don't
you remember? Matron came round to tell us all the
other day. The gas masks are under the beds.'

Sure enough, she could now hear Tom in the
hallway shouting, 'Gas attack! Gas attack! Put your
masks on!'

'Right, we'd better find your gas mask then,' Lily
said with a sigh, and put aside the washing bowl
and cloth.

'I can do that,' Private Piper said, already bending
to scrabble for the mask under his bed. 'You go and
help one of the others, nurse. Like him, for instance.'
He jerked a thumb over his shoulder towards Private
Daniel Orde's bed. 'Poor lad, I don't know how he'll
get a gas mask on. Not over those burns.'

Shocked by the reality of what he'd said, Lily put a
hand to her chest, for her heart was suddenly gallop-
ing. Of course, of course!

Tom came running into the ward, strangely alien in
his rubber mask, straps flapping wildly, and headed
straight for Max Carmichael, since he was one of the

men who couldn't get out of bed to reach his mask. Lily made a note that perhaps masks should be hung on the bed somehow, to make it easier for those who were bed-bound. One of the cleaning staff came in too, also wearing a mask, and helped one of the other men who was struggling.

She hurried to Private Orde's bedside, seeing him perched on the edge of his bed, fumbling to fit the mask over his face.

'I'm all right, thank you,' Danny told her when she tried to help, though she could see from his expression that he was far from all right. 'Why don't you help someone else?'

Uncertain, Lily turned on her heel, but most of the other patients seemed to be coping fine with the new drill. She supposed they had done many gas attack drills in basic training and while fighting overseas. And some would have faced the real thing, in fact.

The thought made her queasy, for she'd heard terrible things about the effects of mustard gas, and knew what it could do to someone who didn't have a mask. People who had endured gas attacks in the Great War had been left in terrible condition, months later, wheezing and coughing, their lungs rattling as they breathed. She could only pray the Germans refrained from using such a terrible weapon in the current war.

'I think everyone else is doing fine,' she said, turning back to him.

Danny glanced at her. 'Where's your mask?'

'Oh, my stars!' In her hurry to help him, she'd forgotten the rule that staff needed to don their masks first before helping patients.

Lily dashed back to her station and fetched the mask from under the desk, rushing back to Danny's bedside while fitting it. The smell was horrid but it didn't bother her. She'd occasionally worn a mask in London during air raids, and had got used to chucking it on whenever people shouted 'Gas!' Only she couldn't quite remember how to tighten the straps on this new type, so the bloody thing kept slipping to one side.

'Here, let me,' Danny said, still not in his own mask, and showed her how to fit it properly. 'That's better.'

The world looked very odd through the round eyeholes of her mask, especially after a few noisy breaths left them misted up at the edges so she could hardly see. But if everyone else was coping, Lily thought stoutly, then she wasn't going to make an idiot of herself by complaining.

'Now let me help you,' Lily insisted, glad to see the mist clearing somewhat as her breathing slowed.

His eyes met hers, and she saw resistance in them. So much stubborn pride, she thought, marvelling at it. Then he grimaced. 'If you must,' he said roughly.

He'd thrown his rubber gas mask aside on the bed. She grabbed it, bringing it to his face, and saw Danny flinch. Then she understood.

'It hurts to wear the mask,' she whispered, 'don't it?'

He didn't bother to deny it but gave a terse smile. 'I suppose a little pain is worth not being gassed.'

'Oh, Danny.'

'Now you're just prolonging the agony, Nurse Fisher.' His smile looked frozen in place. 'You'd better get on with it. Before the gas gets me.'

'It's only a drill.'

'But next time, it could be the real thing.' He nodded for her to continue. 'Go on. You won't break me.'

127

Lily wasn't so sure. But there was no way round it. Frowning with concentration, she fitted the gas mask over his red, swollen facial scarring as delicately as possible, and bit her lip when she saw him wince.

'I'm sorry.'

'Not your fault.' His voice was muffled behind the mouthpiece.

Thankfully, the straps didn't need any adjustment as the mask was already tight enough. But she could see what it cost him to wear the cruel, clumsy contraption over such exquisitely painful burns, every movement an agony for him.

'There you go.'

Matron and Dr Edmund, both wearing masks, had come into the ward to ensure the drill had gone smoothly. They stopped at Bed Three to ask Private Orde how he was coping with the mask over his burns, and Lily expected him to say something. But he just gave them a confident thumbs-up, and they moved on.

'We'll wear the masks for half an hour today,' Dr Edmund told everyone, 'and an hour next time. Speak to a nurse if you have any difficulties breathing.'

When they'd gone, Lily turned back to Danny's bed. But he had lain down again and was staring up at the ceiling in his gas mask, arms folded across his chest.

Poor soul, he must be in such pain, she thought.

It was clear he wouldn't allow her to remove his mask any earlier than the other chaps, so she went back to Private Piper and continued washing his wound, while he told her a muffled anecdote about his first gas drill during basic training, where the sergeant in charge had forgotten to tell them to remove their masks and they'd eventually gone to sleep in them and woken up with red lines all over their faces.

Lily nodded in all the right places and laughed at the private's jokes. But her mind was far away, thinking of Danny's bravery as she blinked away tears.

★ ★ ★

Eva was finding it hard to bite down her growing feelings of frustration. Despite their long talk in the grounds, Max was still refusing to let her visit him on the ward. He had convinced himself that he wasn't good enough for her, or some such nonsense, and that she should walk away from the relationship. Well, he could keep thinking that, Eva told herself defiantly, because she wasn't going anywhere.

But the fact remained that it was an issue.

How to persuade her flight lieutenant that they belonged together, when he wouldn't even speak to her and couldn't seem to see past his injuries?

The longer she thought about it, the more she began to formulate a plan. She would need Max to agree, of course. But she could only deal with one problem at a time, she decided, pushing that fear aside.

She decided that Dr Lewis was her best bet.

So she waited until he was leaving the hall one day, on his way out to his car, and then ran after him. It was a chilly winter's day, the sun hidden behind a mass of grey clouds, the sea lying still and silver in the distance. Eva was glad of her cardigan as the wind blew, hopefully not mussing up her artfully arranged curls, and the raincoat folded over her arm in case of rain later. Though these days the weather was growing cold enough to snow . . .

'Dr Lewis?' When he turned, clearly surprised that she had followed him, Eva gave him her most dazzling smile. 'I'm sorry to disturb you. I was hoping to be able to talk to you alone about something.'

The doctor looked her up and down, frowning. She was in civvies, not her uniform, as it was her day off, and he was clearly wary about fraternising with any of the nursing staff outside work hours. Given Sister Gray's proprietorial hold over him, that didn't surprise her. But she couldn't allow that to worry her.

'I'm afraid I can't, Nurse Ryder. Maybe tomorrow?'

'Or you could give me a lift into town and we could talk on the way. You're always so busy when you come to the home.' She glanced over her shoulder at the entrance door. 'Besides, it's hard to find somewhere private with so many people about. I wouldn't want anyone to overhear us.'

He glanced at his watch. 'Well, I suppose . . . '

'Thank you,' she said before he could elaborate and possibly put her off the idea. She bounded forward to the passenger door of his car. 'This is marvellous of you, I must say. And I love your car. How long have you had her?'

'It's my grandfather's car, actually,' he said, opening the door for her and watching with a faint smile as she slid her legs inside.

'I see.' She waited until he had come round to the driver's side and got inside, then said, 'I noticed Dr Edmund didn't come in today. Is he unwell?'

'Just busy.' He started the engine and set off down the hill towards the town. 'We have to run a surgery for the whole of St Ives too, you know, and the cottage hospital as well. It's not easy keeping up.' He glanced at her sideways. 'So, spill the beans. What's all this about, Nurse Ryder?'

'Call me Eva, please. We're not at work now.'

'All right.' Again, he seemed amused. 'Though you have to call me plain Lewis, in that case.'

'There's nothing plain about you,' she said daringly.

His smile died at her words. The doctor slowed the car almost to a standstill, looking at her in earnest.

'Now, see here, Miss Ryder, I don't know what you've been told — '

'About what?'

'Doctors and nurses getting involved with each other.' He seemed troubled, choosing his words with care. 'I imagine it may happen in other hospitals but not here at Symmonds Hall. I thought you knew the rules — '

'You think a great deal of yourself, don't you?' she interrupted him, laughing. 'And it's Eva, not Miss Ryder. You think I'm making a pass at you. But you're dead wrong.'

'I . . . ' Lewis tilted his hat back to scratch his forehead, then took the wheel again and carried on driving. 'All right, perhaps I deserve that. What's all this about, then?'

'It's about Flight Lieutenant Carmichael. I need to know if there's anything else we could be trying to get him back on his feet. Some other treatment. Or a new approach, maybe.'

Lewis was quiet for a moment, watching the road ahead. 'Where's this come from, Eva? From the patient, or from you?'

'From me,' she admitted. 'Max has given up, you see. He doesn't believe he'll ever be able to walk again.'

She decided not to mention that she'd proposed marriage to Max and he'd refused her. There was no point humiliating herself more than she already had.

'Maybe he won't.'

Eva glared at him. 'So you've given up on him too?'

'The doctors in London already had a good crack at fixing him. They sent him here because there was nothing more they could do.'

'RAF doctors,' she pointed out. 'Hard-working, dedicated men, and I admire them hugely. But they may not have been specialists. Besides, you know how busy those places are at the moment. They're swamped with badly injured men, more coming in every day. Would it be any surprise if they'd missed something about his condition?'

Lewis said nothing.

Ahead of them lay the narrow streets of St Ives, the houses huddled together around the bay shrouded in cool November light. Through gaps, she caught sight of the sea now and then, which roiled under a gloomy sky, its waves flecked white as long rollers barrelled in off the Atlantic. Eva felt the same inside, full of turmoil and despair. There had to be something they could do for Max, there just had to be!

'Well, I suppose that I could write to a friend of mine in London,' he said in the end, grudgingly. 'We studied medicine together. Charles went on to specialise in spinal injuries. He might know of some new research in rehabilitation.'

'Oh, Lewis!' She leant across and kissed him on the cheek, causing him to swerve and nearly hit a lady on a bicycle. 'Thank you. Thank you so much.'

'Here, I say, give over!' He sounded worried. 'People will talk.'

By that, she suspected he meant 'to Sister Gray' and wondered again whether the doctor returned Sister's feelings. If so, he certainly kept his emotions off his face.

They had reached the main street, with St Ives harbour just glimpsed beyond; shop awnings banged and fluttered at each gust here, and people walked into the wind, holding onto their hats. Small ships bobbed about in the water, their rigging slapping musically against the masts.

Lewis slowed down, frowning. 'Now look, don't get your hopes up, Eva. I said I'd write to a friend; I didn't say I could fix him. Your flight lieutenant may be unfixable.'

'I know,' she agreed, beaming at him, and hid her tightly crossed fingers in her lap.

18

The thin glass pane of her bedroom window rattled in the wind, and through it came the unusual sound of tramping feet. Rose, who had been reading a letter from her sister, got up and went to the window.

Elsie's letter had left her confused.

Before Elsie had been conscripted to work in a factory upcountry, she'd insisted that she and Lewis would be married on her return. Rose suspected her sister enjoyed rubbing her nose in their relationship. Yet lately, Elsie's letters had been short and unrevealing, with no mention of Lewis. No doubt factory work was taking all her sister's energy.

Looking down into the yard, Rose saw a small group of orphanage children marching around in a circle, single file. They were not wearing hats or coats, and the wind grabbed at their hair and flapped their clothing. The boys were in short trousers, their legs pitifully exposed to the cold, and the girls' skirts whipped up at each chill gust, making them squeal in embarrassment. Several of them slipped over icy patches on the flagstones as they marched, for it had grown almost cold enough to snow these past few days.

'What on earth?' Rose muttered.

The children looked miserable, their shoulders hunched, heads down. She could hear them chanting something too, but couldn't catch the words.

Was it some kind of game, she wondered? If so, it didn't look like much fun.

Leaning up against the glass, she peered down, and spotted Mr Treverrick in a long, buttoned-up coat, thick scarf wrapped twice about his neck, huddled in a doorway.

Rose was horrified. The orphanage director seemed wholly unconcerned by the icy weather and their lack of warm clothing. She couldn't understand what he was doing, and why on earth he didn't get those poor children inside before they caught their death.

As she watched in disbelief, Mr Treverrick shouted something, waving his arm, and the children all came to a straggling halt, turned wearily about-face, and began trudging in the opposite direction.

It was a punishment of some kind, she realised with a numb sense of shock.

It was a November day.

Yet these young children were being forced to march around the yard in this freezing cold without so much as a coat or scarf among them.

Rose swore under her breath in a most unladylike fashion, then snatched her own coat from the back of the door and stormed out. Reaching the back door into the yard, she pushed through it with unusual force and strode across the icy flagstones, making towards Mr Treverrick.

She still couldn't hear what the marching children were chanting in their small, breathless voices, and as she approached they stopped at a command from Mr Treverrick and stood waiting.

The children looked so cold and wretched; her heart squeezed in pain for them. She wanted to grab every one of them and hold them tight against her, and never let go. But of course she could not. She

135

dared not. Her only course of action was to remain calm and civil with the Treverricks, as far as possible.

Matron had made it clear she was not to interfere with the running of the orphanage. It was not her domain, however protective she might feel towards these unfortunate children. But she could still ask this horrid man a few searching questions, at least.

'Mr Treverrick,' she said, trying to be polite but so furious that her voice was shaking, 'why do none of these children have their coats on?'

Mr Treverrick looked her up and down in amazement. 'I'm sorry?'

'Do the children not possess coats? Or jackets of some kind?' Rose turned to regard the children, who were still marching and chanting, though with bright, curious eyes fixed in her direction. 'How about gloves and scarfs, at least? And where are their hats? They have hats. I have seen the children in hats on their way to church. Why are they not wearing them in this bitter weather?'

'And what business is it of yours?' he demanded without answering her questions. The man had a haughty, authoritarian tone which made her want to kick him in the shins. 'Please return to your patients, nurse, and allow me to run this orphanage in my own way.'

'It's winter. The children must be freezing.' Rose folded her arms, feeling the heat of pure ire in her cheeks. 'And I'm not budging from this spot until those children either go back inside or have coats fetched out to them.'

'Neither of those things is going to happen,' he said, 'so you will be standing there a long time. Though I advise you to leave at once. You are not welcome here and are trespassing. This is not the convalescent home's property, even if we share the cellar during air raids. It belongs to the orphanage.'

'Excuse me if I'm wrong, but I believe the orphanage buildings belong to Lady Symmonds, as does the convalescent home. That makes this her land, not yours. I will move when Lady Symmonds orders me to, and not a moment before.'

Mr Treverrick seemed incensed by her refusal to budge. 'Vile, headstrong woman,' he muttered, trying to turn away and finding her blocking his path.

'My name is Gray, if you have forgotten it. Sister Gray.'

'I'm not interested in your name or your fishwife rantings. You don't understand what you're talking about.'

Her eyes flashed as she followed him into the centre of the yard. 'Is that so?'

'Exercise in the fresh air is good for children. Every fool knows that.' He tightened the knot of his own scarf. 'Hard for their bodies in winter, perhaps. But good for their souls.'

She decided not to address the religious side of his reasoning on the grounds that she might lose her temper too rapidly.

'Perhaps I should ask Lady Symmonds what she thinks of children marching up and down in the cold without coats on. Because I doubt she hired you to torture the orphans in this appalling manner.' Her voice choked, despite her best intentions to stay calm. 'Why, look at the poor little souls! Their hands and faces are turning blue!'

'What a ridiculous assertion. They're merely a little chapped, that's all.' But he clapped his gloved hands, raising his voice so that it rang about the brick yard. 'That's enough exercise for now, children. Back to your classes!'

The children streamed past, clearly relieved to be escaping the cold, several of them shooting Rose a grateful smile as they piled back inside the orphanage.

The last in line was Jimmy, the unhappy little boy from the cellar. His eyes still looked red-rimmed, his face pale and set. But he gave her a significant look before plunging through the door after the others, and she knew for sure then it had been Jimmy she'd seen at the orphanage window during her walk across the fields.

'Happy now, Sister Gray?' Mr Treverrick asked coldly, and turned to follow them inside.

Although triumphant that she had won this small victory, it was with conflict in her heart that Rose watched him vanish inside the orphanage after the children.

She ought to take this incident to Lady Symmonds as she'd threatened to do. But she knew that could mean serious trouble, and not necessarily for the Treverricks.

Matron had already warned her not to interfere with the running of the orphanage, and reporting this to Lady Symmonds would definitely come under the heading of 'interference'.

Her courage faltered a little. She wanted to help the children. Brave young Jimmy, for instance, with his backwards glance at her. But equally she didn't want to lose her job.

If she reported him, it would be Mr Treverrick's word against hers, and in such cases, however unjust and ridiculous, she knew the man was usually believed above the woman. She was not so naïve as to think Lady Symmonds would be on her side simply because her story made better sense.

If she was dismissed, she would have to leave Symmonds Hall and might not see Lewis again for months, perhaps even years, especially if she was conscripted instead to work outside Cornwall, as her sister had been. And then there would be nobody to look out for the children and keep confronting the Treverricks.

Besides, it was not a clear-cut case of cruelty, was it?

There was a chance she could have misinterpreted what she'd seen, and that Mr Treverrick had genuinely not spotted how cold the children were until Rose pointed it out. His rude bluster could have been embarrassment over his poor handling of the situation. After all, he had not refused but had swiftly given in to her demands and sent the children indoors again.

Rose returned briskly to her room, trying not to let her heart rule her head. She would keep a watchful eye on the Treverricks. But for now, it might be wiser not to push too hard.

On her arrival at Symmonds Hall, she had been delighted to find that her room overlooked the orphanage yard rather than the sea, for she loved the innocent sounds of children playing Tag and Hopscotch. Their games and laughter made the war seem so far away.

Yet, perhaps having been an orphan herself meant Rose was not the most impartial judge of what she was seeing and hearing from next door.

19

They had three air raids the next week, the final one lasting for over an hour, which Lily spent kicking her heels in boredom down in the orphanage cellar. She had helped several patients down the steps, including Danny, but soon lost sight of them as the space filled up. Lily had brought nothing except her gas mask, so spent the hour playing with the straps and watching everyone else. Some people dozed the time away, others read books and newspapers, a few of the nursing staff clacked knitting needles, and Eva played a peek-aboo game with two young girls from the orphanage, much to their delight.

When this game grew too loud, Mrs Treverrick, who struck Lily as a killjoy, drew the girls away with a sharp reprimand that left Eva sighing and Sister Gray looking more forbidding than ever.

Finally, the all-clear sounded.

People yawned and stretched, packed away their reading material or knitting, and shuffled up the steps into the gloom of late afternoon.

Lily waited until the end, for she didn't like to push into the queue.

A noise behind her as she crossed the yard brought her round in surprise. It was Dr Edmund, who had been talking quietly to Matron during the air raid. He gave a kind of grunt, clasping his right upper arm as though he'd been stung.

Matron stared at him, looking alarmed, but did nothing.

'Are you all right, Doctor?' Lily ran back to him.

'My . . . heart pills,' Dr Edmund managed to say, his face an awful colour, sweat on his forehead. 'Fetch . . . Lewis.'

Lily was shocked. This was the first time she'd heard anything about the elderly doctor needing heart pills. But she tried to stay calm. There was no point panicking.

'Where are your pills, Doctor?'

But he sagged to the ground in the yard, not answering, and Lily crouched beside him, biting her lip. Was he having a heart attack? She did not know the signs. But it seemed possible.

Matron had still not moved. She was pale, her eyes wide.

Lily looked up at her. 'Do you know where his pills are?' But Matron merely shook her head. 'Look after him,' Lily told her, standing up. 'Loosen his tie and top buttons. I'm going to find Dr Lewis.'

She found Dr Edmund's grandson in Atlantic Ward, helping patients back into bed, and told him succinctly what had happened, though she kept her voice down. There was no point alarming people unnecessarily.

Dr Lewis left the ward at once, his face stern, and Lily followed, though she caught Danny staring after her with curiosity.

In her absence, a small crowd had gathered about the fallen doctor. Dr Lewis, who had fetched his grandfather's pills from his coat pocket in the senior staff room, encouraged most of them to leave, though he called Tom back. 'Bring the ambulance round to the front of the hall, would you? Dr Edmund needs to go to hospital urgently.'

141

'Right away, Doctor,' Tom said, and disappeared back inside.

'Come on, old thing,' Dr Lewis said cajolingly, helping his grandfather sit up in order to take his pills. 'These'll see you right.'

Someone had brought a beaker of water, and Dr Edmund managed to swallow some with two of his heart pills. Gradually, his colour began to return and his breathing became less constricted. He still looked dreadful though, and it was clear that he was too shaky to get up under his own steam.

Sister Gray arrived, the same shock on her face that everyone else seemed to be feeling. She looked questioningly at Dr Lewis, but he merely asked her to go back to the wards and make sure all the patients were securely back in their beds and had been given their evening medication.

For a moment, Lily thought she would refuse.

But then Sister nodded without a word and hurried back inside, chivvying most of the others back to their posts too.

'You need a few nights in hospital for rest and observation,' Dr Lewis told his grandfather, frowning as he checked his pulse. 'Your heart rate's all over the place; I don't like it.'

Dr Edmund tried to protest, but gave up.

His grandson and an orderly supported the elderly doctor between them to the front entrance, where Tom stood waiting by the hall's only ambulance. Soon they had Dr Edmund safely stowed on the bench inside, and Lewis climbed into the back with him.

Lily, who had followed them with Matron, helped to close the back doors of the ambulance while Tom got into the driver's seat.

142

'I'll come back first thing in the morning,' Dr Lewis told them in a clipped voice after checking that his grandfather was comfortable, 'and let you know how he's getting along.'

He saw the look of consternation on Lily's face and smiled grimly. 'Don't fret, Nurse Fisher. This isn't his first attack, and I doubt it will be his last. My grandfather's as tough as old boots. He'll be back on the wards in no time, you'll see, complaining about dirty bandages and soldiers smoking in their beds.' He nodded to Matron, whose lip was trembling. 'You too, Matron. No worrying, you hear me?'

Lily closed the doors, and banged on the side panel, and Tom drove off slowly.

As soon as the ambulance was out of sight, Matron burst into tears. 'I can't lose him,' she sobbed quietly. 'Not . . . Edmund.'

'Here, come on, you heard Dr Lewis,' she reassured Matron. Putting an arm about her waist, she helped the older woman back inside. She'd seen a few women in this state back in the East End after a bombing, too traumatised to speak. But it shook her all the same, because this was Matron, whom she'd only ever seen calm and in control. 'Dr Edmund will be right as rain. Nothing for you to get upset about.'

But she didn't quite believe that herself, and doubted that Matron did either.

Everyone was shocked by Dr Edmund's heart attack once news about it had buzzed around the convalescent home.

Eva herself could not understand how a man made of such stern stuff as Dr Edmund, even given his age, could be laid low in a matter of moments.

She had learned about heart attacks during her basic training, but been taught nothing much beyond the need to make the patient comfortable and fetch a doctor quickly. It was difficult not to worry about her own father, who regularly ate too well and smoked too many cigars, and who wheezed and puffed going up the stairs. But Daddy was considerably younger than Dr Edmund, she considered, and it was perhaps too early to fear that she might lose him to a similar attack.

'Will the doc recover, do you think?' Corporal Smith, whose arm she was moving in slow circles to help him get the circulation going, asked. He shifted uncomfortably as his wound stretched. 'There's been all sorts of gossip; I heard it wasn't looking too good for the old fella.'

They were in the conservatory, where it was so chilly that her breath was steaming like a dragon's. But at least it made a change of scenery for patients on those days when it was too brutally cold to take them outside.

'I know as much as you, I'm afraid,' Eva said, and finished the second set of rehabilitation exercises, returning his limp arm to his side. 'Any improvement in sensation?'

'Oh, I can feel it all right, Nurse. But I ain't got the strength to lift it more than a couple of inches.' He tried on his own, grimacing, and then shook his head. 'Bleeding useless arm!' His gaze flashed guiltily to her face. 'Sorry, pardon my French.'

'No need to apologise,' she said with a grin. 'I'm a professional soldier's daughter; I've heard far worse. Besides, that was a nasty wound. The bullet shattered the bone, didn't it?'

'It did,' he agreed. 'Now there's metal studs holding the whole blasted thing together.'

'Well, then,' she said, ignoring his bad language. 'You can't expect a mess like that to mend in a few months.'

A Cockney and a little rough around the edges, the man settled back against the padded seat back, looking her up and down with admiration. 'You're a good sport, Nurse Ryder. And I don't mind a posh accent when it comes with a figure like yours. Don't suppose you'd ever consider marrying a soldier?'

She laughed, shaking her head. 'Try to get some rest now, Corporal Smith,' she told him firmly, moving on to the next patient on her list.

Eva kept smiling, keeping her head high all that morning. But inside she was far from confident. Her heart was aching, for Max was still being stubborn as hell.

Mary had discreetly left him unattended in the conservatory for five minutes and Eva had nipped in to speak to him alone. But he had refused to relent.

'If I can never walk again, then I'll never marry you,' Max had told her, his jaw set hard, 'and that's final.'

Mulish, obstinate man!

'What if you had to use a stick to walk?' she had suggested, grinding her teeth.

After some delicate persuasion on her part, Max had agreed that walking with a stick would be acceptable. But he still did not want her to visit him, and his chances of ever getting back on his feet were remote unless Dr Lewis helped with rehabilitation techniques.

Now that Dr Edmund was recovering from a heart attack, poor Dr Lewis had his grandfather's patients to cope with as well as his own. She doubted he would have a single moment to spare for her and Max now. It was quite right that he should prioritise his grandfather and his St Ives patients before worrying about them, of course, but the delay still made her uneasy.

That afternoon, she wrote Dr Lewis a note, aware that he was unlikely to visit the convalescent home for the next few days. In it, she repeated her request for information on healing severe spinal injury, though apologised too for bothering him at this difficult time.

To her mind, the longer Max lay brooding in that bed, pushing aside the possibility of recovery, the less likely it was he would ever walk again.

'Tom, could you please deliver this to Dr Lewis at the surgery?' She had caught the orderly just as he was about to drive down into St Ives for supplies, and handed him the letter with a quick smile. 'I'm so sorry to be a nuisance. But it is important that the doctor gets this today.'

'Right you are, Miss,' Tom said with a wink.

Eva turned to go back inside, her white apron flapping in the wind off the Atlantic, but found Sister Gray waiting for her on the steps. It was clear from her expression that she had overheard some of what Eva had said to Tom.

'What was that about? Who is that letter for?' Sister Gray demanded, her eyes fierce. 'Is this because you've been blocked from seeing your flight lieutenant? Are you sending love notes to Dr Lewis now?'

Eva was astonished. '*Love notes*?'

'Relationships between doctors and nurses are strictly forbidden, Nurse Ryder. If I were to inform Matron of this development, both you and the doctor could suffer black marks against your record. Is that what you want?'

'Sister, you've misunderstood — '

But her words fell on deaf ears. Sister Gray had already gone, whirling back inside and slamming furiously through the door into Atlantic Ward.

20

Lily found herself repeatedly drawn back to Danny's bedside, knowing she really ought not to but unable to resist the charm of his wry smile.

'How's the old boy?' he asked next time Lily came to apply the prescribed emollient cream to his scars. 'Dr Edmund, I mean.'

He was lying on top of his cover in his pyjamas and dressing gown, hands behind his head as he surveyed her. She admired the way Danny no longer seemed aware of his facial scarring when he spoke to her, his smile unaffected. It was such a change from his shyness and embarrassment the first time she'd spoken to him.

'I heard he was taken ill after the air raid,' he continued. 'Heart attack, some are saying. Is the doctor all right?'

'I'm sure they're taking good care of him at the cottage hospital,' was all she said, not wanting to gossip about a senior member of staff.

He studied her. 'How old are you, if you don't mind me asking?'

'I do mind,' Lily said tartly.

He grinned, sitting up for his treatment. 'Come on, you can't be much older than me. I'm nineteen years old, though I'll be twenty in a few months.'

Lily set out the equipment, a little unsure of how to respond. But what harm could it do? And his smile really was quite persuasive.

'I'm eighteen,' she admitted shyly.

'And you're from London.'

'Dagenham.' She saw his frown. 'That's on the outskirts of London, in the East End. I lived there with my family before . . . before the bombs started falling. How about you?'

'Me? I'm from over Truro way. Cornish, born and bred.' She must have looked surprised because he added, 'My mum was from London though, so I don't have as strong an accent as some here. Or so I'm told.'

'Get teased for it, do you?'

'The lads like to rag on at me sometimes. They call me Upcountry.'

'Sorry?'

'That's what they call visitors from outside Cornwall.'

'Yes, I remember now. I did hear that expression when I was down in Porthcurno. Though the locals were all so friendly, we never felt like outsiders.'

Briefly, as she cleaned the ridges of his scars with careful, dabbing motions, she told him about her mother's death, and how her family had left London for Cornwall, but things hadn't worked out on her aunt and uncle's farm near Penzance, so they'd moved on again in search of work.

She didn't mention the listening post at Porthcurno, because that was top secret, and she also missed out the horrible experience with her greatuncle. It didn't do to dwell on the past, she told herself firmly. She knew now that girls had to be extra careful with some men or they'd take advantage. But also that not all men were like Stanley. Thank goodness!

'Better hold still.' Lily started to apply the emollient cream to his scars and felt him flinch. 'Does it still hurt bad?'

'I'm not complaining, am I?'

'There's no shame in admitting it hurts.'

'I wouldn't describe it as painful, exactly.' He grimaced, though, as she continued. 'Hard to explain, but it itches and burns at the same time.'

'Itching's a good sign, Dr Lewis says. He says it means — ' But he interrupted her.

'It means that new skin is growing back,' he finished impatiently, nodding. 'Yes, I know. I've heard it all before, nurse. A hundred bloody times or more.'

She fell silent, concentrating on her work.

Danny watched her.

'Sorry, that was rude of me,' he said a moment later, and sighed. 'My blasted tongue. I've just spent so long in hospitals and medical units, seeing doctor after doctor, nurse after nurse, and all of them saying the same things to me. It gets a bit wearing, that's all.'

Lily used her fingertips to gently work the cream in, trying not to press too hard on the raw, swollen skin, and saw his eyes close.

'Why didn't you stay in the specialist burns unit?' She knew she shouldn't pry but couldn't help it. 'They could have treated you far better than what we can. This is just a convalescent home. Most patients come here for a few weeks or months of rest and recuperation before going home or back to their regiments.'

'Oh, there were other men who needed that bed,' he said dismissively, his eyes still shut. 'Soldiers in far worse shape than me. And at least my folks can come and visit me here in St Ives.'

She did not quite believe that excuse. Not least because he'd not had any family visitors yet, to her knowledge, even though Truro wasn't that far by bus, and there was a straight route, too. It could easily be done in a day, there and back, with time to spare for sight-seeing. By contrast, Porthcurno was much further away and harder to reach. Otherwise she would have asked her own family to visit.

'Still, Dr Lewis told me the specialist units can do amazing things these days. I mean, these burns . . . Your face . . . ' She caught his instinctive movement and stopped. 'Are you sure I'm not hurting you?'

His eyes had opened and he was glaring at her. 'I didn't want them to try and fix my face,' he said roughly, keeping his voice low. 'All right?'

Lily blinked. 'Why not?'

'Because I don't deserve to look that good ever again.' He jerked his head round, showing her the still-handsome, untouched side of his face. 'I could have done more to save my friends. I only managed to pull a few out before the roof fell in. The rest of them . . . ' He turned back to stare at the far wall, his jaw clenched hard. 'That's enough for today. Thank you, Nurse Fisher. But I'm tired now, I want to rest.'

Lily packed the creams and equipment away without saying anything, and went back to her station to wash her hands.

Poor soul, she thought, not seeing her hands properly under the running water, her vision too blurred by tears. Poor suffering soul . . .

★ ★ ★

151

'Here you go, Miss. Letter for you.' Tom pushed an envelope into Eva's hands, and walked away down the corridor, whistling cheerfully.

At first, Eva did not understand. Then she saw the familiar black slant of Dr Lewis's distinctive handwriting, and her heart leapt.

'Nurse Ryder?'

She jumped and stuffed the envelope, hurriedly folded in two, into her apron pocket. Turning, she pinned a professional smile to her face.

'Matron?'

But Matron was not alone. Beside her, leaning on a silver-topped cane, was their benefactress, Lady Symmonds.

The wealthy old widow wore a black dress as though still in mourning, ankle-length but with sequins glinting at the square collar. Her silver hair was worn in soft, old-fashioned rolls, loosely set and resting on her shoulders. Eva had only met her once before, and could not understand why some of the other nurses held her in awe. She seemed like such a kindly old lady.

'Lady Symmonds has come to look over the wards,' Matron said in a forbidding manner, a suspicious look on her face, as though she knew Eva was up to something illicit. Which, of course, she was. But only because it was in Max's best interests. 'Would you fetch Sister Gray at once?'

'Yes, Matron.'

'Wait,' Lady Symmonds said clearly. 'I don't need Sister Gray. I'm sure the Sister has enough to do without pandering to the whims of an old lady.' She held up her cane and pointed it at Eva. 'This gal can show me about the place. She looks like a bright young thing.'

'But your ladyship — '

'You won't be needed either, Matron. I'll only be here a short while and I'd rather peek through a few doorways unannounced than have the grand tour.'

Matron glanced uneasily from her ladyship to Eva, and then seemed to give up. The entire site belonged to Lady Symmonds, after all. She could hardly refuse access. 'Very well, my lady. I have some paperwork to do, as it happens. I'll be in my office if you need me.' She gave Eva a significant look. 'Don't tire her ladyship out, Nurse Ryder.'

Which sounded like code for get rid of the *tiresome old bag as soon as possible*.

Once Matron had gone, Lady Symmonds linked her arm with Eva, and gave her a mischievous smile. 'That's better. Now, what's your name, my dear?'

'Nurse Ryder.'

'I meant your name, not your title. I'm Lady Symmonds, but my friends call me Babs. What about you?'

'I'm Eva, your ladyship.'

'Lead on, Eva.' The old lady's eyes twinkled. 'I believe we shall rub along very well together. Just a quick whizz round, and then maybe a cup of tea and a biscuit? You can tell me all about yourself.'

★ ★ ★

Eva showed her briefly around the wards and the conservatory, where some of the men were enjoying their recreation, for it was raining outside.

Lady Symmonds spoke kindly to a few of the patients, who stared at her in amazement, and complimented the nurses on their hard work.

They came across Sister Gray in Carbis Ward, who looked at Eva with narrowed eyes, responding to her ladyship's queries in a tight-lipped way. No doubt she still wrongly suspected her of sending 'love notes' to Dr Lewis.

Finally, at her express request, Eva took Lady Symmonds to the canteen, for it was nearly lunch-time, and fetched her a cup of strong tea with an oaten biscuit nestled on the saucer.

'Ah,' her ladyship said with a sigh, dunking the biscuit into her tea and then eating it before it crumbled. 'How perfect. Thank you, my dear.'

Eva drank some of her own tea, amused by the eccentric old lady. 'May I ask you a question, your ladyship?'

'Please, call me Babs. Hardly anyone does these days. And ask away. I have nothing to hide, most unfortunately.'

Eva laughed. 'That's very kind of you. But when the air-raid sirens go off, Babs, I notice you never come to the orphanage cellar. Aren't you afraid the building may be hit?'

'I have my own shelter, of sorts. It's not very large, but it's big enough for me and my companion, Sonya. An old priest hole, I suppose you could call it. It's underneath my apartment, which overlooks the orphanage yard.'

'I see.' Eva hesitated. 'How long has it been since you endowed part of the hall as an orphanage?'

'Oh, more than twenty-five years, my dear. Far longer than this place. There used to be a poorhouse that took in orphans but that closed in the early part of the century. I only handed over this building to be used as a convalescent home when war broke out. We

154

took in wounded servicemen in the Great War, you know. Though nothing like this. Just a few men, here and there, to help ease the burden.' Lady Symmonds took a sip of tea in a genteel way, her little finger crooked, just as Eva had been taught to do in finishing school. 'Then my husband passed away, and my son George, and then, in the first months of the war, my darling grandson, Francis . . . ' Her voice broke slightly. 'I'm sorry.'

'Please don't apologise. I know you lost him. That must have been quite a blow.'

'And a bitter one. Francis was the apple of my eye. But he died serving his country, and I know how much that meant to him. Silly, wonderful boy.' Sniffing, her ladyship took out a white handkerchief and dabbed at her eyes. 'Oh, how I miss his lovely smile.'

Impulsively, Eva leant forward and touched her hand, forcing a smile to her lips despite the tear rolling down her own cheek. 'This bloody war,' she exclaimed.

'My thoughts exactly.'

They both laughed through their tears.

'But I do like to see the children through my window,' Lady Symmonds continued, blowing her nose before putting away her handkerchief. 'It makes me feel young again. And if we didn't look after them, and help them prepare for adult life, who would?'

Eva murmured her assent, but thought of the Treverricks, who were not the most charming people in the world.

'I do wonder though about the couple who run it,' she said carefully, not wishing to offend her ladyship. 'At times, they seem a trifle off-hand with the children.

155

Mrs Treverrick, in particular. I'm rather glad I'm not an orphan in their care.'

'Aren't we all?' But her ladyship seemed interested. 'All the same, perhaps I should ask for a tour of the orphanage as well, and see how they're getting on over there. In another week or two, perhaps. When I've recovered from the excitement of today's little outing.' She beamed at Eva. 'Would you go with me?'

'Me?'

'Why not? Two pairs of eyes are more useful than one. And I forget things so easily these days. You can remind me afterwards what I saw.'

'Well,' Eva said carefully, 'if Sister can spare me — '

'Oh, I'm sure Sister Gray can spare you. She's a capable woman. So that's decided. Excellent. I shall ask Sonya to make the arrangements at once.' She peered dubiously into her cup. 'This tea is very, erm, invigorating.'

'Isn't it just? Some days, I'm surprised it doesn't dissolve the spoon.' But Eva suddenly had an idea. 'I say, Babs, would you like to come to our Christmas party? We're to have music and dancing, and games, too. Plus tea and biscuits, and possibly a sandwich or two. If that sounds like fun?'

'Oh, how utterly charming. A Christmas party would be just the thing to bring me out of myself. I would love to come.'

'And do bring Sonya with you.'

'I'm sure I can speak for my companion; she'd be delighted, too.' Lady Symmonds patted her hand. 'Thank you so much, my dear. This has been a most entertaining visit.'

Despite its bitter taste, Eva finished her cup of tea with a smile on her face, pleased at the thought of having their benefactress attend the party.

It was only much later, once she'd accompanied her ladyship back to her apartment across the orphanage yard — under the shelter of an umbrella, for it was still raining — that she remembered the letter stuffed in her apron pocket.

Opening the envelope in private, she scanned the short reply from Dr Lewis with hope in her heart.

Dear Eva,

I wrote to my friend in London some days ago, but he hasn't yet replied. However, after receiving your note, I managed to get him on the telephone, and he does know of some new research into spinal injury rehabilitation. He's very busy right now, but will send me a summary of the research as soon as he can. I thought you'd like to know straight away.

Yours, Lewis.

Eva read the note twice, and then clasped it to her chest, closing her eyes as she sent up a little prayer to the heavens.

New research sounded promising, she thought. Very promising indeed.

It was unlikely to be a miracle cure, she acknowledged, and would almost certainly involve hard work on both their parts. But if it brought them even one step closer to getting Max out of that damn wheelchair and back on his feet, she swore that she would be happy.

21

The air-raid siren went off again just as Rose was hurrying downstairs for the start of her evening shift. Night had fallen and dinner had been served to the patients an hour ago, the dirty plates still piled up on a trolley in the hallway. No doubt Tom had abandoned them when the warning sirens sounded from St Ives.

'Oh, for goodness' sake,' she muttered, realising she had come down without her gas mask. She ran back upstairs, passing several other nurses heading down to the shelter, and encouraged them to hurry, and also to help any patients having difficulties.

By the time she got back down to the wards, mask in hand, she found Dr Lewis coming out of Atlantic Ward.

'Oh, hullo there,' Rose said, stupidly blushing. He hadn't been back to Symmonds Hall since his grand-father's heart attack and it was a shock to see him standing there. 'I didn't know you were here today. How's Dr Edmund?'

'Better every day, thanks.' He too was holding a gas mask. 'Why aren't you down in the shelter? You'd better hurry.'

'I always help the men in Atlantic Ward first. The ones who have to shelter under their beds instead. Some of them find it hard to get out of bed alone.'

'I'll do that. You go.'

'Absolutely not.' She was puzzled. 'Where's Tom? He usually helps.'

'Yes, well, I sent Tom down to the shelter with the

others. He shouldn't be expected to risk his neck every time. It's my turn today.' Lewis gave her a lopsided grin, swinging his gas mask. 'Besides, I couldn't stand another stint down there with the appalling Treverricks. That woman's voice could grate cheese. Those unfortunate kids . . . I don't know why they haven't tied the Treverricks up and rolled them off the cliff yet.'

Rose bit her lip, half laughing, half serious. 'They are awful people, aren't they? But look, this is too dangerous. And it's not your job.'

'All the same, I'm here now, and I'd feel better if you were in the shelter.'

'I'm not going anywhere.'

'Fine.' He gave up, with a shake of his head at her stubbornness, and turned to go back into Atlantic Ward. The blackout curtains were in place but the lights were off too, for good measure. He grabbed up a torch from the nurses' station. 'We'd better get cracking, then. Those planes sound bloody close.'

He pointed down the ward. 'Can you help Max over there? Looks like he's the only one not in place. I'll check the others.'

Rose helped the flight lieutenant, who had somehow managed to drag himself out of bed, but was not yet underneath it. 'There you go,' she said with forced cheeriness, handing him some bolsters against possible blast damage. 'Comfortable?'

'Hardly,' Max said with a ghost of a laugh. 'But thank you, Sister.'

'You're welcome.'

She hesitated, tempted to ask about Nurse Ryder, but decided against it. Although Max had not asked if Eva could visit him on the ward again, she had seen them together recently in the conservatory, heads bent as they sat deep in conversation. Rose had lingered in the doorway, giving him a chance to complain about Eva pestering him. But Max had barely glanced at her, and Rose had gone away in the end, troubled and dissatisfied.

She was not convinced that Nurse Ryder had his best interests at heart; Eva's flirtatious ways still reminded Rose too much of her sister for that, and she had distinctly overheard Eva giving Tom a private letter for Lewis Lanyon the other day, even though nurses and doctors were not permitted to fraternise outside work.

Rose had lost her temper at the time, it was pointless to deny it. No doubt Eva had laughed about it with the other nurses afterwards. And she badly wanted to ask Lewis for an explanation of that letter. But in her heart she knew Lewis would never betray Elsie like that. He was too honourable a man.

Rose straightened, and was shocked to see a young boy outlined in the ward doorway. It looked like Jimmy, but without the lights on it was hard to be sure.

'Jimmy?' she exclaimed, hurrying towards him. Fear for the boy's safety made her speak more sharply than intended. 'What on earth are you doing here? You should be down in the shelter.'

He vanished, and the door banged shut behind him.

Lewis joined her, frowning, torch in hand. He shone the beam of light at the door. 'Was someone there?'

'Jimmy, I think.' Quickly, she explained about the orphan boy, and how she'd started to develop a tentative friendship with him. 'But I have no idea why he's not in the shelter with the others. Perhaps he was playing truant when the sirens sounded, and was too late to get into the cellar.'

'That does sound likely, given what you've told me.'

'We have to find him.'

'Right.' But he hesitated, gazing about the dark ward. 'Look, you get under cover here. I'll go and find him.'

'He may not come to you. He...He's not very trusting.' She held out her hand for the torch. 'Let me go instead.'

'Not a chance.'

'Then we'll go together. If the planes start bombing us, we can duck under one of the beds in the other wards.'

Lewis ran an exasperated hand through his hair. 'You are one hell of a stubborn woman, Sister Gray. Did anyone ever tell you that?' But he didn't argue anymore, following her out into the corridor. He shone the torch up and down, his face frustrated. 'Which way do you think this boy might have gone, then?'

A sound made her turn, frantically searching the dark for a small figure. There was no sign of the boy. But the door to St Ives Ward was ajar.

'That way?'

St Ives Ward was empty and dark. All the patients there were mobile and had been taken down to the shelters with everyone else.

Lewis crouched and shone his torch under the beds. 'Jimmy?' he called. 'Jimmy, for God's sake. You're putting Sister Gray in danger by hiding like this. If you come out, I promise nobody will give you a scold for it. I need to get you both to safety.'

It was freezing cold on the ward, Rose realised,

shivering. 'What on earth?' Someone had dragged a blackout curtain aside, and then presumably climbed out of the window, leaving it wide open.

There was only the barest glimmer of moonlight in the sky. She leaned out but could see nobody outside in the darkness.

'Jimmy?'

The menacing drone of enemy planes were so loud, they made her tremble with anticipation. An explosion rocked the nearby town and she felt the shock of it on the air. There was nothing more she could do, she realised.

'He's gone,' she said, closing the window, her heart full of fear for the boy's safety.

'Hopefully he'll be all right.' Lewis had snapped off the torch at the sight of the open window and the faint moonlight streaming in. Now he pulled the blackout curtain across, leaning close to her, and the ward was plunged into darkness once more. But he didn't turn the torch on again. 'We should both get under a bed, I suppose. Much good it would do if this place got a direct hit. But it's the best we can do.'

She nodded, trying not to sound shaky. 'After you, Dr Lewis.'

'You don't have to call me Doctor when we're alone. We've known each other since we were children,' he pointed out, adding softly, 'Rose.'

Again, that foolish blush. Thank goodness he couldn't see it.

'I like to keep things professional.' He said nothing, but her tongue kept on working, stupid and compulsive. 'And it wouldn't be right. There's Elsie to consider.'

'What about Elsie?'

'You two are practically engaged, of course. I know Elsie's not here now, but she'll come home eventually. And when the war's over — '

Another explosion, much nearer, left her breathless.

'Damn it to hell.' Lewis turned on the torch, its narrow light somehow cold and clinical, illuminating his face. She thought she had never seen him look so grim. He dragged her away from the window and pushed her under a bed on the other side of the ward. 'Stay down.'

Rose stupidly hoped that he would join her there, but he moved away, and she lay in the dark, listening as he rolled under one of the other beds.

To her relief the planes seemed to change course, no longer heading up towards their location above the town but moving away again, perhaps back out across the Atlantic. After a while she could not even hear them anymore above the rapid thump of her heart and the rasp of her breathing.

She had never felt so alone in her life.

★ ★ ★

Matron had not seemed quite herself since Dr Edmund's collapse. The elderly doctor's brush with death had obviously affected her deeply. Nonetheless, she sat with a straight back and pursed lips while Rose described seeing Jimmy during the air raid, and then stood, pacing her office briefly.

'And you're sure this boy wasn't a figment of your imagination? One's emotions can become quite heightened during an enemy attack. Especially if you are not lucky enough to be in a shelter.'

'Dr Lewis witnessed it too.' Rose saw Matron turn sharply to study her, and carefully kept her face blank and professional. 'He can verify my account, I'm sure.'

'I see.'

'I'm worried about this boy. His name is Jimmy. And I've seen the Treverricks mistreating the children recently —'

'What do you mean?' Matron interrupted.

'Mr Treverrick was marching them about the yard in the bitter cold. Without hats or coats. The poor little mites looked half-frozen. He claimed they were exercising.'

'That's none of our business. Good God, would you be happy for one of the Treverricks to come strolling in here, telling us how to look after our patients?'

'With respect, Matron, the two situations are not equivalent. The Treverricks have no medical training. But you don't need to know anything about raising a child to know the difference between exercise and cruelty.'

'Oh, stuff and nonsense. Don't be so melodramatic...'

Rose gritted her teeth, and then tried a different approach. 'All right, what about Jimmy wandering about the home during the air raid, then? He doesn't look much older than eight or nine. Yet he wasn't taken down to the shelter with the other children. Nor did anyone set up a hue and cry over his absence. That has to be negligence, at least.'

'I have to admit that's not good. But they have been overstretched with all these evacuees from London, and children en masse can be difficult to control. Especially orphans, some of whom may have grown up without the benefit of a parent's guidance.' Matron

164

hesitated. 'No doubt this boy is particularly troubled and gave the Treverricks the slip.'

'He ran away from them because he's scared and unhappy.'

'You know this? You spoke to the boy?'

'It's my gut feeling.'

'I'm sorry, Sister.' Matron shook her head, her thin brows arched in disdain. 'Regardless of your interest in this boy, I'm not risking a feud with the Treverricks over a gut feeling. I'm ordering you to let this go.'

Rose ought to have accepted that, of course. But she couldn't help herself. 'And I'm telling you that something must be done!'

'I beg your pardon?' Clearly shocked by her outburst, Matron ordered her to return to the wards at once and get about her duties. 'And not another word about this boy Jimmy, do you hear? You're on an official warning, Sister Gray.' She glared. 'One more misstep and you'll be looking for a new posting elsewhere.'

22

Eva loved striding out in the fresh air after spending long hours cooped up on the wards, especially on dry winter days when the sunshine and sea views could cheer her up. Indoors, her senses were often overwhelmed with the noise of patients coughing and chatting or calling for help, the sickly smells of creams and medications, and the cold ocean light streaming in during morning shifts.

She was on a special mission today though, bearing a few small gifts and a card for Dr Edmund Lanyon.

He had been discharged from the cottage hospital and was resting at home under the careful eye of the doctors' widowed housekeeper, Mrs Delaney, who looked after him while Dr Lewis was out on his rounds.

Apparently, Dr Edmund was not a very good patient. 'I believe doctors rarely are,' Matron had told Eva with an indulgent sigh, handing her the basket of gifts. 'Do please convey our deepest wishes for his improved health. But don't stay too long. We don't want to exhaust his strength.'

The two doctors lived together at the end of a short lane near the town centre, their large house overlooking the bay, with a handsome, well-kept garden. It being winter now, most of the branches were bare. But a sturdy holly bush grew near the entrance door, red berries nestled amid the glossy green leaves, and somebody had recently swept autumn leaves from the gravelled drive, a heap of brown and russet in one

166

corner with a rake beside them.

She pulled on the bell and Mrs Delaney soon appeared. She looked on the verge of leaving the house, however, her coat half-buttoned, her greying hair restrained by a headscarf.

'Oh,' she exclaimed in obvious surprise on learning of Eva's identity and mission. 'I was just about to visit the shops. I've heard there might be some ox tongue in the butcher's today.' She glanced at the hall clock, seeming flustered. 'But I suppose you'd better come in. I'll put the kettle on.'

'No need, Mrs Delaney.' Eva untied her own headscarf and checked her reflection in the hall mirror, patting her blonde rolls. 'I can make the tea. You take on the butcher.'

'Are you sure?'

She didn't need much persuading though, and soon the housekeeper was bustling down the drive, a covered shopping basket over one arm.

Eva introduced herself to the well-equipped kitchen, where she found all the ingredients necessary for preparing tea and biscuits. Peering out of the window, she admired the back garden, where she guessed a lawn must have been removed to make way for a vegetable plot. She could see carrots and sprouts growing in neatly tended rows, and leafy-topped mounds beneath which she suspected there might be a few potatoes lurking. At the back of the garden, half hidden from view behind some apple trees, was what looked like a covered seat.

Having made up a tea tray, she carried it through to the living room, where she found Dr Edmund snoring gently in an armchair, his face hidden under a newspaper.

The fire was dying, and the air smelt of wood-smoke, for there was never much coal to be got these days and fresh-cut logs took so long to dry out. A few pairs of socks were strung out on a rack in front of the fire, which spoke of a lack of drying space elsewhere. But the room was cosy enough.

'Hullo, doctor,' she said, and began laying out the cups. He stirred, removing his newspaper, and she looked up to find him staring at her in bafflement. 'Do you take sugar?'

'No, thank you.' Dr Edmund frowned. 'I'm sorry. Where's Mrs Delaney?'

'Gone hunting.' Eva poured him a cup of tea and handed it over. 'No need to look so alarmed. Matron sent me to make sure you're resting. And to give you this.' She set her basket of goodies on the table and showed him a few of its contents. 'Look, a slice of Cook's fruit cake. Plus, a Christmas greetings card, signed by all the staff and many of the patients. Every-one at Symmonds Hall wishes you well, and hopes you make a full recovery.'

'Goodness me,' he said faintly.

'Especially Matron. She's been very worried about you.'

'Oh, nonsense.' With an obvious effort, Dr Edmund put aside his cup of tea and sat up straight in his arm-chair. He tapped himself on the chest and nodded, as though to indicate it was all working fine in there. 'Just a false alarm. One of those things. I'll soon be back at the hall.'

Eva looked at him without speaking, and he sighed.

'Well,' he conceded, 'there may have been a slight flutter. But nothing for Matron to get upset about. I hope you'll tell her so.'

'I shall be sure to give her a full and frank report of your condition,' Eva agreed, and sat down in the armchair opposite, cup and saucer in hand. From his troubled expression, she deemed it best to change the topic of conversation. She had not come to precipitate a further heart attack, after all. 'I say, this tea is very refreshing. Much better than the grim stuff they serve in the canteen. Though it probably helps having a little more milk to hand.'

That seemed to do the trick. For a while, they talked about the terrible state of food supplies in Britain, and the necessary evils of rationing, before moving on to the wider topic of the war and when it might end.

Dr Edmund cheered up after his second cup, but Eva was not fooled. He had been genuinely concerned about Matron and her fears for his health. More so, perhaps, than for himself. She wondered, not for the first time, if the two oldest members of the senior staff were in fact secretly carrying on together. Though she couldn't see why they would need to hide it. Unless they felt embarrassed. She supposed that Matron must be a good twenty years younger, and that might cause gossip in the town. But no more than usual.

Of course, if they got married, Matron would have to leave the profession. Nurses were not permitted to remain at work after marrying. One of those stupid rules presumably dreamt up by men in authority, Eva considered, sipping her cooling tea. But only once the war was over. For the moment, that rule seemed to be on hold.

She spotted a children's book on the sideboard, and asked about it, wondering if he kept it for patients.

'No, we've taken in a couple of evacuees from Hackney. About a fortnight back. They had nowhere else to go. Mrs Delaney doesn't live in, so there was plenty of space. Two young brothers; they share the box room at the back.'

'Isn't that rather a lot of work for you?'

'Oh no, we barely see them. They're at school on weekdays and off adventuring at weekends, you know how boys are. Mrs Delaney looks after them wonderfully. Leaves a good hot dinner in the range before she goes home, or a tureen of soup on the side. And she works miracles with our sugar ration so they can have biscuits or cake twice a week.'

'I think it's wonderful of you to have taken them in.'

'Just doing our bit. They're good lads, clean and polite. Joshua and Benjamin. They read down here in the evenings before bedtime.' He smiled. 'It's good to have the company when Lewis has to go out in the evenings.'

Eva nodded sympathetically. 'The orphanage has taken some evacuees too, of course. But they have rather more room than you.' She hesitated. 'I spoke to Lady Symmonds the other day. She's arranging a tour of the orphanage and has asked me to go with her.'

'And how is Rose getting along?' he asked.

Eva was taken aback by the question. 'Sister Gray, you mean?'

'Yes, sorry.'

'Perfectly well, I believe. I spoke to Sister earlier today, in fact, when she was signing the Christmas card.' She pointed to Sister Gray's neat, precise signature which said, *Rose Gray*, with no mention of her title. 'Pardon me, but why do you ask? Has she been unwell?'

'Not at all, I just like to keep an eye on her.'

Dr Edmund hesitated, then said slowly, 'The thing is, her younger sister Elsie is a friend of the family. Quite a close friend, in fact. Elsie's all but engaged to my grandson.'

Eva put down her cup and saucer, riveted. 'Dr Lewis is *engaged* to Rose's sister?'

'Not officially. They have what my generation used to call *an understanding.*' He frowned, looking away. 'Awkward timing for them, what with the war and all. Elsie was conscripted earlier this year and disappeared off to a munitions factory up near Leeds. So any plans for an engagement had to be put on hold.'

'What rotten luck for them.'

'Perhaps,' the doctor said absent-mindedly, and then realised the implication, hurriedly adding, 'I mean, no point rushing these things, is there? They're both still so young.'

Eva grinned at him. 'You don't approve of his choice?'

'I wouldn't say that.' But she could see Dr Edmund knew he'd been rumbled. 'Elsie's a lovely girl. Plenty of spirit, you know? But she's flighty with it, always pacing around, head full of big ideas. Very talkative too. I've never seen her sit down and listen to anybody. Really listen, I mean.' He looked troubled again. 'A country doctor's wife needs to be a little more . . . '

'Sensible?'

'Well, she ought to have her feet on the ground. And be prepared to take second place to his work. Because she'll have to at times. We have patients demanding house calls at all hours of the night, giving birth at Christmas or dropping dead in the middle of Sunday lunch. It's not an easy life, and I'm not sure Elsie's cut out for the job, that's all.'

Eva searched his face thoughtfully. 'Unlike her sister, Rose.'

'Now don't put words in my mouth, Nurse Ryder.' But he pulled a face. 'I've told Lewis what he should do. Break off with the sister before it's too late. But he's a stubborn lad. Feels honour-bound to stick with Elsie, come hell or high water.'

'Of course he does. And quite right too. But if it's bound to be a disaster . . . ' Eva rested her chin on her hand, thinking hard. 'You know, there's this Christmas party coming up. If we could somehow push the two of them together — '

'Nurse!'

'Don't you prefer the idea of Rose as your grand-daughter-in-law?'

'Well, obviously, but . . . ' Dr Edmund exhaled, looking at her warily. 'Subterfuge? I'm not sure I like the sound of that.'

'Who needs subterfuge when you've got Glenn Miller?' Cheerfully, Eva collected up the cups and carried them back to the kitchen. There was already a plan forming in her head. 'You leave everything to me, Dr Edmund,' she called back over her shoulder. 'I'll soon have those two lovebirds dancing at the Christmas party, you see if I don't.'

'Which two lovebirds?' someone asked, directly behind her in the hallway.

Eva spun on the threshold to the kitchen, tray still in hand.

It was Dr Lewis.

She felt heat flood her cheeks. The very man they'd been talking about! It was a Tuesday, so she'd assumed Lewis would be at the doctors' surgery in St Ives most of the day. But he must have come home for his lunch.

172

'Hullo there, Dr Lewis,' she said loudly, hoping his grandfather would get the message. 'Gosh, what a surprise to see you. We were just joking about Lily and . . . erm . . . one of the patients.' Inspiration struck her. 'Private Orde, in fact.'

'Daniel Orde and Nurse Fisher?' Dr Lewis frowned, unbuttoning his coat. 'I suppose they are about the same age. But lovebirds? I imagine Matron would have something to say about that. Sister Gray too. Lily's still on probation, and you know nurses and patients aren't permitted to — '

'For a dance at the Christmas party, she meant,' his grandfather called out from the living room, gallantly rescuing her from the dilemma. 'Come in here, Lewis. Are you home for lunch? We've just had a pot of tea.'

Eva left the tray in the kitchen and hurried back in time to hear Dr Edmund impatiently telling his grandson, 'We can hardly expect the patients to dance with themselves. Besides, if one can't make an exception to the rules at Christmas, when there's a damn war on, then the world's gone topsy-turvy and that's all there is to it.'

Dr Lewis had taken off his hat and was twirling it about in one hand. He looked from his grandfather to Eva, and scratched his head.

'I wasn't arguing with either of you,' he said mildly. 'Sounds like a capital idea. Though I didn't know Nurse Fisher was sweet on Private Orde.'

'Funny old world, isn't it?' Eva said, and smiled at him innocently.

★ ★ ★

173

About an hour later, Dr Lewis showed her out of the house, offering her a lift back up to Symmonds Hall in his car. 'It looks like it might rain at any minute.'

'I don't mind a spot of rain,' Eva said, refusing his offer. 'I'm happier walking, thanks. To be honest, it's been a tough week. I need to blow away some cobwebs.'

'Can't say I blame you. I shall probably take a walk myself later, before blackout.' Dr Lewis stopped, his eyes widening. 'Hang on a tick.' He limped back inside the house and emerged again a few minutes later, holding up some folded sheets of paper. 'That research you wanted; it arrived in this morning's post. You remember my friend in London, the spinal surgeon? This is what he sent me. I've had a quick read-through but thought you might like to hold on to these papers for now. Since this is your project.'

'Goodness, thank you so much.' Eva had a brief glance through the sheets, and was delighted to see diagrams of physical exercises to be conducted, along with further written instructions for rehabilitating patients with spinal injuries. 'This is simply marvellous. You are a dear, Lewis. And so is your friend.'

'No guarantees those exercises will work, of course. There are so many caveats and provisos. But it's worth a try all the same. Assuming your flight lieutenant agrees to take part in the experiment.'

'Oh, Max will agree.' Carefully, Eva stowed the research sheets away in her covered basket, trying to sound cheerful. In truth though, she was not sure how she would persuade Max even to speak to her, let alone do these exercises. 'Or he'll have me to answer to.'

'I see.' Dr Lewis folded his arms and leant against the door frame to study her. 'I know you're still banned from visiting him.'

'Oh,' she said unhappily.

'No need to look so glum. I was intrigued, so I took a note of the primary exercises. Would you like *me* to approach him with them instead?'

Eva was amazed. 'Would you? That would be perfect, thank you so much.'

'No need for thanks. Your obsession with this has piqued my interest.' He grinned. 'I'm still a sceptic, given the extent of his injuries, but I'm curious now to see if these exercises have any effect.'

'Oh, but you can't just be curious,' she told him sternly. 'You have to believe it will work. With all your heart and soul. That's the only way to get results.'

Dr Lewis blinked, and for a moment Eva thought she had offended him with her forthright manner. Then he said slowly, 'You know, don't take this the wrong way, but I see you and Sister Gray engaged in battle sometimes, and . . . ' He hesitated, tailing off.

'Spit it out.'

'You have more in common with her than you think,' he finished quickly, and then threw back his head, laughing at her outraged expression.

23

Lily was seated on her bed on her morning off, painstakingly piecing together paper chains made from newspaper and magazine cuttings, when Mary knocked at the door.

'I say, that looks fun,' Mary said, coming in to stare at her work.

'Only if you like losing your marbles.'

'Sorry?'

Lily gave up, exasperated, as another link further down the line tore while she was trying to lift the chain for Mary's inspection. 'I mean I'm going crazy here. And this glue absolutely reeks. I've promised to make a dozen paper chains for each ward, but I'm already regretting it.' She glanced at the letter Mary was clutching. 'Here, is that for me?'

Mary handed it over. 'It just came in the post.'

'Thanks for bringing it up, you're such a love. Looks like another one from my Aunt Violet.' Lily dropped the paper chain happily and tore open the letter. Excitement flooded her as she scanned the short letter at speed. 'Oh, my stars!'

'What is it?' Mary perched beside her on the bed, careful not to squash the home-made paper chains.

'It's Aunty Vi's birthday soon. She says she's coming to visit us here in St Ives, and bringing Gran and my little sister Alice, too.'

'That'll be nice for you.'

'It feels like a hundred years since I saw them.' Lily read on, so thrilled she could hardly speak. 'And her friend Mrs Baxter is driving them, along with her son Charlie, so they can bring some of the things I left behind. Oh, I wonder if they'll bring my spare boots, I forgot them when I left.' She looked up at Mary, unable to stop grinning in delight. 'I can't wait to see them all again.'

Mary gave her a hug. 'I can tell. But who's this Charlie character?' She nudged Lily meaningfully. 'He sounds promising.'

'But not my type. We lived with him and his mum for a while back in Porthcurno. Charlie's not much more than a kid, really, and a bit of a firecracker. But he's all right.' Lily summoned up the image of a grubby schoolboy in her memory, with a shy smile but a tendency to yell when he was in a temper. 'He's got a job in a factory at Penzance now. That's probably calmed him down.'

Mary picked up one of the paper-chain lengths, studying them dubiously. Most of the links were still sticky with glue and decidedly lopsided.

'Do you need a hand with making these?' she asked. 'Could you?'

'How long are they supposed to be?'

'Erm . . . ' Lily bit her lip, hurriedly pushing aside her enthusiasm for the family visit. 'Blimey, I hadn't thought to take any measurements. I've just been cutting out rectangles from this lot,' she said, indicating the stack of newspapers and magazines she'd been collecting assiduously from the senior staff room and conservatory, 'folding them over and sticking them together to make a few chains. I never thought how many links there should be in a chain.'

Mary looked at her, then they both giggled.

'I'll go and measure the wards, see how long each

chain needs to be to drape across them. You keep cutting out rectangles, all right?' She handed Lily the scissors and some more newspapers, and then frowned. 'Maybe we could paint a few links to make the chains look brighter. Or we could splash out on some coloured pencils from town.'

'Thank you for offering to help,' Lily told her gratefully.

'My pleasure.' Mary gave her a wink from the door. 'It wouldn't be a Christmas party without paper chains, now would it?'

★ ★ ★

After coming back from lunch, Lily suddenly remembered she'd put herself down on the rota for a bath that day. Swiftly, she grabbed her bath things, and hurried down the hall. She'd washed her hands in the sink, but they were still covered in tiny bits of dried-on glue and faded newsprint. A hot bath would be just the ticket, she was sure.

Somebody was coming out of the steamy bathroom just as she reached the door, and they nearly collided.

'Sorry,' she said, and then realised it was Sister Gray.

Sister looked different in a tatty bathrobe than in her starched uniform, somehow nicer and more approachable. Her skin was pink from the bath, her feet stuffed in old slippers that looked like they ought to have been thrown out years before. She was carrying a towel and her bath bag under one arm.

'My fault,' Sister Gray said in a muffled voice, her head bent, and stepped sideways just as Lily did too, so they both banged into each other again. This time

178

for real.

'Oh bother.' Lily cursed under her breath, embarrassed by her own clumsiness, and shrank back against the wall. 'Sorry, Sister. You go first, I'll wait.'

To her surprise, Sister Gray did not move but gave a strangled sob and put a hand to her face.

She was crying!

'Blimey, did I hurt you?' Lily was mortified.

'No, no.' But Sister Gray was shaking like a leaf. 'It's . . . nothing.'

Lily dropped her bath bag on the rough matting that passed for carpet up in the nurses' quarters, and put an arm about Sister Gray. 'Do you need to sit down?' There was a wooden chair outside the bathroom, and she steered the nurse towards it, carefully putting her towel and bag to one side. 'Take a load off, you'll soon feel better.' She bit her lip. 'It's probably all that bloody steam what does it. Makes me proper light-headed too sometimes.'

Sister Gray sat slumped on the chair, still hiding her face in her hands. 'Thank you,' she whispered. 'But I'm fine. You go and have your bath. Please.'

'I'm not leaving you in this state,' Lily said stoutly.

Sister did not respond.

After a moment, Lily crouched down beside her. She'd never really thought much about Sister Gray before now, except to avoid crossing her. The other girls called her an old dragon. But Lily couldn't bear to see someone in pain, whoever that was. And she was sure she could help.

'Do you want to talk about it?' she asked gently.

Still, Sister said nothing.

Lily's eye was caught by a folded piece of paper sticking out of Sister's bath bag. It looked like

179

a personal letter, and her guess was that Sister Gray had been reading it in the bath, because the paper looked a little damp and crinkled at the edges.

'Did you get post today too?' Sister shuddered, and Lily knew she'd guessed correctly. 'Bad news, was it? I'm so sorry.' She hesitated, not sure whether to probe further or let things alone. In the end, instinct won. 'My old gran says, a trouble shared is a trouble halved. If you want to tell me what's in the letter, I won't tell another living soul. Cross my heart and hope to die.' She made the sign of the cross over her heart. 'It won't go no further, I swear to God.'

Slowly, Sister Gray lowered her hands and looked at her. Her eyes were swimming with tears. 'You promise?'

'I crossed my heart, didn't I?' Lily passed her the letter, nodding. 'You'll feel better getting it off your chest. And that's a fact.'

Sister Gray looked unconvinced. But she unfolded the letter and peered down at it. 'To be honest, I don't know why I'm so upset. It's not bad news, really.' She paused. 'It's from my sister, Elsie. She's younger than me by five years. And she's never lost any opportunity to remind me of that.'

'You don't get on?'

'It's not that, exactly. More like Elsie sees everything as a competition.'

Lily thought of her own younger sister, Alice, who could be quite headstrong, but it wasn't the same. She and Alice weren't even three years apart, and had always been close, especially since their mum's death and their dad's disappearance while serving overseas. That kind of tragedy tended to push siblings together, she felt. They still bickered on like nobody's business when stuck together for any length of time, of course, but she'd always imagined sisters were like that in general.

'We're both orphans,' Sister Gray continued, as if reading Lily's mind. 'We grew up here in St Ives. Our parents died of the flu when we were still young, so my aunt raised us for a few years. But then she grew too ill to look after us, and we went into the orphanage for a few years until she was better. It should have brought us closer, but Elsie . . . Well, my sister's not very good at showing affection. In fact, I think she rather enjoys being mean.' Sister stumbled over her words. 'Whenever there was something I liked or wanted, she would always take it for herself before I could get it. And now . . . '

She stopped, swallowing convulsively.

'It's all right,' Lily reassured her. 'I understand. So what was in the letter?'

'Elsie told me she's coming home for Christmas, that she's got something very special to tell me.' Sister Gray gave a sob and crumpled the letter up in her fist. 'Except I already know what it is.'

'What?'

'She's going to marry Lewis.'

Lily stared, astounded by that exciting nugget of gossip. She almost regretted having promised not to tell anyone else. But it was too late now. '*Dr Lewis*?'

'They were seeing each other before Elsie was drafted up north. My sister knew how much I liked him, you see. So she made him fall in love with her. And it worked. He never looked twice at me again.'

'I'm sure that's not true,' Lily said quickly. She'd seen the looks Dr Lewis occasionally threw Sister

Gray, and although he might not be smitten with her, he was definitely not immune.

'No, it's true. And even if he does feel something for me, he would never leave Elsie in the lurch. He's a good man.'

Lily patted her hand, watching Sister Gray with sympathy.

'I secretly hoped Elsie would forget him while she was away up north,' she continued shakily, 'that she'd find some other man to sink her hooks into. But from this letter, it's obvious she hasn't. Now, I'm going to have to watch them walk down the aisle together as man and wife, and not let anyone see that I'm dying inside.' Sister Gray closed her eyes, tears squeezing out from under her lids. 'I don't think I can bear it.'

24

The bus juddered along the main street and swung around the corner, heading out of town. It was mid-afternoon and gloomy, dusk gathering more swiftly now they had edged into December. The windows were steamed up but Rose could see misty lights around the town, some of them being blotted up as people drew their blackout curtains early. The bus was busy, for this would be the last one of the evening, headlights being generally forbidden after dark.

Rose looked through her basket, checking her purchases again. She did not often go into town, preferring to put aside her salary against some future need. But given that it would be Christmas soon, she had brought her luxury coupons with her this time and gone browsing for a few small gifts.

Dipping into her savings, she had splashed out on a pretty flower brooch for Matron, a few knitting patterns for her closest friends among the nurses, half an ounce of rolling tobacco for Tom, who enjoyed a crafty smoke now and then, and something special for Lewis.

Foolish of her to get the doctor a gift, perhaps. Elsie would be back home soon, and his attention would be on her instead. Since getting her sister's letter, she had told herself to put aside all thoughts of Lewis Lanyon; dreaming about him would only cause them both terrible heartache. Indeed, it had already caused her to weep all over young Nurse Fisher, who must think her an awful wet blanket. She just hoped Lily would keep her word and not tell anyone else.

But then she'd passed the small antique shop in town today, down a side street near the harbour, and not been able to resist looking in.

The glass of the antique shop window had been shattered by a recent bombing raid, but the owner had merely moved his goods further back into the shop and put up boards to protect against bad weather. Rose had stopped to peer through the door, left open for customers, and seen something that snagged her attention.

She removed her purchase now from the basket and cupped it in her hand. A small but exquisite vintage paperweight, its cool glass misting over in the crowded bus.

Rose knew why the unusual object had caught her eye.

Blue was Lewis's favourite colour, he had told her once, as they stood looking out over Carbis Bay together. The colour of sorrow, she always thought, yet also of the open sea and sky. The colour of infinity, perhaps. And these perfect blue-and-white glass rods had been imprisoned within a smooth glass dome, shaped by their creator into flowers doomed never to open and bloom.

She didn't know if he would understand. She wasn't even sure that she understood. But the gesture must be enough.

The bus halted at the crossroads, waiting for a slow farm vehicle to pass.

Up above, a group of school children in hats and coats were hurrying home, carrying satchels, chatting eagerly with each other as they streamed across the road.

Leaning forward to rub a porthole in the steamed-up window, she recognised some of the orphanage children on their way home too, straggling behind the others. Jimmy was among them, looking a little forlorn, but at least he hadn't run away. She feared he would, knowing how unhappy the boy was under the care of the awful Treverricks. It would be a disaster, given how young he was.

New passengers had got on board while the bus was stationary. Now it started up again, chugging slowly up the hill.

'Hullo there, it's Rose Gray, isn't it?'

She looked up, startled, and saw Dick Jeffries grinning down at her.

'Dick!'

He looked just the same as he'd done when they were at school together. A fair dollop of hair above a round face, with a slightly pudgy build, clad now in a serious-looking tweed suit.

'Anyone sitting here?' Before Rose could answer, he had swung into the seat next to her, his knee bumping her basket. 'Sorry.' He placed a briefcase on his own knee and patted it. 'School books. Taking my marking home.'

'Of course,' she said. 'You work at the school now. A teacher?'

'For my sins. Tried to enlist but they wouldn't have me. Damn dodgy eye.' He had a lazy eye, she remembered. 'But you're up at Symmonds Hall these days, aren't you? Last thing I heard, you'd gone away to train as a nurse. That must have been a few years before the war, surely?'

'I trained in Truro at the hospital; I was there for three years. I came back to St Ives just before war broke out, as luck would have it.'

The young clippie appeared and took Dick's fare, handing him a ticket in return. Her curious gaze slid over Rose with interest before she moved away.

'So you're, what now? Nurse Gray?'

'Sister Gray.'

'Practically royalty, then!' Dick doffed his cap with a mock flourish and then replaced it, his smile approving. 'I must say, you look well on it. Bit thinner than I remember. But I suppose all that marching up and down the wards with your tiara on must take its toll.'

The children were lost to view now. Rose guessed they must cross the fields in the gloom rather than take the longer route by road.

'Can I ask you something?' she ventured, a little hesitant.

'Ask whatever you like.' Dick laughed, perhaps mistaking what she meant. 'No, I'm not married yet. Yes, I'm in the market for a wife. And my favourite dinner is liver and bacon.'

Rose blinked, then laughed too, realising that he must be joking. At least, she hoped he was joking. 'That wasn't — '

'Sorry, I'm an idiot. I'm just getting desperate. Still living with my mother, and as you can see, I don't even have a car. Hence the bus.' He saw her confusion and shook his head. 'Forget it. It wasn't a personal question you wanted to ask, was it?'

'I just wanted to know what you think of the orphanage children.'

'The orphanage kids? What do you mean?'

'I'm worried about them.' She bit her lip. 'You won't tell anyone, will you?'

'God, no. Who would I tell? But why are you worried?'

Briefly, she told him about the Treverricks, whom he seemed to know about already, and her fears about their mistreatment of the children, and Jimmy in particular. She swore him to secrecy. 'I don't want them to know I've been asking about them. They might take it out on the children.'

'That's serious stuff, I must admit. Punishing them in the freezing cold? Telling them off for crying when there's an air-raid siren? Well, I can't deny I've seen them wolf down their milk and biscuits at school like they didn't get breakfast. And some of them barely open their mouths in class, which is often a sign that they're unhappy at home.'

'Is Jimmy unhappy, would you say?'

'Jimmy?' He pulled a face. 'The boy is morose, not just unhappy.'

Rose felt a wave of sorrow wash over her. She had half-hoped it had been purely her imagination. There was so little she could do to help the poor boy.

'Tell me, Dick, do you believe in corporal punishment?'

He looked troubled. 'I don't like administering it. But sometimes there's no other way. And the kids expect it, too. If they kick up a rumpus or break a window . . . Well, if you don't dole out the strap every now and then, they see it as a sign of weakness. And once that happens in a full class, you lose all hope of discipline.'

'Yes, I see.'

'But what you've described . . . An orphanage isn't

like a school, Rose. It's essentially a child's home. And they shouldn't be afraid to go home.'

'Yes, exactly.' Rose was pleased that he understood.

'So what are you planning to do?'

'I'm really not sure.' She stared out into the thickening dusk. 'I've spoken to Matron about it but she's forbidden me from investigating further. And I dare not push any harder or I could lose my position at the home.' Rose gave him a grateful smile. 'But thank you for being so helpful. At least now I can be sure that I'm not exaggerating, thinking they're unhappy when they're not.'

'You're welcome. I just wish I could do more.' Dick hesitated. 'Look, why don't we meet for a drink in town sometime? We could talk more about this. I could keep a closer eye on Jimmy and the others, and give you a report.' He grinned. 'A bit like spying, but on the side of the angels.'

Rose knew what he was doing. Trying to get a date with her on the pretext of helping with the orphanage kids. She opened her mouth to refuse, then shut it again. Why should she turn him down? He wasn't so bad looking and he had a steady job. A job of service, like her own. Elsie would be home from Leeds soon, and then it would only be a matter of time before she and Lewis were married. Which would leave Rose lonelier than ever.

Yet she simply couldn't bring herself to say yes.

'I'm sorry,' she said.

He brushed it off, still smiling, but she could tell that he was hurt. 'Not to worry, I can always write you a note if anything occurs that you should know about.' Before she could thank him, Dick peered through the dark and jumped up, briefcase in hand. 'This is my stop. Better dash. Wonderful to see you, Sister Gray.'

And then he was gone.

★ ★ ★

After walking the rest of the way from the bus stop, Rose decided to approach the hall from the side, swinging past the orphanage on her way. Mr Treverrick's dog, Buster, a large mongrel, came tearing out of the darkness, barking madly as she drew level with the front entrance. But he must have recognised her voice or scent, for he stopped barking and whined softly through the fence instead.

'Good boy,' Rose reassured the dog, then stood there a moment, looking up at the orphanage windows. They were dark, the blackout curtains in place, or perhaps the rooms were mostly empty at this time in the early evening. She thought about the small, dimly lit rooms inside, and the grim little dormitories with their cramped beds where she and Elsie had spent several years of their childhood, pretending to be royal prisoners locked away from the world. Though it had been a different couple in charge, back then. Mr and Mrs Cooper, who had been quite friendly in reality, and Mrs Van Dook, a strange old lady with big teeth who had frankly terrified the children. Rose and Elsie had eventually escaped and returned to the sanctuary of their aunt's house.

She wasn't sure what she expected to see through those dark windows. Only that she wanted to be seen by them, perhaps. To put the Treverricks on notice that they couldn't continue getting away with ill-treating the children in their charge, because someone at least was watching.

It wasn't much. But it was all she could do. To bear witness.

Slowly, she walked on along the new fence that bordered the property, and the dog trotted cheerfully along on the other side, following her.

A door creaked open somewhere behind the fence, and after a few seconds a voice whispered through the fence, 'Is that you, Miss?'

'Jimmy?'

There was an odd rustling noise, with a few grunts, and then Jimmy's head appeared above the fence, grinning down at her.

'Careful!' she exclaimed, scared for the boy. 'And watch out for that dog.'

'Buster don't scare me.'

'Well, all the same, please don't fall.'

'I won't fall, I can climb anything, me,' Jimmy boasted proudly, then wobbled and almost fell as she watched, her heart in her mouth. Somehow he managed to steady himself, his wide grin displaying a missing front tooth. 'I saw you through the window, Miss. Why are you out so late?'

She showed him her shopping basket. 'I've been into town. I saw you and the others walking back from school earlier. How are you getting on with your lessons?'

'Dunno.'

'And are they treating you well, the Treverricks?'

Jimmy didn't answer, watching her uneasily, as though he feared she would use whatever he said against him.

'Well,' she continued with a reassuring smile, 'don't worry about that. Have you heard about the Christmas party?'

His eyes widened in awe and he shook his head silently.

'We're holding a party later this month at the home. Nearer Christmas. There'll be carol singing and dancing and games.' She saw his face light up. 'Cook is making sandwiches and special cake too.'

'Cake?' he whispered.

'Plus, there'll be a big Christmas tree with baubles and tinsel. Maybe you and your friends could come over and help us decorate it.'

He looked stunned. 'I've never deco . . . decorated a Christmas tree before.'

'It's quite easy. I can show you, if you like.'

He was looking happier, she thought, with a lightening of her spirits. But at that moment, she heard a man's voice shouting, 'Jimmy? Where are you?' from inside the building.

'That's Mr T,' Jimmy gasped, panic in his voice, and he disappeared again. 'Bye, Miss.' He ran across the yard towards the building, then she heard a door close behind him.

Rose stood listening for several minutes after he'd gone, her heart beating fast. She was prepared to march back to the front door and hammer on it, demanding entrance, if she heard the slightest sound of that boy being abused. But the evening was silent, and nothing moved in the dark windows. Even the dog went back to lie down somewhere. In a kennel, perhaps.

Eventually, she moved on. But her heart was heavy and she felt again the weight of failure. She could only ever help that boy for a few minutes at a time. He would always have to return to the Treverricks, who seemed to terrify him. Was she doing more harm than

191

good by raising his hopes with these fleeting moments of happiness?

Somehow, she had to find a way to make life better for Jimmy. For him and the other children too. Even if it meant being dismissed from Symmonds Hall.

25

Eva stood on the lonely cliff path, enjoying the solitude of the open air, head bent as she read through Hazel Baxter's latest letter again. It wasn't a long letter, but it did bear news of Violet and her father, and she appreciated her friend making the effort to write. She, Hazel and Violet had only really become close after organising the dance at Porthcurno together, and Eva had been knocked off balance by the wrench she'd felt on leaving the other two women behind when she came to St Ives.

Your father is in fine spirits after some of the big wigs from London came to inspect the place. They stayed three days, and Mr Frobisher was run off his feet, whipping up special dinners every night. Violet had to do more than her fair share too, cooking and cleaning. Lily's Gran even came up to help on the last evening, though she gave Frobisher what for when he asked her to mop out the lavatories. 'Beneath my dignity,' she told him, just like the Queen. His face was a picture. Sheila doesn't half make me laugh. I've written to Lily too, telling her all about it.

Eva grinned, perfectly able to imagine the scene. No doubt her father would have been lording it about the place, eager to show off Eastern House to his important guests from London. And it sounded to her like he'd succeeded.

I'm feeling a bit sorry for myself though. This baby is so heavy, and I don't remember getting this tired when I was expecting Charlie. But I was a lot younger in those days, and there wasn't a war on. I'm so round too, I feel like I may pop soon. Last time I saw the doctor, he said he could hear the baby's heartbeat, and he thinks the head may be down. That means it won't be long now.

Eva shook her head, worried for her friend's health. Hazel was a strong and energetic Cornishwoman in her early thirties. But having a baby in these difficult times would drain anyone's strength . . .

'Do you think it will snow soon?'

Eva tucked her letter back into her coat pocket and spun round, surprised that anyone else would have come outside in this chilly weather.

But she knew the voice only too well.

It was Sister Gray standing behind her, wrapped in a thick coat, a hat jammed down over her red hair, clapping her hands together in woollen gloves as though to keep them warm. She looked flushed, no doubt by the cold or the blustery walk from Symmonds Hall, but unfortunately had not been put off by either.

Oh blow, Eva thought wearily. Trust old Graysides to come and spoil her time off. After re-reading Hazel's letter, she'd been planning to take a long walk and contemplate how to unknot the thorny problem of Max's refusal to see her. Dr Lewis had told her that he'd persuaded Max to make a start on those exercises. She was delighted at the news, of course. But she was also convinced that Max would make faster progress with her by his side.

And now she had unwelcome company to distract her.

'Anything's possible, it's certainly cold enough at the moment,' Eva said lightly, and then glanced back along the narrow cliff path. 'Well, I was just on my way back to the hall. Have a good walk!'

But it seemed she wasn't to get off that easily.

'Nurse Ryder, wait,' Sister Gray ordered her in a peremptory tone, and Eva stopped reluctantly. 'I saw you from the conservatory, actually, and came out specially to see you. I'd like a private word.'

Oh no, Eva thought crossly, what now? More complaints about her and Max perhaps, or questions about why she had written that letter to Dr Lewis . . .

'Is that so?' Eva waited, her arms folded. 'I'm not on duty, you know.'

Sister Gray's eyes flashed. 'I'm well aware of that, thank you. This isn't about work.' She turned to look out at the ocean, clearly struggling with herself, and then pointed along the cliff path. There was a rock sticking out of the bracken a few hundred feet away, with a smooth area which often served as a perch for weary hikers. 'Shall we sit?'

Eva was taken aback but agreed.

Seated a few inches away on the hard, cold rock, Sister Gray stared at the sea, its turbulent expanse stretching all the way to America. She said abruptly, still not looking at Eva, 'I have a proposition to put to you.'

Eva resisted the urge to raise her eyebrows. 'Go on.'

'I've been told you're due to accompany Lady Symmonds on a tour of the orphanage soon.'

'That's right. Her ladyship asked me to go along to keep a note of whatever she sees there. Her memory's

not what it was, apparently. Why, is that a problem?'
Eva stiffened, sensing a reprimand on its way. 'I've
already squared it with Matron, so if — '

'I want to go with you.'

Eva opened her mouth, then closed it again. That
wasn't what she'd been expecting to hear. 'Sister?'

'I have an interest there. One of the orphans, a
little boy called Jimmy . . . Between you and me,
I'm not convinced he's being treated properly by
the Treverricks.'

Eva's brows rose steeply, and this time she didn't
try to stop them.

'I just want to see the place for myself,' Sister Gray
continued, gripping her gloved hands tightly in her
lap, her face troubled. 'I need to be sure.'

'Of what?'

'My instinct that he's being ill-treated. I don't want
to rush things and accuse them of neglect if . . . ' She
took a deep breath. 'It could make things worse for
the boy, you see, if I get it wrong or move against
them without evidence.' Then she began to tell Eva
about Jimmy, and various incidents she'd witnessed
that made her fear for his welfare and that of the other
children too.

Eva, listening, thought back to her own fears about
the way the orphanage was being run. From her first
days at Symmonds Hall, she'd heard sounds of children
crying next door, and she'd had ample opportunity to
study the Treverricks in the shared cellar during air
raids. Mr Treverrick seemed to pay his young charges
no attention at all, except to complain when they
spoke above a whisper, and Mrs Treverrick's sharp,
impatient responses to children scared by the sounds
of bombs falling had told her everything she needed

196

to know about that woman's temperament.

'So you want to visit the orphanage too?' Eva considered that request carefully. 'If it were up to me, I'd say yes immediately. But I'm going as Lady Symmonds' guest, and I'm not sure I can extend that invitation to a third party as well.'

'I've thought of that.' Sister Gray turned to look at her for the first time, a defensive look on her face. 'I . . . I was an orphan there myself once.'

Eva was amazed. 'Really?'

She remembered Dr Edmund telling her about Rose and her younger sister Elsie, but the old doctor had never mentioned that the two sisters had been orphaned. It partly explained Sister's barbed-wire personality, if she had grown up in that rather forbidding looking place!

'It's a long story,' Sister Gray said curtly, clearly not willing to talk about her past, 'and not particularly relevant to this situation, except as a way to get me through the door. Perhaps if you were to approach her ladyship and explain that I grew up at the orphanage and would dearly love to see inside the building one more time — '

'Yes,' Eva said, understanding in a flash. 'That would sound plausible.'

The sea rumbled in the distance and the afternoon light began to fail around them, a cold silver shot through with gold streaks. A mass of dark, heavy clouds came lumbering across the Atlantic towards the Cornish coast; Eva shivered, watching them approach, thankful of her coat. Were those clouds bringing snow?

'So you'll ask for me?'

'Why can't you ask Lady Symmonds yourself?'

Sister Gray threw her an eloquent look. 'Why do you think? I was like Jimmy once. I'm not her class,' she said bitterly.

'I'm not her class either.'

'Your father's a colonel. I bet you had a good education, went to finishing school, know all the right things to say . . . ' At Eva's embarrassed silence, Sister Gray nodded. 'Right or wrong, she's more likely to listen to you than to me.'

Eva did not know what to say.

'Look, I'll make it easier for you.' Sister Gray stood up and by mutual consent they began to walk back towards Symmonds Hall. 'You get me onto that orphanage tour and I'll make sure the ban's lifted on you working in Atlantic Ward. How's that?' She gave Eva a sharp sideways nod. 'Yes, and if he agrees, you can even spend time with your precious flight lieutenant without me interfering. That's a promise.'

'I can see Max again?'

'Will you do it? Will you speak to her ladyship for me?

Eva blinked. 'I can't guarantee that — '

'But you'll try? And not mention it to anyone else? Matron is against the idea. She says to leave well alone. If she even knew about this conversation . . . ' Sister Gray gave her a direct look. 'I could get into serious trouble if you blab.'

The fate of those orphans must really mean a great deal to her, Eva realised, to admit such a thing to someone she knew might be her enemy. She couldn't quite bring herself to like the woman, who was so very different from herself, but she was beginning to respect her, at least. Sister Gray was risking her career in nursing, which she obviously loved, for the sake of a few children she barely knew.

Eva was only too happy to get on board with her plan. If the orphans were indeed being ill-treated by the Treverricks, and she felt Sister was right to fear they were, it was vital they found evidence to back up that accusation, so they could rescue them.

'I won't blab,' Eva reassured her, and risked a smile. 'Careless talk costs lives, eh?' She clasped both hands behind her back and strode out across the grassy headland. 'So, assuming you get permission to tag along, what's the plan?'

26

'That's right, dearie,' Cook said cheerfully, nudging Lily's elbow as she paused over the mixing bowl, bag of currants in hand. 'A few more shakes, and that'll do nicely.'

Lily obeyed, and then handed the bag back to Cook, to be replaced in the kitchen store cupboard.

'Ain't there supposed to be more dried fruit in the mix?' Lily wiped her hands on her apron and peered dubiously into the bowl. 'Each Christmas cake has to serve thirty people, at least.'

'There's a war on. They'll make do.' Cook grimaced. 'But you're right, this one does look a bit thin. That's what comes of trying to make a cake with no eggs.' She clucked her tongue, thinking. 'How about we add more grated carrot and breadcrumbs? I can spare a cupful.'

Quickly, Cook set to work grating another carrot with nimble fingers.

'And a silver sixpence for luck,' Lily said brightly, recalling with nostalgia how she had once helped her mum prepare the Christmas fare. How she missed those happy, care-free days before the war!

'Bless your heart, that's for a Christmas pudding.'

'Oh.'

'Here you go.' Cook added another cup of grated carrot and breadcrumbs, and another dash of sweetly fragrant vanilla essence. 'Give it a good stir.'

Lily stirred the strange, stodgy mix with her wooden

spoon. 'Yes, that's better. Though I think it needs more brandy too.'

'It's not the only one,' Cook said drily, but opened the bottle again and let fall a few more drops of pungent alcohol into the fruity cake mix. 'Mmm, brandy. I can smell Christmas already.'

'Oh, don't,' Lily grumbled, stirring again fervently. 'Matron's going to boil me in oil, I'm so far behind with the Christmas party plans. I've hardly any bloody money left from the fund she gave me, all I've got is a ton of paper chains, and I don't know where I'm going to find more decorations this close to Christmas.'

'No need to worry about that.' Cook gave her a wink, taking the bowl away to fold in the flour and spices. 'Piotr's dad told me he can get cut-price decorations for the hall. Right fancy ones, too. You only have to ask and he'll sort you out.'

Lily watched her work. 'Goodness, that's kind of him.'

'Not sure about kind. He runs a stall in the market sometimes. Knows how to get hold of things other people can't, if you see what I mean. But you watch he doesn't over-charge you.'

'He can't take money I don't have,' Lily pointed out flatly.

Matron interrupted, appearing in the doorway to the kitchen. 'Ah, there you are, Nurse Fisher. Just the person I need to speak to.' She nodded stiffly to Cook. 'If you can spare her, that is.'

Cook had scowled instinctively at her entry; she seemed to resent having Matron in her kitchen, though no more than Matron would have hated to see Cook wandering about the wards.

201

'If you'd follow me, Nurse Fisher...' Matron paused, sniffing the air. 'That smells spicy. Christmas cake?'

Cook covered the bowl with a cloth. 'It might be,' she said sourly.

'I promised to help Cook with Christmas preparations in return for help with the party food,' Lily said, hurriedly washing her hands and removing her apron. 'It's my time off, so I didn't think you'd mind.'

'Of course I don't mind, silly girl. But, as it happens, I need to speak to you about the party.' Matron took her into the corridor and closed the kitchen door so Cook couldn't overhear. 'How are the arrangements going, Nurse Fisher? You were supposed to give me a report last week, but I've heard nothing so far. We're only a few weeks away from the big event.'

'Sorry, Matron. I'll get right on it. I've sorted out the food, and the music, and I've been making paper chains for the wards. Some of the girls have been helping me. But I haven't found a tree yet. Or any baubles and tinsel.' She bit her lip. 'Maybe I should buy some from Piotr's dad, who runs a market stall. Cook says he knows how to get hold of things other people can't. I've got a little money left, but — '

Matron's thin nose quivered in outrage. 'You'll do no such thing. Waste good money on decorations from a stall? Don't be ridiculous. You must speak to Tom instead.'

'Tom?' Lily was baffled.

'Do use some common sense, Nurse. Last year, we had paper chains and garlands strung up in the wards, and a large tree on Carbis Ward. After the New Year celebrations, Tom was instructed to pack away all the Christmas decorations in a box. If you apply to him, I

202

imagine he can find them for you.'

Lily couldn't believe what she was hearing. 'Bleeding hell,' she muttered, 'I wish someone would have told me that before I got meself covered in glue and newspaper!'

Matron's face went almost purple with indignation. 'Nurse Fisher!'

'Oops, me and my big mouth. I'm ever so sorry, Matron.' But the older woman still didn't look too impressed. 'I'd better go and find Tom right away. Get them tree decorations sorted, like you said.'

Not even waiting to be dismissed, Lily scurried away before she could be put on a charge for bad language.

'Blimey,' she muttered, walking quickly with her head down.

She shouldn't have sworn in front of Matron. But frustration flooded her, all the same. She'd been doing her best with an impossible task; now she was in Matron's bad books simply through not keeping a strict enough rein over her tongue. Why, oh why, had she taken on the task of organising the Christmas party, she asked herself crossly. Oh yes, she hadn't taken it on, had she? Even though she was the newest member of staff, with the least experience, she'd been given no *bloody choice* but to accept.

She'd always been described as the polite, well-behaved one out of her family. But perhaps she was too polite for her own good. Perhaps it was time she said what was on her mind and stood up for herself, even if it got her into trouble.

Rounding the corner that led towards the conservatory and the orderlies' quarters, Lily nearly collided with someone walking the other way.

'Oh, for God's sake, not again!' Heat rushed to her cheeks as she realised who it was, and she recoiled, biting her tongue for the second time that day. 'Sorry, my fault. I wasn't looking where I was going.'

It was Private Danny Orde.

Danny looked tall and imposing out of bed, and rather dashing in his dressing gown, even if his pyjamas underneath were a trifle rumpled. She thought his facial scars were looking less red and inflamed too, after days of being assiduously cleaned and having the emollient cream rubbed into them. Indeed, she'd overheard Dr Lewis suggest to Matron the other day that Danny could be discharged for Christmas if he showed no further sign of infection over the next week or two.

She wasn't sure how she felt about Danny leaving Symmonds Hall. She knew the young private found being here difficult though, and would probably be happier at home with his family, especially over the festive season.

'You all right?' Danny asked, then frowned, studying her face. 'Hey, what's the matter? You look upset.'

She felt a sudden urge to run away but the passageway was narrow and he was blocking her way. 'I'm fine. I just had a run-in with Matron, that's all.'

'You, Lily?' He looked amused. 'That doesn't sound very likely.'

'Suit yourself.'

Danny laughed at her sharp response. 'Well, well. So you've got claws. And here I was, thinking pretty Nurse Fisher wouldn't say boo to a goose.'

'Oh no, not bleeding you and all?' Lily folded her arms across her chest, glaring at him. 'Excuse me,

Private Orde. You may think this is funny, but I've got work to do.'

'All right, no need to get upset.' He touched her cheek with a long finger. 'You're even prettier when you're angry, did you know that?'

Lily brushed him aside and hurried on, but talking to Danny had thrown her off balance, and she had to duck aside into a washroom first and splash her face with water.

When she found Tom, she asked for the Christmas decorations in a business-like way, and even got him to promise he'd contact the same farmer as last year about a tree for Carbis Ward, which had the most space for people to gather for carol singing and exchanging gifts.

It was a long time before her high flush subsided and her temper begin to cool, and her cheek bore the invisible imprint of Danny's fingertip for hours afterwards.

Lily's head was whirling and she didn't know what to think.

Danny had barely touched her.

Yet somehow he'd left her feeling shaky inside and unsure of herself, unable even to smile at any of the other patients as she usually did when doing the rounds. Why had that one gentle touch left her breathless and frightened?

Lily had a feeling she knew why. But she couldn't bring herself to face it.

27

Rose had spent the morning helping Matron with the paperwork usually undertaken by Dr Edmund. Mostly lists of medication for the log book, but also weekly records of how each convalescent patient was getting along, which were coming due for discharge, and those whose conditions were deteriorating. For these, they had to refer to Dr Edmund's notebook, which Lewis had brought up from the house. Dr Edmund's handwriting was small and crabbed, and often difficult to decipher, especially as he had odd little squiggles as abbreviations for certain medications and conditions. It was dull work but necessary for the smooth running of the home, and Rose's eyesight appeared to be better than Matron's, so she did most of the transcribing while Matron stared into the fire or talked unhappily about how much everyone was missing the old doctor around the place.

Just before two in the afternoon, Nurse Ryder rapped on the door and then stuck her head round it in a peremptory manner. 'Sister, may I speak to you privately?'

Matron looked up in surprise. 'Sister is busy. What is it?'

But Rose was already putting the lid back on her pen and closing the inkwell. She pushed the medications log aside and gave Matron a brief smile. 'I did agree to see Nurse Ryder on another matter. If you'll excuse me, Matron, I'll finish these later.'

Without further explanation, she left the senior

staff room and followed Nurse Ryder down the hallway to where Lady Symmonds was waiting for them. The old lady, wrapped in a black woollen shawl and leaning on her silver-topped cane, straightened as Rose approached.

Her sharp eyes looked them both over with approval. 'Well,' she told Rose, 'thanks to Eva's powers of persuasion, I've agreed that you may accompany us around the orphanage today. But only on condition you don't cause me any headaches, Sister Gray.'

Rose felt anxious. 'My lady?'

'Matron warned me not to agree to this. She told me there's no love lost between you and the Treverricks. But I prefer to take as I find, and you seem a decent enough woman. So I shall give you the benefit of the doubt.'

'Thank you, my lady.'

'But I'll not have any arguments while I'm making my inspection. Is that clear?'

Rose nodded and fell in beside Eva as they headed across to the orphanage under a cold, leaden sky, a few snowflakes whirling about their heads. She was aware of a sudden fit of nerves, her heart beating faster than it should be. So Matron had already stuck her oar in, had she? Well, she was determined to keep to her and Eva's plan. Her main thought was of Jimmy and the other children, and how good it would be to see them and hopefully be reassured that they were happy and not being ill-treated behind those intimidating walls.

'Thank you for talking her round,' she whispered to Eva. 'I'm worried about little Jimmy, and this may be my only chance to see if he's all right.'

'No need to thank me,' Eva replied, also in a whisper. 'I told you, I can't stand seeing children ill-treated. I want to get to the bottom of this too.' She paused. 'Though make sure you don't get caught, all right? Or it's not going to look very good for either of us.'

'I won't get caught,' Rose insisted.

But in the orphanage, it was clear that the Treverricks were alarmed to see her, Mrs Treverrick going so far as to ask what 'she' was doing there, nodding to Rose.

'I don't like to take notes myself,' Lady Symmonds told them, nodding to the small notebook Eva had brought with her, 'so these two ladies are here to help me remember what I see.' She swept majestically past them, through the entrance door and into the main hallway, before stopping and peering up the long staircase. 'It seems strangely quiet. It's a Saturday afternoon, isn't it? There's no school today, is there?'

'No, your ladyship.' Mrs Treverrick stood nervously at the foot of the stairs. 'Not today.'

'So where are the children?'

Mr Treverrick ushered Lady Symmonds further along the hall. 'They're waiting for you in the dining room, your ladyship. They have a song to perform for you.'

'Hmm.' Lady Symmonds glanced back at Eva and Rose, as though checking they were both still there, and then followed him into the large dining room.

As she entered the large, gloomy room, Eva opened her notebook and produced a pencil, while Rose fell in behind her, Mrs Treverrick bringing up the rear.

It was rather like being under guard, Rose thought, unable to shake off the fear that she would never leave again now she was back. Ever since she had set foot over the threshold, she had known herself back in the belly of the beast. Her skin was prickling with uncomfortable memories, her hands clenched into automatic fists by her side.

The children, over twenty of them, were lined up in the dining room in two straggling rows, the youngest to the front. It was one of the larger downstairs rooms, and even larger today with the tables and chairs pushed back against the walls. Lady Symmonds was led to a seat by the window where she could survey the whole room, and Rose stood behind her with Eva, with the Treverricks watching eagle-eyed from the side.

Mrs Treverrick clapped her hands, and the children clasped their hands behind their backs and began to sing in thin, uneven voices, heads held high. They had prepared the hymn 'Jerusalem', the Christmas carols 'Good King Wenceslas' and 'Once In Royal David's City', with two verses of the National Anthem to finish. Some of the children looked blank, others terrified, while a few stared in wide-eyed curiosity at their visitors.

One thing Rose had noticed within seconds of entering the room: Jimmy was nowhere to be seen. Fear instantly took hold of her, but there was nothing she could do about his absence at the moment.

When the recitation was completed, the adults all clapped dutifully. The children sat cross-legged on the floor at a signal from Mrs Treverrick.

'Excellent singing.' Lady Symmonds banged her cane on the floor, and the children stared at it, and her, their attention rapt. 'And some interesting choices there. 'Good King Wenceslas' would seem a particularly apt carol for my visit. Thank you for that. One of my very own favourites.' It was difficult, Rose decided, to be sure if the old lady was being serious or faintly mocking. Perhaps both at once. 'Now, let me hear some of your names.' She pointed to a small child in the front row, whose eyes widened in horror. 'You can start. Who are you and how old are you?'

It took about fifteen minutes to go through both rows, asking each child's name in turn, their age, and how long they had been in residence at the orphanage. Five of the children were evacuees from London, and they looked the happiest and healthiest, perhaps not surprisingly.

Rose felt Eva's gaze on her face and looked round at her.

'Where's Jimmy?' Eva mouthed.

Baffled, Rose shook her head.

Leaning forward, Eva whispered something in Lady Symmonds' ear, and the old lady nodded, asking in a piercing voice, 'And where is this young Jimmy character, about whom I have heard so much?' She glanced at the Treverricks, frowning. 'He does not appear to be among these children.'

'No, your ladyship,' Mrs Treverrick said awkwardly, shooting a poisonous look at Rose, making it clear she knew who was really behind that question. 'Jimmy . . . He's ill, unfortunately. Confined to bed, poor lad.'

Rose did not believe a word of it.

'Where is he?' she demanded, driven by concern for the young boy. 'What have you done to him?'

Lady Symmonds turned her head and looked round at her. Not much of a reprimand, perhaps, but Rose felt the force behind that sharp gaze and buttoned her lips tight. She had promised Eva that she wouldn't cause trouble.

'I can assure you,' Mr Treverrick said, stepping forward to address Rose with a superior look, 'that

210

nothing has been 'done' to Jimmy, as you put it. The boy is ill and upstairs in his bed. And let me tell you, I bitterly resent the implication that we're lying.'

Lady Symmonds got to her feet, and all the children hurriedly scrambled to their feet too, as though she were the Queen. Which, to their minds, she might as well have been, Rose thought.

'I should like to see over the rest of the orphanage now,' Lady Symmonds said in ringing tones, and headed for the door, again without waiting for her hosts to lead the way. 'I'm interested to see how you have spent the maintenance allowance I make you. So, if you could point out any improvements, Mr Treverrick?'

'Of course,' he said hesitantly, adding a reluctant 'your ladyship' after a nudge from his wife. 'Shall we start in the playroom? That's where the younger children spend most of their time. You'll see we've changed the décor considerably since your last visit, and invested in some new toys.'

As soon as they had disappeared, with a train of children shuffling in their wake, Rose looked round at Nurse Ryder, who had waited behind in the hall with her.

'Right, I'm going upstairs to look for Jimmy,' Rose told her.

'I'll cover for you.' Eva gave her a quick grin. 'Though be as quick as possible. I'll try to distract them with difficult questions, like we agreed, but you'll be for the high jump if the Treverricks discover what you're up to.'

'Then you'd better make sure they don't.'

Eva rolled her eyes. 'Yes, Sister.'

Rose nodded and hurried up the stairs alone,

sure she knew her way about the old building well enough to find Jimmy and return downstairs before anyone had noticed she was missing. That was the plan, anyway.

★ ★ ★

The building had been a red-brick annex of Symmonds Hall, built in the early Victorian era for one of the family to live adjacent to the main house. The architect had added a few Gothic flourishes; all the internal doorways were arched, and there were intricately carved finials at intervals along the dark wood banisters, which had effectively prevented the boys from sliding down them. Unless the Treverricks had changed the layout since her time here, the girls' dormitory was the first doorway to the left on the first floor landing, next to the girls' washroom and toilet, while the boys' dormitory lay straight ahead.

Such a luxury it had seemed to Rose and Elsie, to have indoor loos; they had been near speechless when they first saw the girls' washroom with its big tub and wooden-seated lavatory.

'That's how posh folk live, dearies,' her aunt had told them when she brought them to the orphanage, her health problems meaning she no longer felt well enough to look after them herself. 'They don't have to nip out for a wee in the night like us.'

The boys' washroom and toilets were situated upstairs on the second floor, which meant evenings and mornings had always been full of the noise of boots thundering up and down the narrow stairs to the next floor.

Everything was silent now, of course, with the children downstairs. All the children bar one, she reminded herself.

Rose glanced into the girls' dormitory but did not go beyond the arched doorway. A shiver crawled over her skin as she stared down the cramped rows of bunk-beds, all neatly made. The curtains were still partly drawn against the wintry afternoon, the room cold and dark. A cluster of shadows at the far end looked almost like girls, standing about as they gossiped.

Water bubbled in the pipes that ran into the girls' bathroom next door, sounding like voices in the gloom, whispering and giggling.

'Carrot top!'

They had called her 'Carrot top' and 'Gingerbread', those cruel girls — even her own sister — as Rose had been the only one among them with red hair. Elsie's hair had been a pale strawberry blonde in her youth, much admired by everyone. Nothing like her own fierce mop. One evening, after merciless teasing from the older girls, Rose had cried for hours, going with-out supper rather than face them again.

At bedtime, desperate, she had asked her sister to intervene with the bullies. But Elsie had merely laughed in her face, calling her, 'Carrot top!' with all the rest.

After that, Rose had known she was on her own.

A faded Union Jack was draped above the entrance to the boys' dorm, and pictures of spitfires and tanks cut from magazines were pinned above beds. She checked every bunkbed, and even inside the ward-robes.

Jimmy was not there.

Fear seized her. Rose wrapped her arms about

her waist and hugged herself, trying not to imagine the worst.

Where had he gone?

'Sister Gray?' The shrill call from the stairs brought her round in a hurry. 'Where are you, Sister Gray?'

Hurriedly, Rose returned to the landing, where she found Mrs Treverrick waiting for her, her face flushed with anger.

'What do you think you're doing?' Mrs Treverrick spat out. 'You weren't given permission to come upstairs and you know it.'

'I was looking for somewhere to wash my hands,' Rose lied, sticking to the story she had agreed earlier with Nurse Ryder.

'Nonsense. You were in the boys' dorm; I saw you come out.'

Exasperated, Rose gave up trying to wriggle her way out of it. 'While I was up here, I thought I'd take a moment to check on Jimmy. Only he isn't here.'

From downstairs, Lady Symmonds called up, 'Better come down, Sister Gray. I've seen enough for today and I wish to leave.'

Rose clenched her fists, but did not bother to argue. It was not her place to interfere, was it? Lady Symmonds had made that plain. But at the same time, she was deeply concerned for the missing boy.

As she started down the stairs, with Mrs Treverrick following close behind, Rose heard a noise from above their heads. A muffled, rhythmic knocking that stopped and then started again several times.

She halted and stared upwards. The sound was coming from the second floor. 'What's that knocking? Who's up there?'

'None of your business,' Mrs Treverrick hissed, and nudged her in the back to keep going. 'Go, or I'll make an official complaint against you.'

Rose continued down the stairs, but under protest.

In the hall below, Mr Treverrick was waiting with the others. His face quivered with indignation. 'Lady Symmonds, I hope you don't believe my wife and I are doing anything untoward here. We run a tight ship, that's all.'

'I heard knocking up there,' Rose told them.

Mrs Treverrick said quickly, 'Jimmy has been put in a room on the second floor. We think he may have the measles, so we've quarantined him from the other children.' She hesitated. 'He doesn't like being alone, poor mite, so he keeps knocking to be let out. I daresay that's what Sister Gray heard.'

'I quite understand,' Lady Symmonds said soothingly, and gave Rose a quelling look before smiling at both Treverricks. 'As I've suggested, you need to brighten the place up and do a few minor repairs. But other than that, I'm satisfied with what I've seen here today. I look forward to seeing you and the children at the Christmas party.'

Outside the orphanage, Rose whispered in Eva's ear, 'Did you hear that knocking? It sounded like a message of some kind. What do you think it meant?'

'I can tell you exactly what it means,' Eva whispered. 'I've studied Morse code and that was an S.O.S message.'

'S.O.S?'

'Save Our Souls.' Eva gave her a significant look. 'If that was Jimmy knocking, he was begging for help.'

28

Having just finished writing a long letter to her father, Eva was slipping the folded sheets inside an envelope addressed to Colonel Ryder, Eastern House, Porthcurno, when someone tapped softly at her door. She glanced at her watch, a little surprised. It was half past nine, and nearly her bedtime, for she was on an early shift in the morning.

'Come in,' Eva said, and propped the envelope up against a framed photograph of her late mother, to remind her to post it soon.

She half expected to see Mary Stannard wrapped in a shawl, as the two of them had grown close lately and often brought a tray of tea or cocoa to each other's rooms on their evenings off, for a cosy chat before bed.

Mary was a sweetie, she had discovered, and deeply observant. Probably all the reading she did, for she was a dedicated bookworm, always to be found with a book to hand. Indeed, Mary was rather good at impersonating other members of staff and even some of the patients, much to Eva's amusement. Best of all, she could hit Matron's high-pitched voice perfectly, launching them both into giggles.

But it was Sister Gray in the doorway, not Mary. They had barely spoken since the fiasco at the orphanage, after which Lady Symmonds had given them both a sharp dressing-down before disappearing back into her apartment. But Eva knew Sister wouldn't have

216

given up so easily, so was not entirely surprised by her visit.

'May I come in?' Sister Gray asked, and then did so without waiting for permission, closing the door behind her.

'Good evening,' Eva said drily, and nodded to the armchair. 'Take a pew.'

'Thank you.' But Sister Gray didn't sit, wandering to the window instead, although it was covered with a blackout curtain. She was on the night shift and was wearing her uniform, so she must have come upstairs specially to see Eva. 'I'm sorry to disturb you so late, but this couldn't wait.' She turned away and glanced down at the propped-up envelope. 'Writing to your father?'

'That's right. He frets if I don't write at least once a week.'

'You're lucky to have such a loving family,' Sister Gray said hesitantly. 'I have a younger sister. But we're not close. Not anymore.'

Eva looked at her curiously. *Not anymore?*

She recalled how Dr Edmund had mentioned Sister Gray's sister Elsie in passing, and how she was apparently sweet on Dr Lewis. Given the Sister's own interest in the younger doctor, that must make sisterly affection a little tricky.

'What can I do for you, Sister? I was just about to turn in for the night.'

'I understand. Hopefully, I won't take up too much of your time.' Sister Gray sank into the armchair at last, a troubled expression on her face. She couldn't be much beyond thirty, Eva reckoned, but she looked older than usual, her brow furrowed, tiny wrinkle lines beside her mouth and eyes. Worry lines, her father called them. And Sister Gray certainly looked worried. 'It's about Jimmy and the Treverricks.'

'I thought it must be.' Eva settled back against the headboard, playing with the belt of her dressing gown. 'Like I said before, there's not much either of us can do. Lady Symmonds is sympathetic to your cause, but only to a point. As you saw, she wasn't too impressed by you wandering off at the orphanage. And she didn't believe what we said about the S.O.S message. I'm afraid there's no point trying to persuade her without proper evidence. She's old-fashioned, I suppose; thinks tough love is good for kids.'

'That's not tough love!' Sister Gray exclaimed. 'It's cruelty.'

'I agree with you,' Eva told her gently. 'But if you push too hard, you could face more than just a complaint. Matron doesn't back you on this either, does she?'

Sister Gray shook her head, staring at the floor.

'So, you have to ask yourself, is this boy worth getting dismissed over?' Eva mused, and was surprised when Sister Gray looked up at her fiercely. 'Hey, don't bite my head off. I'm on your side.'

'I can't ignore what's going on next door.'

'Then don't. But, equally, don't keep risking your job by behaving like a bull in a china shop.' Eva chewed on her lip, thinking. 'What you need is to employ a little strategy. Come up with a battle plan, in other words.'

Sister Gray sat up straight. 'I'm listening.'

'The Christmas party is coming up, isn't it? The Treverricks will both be here, as far as I know, and they'll be bringing the children. So that's your chance.'

'For what?'

'To get Jimmy alone and have a proper talk to him. Find out what's going on in the orphanage — if they're genuinely mistreating him or if it's just a boy's natural exaggeration.'

'But what if they don't bring Jimmy to the party?'

'In which case,' Eva said slowly, conjuring up a plan on the hoof, 'you can sneak next door and talk to him there. If you're quick, it's doubtful anyone would miss you, and anyway, I can distract the Treverricks if necessary. If everyone from the orphanage is here, there'll be nobody next door to stop you mooching around.'

'That's true.' Sister Gray stood up, her frown gradually clearing. 'I only need five or ten minutes with him, after all. Long enough to gain Jimmy's confidence, and have him confirm if he's being treated poorly. Though I'm sure he must be. Why else knock out an S.O.S message like that?'

'Boys his age are always larking about; they have an odd sense of humour. He may not have thought we'd take it seriously.'

Sister Gray considered that, then dismissed it with a shake of her head. 'From what I've seen, Jimmy's not that kind of boy.'

'Then what kind of boy is he?'

'The kind who's not very good at obeying orders.'

Eva grinned. 'I like him more and more, and I've barely set eyes on the lad.' She jumped up too, following Sister Gray to the door. 'Try not to fret, all right, Sister? If they have been mistreating Jimmy, the Treverricks will know we're onto them now. So they'll be more careful what they do to him in future.'

'Thank you, I hope you're right.' Sister Gray paused on her way out. 'Since you're no longer banned from

Atlantic Ward, have you been to see Flight Lieutenant Carmichael yet?'

Eva ran a hand through her hair, grimacing. 'Not yet, Sister. I've been on the ward again but avoided speaking to him. I'm still working up to it.'

'Worried he may send you packing again?'

'Something like that.'

Sister Gray nodded slowly. 'You can call me Rose, you know. When we're not on duty.'

'In that case, you can call me Eva,' she said cheerfully, and they shook hands like co-conspirators. Which, in a way, she supposed they were.

★ ★ ★

It was Lily's morning off. Yet so far she had done nothing but pore through boxes of tinsel and Christmas decorations, shaking off the dust and wishing Tom had considered covering the boxes before storing them in the attics.

Lily glanced at her watch at half past ten, and decided enough was enough. She pushed away the heap of gold and silver decorations she'd been sorting through, and chucked the glittering tinsel garlands back into the box.

She needed fresh air.

And not just fresh air, Lily thought rebelliously, grabbing her coat and squashing a woollen beret down on her fair hair, not particularly caring how it looked.

What she needed was space and a change of scene.

She had left Porthcurno that summer feeling it had nothing more to show her. But St Ives really wasn't much better. It might even be worse, for she was no longer sure she was cut out to be a nurse. And the frustration of that awareness was eating away at her.

Today, Lily could not seem to contain her restlessness. Deep down, she knew it was more than simple boredom. But she didn't want to look too closely.

Even though there was a smattering of snow on the ground, reminding her that the Christmas party was not so far off, she decided to take a walk in the woodlands within the grounds. It was too close to lunch-time to risk walking to the cliffs today, as her shift started straight after lunch.

But as she skirted the conservatory outside, someone rapped on the glass and she heard her name, 'Nurse Fisher!'

It was Danny, staring at her through the misty glass. Some of the men were taking their tea in the conservatory, huddled around the wireless as they listened to the news programmes and musical intervals.

Danny beckoned her to join them inside.

But Lily shook her head and hurried on, her heart hammering. She heard him call after her, 'Nurse Fisher, come and have a cuppa with us!' but did not look back.

Entering the woodlands, she struck out along one of the narrow, frosty paths, seeking the dark heart of the trees where she was less likely to be disturbed. Her favourite path ended in a clearing beside an ancient kettle hole, a kind of pond whose icy, stagnant water bristled with briars and fallen branches. There was a mossy, fallen tree trunk carved into a bench beside the water, and she sank down there, breathing fast.

Lily did not know what was wrong with her. This wasn't about restlessness and boredom, nor even the gnawing fear that she didn't enjoy nursing as much as she'd hoped she would. Her whole body had jerked in fear when Danny knocked on the window and called her name, almost as though he was about to attack her.

Danny was harmless, and she knew it. So what was this about?

Without warning, a mental image of her Uncle Stanley swum in front of her eyes, his leering eyes boring into hers, and she buried her face in her hands, making a choking noise. 'No,' she whispered, shaking her head. 'No, no, no.'

Finally, she knew what the problem was. Only she wished to goodness that she didn't.

Even though that horrible incident with Stanley was months behind her now, and she'd tried hard to bury it under happier memories of her days in Porthcurno, Lily knew it still lay heavy on her heart. So heavy a weight, in fact, she could hardly breathe whenever it came to mind. And since Danny had touched her cheek the other day, her memory kept flashing back to the awful day in the barn . . .

'Nurse Fisher?' A man's voice brought her upright, wiping her eyes hurriedly on her gloves. 'Lily? Is that you?'

Oh no! It was Danny Orde, come into the woods in search of her. She couldn't let him see her like this. She simply couldn't . . .

But there was nowhere to go.

29

'If you don't mind me asking, Sister, how did Eva — I mean, Nurse Ryder — persuade you to let her back on the ward?' Max Carmichael asked curiously, watching as Rose pulled the screens about his bed to give them some privacy. 'I couldn't believe it when I saw her doing the rounds earlier. Only she sent Mary to take my pulse and temperature, so I guess she must have put me down as a lost cause, after all.'

'And are you?' Rose asked, taking out the folded exercise sheets that Lewis had given her and studying them diligently.

There was only half an hour to go before the end of her shift today, but she intended to use it to help the flight lieutenant if she could. It was only fair that she should help Eva achieve her objective now she had agreed to help Rose check on Jimmy.

'Am I what?'

'A lost cause.'

'Ah, definitely.' Max rubbed his chin, which was dark with stubble, and she made a mental note to send Nurse Stannard over to help him shave. She doubted he would welcome Eva dealing with his personal care for a while yet. 'Anyway, I've been getting on better without her visits. Head-wise, that is.'

That was a revealing comment, Rose thought, putting the exercise sheets aside. 'But not heart-wise?'

He grimaced. 'Eva's a swell gal. But she doesn't want to face reality, Sister.'

'Which is?'

'That I'm unlikely ever to walk again.' He gave a faint smile, leaning back against the pillows as Rose pulled back his bedcovers to reveal his striped pyjamas and bare feet. 'You know, I've been doing these exercises with the doctor too, and I don't see what real good they're doing. What are you hoping to see?'

'It's a gradual process. It's about stretching and moving your legs until you get some feeling back on your own.'

'In other words, you move my legs up and down while I watch?'

Rose looked at him sternly. 'Flight Lieutenant, are you being difficult? Because I know how to deal with difficult patients.'

'I bet you do, at that.' Max gave a laugh. 'Please don't 'deal' with me, Sister Gray. I was just asking a question. I didn't mean to be difficult.'

'Good, because on the days when Dr Lewis isn't here, you'll be doing these exercises with me instead.' She studied the exercise sheet again, and then took his left foot in her hand as shown and began to move it gently back and forth, taking care not to damage his disused muscles and tendons. 'As a matter of fact, the doctor wants to increase their frequency to twice a day.'

Max looked aghast. 'Twice a day?'

'We expect you to exercise in your own time as well. Some of these stretches can be done without assistance, or with the use of an elastic band hooked around your foot.' Rose frowned when he looked unimpressed. 'I thought you wanted to get back on your own two feet?'

'Of course.'

'Then you'll have to work for it, Flight Lieutenant. Which means stretching and exercising your legs regularly.' Rose replaced his left foot on the sheet, and took up the right foot instead, repeating the same exercises. 'With or without someone to help you.'

She worked in silence for a few minutes, following the complicated exercise sheet as best she could. On glancing up, she found his gaze on her face, steady and intent. 'What is it?' she asked.

'I was just wondering how Eva is.'

Rose straightened, his foot still in her hand, staring at him. 'But you expressly asked Nurse Ryder not to come and visit you, Flight Lieutenant.'

'Yeah, I know.' The young pilot pulled a face. 'It felt like the right thing at the time, given the state of my legs. Only I hadn't reckoned on how much I'd miss seeing her face.' His smile was rather charming. 'I guess I must really be in love with her.'

Once, she would have severely reprimanded a patient for admitting to being in love with one of her nurses. But she herself had given Eva permission to visit him again, so it would be the height of hypocrisy to try and separate them after that. Besides, something told her this was a relationship that would find its own path, regardless of what others did to prevent or influence it.

He gave another crooked smile. 'Can't say I blame her for avoiding me even though she's back on the ward, not after the way I behaved. But you've got to understand that I . . . I can't offer her what she deserves. Someone like Eva doesn't need a man who can only lie about in bed all day.'

'Self-pity will get you precisely nowhere in this life.'

225

Rose put his foot down gently. 'So, how was that? Any sensations at all?'

Max sighed. 'And that's another thing, Sister. I have a confession to make.'

'I beg your pardon?'

'I was saving this moment for when Eva came to see me again. But since she seems to have lost interest, there's not much point in waiting.'

He gripped the sides of the bed, frowned ferociously down at his bare feet, and then strained his whole body. His right foot seemed to flex slightly. The big toe moved infinitesimally, then returned to its resting position. Max let out a long breath, and looked up at her, his eyes wary.

Rose put a hand to her chest, feeling winded. Had she just imagined seeing that or had his foot really moved under its own steam?

'Let me get this straight,' she said. 'You've got feeling back in your legs?'

'More of a vague tingle from time to time,' he admitted awkwardly. 'And only in my feet. I'm sorry not to have owned up sooner, Sister. I mean, my legs were dead all through the summer. I'd given up hope of ever feeling anything at all. Thought I'd be stuck like this for ever.' He gave a self-mocking smile. 'But then Eva turned up and started nagging at me. I guess that stopped me feeling sorry for myself and got me trying to move my legs again, just at night, when nobody was looking.'

'Can you move both feet?'

'Watch this.' Max gripped the bed again and Rose watched in stunned silence as he focused on moving the big toe on his left foot too. That seemed to take more effort, his face slightly flushed by the time he

226

got the toe to twitch. 'The left side's not as strong as the right. But I've been working on moving my feet for the past month. It's taken me all this time to get my damn toe to wiggle.' He shrugged. 'Not exactly earth-shattering progress, is it — '

'I need to let Dr Lewis know.' Cutting across his words, Rose checked her watch. 'He's at the surgery in St Ives today. But I'll send a note down with Tom. He'll want to hear about this at once.'

'Now, hang on there, Sister. It's only my big toe . . . '

'Don't you understand?' She stared at him, incredulous that anyone could be so foolish. 'If you can move even one toe, Flight Lieutenant, it means the nerves that were severed are knitting together again and your spine is on the mend. It means you may be able to walk again one day.'

★ ★ ★

She couldn't face Danny, Lily thought, panicking as she jumped up and looked about for some way of escape. But the path had run out, and besides, it was too late.

Private Orde had already come striding into the clearing, a trench coat over his dressing gown and no hat on his head, his hair blowing about in the cold wind. He was still wearing his carpet slippers, now whitened with frost. Matron would go spare if she caught him in that state.

'Are you all right?' He stopped dead, studying her expression. 'God, you look awful. Like you've seen a ghost, I mean.'

'Maybe I have,' Lily muttered.

'Sorry?' His brows drew together, no doubt trying

227

to puzzle her out. 'Why did you run off like that? We were listening to the news on the wireless. I wanted you to come in and sit with us.'

'I . . . I decided to go for a walk,' she said as brightly as she could.

'A walk? In this weather?' He came towards her, still frowning. 'It's perishing. And a bit gloomy under these trees, isn't it? Here, let me walk back with you.'

'No,' she said, and backed away.

'Careful!' Danny caught her before she could tumble into the kettle hole behind her, its dark sinister water gleaming mere inches away. 'Lily, for God's sake, what's wrong?' He stared down into her face. 'Is this all because of the other day? When I touched you? I said I was sorry. What more do you want?'

She shook her head, unable to say a word. Her eyes misted over and she wished the earth would swallow her up. He must think her such a fool, over-reacting to a simple caress.

'I'm sorry,' he said again, this time more softly. 'I mean it.'

'I know you do.' Lily swallowed, very aware of his hands holding her shoulders. He didn't mean anything by it, she was sure. But the panic was rising in her again. 'Only it's nothing to do with that.'

'What, then?'

She struggled, looking everywhere but at him. 'I can't explain, I wish I could, but this thing . . . It's not about you. You've got to believe me, Danny.'

'I want to.' He sounded as tormented as she felt, and she saw pain in his face. 'But Lily . . . ' His voice was husky. 'Is it my face? You need to tell me the truth, even if it feels cruel. The burns are too horrific, aren't they? You can't bear to be close to me, to see them.'

His words were tearing her apart. In truth, Lily did find the sight of his burnt face unsettling. There, she had thought it, and felt the guilt and shame. But she would never put those thoughts into words. His feelings would be so dreadfully hurt, and what good would it do? He would only despair, and Danny needed to feel hope right now, to look forward to a day when he would be able to look himself in the mirror without grimacing. Lily had no idea if such a future would ever come. But he deserved to believe in it.

'No, it's not that either, honest,' she insisted, and dredged up a shaky smile from somewhere. 'I scarce notice them these days.'

'Oh, Lily.'

He drew her close, and the desire to be near to him and to feel comforted battled against her fear. Then he lowered his head and his mouth touched hers. Just gently, a soft brush of his lips. Nothing to be scared of. And yet, as soon as he was holding her in his arms, kissing her, she felt that absurd sense of being suffocated. Panic flared in her chest and she pushed him away, just as she'd done last time. Only this time she pushed a lot harder, knocking him off balance, and fled through the trees; not taking the path but flailing breathlessly through the undergrowth, briars snagging at her winter coat, thin icy branches whipping her face.

By the time she found the path again, Lily was in a right mess, her hat gone, her hair dishevelled, and her cheek stung where she'd cut it.

★ ★ ★

229

Lily ran back to the hall, ignoring several well-meaning people in the garden who called after her in concern, and let herself in through the little-used door near the kitchen block.

Before she could get upstairs unseen, to sort herself out before difficult questions were asked, who should come after her but Sister Gray? And Sister looked cross as hell fire too, her green eyes spitting fury.

'Nurse Fisher, what on earth has happened to you?'

'I'm sorry, Sister,' Lily tried to say but found the words sticking in her throat. Instead, she wept, hiding her face. 'I . . . I . . . went out walking. I didn't mean to . . . ' No, those weren't the right words either. 'Please, leave me alone.'

'Come with me, girl.'

An arm hooked around her shoulder and Lily found herself inexorably swept along in Sister's wake. Soon she was seated in an armchair in the senior staff room, her damp coat hanging on a rack in front of the fire, her wet shoes removed, her soggy stockinged toes drying in the heat.

Rose plucked a few twigs and leaves from her hair, and threw them on the flames. Then she drew up the other armchair and patted Lily's knee.

'Lily, you helped me when I was upset,' she said softly. 'Now it's my turn to help you. And before you try to deny that there's anything wrong, you might as well know that I saw you out of the window.'

'You saw me?'

'I'd just finished my shift when I saw you go into the woods and Private Orde follow you. Then you came running out of the trees like the devil was behind you.' Rose sat back, her gaze on Lily's face. 'So, what happened?'

230

30

Rose was enraged. She had a fair inkling what had happened to Lily Fisher in the woods. And if she was right, she would tear a strip off Private Orde and ask Matron to transfer the scoundrel to some other hospital at once.

Molesting her young nurses! She wouldn't stand for such wicked behaviour.

It was pure luck she'd spotted Lily and got downstairs before anyone else could intercept her. She'd sent a note to Lewis with Tom, letting the doctor know about Max Carmichael's progress, and then gone upstairs at the end of her shift, only to glance out of the landing window to see Lily on her way into the woods.

The poor girl was in pieces now, her face white as a sheet, her hands shaking. Rose watched her with concern. Good God, what she would like to do to men who attacked women . . . Castration was too good for them, she sometimes thought. But she had to admit to being surprised. She hadn't thought Private Orde to be dangerous in that line. He seemed such a nice young lad, who was suffering his terrible burns with fortitude.

Lily began to speak hesitantly, her voice uneven, explaining how she'd gone walking and had been followed by the private without realising, which Rose had already seen. 'We fell to talking, and then Danny . . . Private Orde, that is . . . He took it in his head to kiss me.'

'Did he now?' Rose raised her eyebrows. 'Go on.'

'I didn't want to be kissed, so I ran away.' Lily looked shamefaced. 'I'm so sorry, Sister. Please don't dismiss me.'

'Dismiss you? I should think not. You were not to blame for this incident. But Private Orde must be sent elsewhere as soon as I can arrange a transfer.' Rose got up and fetched a muslin square from the first aid cabinet, poured some water into a bowl, and then cleaned the thin cut on Lily's cheek. It wasn't deep, thankfully, and she did not believe it would leave a lasting scar. 'Though maybe sending him home straightaway would be best for everyone. I believe his treatment is nearly finished.'

'Poor Danny. Does he have to leave?'

Rose was confused. 'You feel sorry for him? After what he tried to do to you?'

'What do you mean?'

'My dear girl, you can't be that innocent.'

Lily's eyes widened, and she sat up straight, twisting her hands together in an agitated way. 'Oh goodness, no. You don't understand. Danny didn't intend to . . . It wasn't like that at all.'

Rose sat down again, completely lost. 'You'd better explain.'

Stumbling over her words, with colour coming back into her cheeks at last, Lily told her about a time earlier in the year when she'd been assaulted by her own great-uncle on the farm where she'd been staying. He hadn't been able to achieve his horrible purpose, thankfully, owing to the timely intervention of her Aunt Violet, who sounded like a formidable woman. They'd left the farm and taken work in Porthcurno instead. But his

232

attempted rape had left a deep and indelible mark on Lily; that much was obvious from the tremor in her voice as she described the attack and its aftermath.

'Ever since then,' Lily finished shakily, wiping her wet face with the back of her hand, 'I've felt awkward around men. And when Danny kissed me, I just . . . I froze at first, and then I had to get away from him. Far, far away. I can't really explain it better than that.'

Now Rose understood.

She got up and put the soiled muslin square to one side for the laundry bag, left the bowl for the orderly to collect, and closed the first aid cabinet.

She was giving Lily time to calm down.

'I see what you mean about it not being Danny's fault,' she said gently, sitting opposite her again. 'But it's still the case that nurses and patients are not permitted to engage in any kind of romantic activity. And Private Orde knows that. I do not hold you accountable for this, as it's clear you didn't seek out his company, and indeed went to extreme measures to avoid it.'

She thought for a minute, studying the deep sadness in the girl's face. Lily was still very young, after all. And perhaps she had some feelings for Private Orde that she was refusing to acknowledge. But that didn't change the basic situation.

'Let me tell you a story,' Rose began, and saw Lily look up at her in surprise. 'It took place a long time ago, and concerns a young woman about your age, maybe a little older.' She took a deep breath. 'She'd just finished her training as a nurse, and was alone on the ward one evening when a doctor asked her to step into his office. She was a bit green, and he was a very respected doctor, a married man in his fifties, so she didn't question it.'

Rose stopped, feeling again the terror of that night, the sheer hopelessness, and worst of all, the guilt and shame. But it was important that she relayed this story to Lily, that the girl knew she was not alone and not to blame for what had happened.

'She wasn't as lucky as you. There was nobody to intervene. Afterwards, she didn't dare tell anyone. She rightly feared that she wouldn't be believed, or might be blamed for leading him on. A tease, no better than she ought to be.' She heard her voice shake, and waited for her heart to stop racing before continuing more calmly, 'But the young woman made sure she was never trapped like that again. Even if it meant people called her frigid and ice queen behind her back.' Her smile was bitter. 'Better frigid than disgraced and dismissed, I suppose.'

Lily sat silently for a while, staring at her, hot-cheeked. Then she jumped up and, to Rose's shocked surprise, gave her a tight hug.

'You poor love,' she whispered, and stroked her hair. 'What a bloody world this is, and no mistake.'

Rose did not know what to say. There was a lump in her throat. She stared into the fire, somehow wishing she could still be as natural and unspoilt as Lily.

But it was too late for that now.

★ ★ ★

As soon as she got the chance, Rose went to speak to Private Orde on the ward. She drew the screens about the bed in a quiet, professional way, as though about

234

to administer a private treatment, and then stood before him with her eyes folded and her eyes blazing with accusation.

'I've just been speaking to Nurse Fisher,' she said.

The young man looked ashamed, as well he might, and sat bolt upright against his pillows. 'I'm sorry, Sister. I don't know what came over me.'

'On the contrary, I think you have a perfectly good idea what came over you. And I won't have my nurses upset.'

'It won't happen again, Sister. I swear it.'

'No need, because you won't have the chance. After what happened today, I'm going to arrange for your discharge as soon as possible.' She saw his face pale, and relented somewhat. He had been severely burnt, after all, saving the lives of other soldiers. Some dispensation had to be made for his state of mind. 'Your treatment is nearly finished and there's no sign of inflammation. You can safely be sent home with a supply of medicaments.'

'I didn't mean to upset her,' he said, his expression wretched. 'She's so sweet and caring. And she seemed to enjoy talking to me. Out there in the woods, I thought . . . ' He shook his head. 'I misunderstood.'

'You thought she liked you?'

'Yes,' Private Orde said earnestly, then turned his head on his pillows, staring at the wall so she was looking straight at the ruined side of his profile. 'Stupid of me,' he muttered. 'I mean, look at this face. I probably seem like a monster to her.' He groaned. 'Please don't send me home yet. I need to apologise to Lily first.'

Rose was disturbed by the heartfelt pain in his eyes. She didn't think there was any harm in the boy. But she had meant it when she said she wouldn't have her nurses upset. That had to be her priority.

'I'll have to discuss this with Dr Lewis and Matron. For now though, you are to leave Nurse Fisher alone. And that's not a suggestion, it's an order.'

31

It was time to stop shilly-shallying about. Eva took a deep breath and marched into Atlantic Ward with her head held high, and made her way straight towards Max.

He was out of bed today, already seated in his wheelchair, reading.

'Hullo,' she said with forced cheerfulness.

'Nurse Ryder.' He stared at her warily, lowering his newspaper. 'I thought you weren't supposed to talk to me.'

'Dr Lewis asked me to bring you to the conservatory.' Before he could refuse, Eva snatched away the newspaper and whisked him around, pushing his wheelchair out of the ward. 'He says it's time for your daily exercises.'

Max looked up at her quizzically but said nothing.

She still felt awkward around him, despite having snatched a few hurried conversations with him in recent weeks. Yes, she'd done a clandestine deal with Sister Gray and been allowed back on Atlantic Ward. But was she truly welcome there? Or was she wasting her time with a man who had given up on her and himself?

In the conservatory, Dr Lewis stood over them both with arms folded, watching critically as Eva removed Max's slippers and then manipulated his legs and feet through all the recommended exercises, testing the full range of movements he would need for walking.

Snow had been in the air for days and it was pretty cold in the conservatory. So cold, in fact, that her breath was steaming and Eva was soon shivering in her thin, short-sleeved uniform. But concentrating on the exercises kept her from noticing too much.

Some of the other patients had gathered round the wireless as the presenter listed news items for the day. Whenever something positive was mentioned — a win for their side in the war, or the extra rations due for Christmas — the men gave a cheer. To any hint of bad news, however, they barely reacted.

Eva supposed they found it easier to shrug off the bad news in favour of celebrating the good. She couldn't blame them, often doing the same herself these days when scanning newspapers or catching a news bulletin on the wireless.

Things were not going well for their side in the war. But there wasn't much they could do about it, except keep their chins up.

'That's enough, nurse, thank you,' Dr Lewis said at last, and crouched down to speak to Max on his level. 'Sister Gray tells me you've made an amazing breakthrough, Flight Lieutenant. Given the extent and severity of your injuries, I'm afraid I'm still a little sceptical. But maybe if you were to give me a demonstration, now that your muscles should have warmed up a bit, I might believe you.'

Eva stared from one to the other, baffled. 'A break-through? What is he talking about, Max?'

Max shot her an apologetic look, a red tinge to his cheeks. 'I didn't think it was worth mentioning . . . I can twiddle my big toe, that's all.'

'*What?*'

238

Dr Lewis grinned at her exclamation. 'Yes, I don't think our friend here quite understands what he's achieved,' he told Eva, and then nodded to Max. 'Let's see it then. This toe-twiddling stunt of yours.'

Max looked down at his feet, which she had just been massaging to get the blood pumping, and gritted his teeth.

To Eva's astonishment, she saw one of his big toes twitch.

Not much, perhaps.

But it was a definite movement up and down.

'That's astounding, I have to say,' the doctor exclaimed, shaking his head. 'Truly astounding. But you ought to have told me you'd got some feeling back in your lower body, Flight Lieutenant. We could have started you on more advanced exercises, maybe even got you out of that chair to build your strength up. Time is of the essence with spinal injuries.'

'I wanted to mention it to you a couple weeks back, doc,' Max admitted, still avoiding Eva's eyes, 'but it's been so long since the bombing, and I kept thinking that maybe I was imagining things. You know how it is. You hope for something so much, you start to believe it's possible even when it's not.'

'Except it *was* possible.'

Max grinned. 'It would seem so, doc.'

'I blame myself for not spotting your improvement. If I'd continued doing those tests to check your responses . . . But what with my grandfather's heart attack, and how busy we've been . . . '

'Don't go taking the blame for this,' Max insisted. 'I pulled the wool over everyone's eyes. It's nobody's fault but my own.'

Eva felt like singing. And crying. Perhaps both at

the same time. 'You can move your toes,' she whispered, a hand to her mouth. 'Oh, Max.'

'I should have told you, I know, and I'm sorry — '

She swooped on him before he could get any further and kissed him on the cheek. All the men in the room cheered, and Eva straightened, feeling a little hot-cheeked. No doubt she'd gone pink, as she usually did when embarrassed. But damn it, Max could move his toes. That was a cause for celebration. Even jubilation.

Dr Lewis gave her a warning look. 'Nurse, what would Matron say if she caught you doing that?' But he was still smiling. 'All right, Flight Lieutenant. Better rest for five minutes before going through the whole sequence again.'

But Max shook his head. 'Wait, I want to try something.'

Eva held her breath.

They both watched in silence as he glared down at his legs, furrowing his brow with concentration. This time, he managed to lift his whole foot. Max only kept his foot in the air for a split second. But it was genuine progress and, best of all, he had done it unaided.

Max gave a breathless laugh. 'Holy smoke, doc, did you see that?'

'I certainly did,' Dr Lewis said. 'Bravo.'

Some of the men watching from nearby let out a cheer. 'Good show, Yank!' one shouted, and there was a smattering of applause. 'Now you just have to do that a few thousand times every day and you'll be fixed,' another said, and everyone laughed.

'Thanks, guys. But I know whom I really have to thank for this.' Flushed with pleasure and excitement, Max looked at Eva. 'My guardian angel, Nurse Ryder.'

The men around them clapped and whistled, and one made a lewd remark under his breath, which gained him a glare from Max and a sharp word from the doctor.

Dr Lewis shook his head. 'I'm sorry, Nurse Ryder. You'll have to forgive them. Some men forget their manners, cooped up in a hospital bed for months,' he said, steering her aside for a private word and turning his back on the others. 'You've done amazingly well with that young man, I hope you realise.'

'I had nothing to do with it. Max did all that on his own.'

'He would never have got the idea of exercising if you hadn't kept pushing. You should be proud of yourself, Eva.'

She blushed and shook her head, uncomfortable with his praise. 'Do you think he'll ever be able to walk again though?'

'If he does, I suspect it'll be down to your sterling efforts.' His brows twitched together and his expression sobered. 'Look, I hear Nurse Fisher isn't feeling too good and has taken a few days off to recover. Should I go up and see her, do you think?'

Lily had been upset by something unfortunate that had happened between herself and Private Orde, that was all Sister had told Eva, and she had not pried further.

Eva had popped in to see her friend a few times, taking her cocoa and even some knitting to keep her hands busy, for Lily had been learning to knit. Not that Lily needed much else to occupy her, as Mary Stannard had brought her books from the lending library, as well as pen and paper to write down any thoughts she might have about the Christmas party arrangements, and even Cook had taken her up some of her spare wool. It seemed the Symmonds Hall grapevine was in excellent working order, even if it was a bit thin on details of what had actually happened to upset young Nurse Fisher.

'Better leave it for now, Doctor,' Eva whispered. 'Least said, soonest mended. Besides,' she added optimistically, 'her family are coming to visit this weekend. That's bound to cheer Lily up.'

Her smile soon faded though when she turned back to find Max chatting easily about sports with the other men around the wireless. He seemed to have completely forgotten her presence.

So it looked like he might be able to walk again, after all.

And she was overjoyed.

Yet he hadn't told her about it before today, and still hadn't made any attempt to renew his flirtation with her. The only logical assumption was that he had changed his mind and was no longer interested in courting her. What had the doctor said? That she had been *pushing* Max. Yes, that was it.

She'd been too pushy and headstrong, and had driven him away.

Eva forced a smile back to her lips when Max turned his head, glancing in her direction. Her heart was in agony, as though it were being clawed and ripped into shreds. But she would keep working to get him on his feet, regardless.

Max being able to walk again was more important than her broken heart.

Rose hurtled away as soon as she saw Lewis coming out of the conservatory, her heart racing with sudden

242

panic. She had been watching through the doorway as he praised Nurse Ryder for her efforts to aid in Flight Lieutenant Carmichael's recovery, and had felt sick to her stomach, battling an attack of green-eyed jealousy.

She made her way to Atlantic Ward, meaning to speak to Private Orde again and ask where exactly he planned to go following his eventual discharge. No date had yet been arranged for Danny, but it was her duty to check he had somewhere to go before drawing up the paperwork. But when she got to the ward, Nurse Hardy was giving him a shave, so she busied herself tidying while she waited.

Lewis had queried Lily's absence from the ward and she'd told him the young nurse was unwell. That was all the doctor needed to know. Besides, Lily's family was coming to visit her soon. That should help her move past the situation with Orde. Though Rose knew from her own experience how hard it could be to shake off such terrifying memories . . .

In the same way, part of her knew that Lewis's smiles for Eva meant nothing. He was friendly towards all the nurses equally. Yet a deeper part of her ached to be special to him in some way, and not just as Elsie's sister.

'Rose?'

She turned, feeling heat leap to her cheeks. Goodness, it was just as well he couldn't read her mind! Lewis had only followed her all the blessed way to Atlantic Ward.

'Hullo, Dr Lewis,' she said as calmly as she could, and folded her arms across her chest. 'How's your grandfather?'

'Much better, thank you. He was talking yesterday

about coming back to work but I managed to put him off.'

'Quite right too. Dr Edmund needs more rest before he even thinks of coming back. What can I do for you?'

'I'm concerned about Nurse Fisher. If she's unwell, shouldn't someone take a look at her? Unless you're satisfied it's nothing serious?' His gaze was sombre and steady. 'I mean, I would never dream of encroaching on your territory. The nurses' welfare must always be your and Matron's concern, not mine. But if there's anything I can do . . . '

'That's very considerate of you, but we can deal with it.'

Lewis nodded slowly. 'Whatever you say.' Yet he stayed there, unmoving. 'I also wanted to talk to you about something else. Privately, if possible.' He came closer, lowering his voice, 'Rose . . . '

'Sister Gray when we're on the ward,' she admonished him, determined not to show any partiality. 'I can spare you five minutes, Doctor Lewis. Then I must go about my duties.'

Torn between her need to remain aloof and curiosity to discover what he wanted to say to her, Rose nodded him towards the nurses' station. The desk and chair were set far enough away from the patients for any conversation to be all but inaudible to them, especially at such a busy time of day, with men coming and going for recreation, or chatting at each other's bedsides.

She sat down and turned over today's medication sheet, pretending to study it. 'What did you want to say to me?'

'Only this . . . ' Lewis stood beside her. 'I've been

thinking about you and Elsie,' he said quietly. 'And me.'

Shocked, she raised her gaze to his. 'I beg your pardon?'

'I can't go on doing this,' he muttered.

'Doing what?'

'Pretending there's nothing between us.'

'Hush.' She stood up, flushed and nervous, unable to look him in the face. 'For goodness' sake, someone might hear.'

'I don't care.'

'You must stop this at once.' Rose put a hand on his arm and then wished she hadn't, electricity seeming to jolt between them. Her arm dropped, and she took a step backwards, aware that some of the patients had turned to watch them. 'This is a bad time. I think you should go; we can talk later.'

'Rose — '

'Look,' she said breathlessly, 'I can already guess what you want to say. I've had a letter from my sister. She told me she'll be back for Christmas.'

He stared at her, arrested. 'Elsie's coming home?'

'You didn't know?'

'I've not heard from her recently.'

'That's typical of Elsie. She does love her little secrets. Well, I'm sorry if I spoiled her surprise this time. But I imagine you and she will be tying the knot pretty soon. So whatever this thing is between us, it ends here.'

'Rose — '

She lifted a finger to silence him, though it killed her to do it. 'Elsie's coming home for Christmas, and she's my sister. I won't do anything to hurt or betray her.'

245

32

As the old converted ambulance juddered to a halt, Lily ran down the steps of Symmonds Hall before the doors were even open, grinning and with her arms wide open.

'Aunty Violet!' she cried, and embraced her aunt as she climbed wearily out of the passenger door. Lily then turned in delight to find her little sister, Alice — somehow mysteriously at least two inches taller than she remembered — behind her. 'Alice!' The two sisters hugged with genuine affection, and Lily only realised in that instant how much she had missed her irritating know-it-all of a younger sister. 'I've been waiting for ages; I thought you would never arrive.'

'Blame Aunty Vi,' Alice said drily. 'She was reading the map upside down.'

'I was not.' Violet looked exasperated, hands on hips. 'But it might help if all the bloomin' signposts hadn't been taken down.'

'Well, of course they have. Can't have the Germans landing in the night and finding their way to the nearest town using our signpost system,' Alice pointed out. 'Do use your noddle, Aunty Vi. I mean, if we leave the signposts up, we might as well throw down a welcome mat for their jackboots while we're at it, and maybe lay on a round of sarnies for the poor hungry dears.'

Charlie, hopping out of the back, gave a shout of laughter. 'Are you two still going on about those signposts? Lily, they've talked about little else since we

246

left Porthcurno. It's driven me mad.'

'You were already mad,' Alice told him disdainfully.

It seemed those two were still into teasing each other, Lily thought, glad that some things hadn't changed at least.

'Hullo, Charlie,' she said shyly.

'You're looking well, Lily. But where's your uniform? I was expecting to see you in your nurse's cap and pinny.' A strapping lad now, instead of the puny boy she remembered, Charlie helped Lily's grandmother climb down from the back of the rickety old ambulance. 'Careful now, Mrs Hopkins. You watch your step there.'

'Gran!'

Lily embraced her grandmother, breathing in her familiar scent of lavender water, and felt tears bursting from under tightly closed lids.

'Did they cut your hair?' was the first thing her gran said, sounding outraged. 'Your beautiful hair, like Rapunzel's, what used to reach almost down to your waist? I don't believe it!'

'I cut it, Gran. And it's not so short.'

'It's short enough. And have they been feeding you properly?' Her gran, clad in the same coat she'd owned for years and with her grey hair covered by a thick woollen scarf, held Lily out at arms' length, casting a suspicious eye over her. 'You're nothing but skin and bones, pet. What you need is a nice meat pie and some taters.'

'And where's she supposed to get 'em, Mum?' Aunty Vi exclaimed, and shook her head. 'Sometimes I think you've forgotten there's a war on.'

'Of course I hadn't forgotten, Vi. What do you take me for, an imbecile? But back when I was running the caff in Dagenham, I wouldn't have let me own flesh and blood go about looking not much thicker than a stick insect.' Gran winked at her, taking the sting out of her words. 'Though still a pretty one at that, bob cut or not.'

'Please don't fuss, Gran,' Lily protested, blushing as they all turned to examine her hair and figure. 'And I only wear my uniform when I'm working, Charlie. It's my day off.'

She wrapped her arms about her waist and hugged herself, glad to have her family around her again, despite the familiar nagging that came with it. It had been so long since she'd seen them all, she felt quite emotional. Or maybe her churning feelings were down to recent events. Events that she didn't intend talking about to anyone, except possibly Alice.

'I'm back on night shift this evening, mind,' she added hurriedly. 'So I only have a few hours to show you round. You didn't say how long you'd be staying.'

'Well, about that . . .' Aunty Violet looked awkward.

But then the driver's door creaked open and Charlie's mum, Mrs Hazel Baxter, finally emerged, looking so happy that Lily almost didn't recognise her. She was heavily pregnant, resting a hand proudly on the top of her swollen belly as she trudged around the vehicle to give Lily a hug.

'Hullo, my lovely,' she said in her warm Cornish accent. 'It's so good to see you again. Your Aunty Vi reads out your letters at work, so I know everything you've been up to. I'm sorry we took so long to get here. I was driving as fast as I dared. But what with your gran in the back, and this little passenger on board too,' she added, rubbing her belly affectionately, 'I didn't want to risk an accident.'

'I don't mind, honestly. I'm just glad you got here safely.' Lily led them into the hall, having got prior permission from Matron to show them round the hall and up to the nurses' quarters. 'Only it will have to be a short visit, which is a shame. I so wanted to celebrate Aunty Vi's birthday properly.'

Lily stopped in the entrance to allow them to take in the dark oak panelling and sweeping staircase ahead, amused to see how her gran's eyes widened at the faded splendour of the old house.

'Now don't fret,' her aunt told her in a hushed voice, also overawed by her surroundings. 'Hazel's cousin Charlotte is putting us up for the night. That's another reason we're late. We stopped there on the way to drop off our bags. So we'll see you again tomorrow before heading back to Porthcurno.'

'How wonderful.' Lily was delighted by that news. 'I'm on night shift again tomorrow, so that works out. I can show you St Ives in the morning if the weather holds.'

'I'd like that,' her gran said approvingly.

'It's a Sunday, of course, so the shops and cafés will all be closed. But we can look in the shop windows and walk along the harbour together. What fun we'll have.'

Lily took them into Atlantic Ward to see Eva, who had also known them at Porthcurno, and to meet Max Carmichael too. The pilot was able to move both feet now and was strengthening his legs in preparation for trying to walk again. With help, of course, for Dr Lewis had said he might never be able to walk under his own steam again, meaning he would always need crutches or a stick to stay upright. Which wasn't too bad, as he'd broken his back, and some people with that injury were bedridden for the rest of their lives.

Lily explained all this in a low voice as she led them into the ward. 'Eva's keeping it quiet,' she finished softly, 'but I think they're sweethearts.'

Eva jumped up at their approach. 'Why, Violet, how lovely to see you again! And my dear Hazel ... My goodness, you look like you might pop at any moment.' She hugged the two women she'd been friends with in Porthcurno. 'I've missed you so much.'

'Hullo, Miss Ryder,' Charlie said boldly, no longer as shy as Lily remembered. He shook her hand, studying Max with hero-worship in his flushed face. 'So you're the pilot, are you? The one who saved Miss Ryder's life in London.'

'I *was* a pilot,' Max corrected him, and smiled at the newcomers crowded about his bed. 'But yes, guilty as charged. Flight Lieutenant Max Carmichael. Very pleased to meet you all.'

Eva embraced Alice too. 'My, you've grown since the summer.'

'Don't say that like it's a good thing. Now she's taller, she keeps pinching me clothes,' Violet complained, and everyone laughed.

Alice rolled her eyes, but said nothing.

'Oh, I nearly forgot,' Hazel Baxter said, and fumbled in her handbag. 'Here you go, Eva. I've brought a letter from the Colonel.'

Turning the envelope over in her hand, Eva looked surprised. 'Daddy wrote to me? But I only sent his letter off a few days ago. He usually takes weeks to reply.'

Max gave her an odd look. 'Maybe you should read it later,' he said, nodding to the company they had, 'after your shift.'

250

'Good idea.' Eva stuffed the letter into her apron pocket, and looked directly at Lily. 'By the way, Private Orde was asking for you earlier,' she said, lowering her voice. 'I told him you were off duty while your family are here but he was most insistent. Why not drop by his bed on your way out, in case it's urgent?'

Lily turned and saw Danny in his bed, the magazine he'd been reading now on his lap as he watched them clustered about Max's bed. Her insides did a little jig, and she felt light-headed, which was silly, but not something she seemed able to control.

No doubt he wanted an explanation for why she had run away from him. But the more she thought about it, the more defiant she became. Trying to kiss her like that! Some girls might have been flattered. But not her.

'Which one is Private Orde?' Alice asked loudly, peering about the ward.

Max pointed him out, and they all turned to stare.

Seeing this, Danny lifted a quick hand in greeting, and then pushed his magazine and sheets aside, swinging out of bed. Was he going to embarrass her in front of her family?

'Goodness, whatever happened to his face?' Gran asked, staring. 'Poor boy.'

'Hush, Mum,' Aunty Vi muttered.

Daniel came towards them, his gaze intent on Lily's face. 'Hello, Lily. I was hoping to speak to you. Nurse Ryder told me you had company coming. Won't you introduce me?'

'He called her Lily,' Alice whispered to Gran, who shushed her too.

Blushing, Lily did not know where to look.

'Erm, this is Danny . . . I mean, Private Daniel

251

Orde,' she told them reluctantly, and then nodded to each of them in turn. 'This is my sister, Alice. That there's my Gran, and my Aunt Violet, and her friend Mrs Baxter, from Porthcurno. And that's Mrs Baxter's son, Charlie.'

'How do you do,' Danny said politely, as they all said hello.

'Were you in a fire?' Charlie asked bluntly, staring at his burnt and disfigured face, and then shuffled his feet. 'Sorry, none of my business.'

'I was in a fire, yes.' Danny answered him calmly enough. 'A very bad fire set off by incendiary bombs. I was lucky to get out alive. Or so they tell me.' He looked Charlie up and down. 'Are you hoping to join up when you're old enough?'

Hazel Baxter's eyes widened, and she grabbed Charlie, pulling him against her. 'My boy's too young for that malarkey, thank you. His dad died this year, fighting for his country. Charlie don't need to do the same, not at his age.'

'I'm sorry, Mrs Baxter, I didn't know. You have my deepest sympathies.' Clearly uncomfortable, Danny turned away. 'Excuse me, ladies. Maybe I could speak to you later, Nurse Fisher.'

Lily watched him go with conflicting emotions, glad that he hadn't said anything revealing to her kin, but also sorry that he'd been made to feel unwelcome. She'd witnessed some of the other patients shrinking from the burns victims, just as she'd done on first seeing Danny's face, an unpleasant and unfair reaction that would follow them for the rest of their lives.

'Mum!' Charlie fought free of her grasp, his tone exasperated. 'I told you before, I'm not a kid. I can speak for myself.'

Hazel Baxter said nothing, her face white, her red lips compressed. Lily could see she was terrified of losing her son to the war, and she couldn't blame her.

Charlie had tried to enlist when he was still little more than a child, falsifying his papers to slip past the recruitment officer's attention. It was only thanks to George Cotterill, now Hazel's betrothed, that the foolish young lad hadn't been shipped out for his basic training and never seen again.

But she could understand Charlie's point of view as well. To escape his mum's over-protectiveness, he'd left home that summer and gone off to Penzance to work in a factory. Yet here she was, treating him like a little kid again as soon as they were back together. And in front of a soldier too.

'Shall we go up to my room?' Lily asked brightly. 'It'll be medication time soon, so we should leave Eva to her job. Besides,' she added with a smile, thinking of the birthday cake she'd helped Cook make this week, 'I've got a surprise for you, Aunty Vi.'

It wasn't a big cake, and sugar rationing meant it wasn't terribly sweet either, but the gesture was important. There might be a war on but people should still be able to celebrate their birthdays.

'A surprise? For me?' Her aunt looked gratified.

'That's a grand idea. You lead on, petal.' Gran gave her a wink, linking her arm with Lily's as they said goodbye to Eva and Max, and headed out of the ward. 'I can't wait to see your room. You're lucky young things, not needing to share . . . So spoilt. When I was your age, and went away for a spot of training, I had to share with three other girls. Three, mind you. And I was the only one who didn't snore!'

253

Lily laughed, but her real focus was on trying not to look at Danny, who had got back on his bed and was reading his magazine again, while secretly studying him from under her lashes.

Private Orde was asking for you earlier, Eva had told her. He was most insistent, apparently.

Sister Gray had insisted she wasn't to speak to him again, nor he to her. Danny obviously didn't care about the rules. But what had he wanted to speak to her about? As if she needed to ask . . .

★ ★ ★

Aunty Violet cried genuine tears when she saw the birthday cake Lily and Cook had made for her. And she was polite enough not to mention that it was slightly lopsided, or that the sponge was tough as old shoe leather. 'My darling girl,' she said, hugging Lily again, 'what a treat. Isn't this the best, Mum?'

'Quite right,' Gran said, nibbling on the small slice she'd been given. 'Not bad for a beginner. We'll make a baker out of her yet.'

'It's a bit dry,' Alice said dubiously. But Charlie jabbed her in the ribs, and she said, 'Ouch!' and fell silent.

Mrs Baxter declined to eat a slice, staring out of the window instead. Gran had told Lily on the way upstairs that she was to be married to George Cotterill sometime early next year, once she'd had the baby, who was due at Christmas. Lily had been surprised. 'So soon? Wasn't she worried to drive you all this way when she's so heavily pregnant?'

'That's what Mr Cotterill said. He had Charlie drive most of the way — he's been learning, you see — and

254

Hazel only took over once they got into St Ives.'

'That's sensible, at least.'

'Charlie shouldn't strictly be driving, of course. But who cares, eh? The rules have all flown out the window these days.'

Lily didn't share her gran's uninterest in the law of the land, but she was glad poor Hazel wouldn't be facing a long drive back tomorrow. She looked so weary, poor dear — and no surprise, given her advanced pregnancy — and her lower back was surely aching, from the way Hazel kept rubbing at it.

She gave Aunty Violet a large stone off the beach at St Ives that she'd painted with a pretty seascape. She wasn't a brilliant artist, but thought she'd captured the waves nicely.

Violet was ecstatic, praising her like she was Michelangelo. 'Oh, Mum, look at this. Lily painted it herself. Isn't it beautiful? Thank you so much, love. And for the cake. What a marvellous birthday this has been.'

They all left mid-afternoon, after taking a walk around the damp, windswept gardens and speaking briefly to Sister Gray, who had come out to remind Lily not to be late for her shift.

'We'll see you tomorrow for a walk around St Ives,' Aunty Violet said merrily, waving out of the passenger window, and then clutched the door in shock as Charlie revved the engine violently. 'If we live that long . . .'

When they'd gone, Lily trudged back upstairs to change into her uniform, exhausted and a little weepy. She hadn't realised how much she missed her family until she'd seen them again, surrounded with their noisy, happy laughter for hours. Had she done the right thing, moving away? She wasn't sure anymore, and was hit by a violent wave of homesickness as she remembered they would all be leaving tomorrow.

But Tom cheered her up, coming up to her at the start of her shift. He'd managed to make a deal with the farmer who supplied last year's Christmas tree. 'He'll deliver a seven- or eight-footer next week,' he told her. 'Just in time for the Christmas party.'

'Thank goodness,' Lily said, thanking him profusely. So that was the Christmas tree sorted. One more thing to tick off her list. After a difficult start, everything was coming together nicely.

By rights, she ought to be happy. So why wasn't she?

Danny asking to see her earlier was still nagging away at the back of her mind. The private would likely be discharged soon, and no doubt wanted to make some kind of peace between them before he left. But Lily couldn't bring herself to speak to him again. Not yet, anyhow. Maybe not ever.

33

Rose was astonished when Tom came to find her in the linen store late in the afternoon, his brow furrowed. 'There's a gent waiting out front for you,' he said, making his disapproval obvious. 'Should I send him away or show him in?'

She put away the clean bandages she'd been rolling up for storage. 'What's this gent's name?'

Tom rubbed his chin. 'Didn't think to ask, Sister. Shall I go back and find out?'

'No, I'll go. Thank you, Tom.'

Rose bustled out, leaving him to lock up the room, and hurried down to the front entrance, intrigued by this mysterious visitor.

Sure enough, she could see the outline of a man in a trench coat leaning against one of the white entrance pillars. There was a distinct chill to the night, and he had his hat tipped forward, the collar of his coat turned up, and was smoking a cigarette.

'Hello?' She ventured outside a few steps, though it was perishing and she was only wearing her uniform. 'You wanted to see me?'

The man straightened and threw his cigarette away at once, coming forward into the pool of light cast by the front door lamp. Then she recognised him. It was Dick Jeffries, the school teacher.

He took off his hat to her. 'Good evening, Rose. I hope I haven't disturbed some important procedure. You don't mind if I call you Rose, do you? Or should it be Sister Gray?' He replaced his hat and nodded to her uniform, smiling. 'The children speak very highly of you.'

'Good evening, Dick. Of course you may call me Rose.' But she was flustered by what he'd said. 'They . . . They do?' She didn't know the children had even noticed her existence, barring a couple of them. 'What can I do for you?'

'It's about Jimmy,' he said. 'You asked me to come and see you if there were any developments.'

Rose's eyes widened. Quickly, she asked him to come in out of the cold, deciding to take him to the senior staff room. There was rarely anybody in there at this time, Lewis having gone home for the night, a hot meal delivered to all the patients, and Tom only waiting to collect the empties before the lights were lowered. There was still half an hour before Matron would begin her final round of the evening.

The fire had burnt down but the room was cosy enough. She swung a cardigan about her shoulders and sat in the armchair opposite him.

'Go on, what do you know?' she prompted him.

'It could be nothing. But he hasn't been in school for some days now. At first, I was told by the other kids that he was ill. But when I started asking what this illness was, they couldn't tell me. The Treverricks sent no note, so I sent one back with one of the children. Only, they never replied.' He settled his hat on his knee, looking at her. 'Then yesterday, this girl Mandy, one of the evacuees who's been housed at the orphanage, she started to cry. And when I asked her what the matter was, she said she didn't like the Treverricks and didn't want to live with them anymore.'

'Poor little mite! Did she say why, though?'

'I couldn't get another word out of her, unfortunately.' He pulled a face. 'But I decided enough was enough. Being a Saturday, I had some errands to run today. You know what it's like, racing around trying to get all your chores done while you're off work. But when I was done, I walked up here and called at the orphanage. I wanted to ask the Treverricks where Jimmy is, what's wrong with him, and why young Mandy's so unhappy living there.'

Rose sat forward, intent on his face. 'And what did they say?'

'Nothing useful, I'm afraid.' Dick shook his head, looking frustrated. 'Mr Treverrick came to the door, looking down his nose at me, and said the children were getting ready for bed so I couldn't come in. He told me Jimmy had been down with the measles, but was on the mend and might be back at school in a week or two. And when I asked about Mandy, he brushed me off. Said she was missing her Ma in London and liked to make up tall tales to get attention.'

'But you don't believe him.'

'Do you?'

'Not a bit of it, no.' Rose stood up and paced the room, filled with a terrible sense of urgency. 'I agreed with Eva — that's one of the other nurses here — that we would wait until the Christmas party and talk to Jimmy then. But if they're not even letting him go to school, they certainly won't let him out for a party.'

'So what should we do? I mean, I'm assuming you want to pursue this.' Dick stood up too, putting his hat back on. 'It's my belief they're holding that boy prisoner.'

'Mine too.'

'Really?' He gave a laugh. 'And here I was, thinking you'd tell me to calm down, that I was imagining things.'

'No, Dick, I think you've hit the nail on the head. I just have no idea why.' She stopped pacing, and glanced at the wall clock. 'It's rather late to be doing much about it tonight.' She heard a noise in the hall, and went quickly to the door. 'But there is something I can do.'

Finding Matron at the door of St Ives Ward, poised to begin her evening round, Rose called her into the senior staff room instead. She briefly introduced Dick Jeffries, and explained why he was there and what he had learnt about Jimmy's ongoing absence from school. Matron listened with polite bewilderment, not interrupting, but it was clear she was not as shocked as Rose had been by what the Treverricks had said. If anything, she was unmoved.

'I see,' she said when Rose had finished her account, and Dick had added a few helpful observations in support of it. 'Forgive me for being obtuse, but why are you telling me this?'

'Because I'm afraid for Jimmy's safety,' Rose said flatly.

'That seems far-fetched, given the circumstances.' Matron had a martial light in her eyes, yet she had spoken with careful restraint; presumably a stranger in the room meant she was unwilling to be outright rude. 'So what do you intend to do? Storm the orphanage and demand to see the boy?'

Rose drew herself up, never more aware of her lack of inches than when looking up at Matron. 'Perhaps. If that's the only way to get answers.'

260

'Poppycock!' Matron shook her head, her self-control snapping. 'It seems to me that you're making an infernal nuisance of yourself, Sister Gray, and worse, you are dragging this unfortunate man into your little charade too. The Treverricks have given a perfectly reasonable excuse for why this boy has not been at school lately, and indeed, if he is infectious, they've done the right thing by keeping him away from the other children.'

'What about that girl, Mandy? The one who was so upset.'

'My goodness, girls her age are upset by the slightest thing. I daresay she's already forgotten what she was crying for. And of course she must be missing her family. They are hundreds of miles away and the country is at war. What child wouldn't be unsettled by that?' Matron went to the door, her look stern. 'I suggest that Mr Jeffries makes his way home, and you continue with your duties, Sister. I shall be visiting my mother all day tomorrow, but I expect to see you in my office first thing on Monday morning.'

'But, Matron — '

'Enough now. Good evening, Mr Jeffries.' And Matron went out, leaving the door wide open as a hint.

Dick looked at Rose, grimacing. 'Well, you tried.'

Rose did not say anything, feeling too furious to trust herself. Instead, she took Dick back to the entrance and said goodbye to him, being careful not to let any light shine out. It was after dark and a mist had fallen about St Ives, making the evening vaguely luminescent. If the moon had risen yet, she couldn't see it.

'Wait. So that's it?' Dick asked as she turned to go back inside the building.

Rose looked round at him. 'There's nothing more I can do tonight. And you saw what happened with Matron. I have to be careful how I approach this. It's possible that Lady Symmonds, who owns the orphanage, might be inclined to listen if I can find real proof of any misdemeanours. But if I get it even slightly wrong . . .'

'You'll be in hot water.'

'Exactly.' Rose gave him a grateful smile. 'Thank you for coming to tell me about Jimmy though. It's made me see how wrong I was to wait for the Christmas party. That could be too late for the poor boy.'

'So you have a plan?'

'Since my options are limited, the only thing I can do now is talk to the police. It may not do any good; I expect you know our local bobby as well as I do, and he's a conservative chap. He may take the same view as Matron, that the Treverricks know what they're doing and should be left to their business.' She gave a helpless shrug. 'But perhaps he can find out whether anything's happened to young Jimmy.'

'Go to the police?' Dick tugged on one ear. 'Phew.'

'Do you think that's an over-reaction?'

'Not if they're mistreating those kids.' But he was looking worried. 'Though if they're not . . . Like you say, that could land us both in serious trouble.'

'I won't mention you,' she said quickly.

But Dick shook his head. 'No, damn it, go ahead and repeat what I told you. In for a penny, in for a pound. This is more important, and I wouldn't trust those Treverricks as far as I could throw them.' He paused. 'Look, do you want me to come with you to the police station tomorrow?'

'Thank you, but I'll be fine.'

He had such a lovely smile, she thought, saying goodnight and closing the door on him, then pulling the blackout curtain across to hide their lights from any enemy planes. She wished again that she could fall for a friendly, uncomplicated man like Dick Jeffries, instead of a man like Lewis, who was not only difficult to know but was already spoken for.

Rose went back to work, helping Tom collect the dirty dinner plates, but found she'd been knocked off balance by Dick's visit and the prospect of a severe telling-off from Matron on Monday morning. Her stomach churned with nerves and she did not look forward to the long peace of the night shift as usual.

Had she really said that she would go to the police?

34

Eva, sitting with Private Fletcher as he struggled to breathe, his head swathed in a towel and bent over a bowl of hot water, heard what sounded like a plane in the distance and froze. It was hard to be sure if it really was a plane, over the private's loud, tortured breathing, but she could not imagine what else that faint drone could signify.

Her body tensed, waiting for the air-raid siren to go off below them in the town. But several minutes passed, and finally Eva realised she could no longer hear its drone. If it had been an enemy plane, flying undetected in poor weather, what could it have been doing? Scouting this part of the coast for possible targets, she thought grimly, and shuddered.

Hopefully, the pilot onboard had not been able to see a thing through the mist. Though that could include the large red cross painted on top of Symmonds Hall, flagging it up as a hospital to anyone flying over — including the enemy.

Not that anyone expected the Germans to play fair.

Private Fletcher began to wheeze and cough, and Eva leant over him to pat his back. 'That's it, old thing,' she told him approvingly, 'cough it all up. That's the ticket.'

Once the treatment was finished, she whisked away the cooling bowl of water, dried Private Fletcher's face, and settled him back against his pillows. Only a few lights were still on, as the other patients were getting ready for bed now. Private Fletcher seemed half-asleep himself, so she removed the screens about his bed and left him to rest.

Eva washed first the equipment and then her hands at the sink near the nurses' station, then sat down at the table. A lamp cast a soft orange light across the various ledgers, but she pushed them aside and retrieved the envelope from her apron pocket.

Her father's letter was crumpled now, but still legible. Leaning on her elbow, she spread the sheet of paper out on her knee to read.

My dearest Eva

I trust this letter finds you well. We are in good spirits here, having just enjoyed a visit from some Very Important People. I would tell you who, but loose lips and all that. Suffice it to say, everything went off swimmingly and your Papa is now basking in the warm glow of official approval. Long may it last!

The reason I'm writing is a queer one. I received a letter the other day from an American pilot, a Flight Lieutenant Max Carmichael. Same cheeky blighter, if I recall correctly, who wrote to you at Porthcurno earlier this year. From what the fellow told me, it's clear you two have been getting rather pally up there in St Ives. Because, guess what? He's only asked permission from me to marry you!

I didn't know it was still the done thing, asking a father's blessing, especially these days. Women in the factories, et cetera. But Americans can be odd fish, can't they?

Anyway, I wrote straight back and put a flea in his damn ear. For starters, he says he's laid up in bed with only the slightest hope of recovery. Not exactly prospective bridegroom material; not for my daughter.

Besides, any man who needs to seek permission before tying the knot isn't worth looking at, my dear. If you're at all interested in a fond father's advice, that is. Which I imagine you're not. Too like your late mother, rest her soul — headstrong, impulsive, and affectionate to a fault.

I shall hope to see you at Christmas for a proper chinwag, but if you can't get leave from Matron, it will have to wait until the New Year. In the mean. time, please stay safe and don't do anything foolish. Never marry while there's a war on. These things are for life, you know.

All my love, Daddy

Eva gave several squeaks at certain intervals during her reading of this letter, and was aware of heads turning curiously in her direction in the darkened ward. But she simply couldn't help herself. Her heart was thudding like a racehorse over the turf and she couldn't believe what she had just read.

Max had written to her father at Porthcurno? Without even telling her? And, most astonishing of all, he had asked Daddy's permission to *marry* her?

She jumped up, clutching the letter and hurried out into the corridor. Mary was there, reading a poster advertising the Christmas party that had been pinned to the notice board. The nurse looked round in surprise as a breathless Eva bore down on her.

'Goodness, Eva, whatever's wrong?' Mary asked.

'I need to see Max — I mean, Flight Lieutenant Carmichael, straightaway. Can you watch Carbis and St Ives Wards while I'm gone? I know I shouldn't ask but — ' She held up the letter. 'Something important has come up.'

'Of course I can watch them.' Mary watched in baffled amusement as Eva strode down towards Atlantic Ward without another word. 'But what's come up?' she called after her in vain. 'And why is it important? Eva?'

Max was dozing, but she dragged the screens around his bed in such a noisy, haphazard fashion that by the time she leant over him, his eyes were open.

'What's the meaning of this?' she demanded, showing him the letter.

She helped Max sit up to read it. As he came to the end of the letter, his glance upwards was full of chagrin. 'All right,' he agreed. 'I put my hand up to writing to your Pa. I had his reply today myself and it wasn't very complimentary.'

'Do you have any idea what I've been going through? I asked first, and you said you didn't want to marry me. Then you've been avoiding me — '

His eyes widened. 'How can a man in a bed avoid anyone? You didn't come to see me.'

'Because you got me banned from the ward!'

'But, honey, that was for your own good. And after Sister let you back on the ward, you sent Nurse Stannard to look after me. You never came yourself.'

'Do you blame me?' Eva shook her head, delighted and exasperated all at the same time. He had called her 'honey' again. 'Good God, Max, you knew what my feelings were. If you wanted to marry me, why not just ask me?'

'I wanted to be sure I was doing things the right way.'

'I beg your pardon?'

'English traditions. I'm okay with some of them. Like the cream before the jam on a scone, or is it the other way round? Anyway, I asked some of the guys about this stuff, and they said I needed to ask your father's permission before popping the question.'

Eva was speechless.

'Was that the wrong thing to do?' Max handed back the letter, looking defeated. 'Have I blown it? Your Pa seems to think so. *Not worth looking at.*' He closed his eyes, running a hand over his forehead. 'Well, that's me, all right. I might be able to move about on my own a bit in the future, but I'll never be what I was. He could do much better for a son-in-law.'

'For goodness' sake, you're a nincompoop!'

His eyes flew open and Max gazed at her in amazement. 'A what? I'm a wh-what?'

'A nincompoop,' she said again, just as crossly.

'And what's one of them?' Max asked, not attempting to repeat the word. 'Because it don't sound too good.'

'It means you don't have the sense you were born with, Flight Lieutenant Carmichael. My father has no hold over me whatsoever. He can jump off a cliff if he thinks he's going to stop me marrying whomever I bloody well please.'

'My beautiful rebel.' But he didn't smile, studying her flushed face with troubled eyes. 'Your Pa gave you good advice in that letter though.'

'Such as?'

'People shouldn't get married when there's a war on. Nobody can make a decision about their future with bombs falling and everyone feeling like it's the end of the world.'

'Oh, fiddlesticks!' Eva said.

But she noticed he didn't propose to her as she'd fully hoped and expected when she brought him her father's letter. Instead, he swiftly changed the subject, asking about plans for the Christmas party.

Max was still determined to be on his feet before he asked her to marry him, she realised with a sinking heart.

But what if he was never able to walk again?

For the first time since she'd discovered her hero was still alive, though badly wounded, she considered the possibility that they might never marry.

And she had to admit to feeling in flat despair about it.

35

Not surprisingly, the small police station was closed and silent when Rose arrived, first thing on Sunday morning. However, a notice on the door told her where she could find the local sergeant in an 'emergency', so she followed the narrow street round until she came to a row of whitewashed cottages with brightly painted front doors.

Locating the sergeant's house by the number on the door, she knocked and was shown into the front room by an elderly lady, who she seemed to recall was his mother.

'I'll fetch him down to you,' the woman said with a disapproving look, and vanished.

Sergeant Pascoe came into the room about ten minutes later, dressed in his Sunday best shirt and dark trousers, still pulling on his braces.

'Miss Gray,' he said in surprise.

'I'm sorry to disturb you on a Sunday morning,' she said quickly, standing up. 'Thank you very much for agreeing to see me, Sergeant Pascoe.'

'Not at all, Miss.' He shook her hand cheerfully enough, a middle-aged man with silvering sideburns who had been a policeman for as long as she could remember. 'It's good to see you again. Let's see, last time we had any dealings with each other, you were about seventeen, and you'd just ridden your bicycle into the front of Mr Hogan's delivery van. You had a nasty cut on your knee, as I recall. But your aunt soon fixed you up.' He grinned. 'Not sure the bicycle ever recovered though.'

'Or Mr Hogan's van,' she said, still embarrassed about that foolish prang all these years later. 'Goodness, what a memory you have.'

'Comes with the job, Miss.' Sergeant Pascoe sat down in a tatty old armchair and signalled for her to take the chair opposite. 'Now, what can I do for you?' He glanced at the clock on the mantel, which showed a little after nine o'clock. 'It must be something urgent, to come chivvying me out on a Sunday morning before church.'

'It is incredibly urgent, yes.'

As quickly and succinctly as she could, Rose explained to him why she was there, leaving Dick Jeffries out of her account except to mention that she'd asked 'at the school' and been told Jimmy hadn't been there for some days, and that at least one of the evacuee children had expressed unhappiness at being looked after by the Treverricks.

Sergeant Pascoe listened thoughtfully, just as Matron had done last night, but at the end of her explanation, he made a face and rubbed his chin.

'I don't see how any of that sounds particularly fishy, Miss. The boy's been sick and is off school, but when he's better, he'll be back.'

'But what if Jimmy isn't sick? I told you about the message I heard. Another nurse was with me, and she heard it too. It was an S.O.S. message.'

'Very likely it was. But it sounds like a boy's trick to me. He'll be just fooling around. No need to worry your head about it.'

'Won't you at least go and ask the Treverricks how he is?' she asked earnestly. 'That might be enough to make them release him.'

'Release him?' Now he threw back his head with laughter. 'Forgive me, Miss Gray. But you say that as if you expect them two to be keeping the lad in a dungeon.'

'An attic room, actually. But yes.'

'And what possible reason could the Treverricks have to lock him up?'

'I'm not sure,' she said, desperately aware that she was failing to persuade him. 'To conceal what they've done to him, perhaps?'

'*Done to him?*' The sergeant stood up with a frown then, shaking his head. 'Miss Gray, that's a very serious accusation to be making about such a respectable couple. Especially when they've been kind enough to help the war effort by taking in extra evacuees at the orphanage . . .'

Rose wanted to scream. He didn't believe her. And meanwhile, poor little Jimmy was locked up in a room at the orphanage under the control of those horrible people.

'Please, Sergeant —'

'I've heard nothing here to make me rush over to the orphanage and demand to see some eight-year-old boy who's probably laid up with the measles.'

He showed her out of the room, where his mother stood waiting by the front door as though she'd been listening to the entire conversation. Which, Rose thought miserably, she probably had.

'But thank you for your report. It's duly noted.' Sergeant Pascoe gave her a kindly smile from the doorstep. 'You take care now, Miss.'

★ ★ ★

272

Weary and depressed, Rose stood outside in the grey morning light, unsure what to do now. A chill breeze tugged at her woollen dress and ruffled her hair while she stood looking up and down the row of cottages.

Seagulls were crying like lost souls above the winding streets of St Ives, and she could hear the strangely rhythmic clink and slap of wires against masts in the harbour. The air was tangy with salt and the smell of fresh fish. She could see heavy clouds massing out at sea and she knew it might snow soon. She caught the rattling note of a boat engine, somewhere beyond the slate roofed houses, and someone shouted a cheerful greeting above its noise.

An old man in a cap was seated outside his cottage, head bent, whistling an old Cornish tune and carving a piece of driftwood. He didn't look up as she passed. A young woman with a baby on her hip peered out at Rose through a gap in the curtains of an adjacent house, then the curtain was whisked shut, as though in disapproval.

It had been worth trying the police.

Hadn't it?

Despondent and unhappy, Rose began to trudge back towards Symmonds Hall, wishing she did not feel like a stranger in the small town where she had grown up.

Most of the young men she'd known at school had gone, and many of the women too, either joining up or going away to work. And she'd never mingled much, so didn't know the younger ones, and many of the older ones, those of her aunt's generation and older, were strangers to her as well. Her aunt had been an odd sort, and not much of a socialiser, although a churchgoer.

It had been no surprise that her sister had jumped at the chance to get away from St Ives as soon as possible, to discover the big world out there and all its excitement. The only surprise had been that Elsie had chosen to keep a toehold here, in the form of Lewis Lanyon, rather than cutting him loose when she left.

A car horn beeped behind her on the hill, and she turned. It was Lewis, who slowed down as he came level with her.

She opened the passenger door and peered in at him, surprised. 'Hello, what are you doing here? You don't usually come up to the hall on a Sunday.'

'Private Fletcher took a turn for the worse during the night.' He hesitated. 'Can I give you a lift?'

She was tempted to refuse, but that would have been ridiculous. And it sounded as though she might be needed at the home, morning off or not.

'Thank you.' She got in and Lewis continued up the road. 'Poor Private Fletcher. He's such a nice lad too. I thought he was on the mend.'

'It's always the same with lung damage. You can never be quite sure if a patient's fully recovered or not, and this damp weather isn't helping.' He looked at her speculatively. 'What were you doing out this early on a Sunday? Don't tell me you're a churchgoer.'

'Not really.' She told him about Dick Jeffries' unexpected visit, the unhelpful discussion she'd had with Matron, and her stupid decision to go to the police. It was hard to admit how humiliated she had felt leaving the sergeant's home. But there was no point pretending her mission had been successful.

'My God.' Lewis was silent for a moment. The sign

274

to Symmonds Hall came into view, and he slowed, turning up the drive. 'So the police aren't going to do anything?'

Rose shook her head sadly.

He parked up outside the home, but did not immediately get out, his head bent in thought. She waited for him, noticing that the old ambulance was back again.

That was the vehicle that belonged to Lily's visitors from Porthcurno; she had seen the heavily pregnant woman driving it yesterday, and was not sure she approved. The steering wheel must press heavily into the woman's tummy, for a start. And what if there was an accident? But she supposed such things would become more commonplace the longer this war went on, with women having to do everything men would usually have done, and their own chores as well.

'Rose.' He turned to her, torment in his face. 'I'm sick of this intolerable situation. I'm going to write to Elsie and break it off with her.'

'What?'

She had foolishly assumed he had been thinking about little Jimmy, and how they were going to rescue him when nobody else seemed to care about his welfare. Instead, he had been thinking about her sister.

'I know your sister will be hurt. But this isn't fair to any of us.'

Panic streaked through her. He belonged to Elsie, fair and square. She couldn't steal him from her sister, not even if he wanted to be stolen. It simply wouldn't be right.

'Lewis —'

But he leant forward and kissed her, sending her body into shock. For a split second, she remembered

Lily describing how she had frozen when Danny kissed her. This was different, of course. She wanted Lewis to kiss her. Yet, at the same time, as soon as their lips met, something inside her felt as though a dam was bursting, and the sheer force of that release terrified her.

She pulled away, shaking her head. 'No,' she whispered, and fumbled for the door handle, then ran inside just as the first flakes of snow began to fall.

★ ★ ★

Twenty minutes later, having splashed her face with cold water and tidied her hair, Rose went back down to the wards. She found Private Fletcher grey-faced but sitting up, and Lewis tending him with Mary's help.

'Can I help?' Rose asked breathlessly, though she wasn't in her uniform.

Lewis did not even look round at her.

'We should be fine now, thank you, Sister,' Mary said, clearly surprised to see her. 'You're not on duty this morning. Did Matron send you down?'

'I just wanted to see if I could be of any use. What happened?'

Wiping her hands on a cloth, Mary took her discreetly aside so they wouldn't disturb Lewis, who was having a quiet conversation with the patient.

'Private Fletcher had a bad turn. But don't worry, he's on the mend.' She studied Rose's face. 'Are you all right, Sister? You look a bit flustered.'

Rose began to make some excuse about having come downstairs too quickly when she stopped and raised a finger, vaguely aware of a distant droning sound. 'Do you hear that?' Several others in the ward had heard it too, she realised, a few voices already raised in query and alarm. 'That sounds like a plane.'

Mary listened, frowning. 'Must be one of ours. The siren hasn't gone off.'

'Or they haven't seen it yet. It's coming from the opposite direction, from down towards Zennor.' Rose swivelled, running to the south-facing window and staring up into the dark sky. For a moment, she could see nothing but a mass of grey. Then a large, grim shape sank out of the snow clouds, inexorably heading their way. 'There!'

She was joined by Lewis and Tom, who both fell back in consternation at the sight of the approaching plane.

'It's the Jerries,' Tom yelled, running to help other men get out of bed. 'Ring the bell, Sister! Get to the shelter!'

'Where are you going?' Lewis demanded, catching at her arm as she would have run after Tom.

'We need to get these men down to the cellar.'

'Forget them. Get yourself to safety,' Lewis told her urgently, propelling her before him towards the door. 'There's no time to lose.'

'But the patients — '

'Tom and I will do it between us. And Atlantic Ward too. You save yourself.' When she tried to protest, the doctor almost bundled her out of the ward door with the others. 'For God's sake, please do as I ask, Rose.' There was torment in his face. 'When will you realise I couldn't bear to lose you?'

Rose squeezed his hand briefly, understanding his pain. But she couldn't let it change her mind. 'We go together,' she insisted, 'or not at all.'

36

Lily's family had returned to meet up with her after leaving Hazel's cousin, and were now all gathered in her small room, Hazel looking weary, and Charlie and Alice squabbling like toddlers as usual. Lily and Gran were just discussing what to see in St Ives that morning when a high-pitched scream from outside brought Aunty Violet up sharp.

'Bloody hell,' she exclaimed, rushing to the window and peering out, 'what in God's name was that?'

Lily frowned. 'One of the kids from the orphanage, by the sound of it. Maybe they're playing a game.' She followed her aunt to the window. 'Can you see anything?'

'There.' Aunty Violet pointed to the far left, then gasped, clearly shocked. 'My stars! What on earth . . .? He'll break his neck.'

Lily had to crane her neck to see what Violet was looking at.

There was a young boy in short trousers, painfully small and skinny, scaling the red brick exterior of the orphanage. He was balanced precariously on a window ledge, the sash window pushed up, as though he had just climbed out of it. He was attempting to stretch out to the nearest drainpipe, presumably so he could shin down it to the ground. But the ground was a good thirty feet below him, by Lily's rough estimate, maybe more. And the drainpipe was icy and treacherous from the snow.

Sickened with fear for the boy, Lily shook her head. 'He must be mad. Oh my Lord, he's sure to fall . . . '

Below him in the yard were three children, staring upwards with mouths open and eyes wide with horror, paying no attention to the snow that was falling. One of them, a small girl with pigtails, gave another piercing scream like the one that had brought them to the window, and shouted, 'No, Jimmy! Go back inside!'

The boy paused, made the mistake of looking down, and then clung to the brick wall in sudden panic.

'God help us,' Gran muttered, nudging past them both to stare out.

Charlie and Alice, unable to see a thing through the adults, ran to the door and vanished. No doubt they were heading down to the yard for a better look.

'Here, love.' Aunty Violet turned aside to let Hazel see what was happening.

After a quick assessing look, Hazel paled and gripped the window sill, her face full of the same age-old fear Lily was feeling.

'That poor boy,' she whispered, glancing at Lily. 'Jimmy, the girl called him. Who is he?'

'One of the orphans. I believe Sister Rose made friends with a boy called Jimmy a while back. Then he disappeared. They said he was ill.' Lily shrugged helplessly, watching as the boy began to inch towards the drainpipe again. 'I guess he's decided to escape through the window.'

'Someone has to stop him. To get him back inside.'

'I think someone's trying,' Aunty Violet said, and pointed. 'She don't look too friendly though. He won't turn back for that face. Silly cow ought to try smiling.'

Sure enough, a woman had appeared at the open window and was loudly remonstrating with the boy, her face an unpleasant mixture of fury and panic.

'I'm going down,' Lily said, and reached for her coat.

Hazel made for the door. 'Me too.'

Then they all stopped and stared at each other, everything narrowed to the terrible awareness of an engine sound, approaching from up the coast.

'That's a bloody plane,' Gran said, her voice shaking. 'One of ours?'

'I don't know,' Lily whispered.

As they stood listening, the air-raid siren went off below in the town, its unnerving wail sending them scurrying for their coats and bags.

'We need to get to the shelter. It's under the orphanage.'

Hazel had slipped her shoes off while sitting down, her feet being swollen, and while Gran and Aunty Violet made for the shelter, Lily waited behind for Hazel to refasten them.

Fumbling with her shoes, Hazel gave a low moan of consternation. 'Don't wait for me, Lily, you go.'

'I'm not leaving you behind.' Lily knelt to help her. 'Here, let me do that buckle for you.'

'Thank you. But that poor boy. He's bound to fall now.' Hazel was beside herself, her breathing laboured as she straightened and reached for her coat. 'Has he gone back inside?'

The buckle fastened, Lily got up and checked out of the window. Snow was falling more heavily now, whirling about on the sea winds. From the heavy drone, it sounded as though the enemy plane must be almost upon them. Below, she could see a steady stream of people hurrying to the cellar, some of the men still in pyjamas, others holding coats over their heads, the trapdoor standing open as children and patients climbed down the steps inside.

To her astonishment though, Jimmy had reached the drainpipe and was shinning down it, clasping the narrow pipe tightly. The woman at the window had disappeared.

'He's climbing down the drainpipe,' she told Hazel, and grabbed her gas mask off the back of the door. 'Like a blessed monkey! He's halfway down already.'

'Oh thank God.'

At that moment, they both heard a high-pitched whistling somewhere far too close, almost on top of them, then the most tremendous, unearthly bang.

The whole building shook, and Hazel stumbled and fell, crying out . . .

★　★　★

Eva, having made sure that Max and the other patients with limited mobility were sheltering under their beds, ran out to the yard with her gas mask in hand. There was a queue to get into the cellar, but it was growing shorter with every passing second as the noise of the approaching plane filled everyone's hearts with dread, people pushing and crowding inside.

Tagging onto the end of the queue, she heard a shout behind her, and turned to see Mrs Treverrick running out of the orphanage with a couple of young stragglers.

'Make way,' the woman said sharply, pushing the children past Eva and the last of the patients. 'It's our cellar, we take precedence.' She threw Eva a vicious

281

look. 'As it was, I couldn't get to all the kids in time. Let's hope they're not in danger, eh? There was hardly any warning.'

Mrs Treverrick said it as though it was somehow Eva's fault that the air-raid siren had gone off so late.

Although stiff with outrage, Eva said nothing; her attention had been caught by something more alarming. There was a small boy climbing down the drainpipe on the side of the orphanage, bare-legged in short trousers, his jacket flapping. He was about ten feet from the ground, snow falling all around him.

Below him stood Dr Lewis, also snow-flecked, exhorting the boy not to let go but to cling on for all he was worth. And at his side was Sister Rose Gray in her civvies, her red hair dishevelled, her eyes quite wild, both arms raised towards the boy as though planning to catch him.

'Jimmy,' Eva breathed, too shocked at first to do anything but stare. Then she ran to Dr Lewis's side, also staring up at the boy. 'What in God's name is he doing?'

'What does it look like, Nurse Ryder?' Rose exclaimed. 'He's *escaping*!'

Eva took a few steps back, unsure what to do. Snow melted against her skin as she peered upwards, shielding her eyes, a sudden terror in her heart. The plane was high above, yet she could almost feel the heavy-duty buzz of its engine in her bones and saw what looked like a dark, ominous body cutting through the snow clouds.

The others had all disappeared and the cellar doors had closed behind them. They might even have been bolted from the inside. But perhaps if they hammered on them loudly enough . . .

'We have to get into the shelter.' She touched Rose's arm. 'We need to go, now, there's no time to lose.'

But it was already too late. The high-pitched whistle of a falling bomb in the immediate vicinity was followed within seconds by a powerful detonation, the earth shaking beneath their feet.

A wall tumbled into rubble at the far end of the orphanage yard, and an outbuilding collapsed along with it.

Perhaps shaken by the force of the bomb's impact, Jimmy released his grip on the drainpipe, and fell backwards with a startled cry. Luckily, he dropped straight into Dr Lewis's waiting arms. Grunting at the impact, the doctor staggered and fell sideways onto the flagstones, yet somehow kept the boy cradled, protecting him from harm.

'Are you all right?' Rose threw herself to her knees beside them both, hurriedly checking Dr Lewis for cuts and bumps. Then her gaze flashed to Jimmy's face. 'You're alive.' She ruffled the boy's wet mop of hair. 'You nearly gave me a heart attack, climbing down that drainpipe. Please don't ever do that again.'

'They locked me up with only bread and water,' Jimmy complained. 'What was I supposed to do?'

Lewis got up, grimacing. It was obvious he had hurt himself in the fall. But he held up a hand against the snow, staring at the collapsed building further down the yard. There was rubble everywhere and a thin dust rising from the bombed-out shell, reminding Eva horribly of terrace after terrace of London houses destroyed in the Blitz.

'I hope nobody was caught under that,' Eva said, also eyeing the rubble uneasily.

'Unlikely,' Lewis said.

Rose helped Jimmy to stand, studying his bare legs with a frown. 'You've hurt yourself,' she said unhappily. 'Let me get you inside and see to those grazes. I doubt that plane will be back any time soon.'

They had already heard another muffled detonation down in the town, then a third one a moment later. Eva crossed her fingers under her apron, hoping to goodness nobody had been hurt or had perished in those explosions.

'For safety's sake,' the doctor said, 'we should wait in the cellar until they give the all-clear.'

'I ain't going in that cellar,' Jimmy piped up defiantly. 'The Treverricks are down there. They'll lock me up again soon as they look at me.'

'Why did they lock you up in the first place, Jimmy?' Eva asked curiously. 'Did you have the measles?'

'I dunno.'

Dr Lewis was rubbing his hurt hip, a pained expression on his face. 'I know you don't want to see the Treverricks again, Jimmy. But we need to get down into the shelter. You stick with me, I won't let them touch you.'

Eva gave Jimmy a reassuring nod, and reluctantly the boy followed them down into the shelter.

Rose led Jimmy to the back of the cellar, with Eva just behind, taking care not to let the Treverricks see him. The doctor brought up the rear, limping heavily and grimacing with every step.

'Rose, wait,' Eva whispered, touching her arm. 'Those aren't just grazes from climbing down a drainpipe.'

Rose turned, frowning. 'What do you mean?'

'Haven't you noticed?' Eva pointed out a mass of faded yellowish streaks across the back of Jimmy's legs. 'Those are bruises. And a week old, by the look of them.' She looked down into Jimmy's evasive eyes and knew the boy was hiding something. 'I'm no expert, but I'd say he's been beaten.'

Rose looked round at Dr Lewis, a hectic flush rising in her cheeks. 'You can't expect me to turn a blind eye to *that*,' she began heatedly, but the doctor gave her a warning look.

'Later,' he said quietly. 'Not now. Not down here.'

37

Hazel had cut her head on the bedstead and seemed to be in a bad way, groaning and clutching her huge belly, as if in pain.

Lily did not know whether to leave her and run to the shelter for help, or stay and do — what? She had no idea, but patted Hazel's hand and said soothing things while trying to staunch the bleeding cut on Hazel's forehead with a pocket hanky. Meanwhile, she kept one ear open for the sound of more bloody planes, for she feared another bomb falling, only this time on their heads.

'I hope that little boy didn't fall to his death,' Hazel said, starting to cry. 'And what about the others? What about Charlie and Alice? Do you think they made it to the shelter in time?'

'I'm sure they did,' Lily reassured her, with more confidence than she really felt. That huge explosion had been so close at hand. Had it hit the orphanage or part of Symmonds Hall? Could it have struck the area above the shelter?

She didn't want to consider the possibility that some of those she knew and loved could be lying dead under the rubble somewhere. She had already lost her mum that way. She didn't think she could bear to lose the rest of her family to the German bombs . . .

It was so quiet now, it made the hairs rise on the back of her neck. She remembered the same eerie silence in the East End after the bombs stopped, when she would sit in the Anderson shelter by candlelight with

Gran and Aunty Vi and Alice, all of them wondering where the bombs had fallen and how many unfortunate souls had lost their lives that night.

Hazel gave a sharp cry and clutched her belly. 'Oh God,' she groaned, and her eyes seemed to roll up white. Then she slumped against Lily, a dead weight.

'What is it? Hazel?' Lily supported her as best she could, cold fear running through her like quicksilver. 'Wake up, Hazel!'

There was no response.

Lowering Hazel gently to the rug, she ran to see if any of the other nurses were in their quarters. But the rooms were all empty, and nobody came out when she called. They must all be down in the orphanage cellar by now, she realised.

She hurried to the top of the stairs, in two minds about whether to run down to the wards for help. Maybe Tom would be sheltering in Atlantic Ward with those men who couldn't get down to the cellar. But halfway down the stairs, she stopped dead and told herself not to be a bloody fool.

It might take ages to find him, and persuade him to leave the patients and come upstairs with her, and what did Tom know about looking after a pregnant woman anyway?

And all the time she was away, Hazel might come to and need her help.

How could she face Charlie if something terrible were to happen to his mum, and Lily hadn't even been by her side at the time?

By the time she ran back into the bedroom, frantic and breathless, she found Hazel conscious again. She had dragged herself to her knees and was leaning against the side of the bed. 'I thought you'd gone,'

Hazel said, rubbing at the tear stains and streaks of blood on her face. Her lip trembled. 'I feel sick. And where's my Charlie?'

'I'm sure he'll be safe in the shelter now.' Lily knelt down beside her. 'Please don't worry. Everything's going to be all right.'

'But the baby . . . It's coming.' Hazel's face contorted in pain. She rocked back and forth on her hands and knees, a hand to her belly. 'I remember this pain from last time. And my waters have broken . . .' She nodded to the wet rug behind her. 'There's no stopping it now.'

'Oh blimey,' Lily said, truly shocked. What on earth were they going to do now? There would be no getting any help until the air raid was over.

Her nursing experience, such as it was, took over. She put a steadying hand on Hazel's shoulder. 'It ain't too early though,' she pointed out. 'The baby was due at Christmas, weren't it?'

'About then, yes.'

'Well, that ain't far off. I daresay you'll be all right.'

'You're a dear for saying so, Lily. I'm glad you're here with me.' Hazel gave a soft cry, her brows dragging together as she dealt with another pain. 'Bertie's child is going to be born at last.'

Bertie Baxter, Hazel's husband, had been killed in action that summer. Lily had never met him, but she'd heard enough about the man to know he'd been a mean husband and a bad father to Charlie.

'George was willing to marry me before the baby was born, you know,' Hazel told her. 'He's such a good man. But I changed my mind. Told him I wasn't walking down the aisle looking like a barrage balloon.'

288

Her smile was strained. 'Now it's coming, at least we can have the banns read.'

Lily squeezed her hand. 'That's the ticket, Hazel, think about something positive,' she said encouragingly, even though her mind was racing and she felt a little queasy herself. She might not have been taught anything about pregnancy and childbirth, but everyone knew that once the waters had broken, the baby wouldn't be far behind.

She helped Hazel onto the bed and tried to make her comfortable, cleaning the blood off her face and loosening her clothing, though all the time her head was buzzing with thoughts and fears.

Hazel had grown calmer now, talking about her first labour with Charlie and how slow that had gone, almost a full day before anything exciting happened, saying that she'd been bored out of her mind. Only, Hazel also seemed to believe subsequent births could be much faster, even as little as an hour once the waters had broken, news which alarmed Lily no end. If this air raid lasted longer than Hazel's labour, how would she cope? Most births were straightforward and uneventful, or so she'd been told by her mother once, but what if there was a complication?

But all the worrying and fretting in the world weren't going to change facts. Until the air raid ended and the others came back from the shelter, there was nothing for it but to help Hazel Baxter have her baby, whether she had a clue how to do it or not.

And she was bloody terrified.

★ ★ ★

Lily had never been so frazzled in all her born days. After a promisingly quiet quarter of an hour, during which Lily began to breathe easier, Hazel suddenly announced that her 'pains' were getting worse. She puffed and panted, complaining that the room was too hot, the room was too cold, she felt sick, she felt restless. At one point she'd tried to climb out of bed and go downstairs, Lily barely able to restrain her.

Lily said calming things, fetched cool water to mop Hazel's brow, and fanned her with one of her women's magazines. Nothing seemed to help.

Then Hazel turned sour and angry. She snarled at Lily that she was 'a child' who didn't know what she was doing. She shouted for her son, and then for a doctor, and banged on the wall with her fist. She knocked over a jug of water and made a more strenuous attempt to escape the room, groaning as her pains rapidly increased.

All the while, she could hear enemy planes flying back and forth across the St Ives area, with the occasional explosion reminding her that at any moment the hall could be flattened, and them along with it.

'Oh, please don't take on so,' Lily urged her patient, to no avail, and had to reach deep inside herself to find the right words in the right tone. 'Hazel Baxter, you get back on that bed and think about your baby. It's coming, and you need to be somewhere safe when it does, not halfway down the stairs!'

Hazel stared at her, wide-eyed, and then subsided onto the bed. 'It hurts' was all she said for a while after that.

'I know, love,' Lily said sympathetically, and held her hand, wishing the all-clear would sound so she could run for Dr Lewis. 'But it'll be over soon.'

'Push!' she was exhorting Hazel a little over an hour later. 'I really think you need to push now, Hazel.'

'I am bloody pushing!'

She had earlier persuaded Hazel to undress and wrap herself in a sheet for dignity, as none of Lily's night clothes would fit her. Soon after that, Hazel had sat up with a jerk, suddenly grunting instead of panting, and Lily, peering down now in a kind of bemused horror, saw a mop of dark wet hair emerging.

The baby's head!

'I-I need to fetch someone,' Lily stammered, trying to get up.

'Don't you dare leave me!' Hazel's eyes were wild, sweat running down her face. She grabbed at Lily's arm with an iron grip. 'It's too late!'

'But Hazel, I . . . I don't know what to do.'

'There's nothing to it, I swear. You just have to . . . ' Hazel threw back her head and gave a gurgling scream, her face a deep purple, eyes straining, as she pushed again with all her might. 'Catch!'

Lily lunged for a clean bath towel and was just in time to scoop up a bright-red wriggling baby, its odd-looking head and pink limbs plastered in some shiny white substance. Even in that first shocked glance, she could see it was a girl, a thin umbilical cord still trailing between their bodies. Then the perfect little face crumpled, the tiny mouth opened wide, and a high-pitched wail echoed about the small room.

Acting on instinct, Lily wrapped the baby in the towel and lifted her for Hazel to see. 'Oh my Lord!' Somehow, she was crying too, her voice choked with tears. 'It's a baby girl. A beautiful, healthy baby girl.'

291

'A girl.' Hazel, exhausted but smiling, collapsed against the pillows, staring at her new-born child. 'Oh, what a little poppet she is. Look at those big eyes! She can't half make a racket too . . . ' She ran the back of her hand across her sweating brow. 'Bloody hell, that was fast. I'm shaking like a leaf. But I'm glad it's over.'

'Me too,' said Lily fervently.

At that moment, the all-clear sounded in St Ives. Lily sat down heavily on the bed, still cradling the baby, and shook her head in disbelief.

'Well, ain't that just bleedin' typical?'

38

A loud thudding at the cellar doors brought everyone round in shock. The all-clear had not yet sounded.

'That'll be the kids who ran off when I was rounding everyone up,' Mrs Treverrick said, looking relieved.

'Someone didn't reach the shelter in time?' Lewis stared at her, aghast. 'And you didn't mention it sooner? We could have gone out looking for them.'

'What, and put yourself in harm's way? If they did as they were told, there'd be no need to make a fuss. But the little blighters scarpered as soon as the siren went off. I thought they'd see sense in the end. But they never came back.' The woman shrugged dismissively. 'Not my fault if they choose to run away instead of coming to the shelter with the rest of us.'

'Hear, hear,' her husband said angrily. 'We're not their parents, and we're not miracle workers either. Some of those kids won't be told what's best for them.'

When Lewis unbolted the cellar doors and threw them open, it wasn't a group of scared children standing outside, but Tom, a flush in his thin cheeks, streaks of dirt across his forehead.

'We need you, Dr Lewis,' he said, sounding breathless. 'You too, Sister. There's a wall come down across the yard, and some of the orphans that didn't make it to safety are hurt. I've carried the worst of them to St Ives Ward.'

Lewis clapped Tom on the shoulder, and the two men hurried away.

'You come with us now, Jimmy,' Mrs Treverrick insisted, making a grab for the boy.

But Rose had Jimmy by the hand, and ushered him out ahead of her. 'He's not going anywhere with you, Mrs Treverrick,' she said coldly. 'I'll be speaking to you later. First, I need to see about these injured children.'

Mrs Treverrick would have gone after her, but her husband pulled her back from the cellar doors, whispering urgently in her ear. More plotting and planning, Rose thought, but paid no further attention. She had more important things on her mind than those two unpleasant schemers.

'Come with me, Jimmy,' she said as calmly as she could, though she felt sick at the thought that some of the orphans could be badly hurt, 'and I'll find you a quiet place to sit while I work. Though I'm afraid this could take a while.'

'I ain't sitting in no corner for hours,' Jimmy told her.

Thoughtfully, Rose looked down at his pale, freckled face. 'Well, would you mind if I left you with a pilot instead, then? An American pilot?' She saw the boy's eyes widen, and added softly, '*An injured* American pilot?'

★   ★   ★

When Tom staggered in carrying the last child, a little girl with bedraggled hair wet with snow, her face and clothes dust-streaked, Rose thought her heart would break.

'Over here, please,' she heard herself say, her voice crisp and devoid of emotion. Because it was no use collapsing in a tearful heap, was it? That wouldn't help these children. Nor would it serve to inspire the other staff, who were equally affected by the sight of these limp, battered children. 'Has somebody made provision for the patients in this ward?'

'They're being found places in Carbis and Atlantic Wards,' someone called back.

'Good.' She examined a young boy who was whimpering with pain, and decided he likely had a sprained wrist. 'Where are those bandages, Nurse Ryder?'

Eva came to her shoulder at once with a tray of bandages, cotton wool and water, plus sterilised needles and sutures for stitching up the deeper cuts and gashes.

There was no time to run upstairs and change into her nursing uniform, as she would have preferred. Instead, Rose washed her hands, donned a white apron over her civvies, rolled up her sleeves, and hurried about the ward, assessing each young body as it was brought in.

Five children walking wounded, three more seriously injured; including one with a bad gash to the head who would need to be seen by the doctor.

Lady Symmonds tottered in at one stage, pale-faced and exclaiming in horror at what she found. Rose dispatched Eva to calm the old lady down and escort her back to her apartment. This was no time to have civilians wandering in and out, disturbing the professional calm of the ward. When Eva came back a short while later, she said Mrs Treverrick was at the back door, demanding to know who had been hurt and how badly, but she had denied her access until tomorrow.

Rose might ordinarily have taken umbrage at such high-handed behaviour on Eva's part; but in this instance, she approved. That woman could go to hell for all she cared!

'Tom, fetch Dr Lewis to that boy with the head wound, would you?'

'Yes, Sister.'

'Nurse Stannard,' she said, 'could you clean up this girl's face, so I can see where to set the stitches?'

'Yes, Sister.'

★ ★ ★

The three nurses worked as a team, moving quietly about the ward, and it was only when Lewis came to her side some time later, blood on his hands, that she realised he'd finally arrived.

'Was someone else hurt?' she said anxiously, nodding to his hands.

'Nothing like that.' Lewis turned away, washing his hands in the bowl of water Nurse Stannard had just brought in and then drying them with a clean towel. 'Mrs Baxter has had her baby, that's all. I went up to see her after treating the boy with the head wound.'

Rose stared. 'Her baby?'

'You remember how worried her son Charlie was in the shelter? He kept fretting because his mother and Lily hadn't made it down to the cellar with the others.'

'I thought they must have been too slow and chosen to shelter in Atlantic Ward with the others.' Rose was astonished, but returned to her work, head bent as she set neat stitches into a cut. 'You're telling me Mrs Baxter gave birth on her own during the air raid?'

'Not on her own. Lily delivered the baby.'

'Nurse Fisher?'

'In the nurses' quarters, no less.' He smiled at her shocked expression. 'A bouncing baby girl. Mother and baby both doing well, thankfully. I've left Mrs Baxter to get some sleep. But she'll need to be brought down to a private room tomorrow. And we really ought to find something to use as a crib.'

'I'll ask Tom if he has any suggestions.' Rose sighed, and shook her head. 'So some good news has come from this awful disaster, then.'

'How's it going here?' he asked softly, glancing down at the girl whose cheek she was gently stitching. The girl, who had been shaking and hysterical, had thankfully fainted as soon as Rose inserted the needle. 'That's a neat job, well done.'

'Thank you.' She finished up, tying off the suture. 'This girl's not badly hurt. Like most of them, she had a lucky escape. If they'd been any nearer the wall that came down . . . ' She shuddered at the thought. 'How about that young lad you were treating?'

'He should live. We need to watch for swelling on the brain but I've cleaned the wound and tried to make him comfortable. This isn't a hospital though, and we don't have all the equipment I'd like.' Lewis gave a helpless shrug. 'But he can't be moved, so it's a case of crossing our fingers now and hoping for the best.'

'Where's Jimmy?' she asked, only now remembering that she'd sat the boy on a bed while she saw to the wounded children. She blinked hard, her vision blurred as she peered at the wall clock. That had been . . . Goodness, three hours ago.

'I sent him off with Nurse Ryder. She looked like

she needed a break.' He followed as she headed over to the sink to wash her own hands. 'As do you.'

'I'll rest when the work's finished.'

'Hey.' Lewis caught her by the arm as she swayed, her mind and body exhausted yet somehow still functioning on automatic. 'There's nobody left to treat. Take a half hour break with me. Nurse Hardy can keep an eye on the children.' He nodded to Harriet, who had arrived on shift while Rose was working. 'We'll be in the senior staff room if you need us, Nurse.'

After washing and drying her hands, Rose trailed wearily after him into the corridor, her head thick with fatigue. 'I should go up and check on Mrs Baxter. Lily, too. What a time she must have had, delivering a baby on her own . . . and in the middle of an air raid. She must be exhausted, poor girl.'

'Come and have a drink first,' he said softly. 'You've earned it. And Lily looked perfectly happy to me. I left her with her family so I doubt she'll welcome our intrusion at the moment.'

Rose nodded sleepily. It struck her that they had both called Nurse Fisher by her first name, Lily, and she had not protested nor even cared about the breach in her own strict protocols.

He ushered her into the staff room, where a small fire was burning. Dusk had fallen while she was working on the children, she realised, and the blackout curtains were up. The room was cosy and inviting, and someone had set a bottle of brandy on the table with several glasses.

Rose stumbled, collapsing into an armchair, too tired to remain on her feet a moment longer. He poured her a few fingers of brandy and handed her the glass. 'Here, this should warm you up.' That was when she realised she was shivering. Not with cold, but with shock. 'Go on, take a sip.'

'I hate brandy.'

'Don't ever let my grandfather hear you say that. This is his emergency bottle; he keeps it locked in Tom's cupboard precisely for occasions like this one.' He poured a small glass for himself and sat down opposite her, nursing it in his cupped hands and inhaling the fumes appreciatively. 'Bottoms up!'

She set the glass to her lips and took a quick gulp, then shuddered. 'Ugh.' But the fiery spirit did give her new strength. Her mind kept circling back to what had happened before the bomb dropped, fury slowly reasserting itself. 'Those Treverricks deserve to be in prison for child abuse. Did you get a proper look at Jimmy's legs?'

He nodded sombrely. 'Those bruises are at least a week to ten days old.'

'They have been beating him, and severely enough to leave marks. A boy that age!' Rose was so angry, she felt like finding the Treverricks right now and confronting them with their crime. 'I asked him which of them did it, but Jimmy was too scared to accuse either of them openly.'

'Maybe he'll tell us tomorrow. He's not under their roof anymore, and if I have anything to do with it, he won't be returned to them.' Lewis swallowed some brandy, and rubbed at his forehead. Rose studied him from under her lashes, noting how weary he looked. What a dreadful day they'd had. And it still wasn't over. 'What does he think will happen if he blabs?'

'I believe they may have threatened to wallop his friends too.'

'Jimmy said that?'

'Not in so many words,' she admitted. 'I was reading between the lines. But those Treverricks are monsters all right. They *claim* he was locked up because he had the measles, but I saw no sign of that.'

'Neither did I.'

'Plus, they kept him on bread and water for days, and had the poor child convinced his only possible escape would be to climb out of a high window.'

'And Jimmy was game enough to do it.' He raised his glass in a silent toast to the boy, and then gave a muffled groan as he sat back.

'Lewis, what is it? Are you hurt?'

'My hip, that's all. The one that was already dodgy. I fell badly on it, catching Jimmy earlier, and ever since . . .' Lewis finished the brandy in two quick gulps, his eyes shut tight, a frown dragging his brows together. Putting the empty glass to one side, he muttered, 'Damn thing hurts like hell.'

'Here, let me see,' Rose said hurriedly, getting up so fast that her head swam. 'Oops.' Somehow, she lost her balance and ended up falling across him. He caught her, bringing her down onto his lap, much to her embarrassment. 'Dear Lord . . . I'm so sorry. I must be more tired than I realised. Or else the brandy — '

'Forget all that,' he said thickly, and kissed her, his arms coming around her.

Rose thought of protesting, as she had done earlier. But her body was having none of it.

She kissed him back, her fingers clutching his short dark hair. If she was going to hell, she might as well do it properly. She had started today by breaking all the rules in going to the police behind Matron's back. She might as well finish it by betraying her sister's trust . . .

After Dr Lewis had finally left, declaring both mum and baby fit and healthy, Lily checked that Hazel was decent again, with an extra blanket drawn up over her tummy to keep her warm, then opened the door to Charlie, Alice, Aunty Vi and her gran.

They had all been waiting outside in the hallway without complaint, clearly shocked by the news that Hazel had given birth so quickly and with only Lily there to help her.

'Charlie, dearest,' Hazel sighed, holding her son close. 'I hope I didn't give you a fright when I didn't come down to the shelter. You must have been so worried.'

'I knew you'd be all right, Mum,' Charlie told her stoutly, and gave Lily an admiring glance, sticking his hands in the pockets of his trousers. 'You had Lily with you, didn't you? Besides, the bomb didn't fall on this building. It fell on an older part of the orphanage.'

'A bomb fell on the orphanage?' Lily was horrified. 'But Dr Lewis didn't say a word about that.'

Her Gran looked up from cradling the baby, who was now fast asleep, no doubt as exhausted as Lily felt. 'I expect he didn't want to upset you, love. You or Hazel.'

'That's awful news.' Hazel sat up gingerly. 'Was anyone hurt?'

Charlie hesitated, glancing back at Lily's Aunt Violet. 'Erm . . . '

Violet sat down on the bed next to Hazel and gave her hand a quick squeeze. 'Now don't fret, love. A few of the kids were hurt, but not seriously.'

'Poor little mites!' Hazel exclaimed.

'It was an old outbuilding they use for storage. Some of the men were talking about it downstairs. A few of the kids were sheltering in there when the bomb dropped. Hiding from the couple who run the orphanage, or so I heard.'

'What happened?' Hazel asked breathlessly.

'The whole place collapsed,' Charlie said, a little too enthusiastically. 'It's a right mess. I saw three kids covered in blood, and one of them — '

'Hush now, Charlie,' Aunty Vi said sharply, and drew him away. 'Your mum's got enough on her plate without worrying about that too.'

'But she asked!' he said sullenly.

Gran handed the baby back to Hazel with a smile. 'She's a real beauty,' she said softly, then turned to Charlie. 'How about we go and look at the conservatory again, give your mum a chance to rest up? I saw a wireless down there while we were being shown round yesterday.' Gran steered him out of the room, and took Alice along with her for good measure. 'Maybe there'll be a musical programme on that we can listen to. Come along, ducks.'

Once they were alone, Hazel begged to be told how the hurt children were faring. But Violet refused to answer, sitting beside her. 'Let's talk about you first. Dr Lewis said you might be here as long as a week, so he can keep an eye on you and the kiddie. Are you feeling all right? Is there anything I can bring you from home?'

'No need to put yourself out,' Hazel said. 'Though I'd be happier if I could see George. Will you let him know what's happened?'

Aunty Violet nodded sympathetically. 'I can ask to

use the telephone here and I'm sure Colonel Ryder will pass on the message to George. He might be able to come over first thing tomorrow, if he can be spared from his duties.'

'Thank you.' Hazel bit her lip. 'But how will you lot get back to Porthcurno, now I can't drive you? It's so late, and you'll need to be back in time for work tomorrow.'

'Charlie can drive us back, if you'll allow him.'

'Charlie? Are you sure?'

'I know he don't have a licence. But he's been learning six months now and he ain't a bad driver.' Aunty Violet hesitated. 'Not that I want to abandon you, love. But our Lily will do you and the baby proud.' She winked. 'That Dr Lewis is a bit of all right, ain't he?'

Hazel gave a gurgling laugh. 'You're so naughty.'

'Oh, I've an eye for a good-looking bloke. My Joe, for instance. That man's a proper dreamboat, just like in the pictures.' She glanced around at Lily proudly. 'Joe Postbridge and me, we're walking out together. Did Alice say?'

Lily grinned. 'She did mention it. I'm glad for you, Aunty Vi.'

After a little while, Charlie came back with Gran and Alice, with tales of Gran dancing about the conservatory to some big band music on the radio, and Aunty Violet went off, chuckling, to telephone the Colonel at Eastern House.

She came back, reporting, 'Mission accomplished!' and they all decided to head straight back to Porthcurno before the snow started to lay down thick, with Charlie at the wheel, agreeing to drive carefully, for once.

Lily went downstairs with them after a round of tearful farewells, so she could collect Hazel's things from the back of the old ambulance. Now, at least, her patient would have her own nightdress and washbag with her.

She kissed her aunt and gran goodbye, and gave Alice a hug too. 'You look after them for me,' she muttered in her sister's ear. 'You hear?'

Alice put her tongue out. 'Who died and made you queen of the universe?' she demanded, but laughed at Lily's expression. 'Of course I'll look after them, ninny head. Nobody else is going to do it, are they?' She hugged her back warmly. 'Say ta ta to Eva for us, would you? I've not seen her today.'

'You done a good job there with Hazel and her baby,' Gran told her approvingly. 'And here's a bit of advice,' she added, tapping her nose. 'Empty out a drawer, line it with a soft blanket to keep out the draught, and baby will be as snug in there as in a crib.'

'Thanks, Gran.'

Then they all drove off, Charlie waving excitedly out of the driver's window.

Lily stood on the steps in the chill winds until the old ambulance was out of sight, clutching Hazel's bag for all she was worth.

She had brought a new soul into the world today.

And, despite all her fears, perhaps she had found a new vocation.

39

Eva was sitting with Max in Atlantic Ward, holding his hand, while both of them watched the small boy wriggling around at the end of his bed, trying to get comfortable.

'If this is what it's like to be a parent,' Max said, 'I'd rather pass, thanks.'

'Our child would be very different,' Eva reassured him, then smacked at his hand when he went to pick up the newspaper he'd been reading. 'You can't read, Max,' she hissed, nodding towards the boy. 'We're meant to be looking after him.'

'No, *you* are meant to be looking after him. I'm a man. Men read the newspaper while women look after the children.'

'Is that so?' she asked ominously.

Max, about to give her another of his glib responses, seemed to catch the warning eye of Raymond in the bed opposite, and pushed aside the newspaper, smiling at her instead.

'Darling, how can I help you? I want to, obviously. But I'm stuck in this bed, and — '

'That's a whopper,' she interrupted him.

'Yeah, she's right, it is,' Jimmy said, suddenly perking up. He sat up and stared at them both. 'You told me the doctor said as how you'd never walk again, only then you proved everyone wrong by being able to wiggle your toes, and now you can get out of bed on your own anytime you like.'

'I didn't exactly say that,' Max protested.

Eva raised her eyebrows at him. 'You can get out of bed anytime you like? Let's see this miracle, then.'

'He's exaggerating. I said I could probably get out of bed on my own,' Max spluttered, then swore under his breath. 'Honestly, isn't there a room he can go to? It must be past his bedtime.'

'I don't have a bedtime,' Jimmy stated confidently.

'Now that is a whopper,' Eva told him, 'and a big one too. Your friend Sally told me you all have to be in bed for six-thirty at the orphanage.'

Jimmy blinked, and then picked at the sheet, his head bent. 'How . . . How is Sally?'

Sally was one of the young girls hurt in the bombing at the orphanage. Thankfully, she'd been relatively unharmed, only a few cuts and bruises. Eva had patched the girl up herself.

Since Matron had gone to visit her mother in Penzance, they were a little short-handed, and though Tom had offered to drive over to fetch her back, Rose had refused, saying they were well able to cope.

'Sally is going to be fine. She wasn't seriously hurt,' Eva reassured him, and saw his head come up, his eyes brightening in relief. 'I cleaned and bandaged her up and she was well enough to go back to the orphanage afterwards.'

Jimmy stiffened at that information, his eyes wary as he looked from her to Max. 'Will I have to go back too?'

'I don't know,' she admitted. 'But if you're staying here tonight, you'll need somewhere to sleep. Perhaps we should go and ask about a bed for you.' She got up and held out a hand to him. But he merely clung onto the sheets, clearly unwilling to leave the little

306

sanctuary he'd made for himself there. 'You can't sleep on Flight Lieutenant Carmichael's bed all night.'

'I'll be good. I won't make any noise, honest.'

'No, you won't, Max agreed firmly. 'Because you won't be there.' But his frown disappeared when he saw the boy's fear. 'Look, Jimmy, I freely admit to not being much of an expert on children. But I do know Nurse Ryder, and I've got to know Sister Gray quite well, too, over the past few months, and I can assure you, neither of those two ladies will allow you to return to the orphanage. Not while the Treverricks are in charge, at any rate. So you might as well go along with Nurse Ryder and find somewhere comfier to sleep than the end of my bed.' He gave the boy an encouraging smile. 'All right?'

Eva blew Max a kiss, and led the little boy back down the corridor to the senior staff room, where Dr Lewis had told her to take Jimmy once he was ready for bed. But she heard raised voices as they approached and found the door open.

Mr Treverrick was inside, arguing hotly with Rose and Dr Lewis. To her surprise, there was also a policeman in the room.

'How dare you barge in here at this time of night?' Rose was saying, her face flushed, her hair untidy.

'Ain't nobody barging, Miss,' the policeman replied, though his Cornish accent was so strong, it was difficult for Eva to completely understand him. 'I come up on account of the bomb, see? And Mr Treverrick here, he has every right to make a complaint against you, given what's happened.'

'There he is!' Mr Treverrick had spotted Eva and Jimmy in the doorway. 'Right, I'm taking that boy back where he belongs.'

'No, you're not,' Rose said coldly.

'Now, Miss Gray, you don't have no right to stop him.' The policeman stood in her way, and Eva could tell that he didn't like Sister much. 'Legally, this boy's under his charge. Not yours.'

Rose turned on the policeman. 'And does his charge include beating the boy so badly, he has to be locked in his room for several weeks until the bruises have disappeared?'

'That's slander,' Mr Treverrick blustered. 'I'll have you up in court even for suggesting such a disgraceful thing.'

'Take a look at the boy's legs, Sergeant Pascoe,' Dr Lewis said calmly, and gestured for Eva to bring Jimmy into the room. Jimmy shrank back, trying to twist free of her hand, but the doctor smiled at him. 'It's all right, lad,' he said gently. 'Turn around and let us see the backs of your legs. The officer needs to know what kind of care you've been getting at the orphanage.'

Jimmy turned around, though Eva could feel him trembling. She squeezed his hand comfortingly, and gave him a wink.

'We'll soon have you out of here, don't worry,' she whispered.

The policeman bent to scrutinise Jimmy's bruises, then straightened slowly. 'Aye, well, that doesn't look good, I must admit.' He scratched his head, clearly reluctant to make a decision. 'I'm not sure it's enough to warrant taking the boy away though. Maybe he fell and hurt himself.'

'Sergeant Pascoe,' Dr Lewis said, in an authoritative voice, 'if I tell you that among the children I treated here tonight were several others who showed signs of bruising to the arms and legs, will that change your mind? And that's not all. One boy was so thin, his ribs were showing. I asked when he'd last eaten, and he said the Treverricks had taken away his meal privileges for three days after he'd made too much noise at bedtime. Apparently, it was not the first time they'd starved him — or the other children — as a punishment.'

'That's not true,' Mr Treverrick said quickly, a hunted look about him. 'That is, we do punish the children with loss of meals. But only for one day.'

'Oh, is that all?' Eva muttered, and saw his angry gaze flash in her direction.

'I'm taking that boy back with me,' Mr Treverrick insisted, picking up his hat, but the police sergeant intervened, his face reluctant.

'I don't think that would be a good idea, Fred,' he told Mr Treverrick in a warning tone. 'Doctor's right. Now a complaint's been made, there'll have to be a formal investigation. And while that's ongoing, young Jimmy will have to stay elsewhere.'

'This isn't a fit place for a child,' Mr Treverrick exploded. 'It's a convalescent home.'

'He can stay with me and my grandfather,' Dr Lewis said unexpectedly. 'We have two evacuee boys at the house already. They'll make Jimmy feel at home while this business is sorted out. And my housekeeper will make sure he's properly fed and watered.'

Sergeant Pascoe smiled grudgingly. 'That's generous of you, Dr Lewis.'

'It's the least I can do.'

Mr Treverrick was shown to the front door by Tom, who had been unobtrusively loitering in the corridor during this fracas, and the sergeant followed him out.

When they'd finally gone, Rose clapped her hands, her face lit up with a strange glowing joy. 'We did it,' she breathed. 'We finally got Jimmy out of that god-forsaken place.' She turned to the doctor. 'Thank you.'

Eva, watching the exchange, got the feeling that something had happened between them tonight. And about time too, she thought with an inner smirk. She fell back discreetly, talking to Jimmy instead, who was limp with fatigue but excited to be leaving with the doctor.

Dr Lewis waited until the coast was clear, and then shepherded Jimmy out into the chilly night, the boy almost drowning in his overcoat.

'I'll be back in one hour,' he told Eva and Rose at the door.

After the door closed behind him, Eva drew across the blackout curtain and looked at Rose in surprise.

'The doctor's coming back?' she queried. 'But he looks done in. I thought he was going home for the night.' Before Rose could respond, a high-pitched cry split the air from somewhere upstairs, and Eva spun in astonishment. 'What on earth's that?'

'That is Mrs Baxter's baby,' Rose said, leaning back wearily against the blackout curtain. 'She gave birth to a little girl during the air raid.'

'Oh my God. Poor Hazel. I wondered why she didn't come to the shelter with the others.' She frowned. 'But if she went into labour during the air raid, who on earth delivered the baby?'

'Nurse Fisher, I'm told.'

'*Lily?*'

Eva stared at Rose in horrified disbelief, a hand at her mouth, and then they both dissolved into helpless giggles.

Early the next morning, mother and baby were found a private room near the wards and left there to rest, the baby tucked up in a cosy, lined drawer just as Gran had advised while Hazel peered down at her, smiling sleepily.

'The old quarantine room,' Dr Lewis called it as he gave Hazel and her infant another postnatal check. 'Nobody should disturb you here, Mrs Baxter. Though if you need anything, just ring the little bell on the side table.' He ushered Lily out into the corridor and closed the door quietly behind him. 'Nurse Fisher, you look like you barely grabbed a wink all night.'

'I didn't,' Lily admitted sheepishly.

'Welcome to my life,' the doctor said with a grin, and patted her on the back. 'Look, you should take the morning off and rest instead. You'll be no good to Sister Gray in this state. And you can tell her I said so. Doctor's orders!' He glanced at his watch. 'One more errand to run this morning. Ah, well, no rest for the wicked.'

He left the hall and a moment later she heard the sound of his car departing.

Lily staggered outside to look at the dawn, the sun barely risen over a cold and misty Cornwall. There was still snow on the ground from last night. She stretched and yawned for a bit, and then sank down onto the top step despite the damp under her bottom, wrapping her arms about herself in the chill air.

She felt happier than she'd done in years. She had done something special, she thought. She had helped deliver a child, and now that baby was sleeping peacefully by her mother's side, and everything looked different to her.

The whole world had changed.

She'd always feared nursing was beyond her, finding it difficult to relate to patients at the convalescent home and deal with their needs. But perhaps that was simply because she had never considered *other* kinds of nursing. There was midwifery, after all. That was all about looking after pregnant ladies and helping them deliver and care for their babies. Perhaps she could do some training in that area when the war was over.

Lily started, hearing a car engine slow for the turn into the drive, and jumped up as George Cotterill's car swung into view.

'How is she, Lily?' George looked awful, his chin stubbly, his eyes bloodshot. 'I couldn't get away sooner. There was a blasted air raid about ten minutes after your aunt's call came in last night, and we were stuck in the tunnels for hours. Then the snow started to fall . . .'

'Come and see for yourself,' Lily said, smiling, and led him inside.

'Oh, George,' Hazel breathed on seeing him, and sat up in bed. She had fetched her baby from the makeshift crib and now held her out to him, her face aglow with pleasure and satisfaction. 'It's a girl. Look, isn't she adorable?' She paused, glancing past him to Lily in the doorway. 'I couldn't have done it without Lily. She was amazing.'

Lily closed the door with a shy smile and left them to it. She was so tired now she could barely stand, and she staggered up to bed like a drunk.

In the merciful silence of her bedroom, she kicked off her shoes, threw a blanket over the crumpled

312

sheets, and then flopped face-down on the bed without even bothering to remove her clothes. She felt bloody awful. Her ears were buzzing and her eyes were blurry.

But inside she was singing.

40

Rose was fifteen minutes late for her shift by the time
she'd struggled out of bed and got herself downstairs
the morning after the orphanage bombing. This late-
ness was unheard of, so she came in for some ribbing
from some of the patients.

She looked in on Mrs Baxter first, who was sleeping,
and nodded to the very correct-looking man seated
beside her, wearing a suit and cradling the new-born
baby in his arms. He introduced himself quietly as Mr
George Cotterill, Mrs Baxter's betrothed, and gladly
accepted Rose's offer of a cup of tea. She organised
that with one of the orderlies, and moved on with her
inspection.

The men who would normally have slept in St Ives
Ward had bunked up in Carbis and Atlantic Wards
for the night, either sharing beds or rolled up in blan-
kets on the floor. But clearly that situation could not
be allowed to continue. Their patients were supposed
to be convalescing at Symmonds Hall, not camping
out like Boy Scouts, as she told a harassed-looking
Nurse Stannard, who was pouring herself a cup from
the steaming tea urn. Displaced men were eating
breakfast on the floor or in the conservatory, and that
simply wouldn't do.

The children were all sitting on each other's beds
and chatting by the time she reached St Ives Ward
and swept in, clapping her hands.

'You noisy lot seem to be recovering,' Rose said
loudly as one boy dived back to his bed with a toothy

grin, his precautionary neck brace askew, 'otherwise you would hardly be scampering about in this excitable fashion.'

Only one child was not sitting up, and that was Harry, the boy whose head had suffered a nasty gash. But he was conscious, at least. She checked his chart — nurses had been keeping an eye on him by rota during the night — and was satisfied by what she saw. Nonetheless, she took his vital signs, and smiled down at him while taking his pulse, which was a little fast, but nothing out of the ordinary for a child.

'How are you feeling, Harry? Any more pain?'

He nodded. 'It hurts, Miss.'

'I'm Sister Gray,' she said, bending close to examine the bloodied bandage on his head. The blood was dried, at least, not fresh, and the boy's colour was much healthier than last night, when she'd very much feared they might lose him. 'But you can call me Rose,' she relented.

'I like Rose. That's a nice name. Like the flower.'

She popped a clean thermometer in his mouth. 'Keep still for a moment and no talking.' She counted silently, amused by his wide-eyed stare, then checked his temperature. It was normal, which meant no infection or inflammation. 'Goodness, you're practically all better.'

'Does that mean I have to go back to the orphanage today?'

Rose studied him. 'You get to stay here a little longer. Would you like that?' When he nodded silently, she smiled at his pleased expression and tucked the boy back under his covers. 'In that case, you'd better get some more rest.'

'Don't I get breakfast?' He was looking wistfully at

the other children, who were tucking into a hot meal provided by Cook.

'Not until the doctor has given you the all-clear, I'm afraid.'

Rose straightened at the sound of her name being called in an angry tone, and turned to find Matron had entered the ward.

'Sister Gray,' she repeated coldly, 'had you forgotten that I wished to speak to you first thing this morning?'

'Of course not, Matron.' Rose followed her out of the ward and down towards Matron's personal office. 'I'm sure you must have seen; we had a bomb fall on part of the orphanage yesterday. Children were wounded and a rearrangement of the wards had to take place to accommodate them. Circumstances have been difficult.'

'Tom explained everything to me when I arrived this morning. A most unfortunate situation. We must thank God nobody was killed.'

Matron ushered Rose into her office and closed the door. She sat behind her desk and Rose stood straight before her, hands clasped behind her back. Matron kept no chairs in her office, except for her own; she only ever brought staff in there to give them a trimming, and seemed to prefer making her nurses stand while they were reprimanded.

'So, let me see. I returned to the Hall at seven this morning, completed my rounds, spoke to the children, and then came here to wait for you. But you did not appear.' Her tone was acidic. 'I fail to see why a bomb falling yesterday means you are unable to tell the time today, Sister Gray.'

'I apologise, Matron.'

'There is also a female in this convalescent home

who appears to have given birth here, and is accompanied by a man who is neither her husband nor her brother.' Matron tapped a fingernail on the desk, glaring at her. 'Has Symmonds Hall changed ethos while I was away? Have we become a maternity hospital now?'

'Mrs Baxter is a friend of Nurse Ryder's and was visiting yesterday. She went into premature labour during the air raid. Under the circumstances, I didn't feel I could usher her out of the door.'

'I would have done,' Matron said sharply. 'The cottage hospital is a far better place for the woman. Especially given her dubious marital status.'

'The birth was over by the time we came out of the shelter, and by then Tom was already bringing in the wounded children. There was simply no time to worry about such considerations. Besides, Mrs Baxter is a widow. The child was her late husband's. I'm told he was killed in action earlier this year.'

Matron harrumphed under her breath. 'And the gentleman with her? I trust he didn't attend the birth.'

'He arrived this morning, he told me. A Mr Cotterill, her betrothed.'

'She's already engaged to another man?' Her thin brows shot up. 'Mrs Baxter doesn't waste much time, does she?'

Rose stared hard at the row of porcelain figures on the shelf behind Matron's desk, and tried not to let her distaste for the woman show.

'I'm also led to understand,' Matron said, 'that you defied my orders, spoke to the police yesterday, and then later removed that boy Jimmy from the orphanage. He was not harmed by the bomb blast, I take it?'

It seemed Tom or one of the other nurses was a tattle-tale, Rose thought.

Rose told her shortly, 'Jimmy had been locked into his room during an air raid. In trying to reach safety, he nearly fell to his death.'

'Good grief.'

'Besides which, Dr Lewis has supported my case for removing him from the orphanage. The boy has been starved and severely beaten. We believe that was why he was kept hidden away,' she added, looking directly at Matron in an attempt to appeal to her humanity. 'To conceal what had been done to him.'

Matron said nothing, but her mouth was a thin line.

Briefly, she told Matron about the other children, the bruises and the starvation, and hoped she was getting through to the woman. 'I know you believe that discipline is good for the young. But Jimmy is only eight years old. Whatever his misdemeanours, no child deserves to be beaten and starved for them.'

'I can see you feel you are on the side of the angels where this boy is concerned, Sister Gray. But there is still the matter of your insubordination towards me. I expressly forbade you to get involved. Nonetheless, you went to the police behind my back, and I'm told you also had some kind of altercation with Mr Trever-rick last night, within the home itself, disturbing the peace and quiet of our patients.'

The door behind her opened, but Rose did not look around.

'If you are unhappy with my behaviour, Matron, despite what I have told you in my defence, then I must regretfully tender my resignation immediately.'

'Resign?' The deep tones of Dr Edmund made her turn, startled. 'You shall do no such thing, my dear

Sister Gray. Quite out of the question. Nurses of your calibre and experience don't grow on trees, you know.'

'Dr Edmund!' Matron had jumped up, looking flustered. 'Whatever are you doing here? I thought you were on home rest for at least another six months.'

'Oh, fiddle to that.' The old doctor strolled in, looking ridiculously healthy for a man who had recently suffered a heart attack. 'I came to see this boy who got his head bashed in during that bombing yesterday. My grandson drove me up. Skulls have always been my speciality. And I also heard that Nurse Fisher delivered a baby here yesterday.' His smile beamed. 'What a delightful thing! I intend to convey my congratulations to the mother, and of course, to young Lily herself. Nothing like bringing a child into the world to make you feel a sense of hope. Especially in wartime.'

'Oh, quite,' Matron said hurriedly.

'And we have a new addition to my own household. Charming young chap, gets on with our two evacuees like a house on fire.'

'I beg your pardon?' Matron looked confused.

'Dr Lewis took Jimmy home to stay with him last night,' Rose explained, and was gratified to see a blush on Matron's cheeks as she realised the impossibility of her situation.

'I see.' Matron put a hand on Dr Edmund's arm, smiling up at him in a conciliatory fashion. 'Well, how lovely. I only hope these boys won't tire you out. You must have quite a houseful now.'

'On the contrary, they keep me young. Always asking questions, taking an interest in the world. And Mrs Delaney does the housework, so it's really no bother.' Dr Edmund winked at Matron. 'You must come to tea and meet them one day.' Then he turned towards the door, where Rose could see Lewis hovering in the corridor. 'It's good to be back. I should like to see this new-born baby first. Then a pot of tea with you, Matron, while we discuss my return to work. And Lewis is going to show me this boy with the head wound.'

The old doctor and Matron headed off down the corridor together.

Rose turned to Lewis in astonishment. 'Is Dr Edmund really well enough to be here? I'm grateful to him for getting me off the hook — the way he handles Matron is superb — but he needs to look after his heart.'

'When I told him what had happened yesterday, he was itching to come back. I tried to stop him, but you know my grandfather. Stubborn as an old goat.' His smile faded as he gazed down into her face. 'Rose, about last night — '

'We shouldn't have let it happen.'

'That wasn't what I meant. Maybe it was wrong. Here, at work.' He ran a hand through his hair, looking frustrated. 'But that bomb dropping so close to the Hall . . . It showed me what's really important in my life. And that's you.'

She buried her face in her hands. 'Lewis, I can't . . . '

'It's too late. I've already written to Elsie, breaking off our engagement, and handed the letter to Mrs Delaney for posting. This is my responsibility, Rose, and I won't shirk it.'

Rose shuddered, terrified into silence by what he'd done. Essentially, she was stealing a man from her own sister. Never mind that Elsie had stolen him from her first. Her possessive sister wouldn't see it in those terms. What would Elsie say when she received his letter? Would she ever forgive them?

'But now that's done and I'm a free man again,' he continued, studying her uncertainly, 'dare I assume you have feelings for me? That you wish to take this further?'

She gave a croaky laugh at that foolish question, her shoulders shaking. 'Oh, Lewis! For a doctor, your observational skills leave much to be desired.'

He began to say something, but they were interrupted by Lady Symmonds, who appeared at the end of the corridor, accompanied by Tom, who must have let her in.

'Sister Gray,' she called imperiously. 'Ah, and Dr Lewis too. The very people I need to see. I have been speaking to Tom and he's told me the truly appalling things that have been happening right under my nose at the orphanage. It's downright wicked. You were quite right to explore further, Sister Gray. We ought to have looked higher than the ground floor.' Her sharp gaze interrogated Rose's face. 'You were a resident there yourself as a child, I seem to recall.'

'That's right,' Rose said, pulling herself together. 'Before the Treverricks' time. It was never a wonderful place, but I was grateful for a roof over my head, and at least we were properly fed and cared for.'

'Quite so. That's why I've sacked the Treverricks and — '

'I beg your pardon?'

'Oh, did I not say? I've told them both to pack their bags and be out by tonight, and have asked my lawyer to advertise for a replacement.' Lady Symmonds mimed dusting her hands off. 'Good riddance to bad rubbish, don't you agree?'

Rose put a hand to her mouth, shocked.

'In the meantime,' Lady Symmonds continued, 'some of the local ladies' circle in St Ives will be taking turns to look after the children during the day. And until suitable new directors can be found, I shall move into the building myself, with Sonya, so they're not alone at night.' Lady Symmonds raised her brows at Rose's blank astonishment. 'No need to look at me like that, young lady. I know how to tell a bedtime story as well as anyone else, I daresay.'

'I–I'm sure you do,' Rose stammered.

Lewis gave the old lady an incredulous smile. 'I think that's absolutely marvellous of you, Lady Symmonds. What a brick you are!'

'I will assume that is a compliment and say thank you.' Lady Symmonds smiled graciously and then turned, seeing the tall, middle-aged woman who had wandered into the home, carrying a crate before her. 'Ah, there's Sonya.' She raised a hand to her companion. 'I've had her look out the toys and books my grandson loved as a boy. We're taking them over to the children straightaway. They seem to have so few toys. Well, goodbye. I'll see you both at the Christmas party.'

★ ★ ★

When her ladyship had gone, Lewis's smile slowly faded. 'That's wonderful news. You must be pleased. But I suppose it means Jimmy can go back. He'll be safe with the Treverricks gone.' His face was troubled. 'Jimmy and my grandfather hit it off straightaway — the boy's a real live wire. It would be a shame to send him back.'

Rose was finding it hard to breathe, she was so happy. Happy and scared at the same time. Everything was going to change. New people in charge of the orphanage, Jimmy safe at last, and Lewis looking at her with new emotion in his eyes. Yet there was still a furious Elsie to face, and the war was raging out there, the threat of bombs and an enemy invasion growing ever more menacing.

'You should ask Jimmy what he wants to do,' she pointed out.

Lewis looked deep into her eyes. 'I'll do that as soon as I get home. But what do you want, Rose Gray?'

She clasped both hands to her cheeks, aware that she was blushing. 'I don't know,' she whispered. 'I really don't know.'

41

'Bloody hell,' Lily said anxiously, watching as Eva leant forward precariously to balance a shiny star on top of the Christmas tree. 'If you fall off that ladder, I'll never forgive myself. I told you I should go up there.'

Eva laughed, shaking her head. 'I'm fine, don't be such a wet blanket. Now hand me another strand of the gold tinsel. I might as well decorate the top of the tree while I'm up here.'

She held up the tinsel and Eva bent for it, setting off wolf whistles from around the ward as her uniform skirt hiked up an inch. 'Oi, you cheeky lot,' Lily exclaimed, looking around angrily. 'No more of that. Or there'll be no Christmas punch at the party. And that's a promise.'

'Sorry, ladies,' one of the patients who'd whistled called out. 'Didn't mean to cause offence, but it is the festive season. We got carried away.'

The others grinned.

Eva wound the tinsel about the top, set a few more baubles among the highest branches, and then came down the ladder.

'Pay no attention to them,' she told Lily, seeming unbothered by the men's attention. 'Where's Jimmy? I thought he was supposed to be helping decorate the tree?'

At that moment, Jimmy burst back into the ward, making what was clearly supposed to be the noise of a spitfire, and tilting his arms like wings, a length of Lily's homemade paper chains hanging out of the back of his trousers.

Eva grabbed him and disengaged the paper chains, shaking her head. 'You're meant to be putting these about the ward, Jimmy, not trying to rip them to shreds.'

'That was my smoke trail,' Jimmy explained, unbothered by her scold. 'I'm on fire.' He stopped and blinked up at the huge Christmas tree, now decked out with last year's tinsel and baubles. 'Blimey, that's a belter of a tree!'

'Hey, language!' Lily propelled Jimmy back to the ward door. 'You're no help at all. Matron will be doing her rounds soon, and we'll all catch it if she finds you running wild about the place again. Isn't it about time to beg yourself another biscuit from Cook?' She ruffled his hair. 'Go on, hop it!'

Eva stood back, admiring the tree. 'He's right though. It is a belter!'

'I like Jimmy, I really do, but he does get underfoot.' Lily began to tidy away the box of unused tinsel and paper chains. Some of them could be used in the other wards or the conservatory. 'I thought he'd be going back to live at the orphanage now the Treverricks have gone.'

'I think he asked to stay on with the two evacuees at Dr Lewis's house,' Eva said, and spotted a lost bauble that had rolled away under a bed. 'For the moment anyway.' She used a broom handle to knock it out, and then hooked it on the tree with the others. 'I expect it's more comfortable sharing with two kids than twenty.'

'I hadn't thought of it like that.'

'Besides, it's nice for Harry to have some company

in the daytime.' Eva swept the floor around the tree, and then put away the broom. Harry's head wound was much improved, and there was no more sign of swelling, but Dr Edmund had still decided to keep him at the home until after the Christmas party. 'Maybe Jimmy will go back after the party, when Harry is finally discharged.' She looked round curiously at Lily, who had sat down at the nurses' station and was checking the medications log. 'Talking of discharged patients, have you heard from Danny yet?'

Private Daniel Orde had been discharged to his family home the week before, but had asked if he might come back specially for the evening of the Christmas party. Matron, in an unusually charitable mood, had apparently approved this request. Eva knew something had gone on between Lily and Danny, but had never pushed for more information than the young nurse wished to give.

However, sometimes when the two of them were in the conservatory with Max, working with him on strength-building exercises, and a romantic tune came on the radio . . . Oh, then Lily's face would change, and she would look wistful, staring out at the wind-swept woodlands with a faraway expression.

Now Lily looked merely flustered. 'Of course not. Why would Danny write to me? We're not sweethearts, you know.'

'Sorry, my mistake.' Eva swiftly changed the subject, realising that she had touched a sore point. 'Are you all ready for the party tomorrow night? I heard the Ministry forked up some money, and we might actually get turkey sandwiches.'

'Who told you that?' Lily's eyes widened. 'There won't be much in the way of turkey at Christmas,' she

326

added in a low voice so the patients wouldn't hear, 'let alone at our party. Better watch what you say or you'll start a bleedin' riot.'

'Fish paste all round, is it?'

'Meat substitutes,' Lily said darkly, and shuddered. 'Like we had at the dance in Porthcurno.'

'I'm sure none of us plebs will notice,' Eva said with a wink.

'With tinned fruit and custard for afters.'

'Sounds heavenly.'

Lily eyed her with suspicion. 'You taking the mickey?'

'Goodness, of course not.' Eva hugged her warmly. 'You've done the most amazing job, Lily. I've got to hand it to you. This party's going to be a blast and a half.'

'Well, I couldn't have got the musicians sorted out without you. And the kids from the orphanage are going to sing some carols to kick us off.'

'I can't wait. And neither can Max.'

Lily gave her a sly smile. 'You and Max are very close these days. You need to watch that or Matron will have you in the dungeons for fraternising with a patient.'

'No, she won't,' Eva said with a half-laugh, and then bit her lip. 'Look, can you keep a secret?' she whispered, checking nobody else was listening.

'Cross my heart and hope to die,' Lily whispered, turning towards her with curiosity burning in her eyes. 'What is it?'

'We're getting hitched. Me and Max. But it's still a secret.'

'Congratulations!' Lily looked enchanted, clasping her hands together. 'How wonderful for you. So he finally asked you to marry him?'

Under that innocent stare, Eva felt warmth in her cheeks and couldn't hide her embarrassment. 'Well, not quite.'

'Sorry?'

'He cleared the proposal with my father, which was delightfully old-fashioned of him, but he hasn't actually asked me yet. I think he plans to pop the question once he can walk with a stick. But who knows when that will be? Before Christmas, I hope.' She crossed her fingers, though in truth she was a little concerned. Max could move his feet now, but so far had not been able to put any weight on them. 'As soon as we're married, I'll be leaving Symmonds Hall.'

'Oh no! Why?'

'Because married woman can't be nurses, silly. It's against the rules.' Eva grinned at her shocked expression. 'So I can blow a raspberry to Matron on that day and do whatever I like.'

They both giggled, imagining Matron's horrified face . . .

The door to the ward banged open, and they both straightened, expecting to be reprimanded by Matron for chatting on duty. Eva hurriedly wiped the smile from her face while Lily shut the medications log and stood up, tidying her uniform.

Except it wasn't Matron.

It was Rose.

'And what exactly have you two nurses been up to?' Sister asked in a peremptory tone, folding her arms across her chest as she studied the Christmas tree, which was wreathed in shimmering tinsel and studded with bright baubles. 'This doesn't seem terribly industrious to me.'

'Nurse Fisher and I have been decorating the tree in advance of the festivities.' Eva felt disappointed at Rose's distant manner; she wondered if it was hostilities as usual between them now that Sister Gray had got her way over the orphanage. 'Nothing wrong with that, is there?'

'Only one thing. You appear to have missed a bauble,' Rose pointed out coolly, pointing to a shiny red ball which had somehow found its way under another of the patients' beds. Only this one was right at the back, against the wall.

'Oh, not another escapee,' Eva said, and this time got down on her hands and knees to retrieve it. By the time she stumbled back to her feet, her apron was askew, her face felt flushed, and a few stray strands of fair hair were dangling out from under her lopsided cap. 'Oops.'

Rose looked at her dishevelled appearance, and her lips twitched.

Lily bit her lip, her eyes wide.

'Allow me,' Rose said, plucking the red bauble from her hand and carrying to the tree. She hesitated. 'I think it should go . . . there.' Attaching it to a branch, deep among a sea of gold tinsel, she glanced round at them. 'What do you think, Lily? Too much?'

Eva's jaw dropped at her use of Lily's first name. Sister Gray was usually so strict about the use of titles only on the ward. Was chilly Rose thawing at last?

'No,' Lily said encouragingly. 'It looks perfect.'

'Hmm, let's see.'

Rose took a few steps back, her head tilted, as though to view the whole tree from crepe-covered pot to sparkling star.

Eva came to stand beside her right shoulder, and Lily, smiling shyly, appeared on Rose's other side.

Standing in a row, looking up, they admired the Christmas tree together.

'Not bad,' Rose said after a moment's serious consideration, and nodded. 'Not bad at all.' To their amazement, she patted each of them approvingly on the shoulder. 'Excellent work, Lily, Eva. I'd say Symmonds Hall is almost ready for its Christmas party.'

'Look at you three lovely ladies,' Sergeant Bottomley said with a grin, as he was pushed past them in his wheelchair by Mary Stannard. 'You remind me of my three sisters. They were always up to some mischief too!'

And everyone laughed.

★ ★ ★

About an hour later, Eva was boiling some medical instruments in the nurses' washroom when Rose came in and stopped on the threshold, staring at her.

Eva looked at her curiously in the mirror, wondering why she seemed so uncertain. 'Did you need me for something else, Sister?'

'Ah, Eva,' Rose said hesitantly, and then bit her lip. 'Yes, erm . . . '

Eva turned off the heat under the vat of boiling instruments and carefully washed her hands before turning to face the door. The two of them felt like friends now, so she wasn't worried that she might be in trouble. But her brows twitched together and she felt oddly troubled inside. It wasn't like Sister Gray to

330

behave like a novice around her.

'What is it, Rose?' she asked, drying her hands on a towel. 'You look funny. What's the matter?'

Rose grimaced. 'To be honest, I don't know if I should tell you. It may be a secret, I'm not sure.'

'What may be a secret? What are you talking about?'

But Rose fell silent.

'Look,' Eva said in her forthright way, 'you've let the cat out of the bag, coming in here with that mysterious look on your face. No point trying to pretend otherwise. So come on, spill the beans. What's all this about?'

'It's your pilot . . . Flight Lieutenant Carmichael.'

'Max?' Eva felt winded, as though her heart had stopped. 'What . . . What about him?'

'I think you should come with me,' Rose said.

Without another word, Sister Gray left the nurses' washroom, and Eva, her heart thudding erratically now, followed her down the corridor. They did not turn into Atlantic Ward, however, but made for the conservatory instead, where the men often gathered to listen to the wireless and to play board games.

It had been snowing again outside, just a smattering, but the conservatory was steamed up. Eva could see a crowd of patients inside, some of them calling out rowdily, others clapping and grinning.

But when she would have gone into the room, Rose stopped her.

'Wait,' she whispered. 'Just watch.'

Perplexed, Eva studied Rose's face, but still couldn't work out what was going on. So she turned to stare through the misty glass door instead.

Inside, the crowd parted momentarily, and she

could just make out Max, in dressing gown and slippers, standing upright and gripping the metal walking frame Dr Lewis had brought up to the hall for him a few days before.

'Oh my goodness!' Eva gasped.

Max was standing on his own two feet; for the first time since the bombing, she felt sure.

'He might fall and hurt himself,' she said, instinctively afraid for him.

Again, her hand shot to the door handle. And again, Rose stopped her, this time putting an arm about her shoulder in a reassuring way.

'Wait,' she repeated, nodding towards the door.

Eva leant close to the glass, watching in apprehension as Max clung to the metal walking frame. His face was determined, his jaw set hard. She knew how much it must be costing him to carry his own weight like that, with his legs barely working yet . . .

Behind him stood Dr Edmund, patting him on the back and exhorting him loudly, 'Keep going, man!'

As Eva watched in astonishment, her flight lieutenant dragged one slippered foot along a few inches, and then another, and jerked the frame forward another step.

It took a few seconds, then she realised what she was witnessing.

He was walking! Really, truly walking . . .

Eva gave a heartfelt sob, calling out, 'Max! Oh, Max!' After everything they had both been through, she did not know whether to laugh or cry. But happy tears spilled down her cheeks as she pushed the handle and stumbled into the conservatory, the patients hurriedly making way for her as Max looked up with a grin and their eyes met . . .

'So, what do you say, Miss Ryder?' he asked, a little breathless. 'To me making an honest woman of you, I mean?'

42

As the children standing beside the vast Christmas tree launched into the final verse of 'Ding Dong Merrily On High!', Lady Symmonds turned to Lily, her face wreathed in a smile, and clasped her hands tight.

'Dearest girl,' she said in a quavering voice, 'I cannot praise you highly enough. These little angels . . . How their sweet voices bring tears to my eyes. This is the best Christmas party I have ever attended, war or no war. Your decorations are magnificent. The band had my feet tapping earlier, and I can tell you, that doesn't happen often at my age. And the food has been inspired.'

'Wait until you taste the Christmas cake,' Lily muttered. She had helped make it and knew how few traditional ingredients had made it into the mix.

'What was that, dear?'

But luckily her ladyship's attention had been drawn away by Cook carrying in the first bowls of tinned fruit with custard. Her paste sandwiches had gone down surprisingly well with a mug of strong tea.

The children had all brought their own home-made paper hats, the product of many hours' work, and some to spare for the staff too. Lily had a princess's pointed hat instead of her usual starched cap, and Sister Gray was sombrely wearing a silver creation with tassels that looked suspiciously like they'd been stolen off a cushion.

Everyone devoured the tinned fruit, chatting above the carol singing, and then the empty bowls were collected while the children performed a touching nativity scene that even had some of the patients wiping away a tear.

Afterwards, Dr Edmund tapped a spoon against his bowl to get everyone's attention, and conversation swiftly died away, all heads turning.

'Three cheers for Cook and her wonderful Christmas fare,' Lady Symmonds called out, and everyone applauded Cook, who looked suitably pleased and embarrassed at the same time.

'And bravo to Nurse Fisher,' Dr Edmund added loudly, raising a glass in her direction, 'who organised this party for us. We owe you a debt of gratitude.'

Everyone in St Ives Ward clapped and cheered her, and some of the assembled men whistled and stamped their feet, until Lily could hardly think for the ruckus.

'Speech!' Mary Stannard yelled from the back, and then burst into giggles. Lily rather suspected she had been on the punch.

But the call was taken up by Dr Lewis and some of the patients too.

'Speech! Speech!'

Lily was horrified. She turned to Sister Gray in dismay. 'I didn't prepare anything. I wasn't told there'd be a speech.'

'Just be yourself,' Sister told her, and pushed her forward.

Lily looked about at all the expectant faces watching her as the ward settled into quiet anticipation — a few people whispering, others laughing — and she panicked.

She couldn't think of a single bloody thing to say!

Then she saw Hazel Baxter grinning from her seat beside the Christmas tree, newborn babe in her arms, and George Cotterill standing behind them, and that put new heart into her.

On the edge of the crowd were Eva and Max, smiling at each other, love in their eyes. He was still in his wheelchair for now, but everyone was talking about how he'd managed a few steps with a walking frame, and had finally asked her to marry him right in front of Dr Lewis and all the other patients.

Eva had said yes, of course.

Then there was Harriet, drinking a cup of punch, who'd shyly asked Lily's advice tonight about a man she'd been walking out with recently. And her only seventeen!

And over by the door was Private Danny Orde, who'd been medically discharged to his parents' home, yet had come back specially for the party. He had kept a respectful distance so far, but she really ought to speak to him before he left for good. It wouldn't be fair to leave the poor lad thinking she'd rejected him because of his injuries.

Then there was Sister Gray, whom she'd caught secretly kissing Dr Lewis under the mistletoe this morning, and who seemed to hold everything together on the wards without ever once raising her voice. She seemed happy too.

And Matron, who could be a difficult person to like at times, but who was clearly in love with old Dr Edmund, yet couldn't quite bring herself to admit it. There was hope for her yet.

Finally, there were the children from next door, some fidgeting and staring, others sitting

336

cross-legged around the tree, orphans and evacuees alike waiting hopefully for their presents. *Little angels*, Lady Symmonds had called them. And maybe they were, for they had made the old lady sparkle tonight, her hair dressed with tinsel as she tapped out the dance tunes with her feet and cane.

'I think we all owe each other a great big thank you,' Lily said, nervous at first but growing in confidence as she spoke. 'For friendship, for being there for one another when needed, and for realising everyone has a part to play. We certainly wouldn't get very far on our own, that's for sure. I wasn't alone in putting this party together. I had help from Cook, and Sister Gray, and Eva — I mean, Nurse Ryder — and Tom. And Lady Symmonds, of course, who made sure we had the funding from the Ministry. And all the kiddies who helped make party hats and paper chains, and who decked the wards with decorations.' Lily stopped, not sure what else to say. Then Dr Lewis put a glass of punch in her hand, and she raised it in a toast. 'Merry Christmas to us all!' she said in a ringing voice. 'And Merry Christmas to all the men and women fighting for our country tonight!'

Everyone shouted, 'Merry Christmas!' and those who had drinks raised them.

★ ★ ★

'Well done,' Eva said later, coming to give her a kiss on the cheek. 'That was a marvellous speech. My father couldn't have given a better one, and he's led troops into battle.'

Lily grinned at that compliment, though she didn't quite believe it. It was hard to remember how much in awe of Eva Ryder she'd been once, a posh girl who'd been to finishing school and seemed to know everything. Now she counted her as a good friend, and not too plummy at all.

'You'll be seeing your dad soon, won't you?'

'Not long now. I've been given a three-day Christmas pass to go home. Will you be coming back to Porthcurno too?'

Lily nodded. 'Same as you, back here for the twenty-seventh.'

The band was playing again, a lovely wistful tune by Vera Lynn, 'We'll Meet Again.' She could see Stuart Shrubsole with the other musicians he'd brought, scraping away on his fiddle with an intense expression, ginger beard glinting under the lights. The woman singing the lyrics was very good, though not in Vera Lynn's league, of course.

Like others around the ward, Lily sang along to the lovely tune too, thinking fondly of her aunt and gran, and her sister, too. She only wished she knew where her father was this Christmas, whether Ernest Fisher was still alive or had perished somewhere abroad.

It made Lily so sad to think of her daddy out there, unable to contact her, not even at Christmas, perhaps wounded or in a prisoner of war camp. Even that fate seemed preferable to imagining him dead, because if he was alive, there was still hope she might see him again one day. She'd already lost her mother to this horrible war. She didn't want to lose her father too.

'We must travel home together.' There was a bloom in Eva's cheeks. 'My father's sending a car. I'm taking Max back with me to meet him.'

'Gosh, thank you.'

'I see your Danny has turned up tonight. I wasn't expecting to see him again.'

'He's not my Danny,' Lily said with dignity.

'I hope he knows that. Because he's coming over.' Eva lowered her voice. 'Do you want me to get rid of him?'

Lily took a deep breath. 'No, I need to speak to him. Might as well be now.' As Eva melted discreetly away into the crowd, she turned to face Danny with a cool smile. 'Hello, Private Orde.'

'Oh, we're back to Private now, are we?' Danny sighed and stuck his hands in his trouser pockets. 'You don't need to worry I'm going to make another pass at you. I tried to see you before I was discharged to apologise, but . . . ' He stopped and made a face. 'Look, I was an ass and I'm sorry. The truth is, I was a little lonely and just wanted a kiss. I didn't mean to upset you. Am I forgiven?'

The local musicians had changed tempo, playing a cheerier big band song. Kids were jogging about together, giggling and falling over. Matron and Dr Edmund took to the floor, moving at a dignified snail's pace, and several other couples followed them. Private Fletcher, whose lungs were much recovered, whirled Eva about to the music, grinning at Max's annoyed frustration from the sidelines. And Rose and Dr Lewis were dancing discreetly behind the Christmas tree, with only Jimmy and some of the other kids as their audience.

The sight of Rose dancing with Dr Lewis filled her with joy, especially as Eva had told her it was a secret wish of hers to get them together at the party. Though, as far as she knew, Rose's sister was still engaged to the doctor.

339

Oh, what a muddle everything became when people started to fall in love . . .

'I suppose so,' Lily told him with an effort, her eyes still on the dancers.

'Would you like to dance?' he asked tentatively.

'I would, as it happens,' she admitted after a moment's thought. 'But don't read anything into it. It's Christmas, that's all.'

'Understood,' Danny agreed, and swept her into a whirling dance that left her breathless and giddy.

When the music ended, he brought her back to a standstill but didn't immediately release her, his gaze on her. She looked up into his face, so oddly handsome and yet scarred, and wished there was something she could say or do to make him feel better. But one thing she'd learned since coming to Symmonds Hall was that there was often no way to make a situation 'better'. Sometimes, you just had to make do with what you'd got.

'Thank you,' she said politely, and took a step back. 'That was fun.'

He smiled a little sadly, and let go of her hands.

'Wait,' she said impulsively, as he turned away. 'It wasn't you, Danny. I wasn't scared of you in the woods,' she blurted out hurriedly, before she could change her mind.

He frowned, looking back at her. 'What, then?'

Briefly, in a halting voice, Lily told him about her uncle's attack on the farm, and how it still haunted her. His face darkened, but he did not interrupt. When she had finished, he nodded slowly.

'He must have hurt you very deeply.' He looked angry on her behalf. 'That swine!'

'It's over now,' Lily told him, her chin up. 'I don't

want to think about it anymore. Or him. But I needed you to know what happened that day. That it wasn't you. It was me.'

'It wasn't this face, you mean?' Danny asked huskily, tapping his burnt ridges.

'No,' she said honestly.

He inclined his head, looking almost relieved. 'Thank you for telling me that. I know what it must have cost you. And it won't go any further. God bless you, Lily.'

And with that, Danny turned and walked away.

Behind her, the children began to shriek with delight, jumping up and down, and clapping their hands. Lily turned, exhaling slowly, and saw Santa Claus heading across the ward to the Christmas tree, a bulging red sack over his shoulder.

'Ho ho ho,' Santa boomed, and swung his sack down onto the floor. 'Who's been good this year, then?'

'Me, me, me!' the children all cried earnestly.

Jimmy too was shouting, 'Me, me, Santa, I've been good!' with all the rest, flushed and excited.

The boy looked so happy, Lily thought, and she smiled to see him receive a gift from Santa. His face was intent as he unwrapped the present, revealing a harmonica, which he instantly set to playing, a wild cacophony of notes to accompany the other children's shouts of wonder.

Sister Gray had come to stand beside her, also watching Jimmy.

'Santa seems vaguely familiar,' she remarked, nodding to the white-bearded figure in red with his oddly stout middle and skinny legs, who had now begun doing the rounds of the patients, handing out letters and parcels from home, pouches of tobacco and other small gifts arranged by the senior staff, all accompanied by great guffaws and, 'Ho ho ho's!'

'Tom,' Lily whispered.

'Dr Edmund is usually our Santa. But I doubt his health would have allowed it this year, and Tom is an excellent substitute. Though how on earth did he come by all that stuffing round his middle?'

'Two pillows tied together. My idea.'

'Of course.' Rose laughed, her face suddenly relaxing. 'You know, I don't recall ever enjoying a Christmas party this much before.' She touched Lily on the arm. 'It must be the good company.'

Everyone did seem to be having a good time, Lily thought, looking about the crowded ward with satisfaction. The band had started to play again, patients were opening letters or tucking into the wafer-thin slices of Christmas cake doing the rounds, and the children were playing with their presents.

'It must be,' Lily agreed, and yet secretly found herself wishing for home and family. Not long now, she told herself. 'Merry Christmas, Rose.'

'Merry Christmas, Lily.'

A slight commotion at the door made Lily turn in surprise, frowning to see what was happening. Was there something she had forgotten?

'What on earth is it?' Rose asked at her shoulder, standing on tiptoe as she struggled to see above the heads of the patients.

Then she fell silent, and Lily saw how pale her cheeks had turned.

'Are you all right, love?' Lily asked her, concerned.

But Rose shook her head, her gaze fixed on the woman who had just walked in.

She was about five foot in stature, same as Rose, and stunning in a fancy dress and fur-trimmed coat, all big eyes with thick dark lashes and strawberry blonde curls about a heart-shaped face. The men's heads had turned at her entrance, and several let out appreciative wolf-whistles as the woman sauntered across the ward towards them like she was a film star.

'Hullo there, Rose,' the woman drawled, and kissed the Sister on the cheek, leaving behind a smear of scarlet lipstick. 'How marvellous to see you again. Have you been sleeping properly? You look tired.' She turned to study Lily, who was staring at her, and raised her eyebrows. 'Rose, I take it you're not going to introduce me to this nice young nurse, then? Well, I'll do it myself.' She held out a hand to Lily, with beautifully smooth fingers tipped with scarlet nails to match her lipstick. 'How do you do? I'm Elsie, Rose's little sister. Though I daresay she's never even mentioned me.'

'Oh, she's mentioned you, all right,' Lily replied coldly, bristling in defence of her friend, and looking Elsie up and down with disdain. 'I know exactly who *you* are.'

43

Rose felt like death. Her heart was racing, her body cold to the touch. She was trembling, she realised, as she paused for a deep breath before entering the senior staff room. Lewis had escorted her sister there for a 'chat' some twenty minutes ago, and then sent Tom to find her at the party, saying she was needed.

She walked into the room with her nerves in shreds, half expecting to find Lewis embracing her sister. Why not, after all? They had been engaged unofficially for ages, and there was every chance Elsie had managed to change his mind in the twenty minutes she'd been alone with him. She knew how potent her younger sister's wiles could be when Elsie decided she wanted a man.

Instead, she found Lewis standing by the unlit fire, his face abstracted, and Elsie checking her make-up in a pocket compact. Her sister saw her in the mirrored compact and snapped it shut at once, turning.

'There you are at last, Rose. Trust you to take forever to appear. I'd almost given up hope. And this is such a nasty, dank little room to wait in. Mid-December, and there's not even a fire lit.'

Elsie looked oddly glamorous, Rose realised for the first time, considering she had gone north to work in a factory. She looked her sister over slowly, struggling to understand what she was seeing. Elsie's thigh-length coat had a dark fur collar and cuffs, and she was wearing a very fetching silver pendant necklace that Rose did not recognise. Her black heels looked terribly smart too, and were surely new. They must have taken ever so many ration coupons to acquire.

But Elsie had always enjoyed a taste for the finer things in life, Rose thought, even when she couldn't afford them.

'It's a large building, we have to be sparing with the number of fires we light.' She could feel her heart pounding now, and did not dare raise her eyes to Lewis, who had turned to watch them. 'I wasn't expecting you so soon, Elsie. Your letter said Christmas. There's still ten days to go.'

'Surprise!' Elsie gave her a wan smile. 'When you've heard what I have to say, you'll understand. Just like Lewis did.' She pulled back her coat, and Rose gasped, stepping back in shock. 'Yes, I'm in the family way.'

'But who . . . ? Are you even . . . ?'

'Married?' Elsie rolled her eyes, as though Rose were being boringly old-fashioned. 'Yes, it's all legal and above board.' She flashed her ring finger, which Rose now realised bore expensive-looking engagement and wedding rings. 'As I've been telling Lewis, our engagement was old hat, so he needn't have sent his dreary little letter breaking it off with me. Like I was going to be bothered by that!' She tittered. 'His name's Alastair. He owns the factory where I was working, and I've left him in the car, so he's probably wondering where on earth I've got to by now.' She tittered again. 'I promised him I'd only be fifteen minutes. Poor Alastair, he must be so bored.'

'You married the factory owner?' Rose stared. 'But when? Why?'

'We got hitched last month. When I got Lewis's letter, I thought it might be fun to come and visit.' Elsie pinched Rose's cheek, laughing. 'No, tell a lie, I

345

actually wanted to see your face. And Lewis's.'

'How did it happen?' Rose asked in a shaking voice.

'You're a nurse. Figure it out for yourself.'

'Elsie, for God's sake . . . How old is this man you've married?'

'Sixty-three,' she said, and shrugged at Rose's scandalised stare. 'The short version is, we were thrown together one night in the factory shelter, one thing led to another, and later I realised I was expecting. Luckily, Alastair had just lost his wife. So I was able to comfort him. And give him an heir. His wife couldn't have babies, you see.' Elsie gurgled with laughter. 'But I seem to have had no trouble at all conceiving.'

She prattled on about their house and the factory, oblivious to the looks Rose and Lewis were exchanging.

★ ★ ★

Eventually, Elsie grew bored taunting her sister and took them outside to meet her husband instead. Alastair was a huge, silver-haired man in a smart burgundy Bentley, who got out and shook their hands politely, seemingly relieved not to face any hysterics over their rushed wedding.

'Are you staying in St Ives?' Lewis asked them.

'Can't spare the time away from the factory, unfortunately,' Alastair told them in a rolling northern accent, looking embarrassed. 'We're only here for the day. This was a special favour to Elsie. She wanted to come down and collect some things she left behind. And to see you, of course, Miss Gray.'

'Rose, please,' she told him, feeling a little sorry for the man, who was likely to have quite a difficult existence as her brother-in-law.

'I couldn't let my wife travel alone. Not in her condition, and with a war on.' Alastair put his arm around Elsie, who gave him a simpering smile. 'We'll stop at Exeter tonight, get an early start tomorrow, and hope to be back in Leeds before nightfall.'

'So soon? She must be a fast runner,' Lewis said, admiring the Bentley.

'Oh, she's a beauty,' Alastair agreed enthusiastically.

Elsie took Rose aside while the men talked cars, saying in a low voice, 'Listen, I dropped by the vicarage on our way up this morning and collected my things. So there's nothing here for me now. I doubt I'll ever be back.' She looked down at the small town of St Ives, which was looking rather battered in grey, stormy light today. 'I've left Lewis a bit shocked, I could see that when I told him about the baby. But I can't say I'm sorry.' She put a hand on Rose's arm. 'You'll look after him, won't you?'

Rose opened her mouth, and then shut it again. Better not, she decided. 'Did you take everything of yours that was in storage?' she asked, changing the subject.

When their aunt's house had been sold, any items they had wanted to keep but couldn't take with them had been stored in an outbuilding at the vicarage, their aunt having been good friends with the vicar's wife. Rose had collected her own few precious possessions long ago, but Elsie had never bothered, leaving some old clothes and jewellery there that had belonged to their mother. The jewellery was only paste, but all the same . . .

'Yes, it's all cleared out now.' Elsie shivered in the wind, pulling her posh coat about herself. 'Silly to be sentimental, but now that I'm to be a mother myself, I wanted something to remind me of Mother. Do you understand?'

'Perfectly natural.'

'I know I said I'd be coming to you for Christmas, but I've changed my mind. I want to spend this first Christmas with Alastair. He has ever such a big mansion house on the outskirts of Leeds, with huge grounds and a fountain on the front lawn. And *three* servants!' Elsie smiled in triumph. 'You must come and visit us next year when the baby's born. I mean, this war can't go on for ever, can it?'

Rose wished she shared her sister's optimism.

★ ★ ★

When her new husband had turned the Bentley around, Elsie wound down the window and waved, shouting, 'Merry Christmas, Carrot-Top!' as they drove away.

Before the car was even out of sight, Rose and Lewis ran up the steps to get out of the wind, and stood there in the sheltered porch a moment, staring at each other. From inside the hall, they could hear everyone singing a carol, the sound of festive voices drifting across the snowy landscape.

'We should go back to the party,' he said slowly.

Her heart was thudding hard and she was finding it hard to breathe. 'You're free now,' Rose whispered.

Lewis held out his hand, and she touched it, but only with her fingertips.

'We're both free,' he told her.

44

'Are you sure I can't help?' Rose asked, for about the fifth time.

Lewis turned her about and steered her out of the steamy kitchen, just as he had done the other four times. 'I told you, it's all in hand.'

'But I feel so guilty. When you invited me to Christmas lunch, I assumed Mrs Delaney would be cooking it for you.'

'Even Mrs Delaney gets a few days off at Christmas. She's gone to visit her relations. Now stop fussing. I know we are but lowly males, but I assure you we are more than capable of cooking up a family dinner.'

She laughed. 'You and Dr Edmund are very far from lowly males. And I wasn't casting aspersions on your ability to cook. I just hate not being able to help.'

'If you want to help, go and sit with the boys. Entertain them so they don't keep running into the kitchen while we're boiling vegetables.'

So, Rose sat and watched the boys play some Christmas games instead, loving to see Jimmy's big grin as he trumped the other boys, who were both older than him but didn't appear to have enjoyed quite such a misspent youth. Every now and then, there was a clattering noise from the kitchen, and some muffled cursing, which made her worry that the boys would hear and pick up bad words, but if they did, there was no change of expression.

Eventually, Edmund tottered out with the half goose Mrs Delaney had somehow wangled from the butcher, for which she had left precise instructions on how it should be prepared, and the boys sprang up in hungry excitement. Lewis followed with sprouts, roast potatoes and a large bowl of well-steamed carrots, all from their own back garden, plus a generous jug of gravy, and they all sat down to eat. There was even wine for the adults and a syrupy home-made cordial for the boys, heavily watered down.

'Well?' Edmund said, leaning towards her expectantly as Rose pushed away her plate afterwards.

'Delicious,' she said sincerely. 'You're a brilliant cook.' When Edmund crowed with laughter and Lewis cast his eyes to heaven, she corrected herself hurriedly, 'I mean, you're both brilliant cooks. Aren't they, boys?'

Joshua and Benjamin both politely concurred.

'The best!' Jimmy agreed, and waved his knife merrily, sending gravy flecks spinning across the table cloth.

'Thank you,' Edmund said with a pained expression, 'but try not to gesticulate with your cutlery, dear boy. It's not good manners.'

Rose met Lewis's eyes across the table and could not help smiling.

After their empty plates had been cleared, leftovers of Christmas cake from the party were brought out, which Cook had kindly put aside for the doctors, knowing they had three children to feed now. Then they played nursery rhyme charades at the table, which had the boys in stitches, until Edmund declared himself exhausted and dropped off to sleep in his armchair.

'Why don't you take your presents upstairs?' Lewis told the boys with a wink, and handed them a small orange each. 'Give us grown-ups a bit of peace and quiet.'

They all headed upstairs, though Jimmy turned at the top of the stairs to give Rose and Lewis a cheeky wink of his own, as though to say he knew precisely why they wanted to be alone.

'Those boys . . . ' Lewis ran a hand over his face as soon as they'd vanished into their room, and pretended to sag against the wall in mock exhaustion. 'I can't keep up with them.'

'Of course you can,' Rose told him, and glanced back into the front room, where Edmund was now snoring gently. 'It's your grandfather I worry about.'

'Oh, he's all right. They keep him young. I'd be more worried if he had nothing to do all day but sit in that armchair.'

Rose hesitated. 'Shall I start the washing up? I'm afraid there must be dozens of dishes to clean and dry after that extravaganza.'

'More like hundreds, I should imagine.' But he shook his head. 'No, let's stretch our legs with a walk around the back garden.'

They both donned coats and headed outside. The weather was uncertain, but they did not stay in the wind for long, Lewis leading her through his grandfather's vegetable patch to a covered seat beside some apple trees, out of sight of the windows. It was quiet there, although the house next door had their wireless on with the kitchen window ajar.

They sat together in silence, looking up into the grey Cornish sky. After a moment, Lewis put his arm about her, and Rose did not protest or move away.

If they married, she would have to give up her nursing career, she thought with a sudden twinge.

But she'd be glad to do so if they had children, and until that happy event occurred, she knew the government would find suitable work for her.

'I love you,' Lewis said simply.

Rose turned to smile at him, and he kissed her in a leisurely fashion.

'Are you going to marry me?' he whispered.

She raised her eyebrows. 'I don't think I've been asked yet. Not properly.'

'Oh hell.' Lewis disentangled himself and dropped to one knee before her, knocking back his springing dark hair before taking her hand in his. 'Miss Rose Gray, will you do me the honour of becoming my wife?'

'I will,' she agreed, smiling shyly.

'Thank God, I'm not sure what I would have done if you'd said no. I don't have a ring with me, I'm afraid,' he added, patting his pockets. Then his smile faded, and his gaze stilled on her face. 'But there's one in the house I'd very much like you to wear, if you're happy to do so. My mother's engagement ring.'

'Oh, Lewis.'

Then he kissed her again.

★ ★ ★

Some time later, sitting hand in hand, her head on his shoulder, Rose said quietly, 'Once we're married, I'd like to ask Lady Symmonds for permission to run the orphanage. Would you mind?'

'I've never been interested in women who only want to stay home and play house. It's a brilliant idea. Not too much work for you, though?'

'I'll have help,' she said firmly. 'And I've never been

352

afraid to get my hands dirty. It will be a challenge.' She paused, and then said daringly, 'I'd also like us to adopt Jimmy. Make him our son. What do you think?'

He lifted her hand, pressing it warmly to his lips. 'I think I love you more than ever, Rose Gray. And yes, I'd been thinking that myself, and wondering what you would say to the suggestion.' He laughed. 'I should have known you'd be three steps ahead of me, as usual.'

She sighed, knowing that everything would change from now on, and strangely content with that thought.

'I hope Elsie will be happy with her new life.'

He smiled down into her eyes. 'Your happiness is the only thing that's important to me now, Rose. Yours and Jimmy's.'

'Everything's going to be all right,' she whispered, 'isn't it?' She closed her eyes on that optimistic question, as though to freeze it for ever in time, while from next door came the festive strains of Christmas music on the wireless.

Epilogue

Holding her posy in both hands, Lily walked down the garden path at Porthcurno under a chilly mid-February sky, too nervous to look up at the army truck waiting at the gate, afraid she might trip and dirty her finery. Not accustomed to wearing high heels, she felt rather like a giraffe in the elegant pair borrowed from Eva. There was a smattering of snow on the ground too, for the weather had turned nippy in recent days, and she had to be careful not to slip on the icy path. If she dislodged the spray of silk flowers in her hair, she'd be in trouble with her aunt, who had spent nearly half an hour arranging it just so.

'Oh, ducks, you look just like your mum, God rest her soul. If Betsy could see you now . . . ' Her gran's eyes filled with tears. Then she turned and bellowed into the house, 'Alice Fisher, if you don't get your backside down those bloomin' stairs in the next thirty seconds, we're leaving you and your aunt behind, I swear to God!'

The soldier waiting for them in the army truck straightened in surprise, his eyes widening. 'I'm sure they'll wait for you at the church, Mrs Hopkins.'

'Nobody asked you, young man,' Gran told him shortly, and turned to tweak Lily's dress. 'Both my beautiful granddaughters as bridesmaids. What a day this is!' She pulled an already damp hanky out from her sleeve and blew her nose. 'I can't wait to see the bride.'

'Don't you mean brides, plural?'

354

'Oh yes, of course. Silly me. A double wedding. Well, I suppose it saves money on the cake and sandwiches after. But I've hardly seen anything of the other bride, so you can't blame me for forgetting. Dearest Hazel though, she's like family.'

Alice came stumbling down the stairs clutching an early spring posy, the silk flowers in her hair already askew, a mulish expression on her face. Their outfits were not matching, as that would have been too expensive, but they were similar styles, both knee-length dresses in a soft blue shade.

Lily thought her younger sister looked oddly mature with lipstick and face powder, almost grown-up at sixteen years old. She herself wasn't used to wearing make-up either, as it wasn't permitted at work.

'Where's your Aunty Vi?' Gran demanded, ready to lock up.

'I'm coming, Mum,' Violet called, appearing in the doorway in a stunning blue dress with a white collar, its neckline rather daringly low to Lily's mind. 'Will I do, do you think?'

'Joe will think he's died and gone to heaven,' Gran said.

'Not too risqué?' Violet pulled on a white jacket over the dress and then settled a blue hat on her soft fair curls, tilting the wide brim to the side. 'This neckline shows off a bit more than what I'm used to.'

'If it helps keep a man interested,' Gran told her bluntly, with a sideways wink to the girls, 'why the hell not, eh?'

'Couldn't have put it better myself,' the soldier in the truck agreed, grinning.

'Mind your own business!' Gran and Violet chorused at the same time, and Lily was amused to see the soldier pull a face but say nothing more.

The truck rattled into life. It was time to leave.

'Hop in the back then, girls,' Gran said, clapping her hands, 'and don't dirty your dresses, for Gawd's sake. It's not the posh car I'd envisaged for this wedding, but at least the Colonel remembered us and it's better than Shanks's pony.' She meant walking, of course. 'I'll ride in the front with Vi.'

'But we're the bridesmaids,' Alice protested, staring appalled into the back of the truck as the soldier came round to help them climb aboard.

'All the more reason to get your skates on,' Gran told her with a wink, and followed Aunty Violet up into the cab of the truck.

★ ★ ★

At the parish church, they found the congregation already seated inside, apart from a few latecomers, and the two brides waiting nervously outside the porch. Hazel was wearing her wedding dress for the second time, this time without the veil, she had told them earlier. Her dress fell to just below her knee, a simple cream linen that looked both smart and thrifty at the same time. The men's jackets flapped on a sharp breeze that brought tiny flurries of snow every now and then, the ground underfoot treacherous with ice.

Hazel looked rosy with health, Lily thought, smiling as she remembered the long night when she had helped her baby girl enter the world.

Baby Lily.

How humbling it was to have a child named after you. Her heart had missed a beat when George and Hazel had told her the name they'd chosen for their little girl. She wondered if the child would like her name when she grew up, and hoped she would.

'Lily, stop gawping at nothing and get into line,' her grandmother told her impatiently, pulling her forward to stand next to Alice.

'Sorry, Gran.'

Hazel's Uncle Trevor took his niece's arm and tucked it through his own. 'You ready, love?' he asked gruffly. She had lost her father, so her uncle would be giving her away instead.

'As ready as I'll ever be,' Hazel said, though she looked almost stunned, staring straight ahead at the open church door.

The vicar, Mr Clewson, came rushing out of the door in a frazzled state. 'You're late,' he told Hazel accusingly, who ignored him with dignity. 'And where's the other bride?'

Lily looked round in time to see Eva step out from behind her father and say clearly, 'Here I am, Reverend. Sorry to have caused you any trouble. We're all set now.'

Lily thought she had never seen Eva looking lovelier, her soft blonde curls glowing, her skin flawless, her lips scarlet. Her dress was RAF blue, to match her husband-to-be's uniform, with an unostentatious frill at the hem and cuffs, and shoes to match.

'It's the bride's prerogative to be late,' Gran pointed out loudly; she had never much liked clergymen since the vicar at her own wedding had apparently turned up drunk.

Mr Clewson ignored her.

The Colonel came forward and took Eva's arm. His whiskers had been brushed, his buttons polished, and he looked very smart in full dress uniform, though a little intimidating too.

Lined up a short distance from the church, currently standing to attention, were six soldiers from Porthcurno who had volunteered to form a guard of honour for Eva and Flight Lieutenant Carmichael as they emerged from the church as man and wife. They had no airmen stationed at the camp, but Max had seemed moved by the gesture, nonetheless.

'Still sure you want to go through with this, m'dear?' the Colonel asked.

'More than ever,' Eva said firmly.

Eva had told them how her father had relented and given the couple his blessing when they arrived at Porthcurno for Christmas. Apparently, any man who could do what Max had gone through to win Eva's hand in marriage 'deserved his little girl'. Of course Alice had snorted when she heard that, but Lily thought it was madly romantic.

The church organ began to play inside. Gran nodded violently for Lily and Alice to start walking, and then darted into the church to take her place with Aunty Violet.

Lily exchanged a quick, panicked glance with Alice, wishing they weren't at the front, then suddenly they were moving. They passed under the shadow of the porch and into the body of the church. In front of them stood the congregation, local women in their best hats and frocks, the men and boys with their hair combed and boots polished, who had all turned to watch as they entered.

The church interior looked lovely. Gran and Aunty Violet had helped the vicar's wife decorate the pew ends with bunches of spring flowers and bright green sprays, with a twist of gold paper here and there, to brighten everything up.

There was Charlie, right at the front, grinning like a fool as he waited for his mum to be married, with his baby sister Lily sleeping in the arms of one of their neighbours, and George Cotterill beside the first pew, wearing his best suit as he waited for his bride-to-be.

At the end of the flower-draped pew on the other side was Max Carmichael in his RAF uniform. Only he was seated in the wooden pew, not standing like George.

As Lily began the approach to the altar, treading at a measured pace in time to the music, she saw Max rise to his feet, a determined look on his face. Slowly, and very deliberately, he took three steps into the aisle, and waited there for his own bride-to-be, leaning on a cane for his only support.

Somewhere behind her, she heard a muffled sob, and realised it was Eva, who must have seen her bridegroom getting to his feet in preparation for the ceremony.

Tears started in Lily's own eyes, and the posy shook in her hand as she battled the urge to weep. Max had insisted he would not marry Eva until he could stand at the altar beside her.

To admit the truth, Lily had not believed it could happen. The flight lieutenant had been so badly injured, it had seemed an impossibility, and she had heard Dr Lewis say so himself, on more than one occasion. Yet Eva had never given up hope, never even countenanced giving up on Max. And now there he was, on his feet again, waiting to marry her.

How beautiful it all was, she thought. How marvellously romantic . . .

'Lil, whatever's the matter?' Alice demanded in a piercing whisper, staring sideways at her with obvious bewilderment.

'Oh, hush,' Lily whispered unsteadily, as a tear rolled down her cheek. 'You'll understand one day.'

She wasn't the only one crying, she realised, spotting other tear-streaked faces in the congregation, and a flurry of white hankies.

Gran was crying, and Aunty Violet too, along with the other cleaners from Eastern House. Even some of the men looked moved, clearing their throats and shuffling their feet. She saw Joe Postbridge standing next to Aunty Violet, and he had an odd look on his face too. Then he glanced at Violet with a smile, and she smiled back, her face radiant under the wide brim of her hat.

Those two will be next to walk down this aisle, Lily predicted with absolute certainty, and had to suppress a laughing sob.

Everyone seemed so happy and carefree today, smiling through their tears at these two couples getting married.

The weather was perishing cold across the country, they were still at war, and life was getting harder every day, what with rationing, and air raids, and bombs constantly killing innocent people, and the growing threat of a land invasion by Germany. But this was Cornwall, Lily reminded herself, one of the mildest corners of the British Isles. It was almost spring outside, the promise of warmer weather mere days away.

Snowdrops had forced their green stalks through the wintry earth last month, birds were beginning to build nests, the first lambs were frolicking in the fields, and men and women were taking each other to church, undeterred by the hardships of war.

They had nearly reached the vicar.

She and Alice stood to one side, as they had practised at the rehearsal, and the two couples stepped forward under the glow of the stained-glass window behind the high altar.

'Dearly Beloved,' Reverend Clewson began his address, suddenly benign and welcoming, and everyone in the congregation gave a collective sigh of joy.

What a topsy-turvy world this was, Lily thought, clutching her spring posy with a tremulous smile. Just when things were at their darkest and most grim, love came along to light the way. Which was exactly as it ought to be.

WARTIME WITH THE CORNISH GIRLS

Betty Walker

When Violet loses her sister in the Blitz, she must take her nieces to safety in Cornwall. On the coast, she meets carefree chorus girl Eva, who is also running from the dangers of London. But Porthcurno hides a secret military base, and soon Violet and Eva realise there's a battle to fight in Cornwall, too. Together with local Hazel, who works on the base, they must come together to help the war effort. But will their friendship be enough to keep them safe?

AN ANGEL'S WORK

Kate Eastham

England, 1941. As nurse Jo Brooks arrives at Mill Road Hospital, a ward takes a direct hit from a bomb. Pulling herself from the rubble, Jo's first priority must be her patients . . . but she can't stop herself frantically searching for her friend Moira. When she eventually finds her, Moira is barely clinging to life. Jo makes a solemn vow: she will do whatever it takes to help the Allies win the war, even if it means sacrificing her own safety.

But when Jo makes the acquaintance of a handsome American soldier, she feels her heart skip a beat, and all her promises are put to the test. Because sacrificing everything is so much more difficult when suddenly you have so very much to live for . . .

THE SPITFIRE GIRLS

Jenny Holmes

Mary is a driver for the ATA, and although she yearns to fly a Spitfire, she fears her humble background will hold her back. After all, glamorous Angela is set to be the next 'Atta girl' on the recruitment posters; Bobbie learned to fly in her father's private plane; and Jean was taught the Queen's English at grammar school before joining the squad. Dedicated and resilient, those three girls rule the skies, weathering storms and dodging enemy fire. Mary can only dream of joining them — until she gets the push she needs to overcome her self-doubt. Thrown together, the girls form a tight bond as they face the perils of their job. But they soon find that affairs of the heart can be just as dangerous as attacks from above . . .